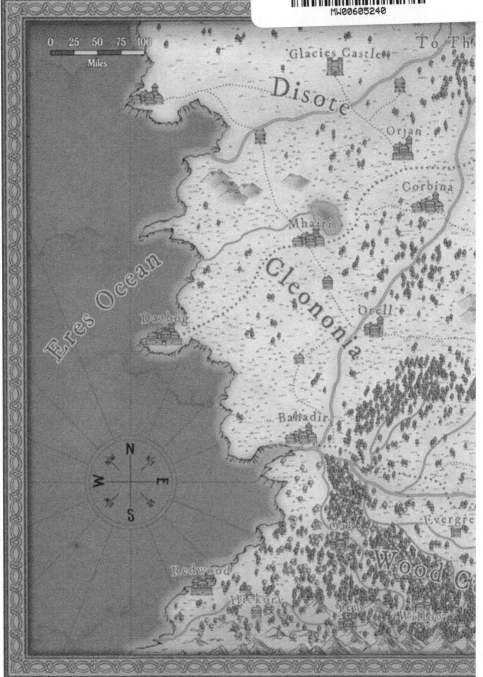

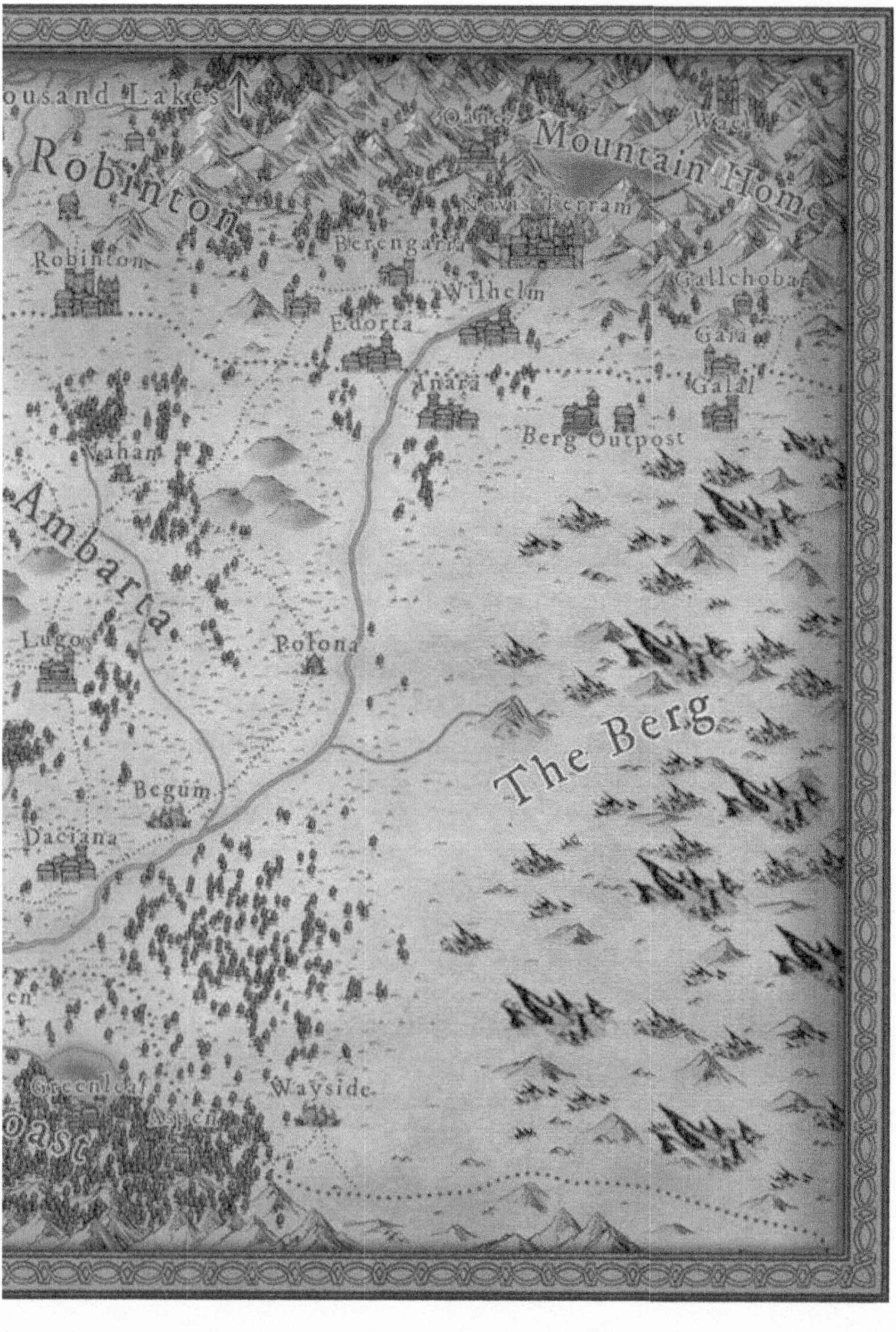
ousand Lakes
Robinton
Mountain Home
Wael
Novis Terram
Berengaria
Robinton
Gallchobar
Wilhelm
Edorta
Gaia
Inara
Galal
Berg Outpost
Nahan
Ambarta
Lugos
Polona
The Berg
Begum
Daciana
Wayside
Aspen
oast

THE POWER OF THE BROKEN

BOOK 2 OF THE KIMORAE RIFT TRILOGY

CAMERON C. PORTER

CONTENTS

PROLOGUE

King Radomir, Lord of Mountain Home, strode impatiently down the long hallway that served as the main thoroughfare through the castle. Lining the hall were tapestries, banners, and other works of art all centered around the principle of balance. Unconsciously he began to mentally recite a portion of the oath he had taken when he had been crowned King: *...to seek balance in all things – balance joy with sorrow, for without sorrow joy has no meaning. Balance love with hate, for not all things are made for every man. Balance patience with urgency, trust with vigilance, compassion with expectation, pity with respect.*

That was all well and good, but he didn't feel particularly balanced right then. Surrounded by his customary retinue of guards, he hurried to the Chordus audience chamber. Despite being in his late middle years -- 85 to be exact -- and largely confined to the castle by his duties, he was only a bit overweight, his gut hanging slightly over the belt tied around the middle of his green velvet tunic. He reached the double doors and continued so quickly the guards barely had time to push the doors open and step out of his way before he came through.

"Comperr did not agree?!" He barked as he entered, looking from one abashed face to another.

The Chordus chamber was much smaller than the grand hall, and was designed for an audience just like this, where the meeting was more of a dialogue and decision-making process as opposed to a petition. The room was almost perfectly circular, with nooks carved in the walls every so often to make room for a pot from some faraway country or a wildly impractical helmet that was so shiny and unmarred it had clearly never been used in battle.

Some prior king or -- more likely -- queen, had gone to the trouble of having the walls of the Chordus chamber painted a light blue. His own queen, Oana, loved the color. For himself, he saw no meaningful difference between the white of most of the rest of the castle and this blue.

In the center of the room was a large circular table just shorter than his waist. It was around this that those who had gotten here before him were gathered. His emissary to Comperr, an old friend named Kaapo, was present with his two assistants. Captain Bagon, the leader of all of Mountain Home's armies, and the freshly-appointed Captain of the Castle Guard Timot Kimorae filled up the rest of the small room.

"My king," Kaapo began, "It's the armistice. Now that Cleononia and Ambarta have signed an agreement to stop the fighting, Comperr's Head Wizard Metnal says they will not act."

"Is it not still in their best interest?" King Radomir replied snappishly. "All we need is a few wizards to aid ours in subduing Ezmith Kimorae!"

Before he could stop himself he looked at Timot. He looked away immediately and noticed that everyone else was pointedly *not* looking at Captain Kimorae as well. The new Captain of the Castle Guard raised his hands placatingly.

"It's all right. We can address the boar in the barn," Captain Kimorae said. "Ezmith is my son and Lady Virtesa my former wife. I do not condone any of their actions after I left Ambarta and I intend to help see justice done. I will provide what insight and knowledge I can. There is no need to walk softly around this issue."

This sort of thing was exactly why King Radomir had chosen

Kimorae for this position. Not his knowledge of the greatest threat currently facing Mountain Home – though that was of value as well – but his confidence in speaking freely in situations where most men would stay silent. Radomir had no doubt that Timot would tell him when he was making a bad decision, and that was more valuable than anything else a captain could bring to his king.

He nodded to Captain Kimorae. "Now that that's all cleared up, someone tell me why Comperr isn't willing to interrupt the leisurely reading of a handful of wizards to save the entire Western region!"

Captain Bagon, a few years younger than Radomir but looking much his senior thanks to the decades of soldiering out in the sun, snow, and Ankon-knew-whatever-else, spoke next.

"Isn't it one of the express purposes of the Guild of Wizards to combat any magic user who engages in warfare?" He asked, directing his question to Ambassador Kaapo. "This should have been nothing more than a courtesy notice for them to do what they always do."

Kaapo tossed his head angrily. "Thank you for that penetrating insight, Captain. That is exactly how I approached it, and Metnal promptly told me to climb a tree. King Raanan was even less help; all he said was that it was Guild business and he wasn't going to get involved."

Radomir had to admit that part of their reluctance was easy to understand – Comperr had just lost a war that they themselves had started and it had been Mountain Home who'd defeated them. Now Comperr might feel like the country who thumped them wanted even more concessions out of them than originally agreed upon. Still, Radomir felt as though he were missing something…like there was a piece of the puzzle he wasn't understanding.

"Go back," he said to Kaapo, who immediately looked indignant. "I know it's a long journey, but there's too much riding on this horse to just leave it alone." He turned to Captain Kimorae. "Go to wizards Mellion and Paavali. See if there's anything they can do to help Kaapo and his company travel faster. Also tell them to come see me to discuss how and when they will get to Cleononia to reinforce their wizard.

Lord Perivon assures me that Cleononia can stand against Ambarta as long as Ezmith is removed from the field."

He shook his head. It was still strange to discuss Ambarta in such terms. Four years ago, even one year ago, the idea that the greatest threat to both Cleononia and Mountain Home would be Ambarta was laughable. Times changed.

It also belied what he thought he knew about magic that their two wizards working together with Leir could not subdue Ezmith on their own. It grated to need Comperr's Wizard's Guild; if he had his way they'd never deal with any snakes from Comperr ever again.

What would happen would happen, and they would deal with it as it came. He just hoped it didn't come to another war on Mountain Home's borders.

Head Wizard Metnal sat at his desk in his private office, surrounded by the trappings that befitted his station. Everything in this office was ornate: his desk hand-carved from a single massive tree, his chair meticulously engraved with a scene from a battle hundreds of years ago, and several massive paintings in the *ocule* style on the walls.

Ocule art was the latest fashion, and was noted by the artist placing a single gem somewhere on the canvas and painting out from it so that whatever the painting depicted, the area of focus, or where the eye was supposed to go to understand the meaning of the painting, would be the gem.

Only the most prestigious artists were doing *ocule*, likely because of the upfront expense of acquiring the gem unless it was commissioned by someone. He scoffed as he admired his paintings. Commissioning art was foolish; art was supposed to open your mind and expand your thoughts. How could it do that if it came from your mind to begin with?

No, he had purchased these pieces after they had been done, and they drew his attention far more than the sweeping landscape viewable from his window a hundred feet off the ground. His favorite, a depiction of a sunset using a pure orange garnet left rough and unpolished, showed power in the sky, with death and destruction on one side and health and happiness on the other.

He stood up, walking over to the sunset *ocule* and looked, just looked, as he often did, seeking meaning in every brush stroke. He'd only been there a moment when a soft chiming noise sounded in his head. It was a spell of his own design that he maintained to warn him when someone entered his office. Originally, he'd only bothered to maintain the spell while he was away, but since Ezmith Kimorae – 'Virtesa', he supposed – had shown the ability to appear anywhere at will, it had seemed prudent to maintain it even when he was here.

Hearing it now, without any sound of the door opening or footsteps, meant that the Virtesa boy was likely standing right behind him, having just stepped out of one of his Folds. Ezmith refused to teach anyone else that trick, despite (or perhaps because of) how useful it would be. Well, turnabout was fair play, so Metnal stared forward, giving no indication that he knew Ezmith was there until speaking.

"Ezmith, I did not expect you today."

Only then did he turn and look at him, so it was obvious that he had known Ezmith was there despite the silence of his entrance. Let him chew on that for a while.

"That is why I came today," the boy replied. A boy in truth, having not even reached his 30th year, yet more powerful and competent than any wizard Metnal had ever seen.

"When was the last time the Mountain Home ambassador visited you?" Ezmith asked him.

"About a month, though I've received word that they're on their way back," Metnal replied, sitting behind his desk casually as though Ezmith was no more intimidating than any other petitioner.

"You've nothing to fear, Ezmith. My answer will be the same. No guild wizard will come to the aid of Cleononia."

Ezmith eyed him with a hint of suspicion, and Metnal only just stopped himself from sighing; anything approaching loyalty for loyalty's sake seemed beyond the boy's understanding, a fact Metnal made a point of trying to remember. Rather than let Ezmith ask the question and put him on the defensive, he explained:

"We remember the assistance Ambarta gave us in the war with Mountain Home. That we eventually lost is irrelevant. You provided us access through the Berg and kept the other western nations from coming to Mountain Home's aid, and we are returning that assistance with loyalty and gratitude."

"In hopes that such assistance might come again when needed," Ezmith said, nodding as he molded the concept of loyalty into what fit into his own pragmatic worldview.

Metnal was not bothered by that interpretation – it was mostly true, after all – though it didn't include the simple fact of gratitude and a sense of indebtedness. The real core of his loyalty was even simpler than those, however: Ezmith could appear at any moment and murder him on a whim, therefore he would not move against Ezmith in any detectable way.

They talked for a little longer, but as Comperr was not directly involved with Ambarta's plans, there was little of value to discuss, and Ezmith left after only a few minutes.

As soon as he was gone, Metnal got up from his desk again and went back to the sunset *ocule*. He stared until his feet ached, pulling meaning from every drop of paint, trying to understand why a depiction of moral good and moral evil was so potent to his mind when he knew that there was, in fact, no such thing as either.

How long would Ambarta's armistice last?

Two years later and some 800 miles to the west, the Lady Virtesa stood on the highest balcony outside the Palace of Orjan, looking south and west towards Dazbog. She couldn't see it, of course; it was yet another 400 miles further west than she herself was. Even so, she had seen it before and knew she would again. Though the frustration from their defeats had long since faded since the tenuous armistice had been signed nearly two years ago, her resolve had only gotten stronger.

Cleononia was the only nation, besides Mountain Home, of course, that had not yet fallen to her army...and it grated. The ruling families of each of the smaller nations had mocked and belittled her before she had brought them to heel, but Cleononia had used intimidation and even force to keep her people poor and insignificant. While there had been a satisfaction in conquering the other nations, taking Cleononia would be the pinnacle; not even the conquering of Mountain Home would overshadow it.

She heard footsteps approaching behind but did not look back. It would be her eldest son Ezmith; he was the only one here who would approach her while she stood on the balcony. The servants had learned how much she valued her solitude.

Despite herself, she couldn't help but feel more than a hint of fear at having Ezmith being behind her. It wasn't particularly rational; if he wanted to kill her, he would hardly have to come from behind to do so, but there was something more disconcerting about not being able to see what he was doing. She didn't want to believe that he would ever actually do her harm, but pragmatism required a certain amount of caution in dealing with him.

She forced herself to continue looking forward, projecting the utmost confidence. Ezmith was widely recognized as the leader of Ambarta's military forces, but *she* was widely recognized as the ruler of all the conquered lands. *She* was the authority in this conversation. She looked over at him as he joined her at the stone railing, leaning as she did with his arms folded, resting on the top.

At first glance, despite his height and broad shoulders, you would never expect him to be the leader of an army; generals as a rule were older, gruff, scarred men. Ezmith, on the other hand, was pristinely groomed – his hair cut short and combed, his face clean-shaven and his clothes immaculate. Even here he wore a formal wizard's robe of deep green. He'd worn little else for years, even in the most informal of circumstances.

He said nothing, and she was in no hurry to begin a conversation; the day had been another full of planning, negotiation, and strategizing to work out the latest problems with the movement of goods to, from, and through her lands and -- as if that weren't enough -- the news she had received that day enveloped her mind. After a long moment, however, Ezmith broke the silence.

"I have just received word from Guillame. Every ship in the Redwood fleet has been inspected and is ready for battle."

Lady Virtesa's heart started beating faster. This was good news from the Redwood wizard, she supposed, though she had never been confident in that part of their plan. The armistice had been signed because they had reached an impasse with Cleononia; Cleononia could not stop Virtesa's army on land, but they had used their unmatched navy to blockade the port at Redwood, which Ambarta could do nothing about.

Over the last two years, they had built up their own navy at Redwood to fight back if there was another blockade. There were plenty of sailors in Redwood, as it had been a trading port for hundreds of years, but very few of them had experience in naval combat beyond the occasional encounter with pirates, largely *because* of Cleononia's naval might.

Even if they had tried to match Cleononia's numbers on water (which they had not), it was still more likely than not that her inexperienced forces would be quickly defeated, but Ezmith had been confident in the move. According to him, it wasn't so much about defeating Cleononia on the water as it was about making sure their land forces had enough time to take both of Cleononia's ports – Dazbog and Bahadir. Once they had control of all the ports on this coast, the Cleononian navy would have nowhere to dock for resupply or repairs. The stranded ships could still blockade the ports, sure, but they'd run out of food and supplies far sooner than Virtesa's people felt the stoppage of overseas trade too keenly.

The plan was simple enough, but as she tried to rehearse it in her mind, her thoughts continued to go back to Mountain Home and to the news she had received that day.

"Your mind is far away from this, isn't it?" Ezmith asked, once again surprising her with his observance.

Virtesa nodded, holding her back straight and her head high.

"They can still be killed." Ezmith's voice was earnest, with a hint of confusion.

Virtesa sighed internally. Only Ezmith would think she would be comforted by that statement after hearing that her youngest son and former husband were still alive. How strange it was that Ezmith could so quickly identify what a person was feeling by outward signs and yet still completely miss the mark on *why* the person was feeling that way.

That said, the earnestness in his voice assuaged her fear that he would harm her. He clearly still either cared for her or craved her approval. It was good to get those reminders on occasion.

Following Ezmith's reasoning, it was clear that he assumed she was disturbed by the news that her former husband and youngest son were not only alive, they were also entrenched with the royal family of Mountain Home. Her husband, Timot, was Captain of the Palace Guard, and *had been for two years!* Ezren, whom she had last seen when he was only ten years old, was attending the royal academy alongside the children of the wealthiest and most powerful families in the region.

Knowing she was disturbed by the news would only be the first step in his reasoning, though. It would never occur to her eldest that she was conflicted by the news; part of her being pleased that they yet lived, part of her feeling relief of a burden of guilt she had carried for six years, while yet another part of her was angry at her other two sons for lying to her about Timot and Ezren's deaths.

Overshadowing all of it was pure shock, as though the floor had suddenly disappeared from under her and she'd plunged into icy water.

No, Ezmith would never guess any of that. He would assume that she was worried about how their survival might threaten their plans. And yes, that was certainly a part of what she was feeling, but the idea that she would find *comfort* in his saying Ezren and Timot could still be killed was almost laughably obtuse. Almost.

But how to respond...Talking with Ezmith was, at best, a juggle to rival any entertainer she had ever seen and, at worst, a blind walk down a path that could either lead to death or victory. His magical abilities would allow him to crush her as a grape underfoot if he had the inclination, so she had to continually prove to him that he needed her while never, *ever* making it appear that that's what she was doing.

She did not think she could speak without crying, and letting Ezmith see such an emotional display was a dangerous proposition, so she opted to remain silent, continuing to stare forward.

Ezmith had watched her closely since his last statement, no doubt trying to analyze the effects of his words as though she were the subject of some experiment.

"Perhaps we can discuss it more later," he said finally. "I will begin preparing the troops to move on Mhairi and instruct Guillame to move the fleet out to protect trade through Redwood port."

He waited another moment until she nodded, then turned and left, his footsteps fading as he went further away.

Once she could no longer hear his footsteps, she leaned back away from the rail, putting her hands on the top and looking out at the sun that had just finished setting. The darkness settling on her soon obscured the wet drops of her tears on the railing.

She had thought this thing over and done with.

She had come to terms with living the rest of her life with the pain of knowing she had sacrificed her husband and youngest son to achieve her life's calling.

They had stood in her way once, and she'd been forced to order them killed. Now...would she be forced to do it again? Could she?

CHAPTER 1: CASTLE LIFE

E zren Kimorae stood in the training yard, in a row with the other boys in his age group, one leg forward in a lunge, his pike thrust forward, up at a slight angle. His dark brown hair had grown a little longer than he usually let it get, but it still wasn't quite getting in his eyes. He was of average height and build, but with the slightly darker skin and brown eyes that marked him of Ambartan descent.

The boys were all in a single row, all 16 of them, and they were supposed to have their pikes thrust at the exact same angle. The intent of this thrust was to catch a swordsman in the throat where their armor was likely to be weaker.

The Royal Academy didn't spend much time on polearms, which did not bother Ezren. Polearms were boring and simple. Effective yes, but the Academy wasn't a military school; it was among the most prestigious and rigorous schools on the continent.

With the Royal Academy's emphasis on disciplinary balance, it wouldn't make sense to spend more time training with a weapon than necessary to establish proficiency, and proficiency could be established quickly with a polearm. They spent more time on swords.

"Thrust!" yelled the instructor, and Ezren stepped forward with his rear foot into another lunge and thrust his pike up at the same angle.

The rest of the boys did as well, all with varying degrees of success. Besides Ezren, it seemed none of them saw any value in training with polearms, and only a few bothered to hide that fact.

Ezren had his first introduction to the utility of a polearm when he was only eleven. He had managed to trap a bear and the only way to get in close enough to kill it was for his father to use a spear. Just because it was relatively easy to master did not mean it wasn't important, and Ezren applied the same focus and concentration on these lessons as he did any other.

That didn't mean he couldn't understand their apathy; today especially he found it hard to keep on practicing, going through the same routine over and over.

"Thrust!" the instructor yelled again, and Ezren took another step forward and thrust his pike forward again, his pike's angle matching the previous two thrusts almost exactly.

The other boys scoffed at most of their lessons – when, they would ask, would they ever need to know things like how the stars changed throughout the year or how to calculate how far an arrow would shoot from a bow held at a certain angle? These were the sons of Mayors, other Captains in the Mountain Home Guards, and other nobility.

Take Nicov, for example. He held his pike lazily, earning a swat from the rag held by Master Juildar. He was the only son of the Lord and Lady of Disote. Were they still called the Lord and Lady now that they were vassals to his mother, the Lady of Ambarta? Regardless, Nicov despised Ezren and demonstrated it every chance he got. Perhaps Ezren should be grateful Nicov didn't take his weapons training seriously.

"Back and thrust!" came the command, and Ezren took one step back in unison with the rest of the boys and thrust his pike again.

Most of the boys didn't like Ezren, though he wasn't sure why. He was friendly enough when he found time for it. He supposed it had to do with his family. Despite his father's position as Captain of the

Castle Guard, a lot of the people around here were suspicious of him and his loyalties. No matter that he and his father had escaped an attempted execution and then lived as refugees for years before coming to Novis Terram. No matter that his father was a hero of the Border War and had been appointed to his current position by King Radomir himself.

"Back and thrust!"

As he moved habitually, Ezren wondered if he would have been just like these boys if he'd grown up as he was supposed to in the castle at Lugos in Ambarta. The sons of soldiers seemed to take the weapons training more seriously, while the children of mayors and nobility seemed to accept the value of only their grammar and arts lessons even if they didn't necessarily enjoy them.

Most of all, the problem seemed simply to be that they didn't want to put in the work to learn it all properly. They obviously had never had to travel alone by horse in the middle of winter, or they would have seen the value of knowing the stars. They had obviously never used a bow to defend themselves against goblins or they would memorize the calculations of an arrow's trajectory by heart as Ezren himself had.

"At ease!" Came the final command, and Ezren stood up straight and angled his pike up.

Master Juildar, of average height with a thick head of light brown hair wearing the dark green, almost black tunic of the Academy instructors, dismissed them to go back to their classroom. Each day at the Academy was broken up into classroom sessions and weapons training, seemingly with the intent of using one to give the students a break from the other.

Ezren took a moment to breathe the spring air deeply and just enjoy the cool breeze coming off the mountains. A breeze always came off the mountains in the mornings and was always gone by the middle of the afternoon, and it was most prominent during Planting and Harvest. He closed his eyes, relishing the breeze, in no hurry.

Their second morning lesson today was to be on geography and history. These two subjects seemed to be somewhat intertwined, and they were always paired during instruction.

Ezren followed the rest of the boys up the cement stairs out of the training yard to the wall walk and along the balustrade to the wooden door at the end.

As he walked down the hallway trailing the rest of the boys, a group of girls from the age group below his own walked the other way. One of them, a girl Ezren had met before he even lived in the castle, had a big smile for him and stopped to talk. He smiled back and stopped as well.

It was Asteri, the princess of Mountain Home. Of all the students in the Academy who had reason to distrust or look down on Ezren, she had the most. And yet...she had always been friendly with him. If he hadn't known it was impossible, he would have thought she was trying to win his approval.

Despite the fact that she was on her way out to the training yard for whatever girls did in lieu of weapons training, she looked...well...glamorous. As odd as it was to attach such a word to a girl of only 14 years, it was the one that fit best. Most likely her parents or other keepers insisted that as royalty she had to be the most radiant student in the Academy. Her hair was done up at the back of her head, her face shone with whatever had been rubbed on it, and even her clothes, while appropriate for exercising, looked more like the flowy loose pants and shirt that Ambassador Bura always wore than the varyingly simple cotton that most students sported.

"Hi, Ezren," she said with a big, bright smile.

"Princess," he replied, bowing deeply with a smile.

"Oh, yes, you're so funny. Ha ha," she said sarcastically, smacking his shoulder.

He shrugged, unable to keep a grin from his face. "I just wouldn't want anyone thinking our relationship was anything but the most formal, that's all."

Asteri's face turned a bright red, clearly remembering the circumstances in which they'd been discovered when they had last spoken.

Ezren had complained of an itch on his back, so she had pulled him aside and lifted up his shirt to see if there was a tick there. At that moment, her caretaker, an old woman in her hundreds named Vivi had come around the corner and shrieked, coming to the worst possible conclusions and sending the entire castle into an uproar.

Once Asteri had had a chance to explain what had happened to the king and queen, the uproar had blown over, and it was easy for Ezren to find the humor in the situation. Vivi had always disliked him and his father for being Ambartan anyway, so now she just disliked him more. For some reason, though, Asteri had found it far more embarrassing than he, which just gave him even more enjoyment from teasing her over it.

"I think my father has just barely begun to believe me," She said, looking up and down the hall. She looked back at Ezren, shaking her head. "You've been getting me into trouble since the first time we met, Kimorae."

He laughed, remembering the occasion clearly. He had dropped from a rooftop into a puddle, showering her in muddy water.

He had no retort, so he nodded towards the training yard and asked, "what do you do out there? You don't train with weapons, right?"

"Ye-, no, you're right we don't train with weapons. We, um, we do a lot of different things." She stood up straighter and stared at him defiantly. "I believe today we're dancing."

Ezren's eyebrows shot up in amazement. "They teach you *dancing*? Why? Why wouldn't they teach you to fight?"

Asteri giggled. "They teach us some things, with knives and the like. I think most of the girls would fall to pieces if they did more than that. Besides, when will any of these girls ever need to swing a sword around? Most of them are growing up in wealth and plan on marrying into even more wealth."

Ezren shrugged. "Just seems like something everyone should know, that's all. There's not always someone else to protect you."

"Just because we don't learn it at the academy doesn't mean we don't learn it at all," Asteri said cryptically.

Ezren held out his hands bracingly. "Fair enough. Enjoy your *dancing*, and I'll try to stay awake through..." he thought for a moment, trying to remember what subjects he had next.

"-geography and history," she said, interrupting him. Then she looked at him with wide eyes, said, "Bye," and walked quickly away. He stared after her for a moment, somewhat bewildered.

She did things like that sometimes -- blushing at odd times, abruptly ending the conversation, that sort of thing..

As soon as Ezren was in class, Professor Verna, a graying woman of average height wearing a thick sweater despite the warm weather, jumped right into a lecture on Disote.

"When the Settlers first arrived at Disote, the glacier extended much further than where it does now. In fact, only the topmost spires of Glacies Castle were visible above the ice. Glacies Castle was slowly unfrozen as the glacier retreated over the next 800 years. No one knows who built it, but the library of Glacies Castle has proven itself a treasure trove for the last 200 years, though many of the books are either written in an unknown language or seem to be nonsensical."

She turned and pulled down on a string, unrolling a large map of the Western Region. She pointed her stick at where Disote was in the upper-right corner. "With no mountains to shield it from the northern winds, Disote experiences a winter that lasts most of the year, and only a short summer."

Ezren looked down at his map on his desk, noting Glacies Castle at the north end of Disote. Now *that* sounded interesting. A castle that had been frozen in a glacier for however many thousands of years with books written in languages that no longer existed? He thought wistfully of going *there* instead of being in this classroom.

"The extended winters make Thousand River too treacherous for trade, and the Bay of Delfos usually experiences at least one hard freeze every year, stopping Disote from building a port there," Professor Verna continued.

Dinevan raised his hand. "That's why Orjan was built, isn't it? A city on the main highway to facilitate exports and imports."

"Yes, Dinevan, that's correct," Professor Verna responded.

Ezren let himself look out the window. The mountains that came right up to the city walls blocked most of the view, but due East he could see past to some of the more distant mountains. A late-spring snowstorm was caught a few peaks away. From here it just looked like a cloud that extended downward in barely visible lines. He briefly imagined being caught in the storm and having to ride at a gallop to avoid being caught in a treacherous pass in heavy snow.

Professor Verna droned on nearly uninterrupted for the remaining hour of class, but Ezren forced himself to pay attention to every word, and even to take notes. By the end of the class, he had filled up an entire page of notes.

That didn't mean he didn't continue to catch himself looking out the window, however, and one of those times he saw a small procession heading towards the city, flying the flag of Mountain Home, a grizzly bear's head on a green background. Ezren smiled. Fiona was back!

∽

Captain of the Castle Guard Timot Kimorae stood with his back against the corner of the wall, cloaked and hooded, taking notes as he listened to the voice just on the other side. He shouldn't have been this close, but he needed to hear this conversation.

"...no one's even there after they lock up for the night. You can get us in and we can get it all," finished the voice that Timot wasn't particularly interested in.

"But if I get us in and then things go missing it will be obvious it was me," replied the voice that Timot *was* interested in – the voice belonging to Sergeant Lanpart.

"We'll be halfway to Galal by then, Crof. Come on, you know I'm going to take care of you, just like you did for me when ma died."

Oh, it's his brother? That made more sense. Sergeant Crof Lanpart was a good, if unremarkable, soldier, and Timot had not understood what would make him risk so much to try and rob one of the collection vaults. Now all he needed was a date. It would be cleanest if they could simply catch them in the act.

"You've got everything ready?" Sergeant Lanpart asked his brother.

"It's all ready to go right now. I've got the cart, the chests, and the horse. I could have the cart horsed up and outside the castle with an hour's notice."

There was silence long enough that Timot almost looked around the corner to see if they'd snuck away to have the rest of their conversation in a more private place, which they should have done in the first place. It was lucky he did not, though, because Sergeant Lanpart's response sounded like it came from only inches away:

"Alright, fine. Let's do it tonight."

"Oh, wait, *tonight?* Are you sure?"

"Yes. If we wait any longer, I'll lose my nerve. Get everything ready and meet me right at sundown."

"All right, brother. I will be here."

That was all Timot needed. He silently pushed off from the wall and walked the other way, the rough woolen cloak an adequate disguise to make him look like any other passerby. He had not taken more than a few steps before Lanpart's brother walked by at a faster pace. Timot was not wearing the trappings of his position and was emphasizing his limp: the sergeant might have recognized him if he looked closely, but there's no way the brother would, and it seemed Lanpart had gone the other way.

This was going to be almost absurdly easy. He'd alert his men to catch Sergeant Lanpart in the act and arrest them both. He would provide his record of what he had learned tailing him and the name of the informant who had tipped him off originally, but in this case there would be little cause for doubt. Timot trudged up the cobblestone street that ran alongside the inner castle wall and turned in at the next gate to go up to his office.

He looked around to make sure the brother was indeed out of sight, then straightened and took off the cloak; the day was getting too warm for wool cloaks. In the middle of the massive courtyard, a party appeared to be just arriving. As he looked to see who it was, a smile grew on face. There was no mistaking that shapely redheaded woman at the head of the party. Fiona was back.

He walked briskly over to where she was dismounting. She saw him approach as she beat the dust off her traveling cloak with her gloves and smiled mischievously.

"Captain Kimorae, good to see you again," she said, the dimple in her cheek belonging on a much younger woman.

"Ambassador Bura," Timot said formally. "It is good to see you...we have all been awaiting news from Comperr."

"And that is why it is good to see me, is it?" She asked, drawing herself up.

Timot grinned. "Yes," he replied simply, then walked away. He looked back over his shoulder as he walked, still grinning, and saw her shaking her head with a smile. If only every woman understood him the way Fiona did. He could not count the number of times Kimaya had gotten upset at one of his jokes.

His feet took him up the circular cement staircase that would eventually lead to one of the parapets if he took it all the way up, but he got off on the second level. His footsteps echoed down the hallway that lit just well enough by the arrowslits that lamps weren't necessary until the sun went down. He went through the door at the end of the hall and into the offices of the Captain of the Castle Guard.

His office was here, of course, as were both offices for his two lieutenants and for his secretary, a squirrely little man named Werbal who jumped up the moment Timot walked in. He had a small stack of papers in his hand. Luckily, he had the sense not to start talking about what was in those papers until they went into Timot's office and closed the door.

Timot considered his office the best in the entire castle. It was on the back wall of the fortress, facing the waterfall and the pool where the waterfall accumulated before splitting into the two rivers that merged further down in the city. Because there was almost no risk of attack from this direction, his office had been designed with a window as wide as he could spread his arms, with clear glass that let him see the beauty of the falls.

Even though he'd never really put thought into decorating his office, he'd been there long enough that it had happened gradually over time. He had little trinkets on his desk from the various places he'd visited, some paintings on the wall that he'd been gifted, including one that Fiona had brought back from Comperr that had a gemstone secured in the center-right of it.

As soon as he could get the door shut, Werbal began rattling off the different matters that needed Timot's decisions.

"First, we have the issue with the emissary's guard from Ilarp. The guard has been detained for three days already, and the emissary is supposed to leave on their return trip to Ilarp tomorrow."

"They're leaving tomorrow?" he asked.

Werbal nodded.

Timot shrugged. "Release him then. We cannot prove that he did *not* act in self-defense, so assuming the emissary will take him back, we'll let him go."

Werbal nodded, jotting a note on the first paper.

The rest of the papers represented similar little things that should not have required his decision but did. After all, *someone* had to decide these things, and that was one of the main reasons his position existed.

As Werbal continued rattling things off, Timot settled back in his chair, forcing himself to pay attention. This was potentially his least favorite part of being Captain of the Castle Guard. First and foremost, he was responsible for the safety and security of the royal family and the entire castle. Should the rest of the city fall, he would be expected to hold the castle until help arrived.

As grave as that first responsibility was, on a day-to-day level, it required very little of his time. He ran his battalion through drill after drill covering every scenario he could think of, but there was only so many drills that required his direct supervision. His second responsibility, less well known, was policing the castle complex and the barracks complex.

The Battalions-on-the-Wall handled policing for the rest of the city, but anything that happened within the castle or barracks were his to deal with. As if that weren't enough, King Radomir had entrusted him with a third responsibility that no one besides the two of them knew about. The world had become a far more dangerous place in the last few years, and after an attempt on the Queen's life, King Radomir had tasked Timot with predicting, discovering, and thwarting other attempts.

Since the first attempt there had been two others. In neither case had they been able to confirm who had ordered the assassination, but Timot believed it had been Ezmith and Kimaya, the First General and Lady of Ambarta, respectively, who now controlled everything west of them except Cleononia.

A knock at the door interrupted Werbal's droning voice.

"Enter," Timot said immediately, grateful for the reprieve.

Lieutenant Kindo poked his head in the room. "Captain, the king is receiving Ambassador Bura."

"Right now?" Timot asked incredulously. Fiona had just arrived. If they were already meeting, there must be urgent news.

Kindo nodded. "Yes, sir. I was sent to fetch you."

Timot rose quickly to his feet and donned his uniform tunic – a white tunic lined with blue that had the roaring grizzly head on the front. A set of scales was embroidered above the left chest, with four swords on each side signifying his rank. Only one man in all of Mountain Home had more swords than him, and that was Captain Bagon.

"We'll have to finish up later, Werbal," Timot said as he grabbed his sword belt and went out the door, buckling it as he went.

He could imagine Werbal's look of disappointment as he left, though he had learned not to look back. The man seemed to enjoy everything dull in life.

He was halfway down the hall before he realized he forgot to ask where the meeting was. He stopped, went back, and asked Kindo, who confirmed that it was in "the blue room", by which he meant the Chordus Chamber.

The delay meant that he was the last one in the room, and that the briefing had already started when he arrived.

"...is more amenable than Metnal. He also illuminated me on why Metnal is so reluctant to pledge any aid against Ambarta," Fiona was saying as he entered.

King Radomir looked to Timot. "Ah, Captain, glad you're here. I hope you don't mind we started without you."

Of course he minded, but it was no matter. He could simply ask Fiona to fill him in on anything he had missed after the meeting was over.

"Continue, Ambassador," the king said, gesturing to her.

"Some of it we already knew, like how Ambarta had secured their passage through the Berg at the beginning of the war, but apparently Ezmith Kimorae has the ability to instantly and silently travel wherever he would like. Vewen strongly suspects that Ezmith has visited and threatened Metnal if he does anything to aid us."

Timot felt his face tighten. He held his tongue, but barely. He had told them about Ezmith's Folds *years* ago, but the two wizards here in Novis Terram had been adamant that such a thing was impossible, and that it must have been some kind of trick or illusion. With nothing but his general explanation of what he had seen Ezmith do put up against the expertise of the wizards, King Radomir had sided with them.

One of the reasons Timot was so sure that the assassination attempts had come from Ambarta was that all three of the assassins had made it to right outside the king and queen's chambers without raising any kind of alarm or silencing any guards. There were limitations on the Fold's, and Timot remembered Ezmith being either reluctant or unable to attempt Folding somewhere he had not been before, so it was entirely possible that the assassins had been Folded to one of the audience chambers. This would bypass most of the royal family's protection, and explain how the assassins had gotten so close.

Despite Timot's many attempts to persuade him, King Radomir had refused to place soldiers on guard more densely throughout the castle. Perhaps now they would listen to him.

The king replied to Fiona: "Vewen said this? About Ezmith being able to travel somewhere instantly?"

She nodded soberly. "He's seen it with his own eyes."

The king half turned to Timot. "Well, Captain, I owe you whatever a king is supposed to offer in lieu of an apology. A sincere one."

Timot dipped his head in acknowledgement. "Thank you, your majesty, and I humbly accept whatever a king is supposed to offer in lieu of a sincere...heartfelt...passionate apology."

King Radomir grunted with a smile and turned back to Fiona. "What else?"

"According to Vewen, the entire guild is against Metnal on this issue to some degree. To them it is simple: Ezmith is using his magic to not only gain power, but to subjugate entire nations to his will. Therefore, he must be stopped."

"This is wonderful news, Ambassador. When will they arrive?"

Fiona shook her head. "As long as the armistice holds, Vewen says the situation is not urgent enough to defy both the head of the Guild and King Raanan. If and when violence resumes and Ezmith takes an active role in the battles, he believes he can muster at least a few wizards to join with our own and capture Ezmith."

Captain Bagon stepped closer from the other side of the table. "And what of the reports of merchant caravans attacked? Has Raanan agreed to investigate whether it really is Comperr soldiers?"

Fiona shrugged. "Yes, Captain, but he has said as much on previous visits as well. It does not seem he sees much value in devoting resources to protect Mountain Home merchants."

Timot shook his head nearly in unison with the others in the room. This was ridiculous. Comperr had attacked *them*. Comperr had thrown everything they had at Mountain Home, were beaten back, then sent running home with their tails between their legs. No one in Mountain Home had any lingering appetite for war by then, so the negotiators were sent in to bring a final resolution to the conflict.

The negotiations had seemed to end in their favor, with Comperr waiving their normal tariffs for any goods passing through their lands for merchants with Mountain Home papers and signing a peace pledge. So much for all that; a load of stercore.

After a long moment of thought, King Radomir spoke. "I'd like you to pen a letter to King Raanan, Ambassador, speaking with my authority. Remind him that as the ruler of Comperr it is one of his responsibilities to keep trade routes free from bandits, marauders, and other threats. Until we receive a written commitment of a specific size, number, and frequency of patrols along the Northern Highway we will dispatch our own soldiers to provide protection to our merchants through Comperr and claim payment from King Raanan for their services."

"Are you sure you don't want to write this letter yourself, sire?" Fiona asked.

The king shook his head. "I don't want Raanan to think I consider him worth my time. Also, imply that we may have to establish semi-permanent outposts along the Northern Highway to ensure the safety of our traders unless he keeps the road safe. Send it by pigeon if it's short enough, with Rider if it's not."

"Rider should be back tomorrow, he's been searching for the hideout of a band of thieves in the Southern Hills," Captain Bagon chimed in.

"That should work out perfectly. I'm sure Ben won't mind heading straight back out," King Radomir replied.

"Indeed," Bagon replied. "He will probably take the opportunity to shock us all with how quickly he can get there and back."

After a chuckle, the king dismissed them.

Timot left the chamber with Fiona and they walked together towards one of the curving staircases.

"Ambassador Bura, might I inquire as to your evening plans?" He asked formally.

She gave him a wry look. "Why, Captain Kimorae, what interest could you possibly have in my evening plans?"

"As Captain of the Castle Guard it is my duty to ensure that all those who serve at the King's pleasure are properly accommodated during their stay here," Timot replied.

She rolled her eyes. "Oh do shut up, Timot. Of course I'll join you and Ezren for dinner. Let the kitchens know to bring up a third plate to your apartments."

Timot laughed. "As you wish, Ambassador."

She threw up her hands as he went down a side hallway that would take him more quickly back to his office.

As he walked back he could not keep the smile from his face. Fiona truly had worked a miracle on both Ezren and himself over the last year. When King Radomir had been convinced that Ambassador Kaapo was a walking disaster, he had asked for recommendations for his replacement, and Timot had been quick to suggest Fiona Bura, one of the tax collectors that he had been quite impressed with during his time as the lieutenant over the collection brigades.

The king had taken his recommendation, and they'd been working closely together ever since. He considered how different he and Ezren had been just a year ago before Fiona's efforts. He could acknowledge now how much the war with Comperr had taken from him; some of those scars he would carry with him the rest of his life. That said, Fiona had brought a light and happiness back into him that made his smiles natural instead of forced, reinvigorated his sense of humor, and made him more open to the idea of *fun*.

And that was only a patch on what she had done for Ezren; she may not know it, but the boy was beginning to see her as more of a mother than the one who had raised him for the first ten years of his life. On the rare occasions when Ezren and Timot argued, she'd been someone both of them could go to for a second, *usually* reasonable, opinion.

Back at his office, Werbal was waiting. Timot entered with a sigh and focused his mind back on his work. The time went by quickly enough, and soon it was time to head home to the apartment he shared with Ezren.

∽

After the day of classes was over, Ezren went straight to the castle stables, where his horse Asteri stood in her stall awaiting him. His horse sharing the name of the princess was a coincidence, and while he'd had years to get over the humor of the situation, the princess' indignant squawk when she had first found out still occasionally brought a smile to his face.

He visited Asteri every day and either rode her or let her roam. There were too many horses in the castle stable to allow them to roam around a pasture all the time, so it was especially important that Ezren get down here to take care of her. Rund, one of the stable hands, greeted him with a casual wave as he walked out the other end carrying a saddle in one arm.

Rund and the other hands had taken it personally at first when Ezren insisted on taking care of Asteri on his own. It was their job, after all, but they'd grown used to Ezren's persistence and were reasonably friendly now. He wouldn't mind becoming better friends with them, assuming he could find the time; Ezren didn't have time for many friends.

He'd taken Asteri to the farrier for new shoes only a tenday ago, but he checked the hooves anyway. He ran through the daily checklist that he had learned from Ben Rider, thoroughly inspecting his horse. Once finished, he saddled her and took her out to the round pen equipped with obstacles for horses to jump over and run around.

Asteri seemed itching to get moving, and Ezren was as well. The moment the saddle was properly placed, he was in it, and they were trotting around the pen. After some warm-up, Ezren took Asteri around to jump the obstacles, first a trot, then at a canter, then at a gallop. Since he wanted Asteri to always be ready in case they had to leave at short notice, he tried to exercise her for as long each day as he could, at least an hour and sometimes as much as two.

His first time taking the jump at a gallop, he felt a surge of annoyance at how quickly he had to pull up on the reins to stop from hitting the fence -- the fence that kept them in. He took Asteri around again, completing a second and a third jump. Each time, he found himself unduly annoyed with the fence that had always been there, every day, for the last two years. Even if he diverted Asteri instead of stopping, they would just run in circles. He looked around, seeing all the implements in the corral.

There was just enough room to gallop for a bit, a few obstacles of different heights to practice jumping, plenty of straw and space in the stable.

Everything a horse needed to stay healthy.

As long as the horse stayed within the walls.

As long as he stayed in the cage.

He found himself very frustrated on his horse's behalf. After all, she spent all this time practicing, training, dealing with other peop-... horses, and for what? To do it again the next day? To see the same stall, the same faces, the same walls over and over again? Surely Asteri felt useless, watching the older horses go out doing meaningful things while she just waited day after day for Ezren to come exercise her.

Yes, Ezren decided. Asteri needed to get out of the city for a while. She needed something important to do, some way of contributing. She would love a chance to see one of the elves they talked about in school, or a dwarf. Ancient ruins of times before the War of the Intelligences, great libraries like the one in Glacies Castle, or wonderful art houses full of the greatest works of artists from around Quilara like the Royal Art House in Comperr or one of the museums of Admone.

Then an idea came to his mind. Fiona was back! Maybe he could ask if he could bring Asteri along and go with her on her next voyage out to Comperr. Sure, it wasn't everything he wanted but it was a start. Ezren and his horse would be expected to take turns at watch during the night, help fight off any bandits or marauders foolish enough to attack them, and do plenty of other exciting things.

It was exactly what his horse needed.

He looked up to check where the sun was in the sky. Fiona always did dinner with them the first night she got back. He had time to take Asteri through a few more paces before heading up to their apartments for dinner. With renewed vigor, he nudged the horse with his heels to get her moving again.

The dinner hour came quickly, but Ezren was already in their apartments waiting. He'd gotten used to the accommodations, but when they'd first moved in he had been wide-eyed at how much space they had. They had their own latrine, which used the running water from the Novis waterfall to whisk away their waste, a whole room for just greeting people at the door, a separate dining room and kitchen, a spare bedroom, and another small room they used as a library.

He paced in the front room waiting for his father and Fiona to arrive. He looked around at the furnishings and decoration. His father and he never really thought about decorating, so most of the things on the walls had come from Fiona. A piece of art on this wall, a vase on a pedestal in that corner, the pillows on the sofa, and even curtains on the kitchen window were all from her.

As he continued to pace, he thought about how he was going to bring up his plan. On one side of the scale, if he made it seem like a big request, they might be more likely to see it that way. On the other side, if he didn't make it clear how badly he wanted to go, then they might not be willing to go through the trouble to make it happen. He would wait until dinner was brought up from the kitchens (another big perk they'd gotten used to over the last two years), and then ask about how the last trip went.

Yes, that would lead nicely into when the next trip was happening and then he could make his ask.

He heard a key in the door and it came open, revealing his father and Fiona talking and laughing as they came in. He grinned happily and went to give Fiona a hug. She smelled just as he remembered, and she seemed just as happy to see him as he was to see her. He'd been taller than her for a while now, but he still didn't think of her as shorter than him.

"Ezren!" she said as she hugged him back. "Oh, it's so good to see you!"

She pulled away and held him at arms length. "It seems like every time I come back you're taller. Do you plan on stopping anytime soon?"

He wanted to say something witty or clever, but he couldn't think of anything and the moment passed him by. No sooner had the door shut behind them than a knock came at it announcing the arrival of dinner from the kitchens. His father opened the door and Euleny, one of the cooks, pushed a cart in and made a beeline for the dining room.

Euleny was an old woman who had just celebrated her 130th birthday, but she often said she felt as spry as she did 70 years ago. She tsked as she looked in the kitchen and saw that, once again, there was no sign that it had been used at all. Like many in the castle, she had made it her matronly duty to look after Timot and Ezren, and she had good-naturedly ribbed his father and he about never cooking for themselves.

Apparently most people who lived in the castle cooked for themselves after a while because the castle kitchens stayed on a cycle that repeated meals each month, with the only differences being what was in season during the year. Ezren and his father had never started cooking for themselves and had no plans to. Even when they had lived in the barracks and they had to walk to the barracks cafeteria for every meal, they had never cooked.

His father joked that if he never had to cook another meal in his life, he'd be happy. Ezren didn't mind, especially now that they could eat in their apartments.

It was a stark difference from the way his best friend Raban and his father, Sergeant Kennard, cooked all their own meals, though they were still in the barracks complex where they had been for years.

Euleny put out the food on the table and Ezren, his father, and Fiona got out plates and silverware from the kitchen. They sat down to eat, and Ezren was able to get started on his plan.

"So, Fiona, how did this trip to Comperr go? Did they finally say yes?" Ezren asked.

Fiona looked at his father with a raised eyebrow, and his father shrugged. Ezren had no idea what was being communicated.

She looked back at Ezren. "No, Metnal and Raanan are just as stubborn as ever, and seem to resent even being asked. However, I did speak with one of the other wizards in the guild, and he agreed that *if* Ambarta breaks the armistice *and* Ezmith joins in the fighting, then he and several other wizards would feel obligated to act even without approval from the Guild."

"So that's good, right?" Ezren asked as he put more potatoes on his plate.

Fiona nodded, chewing. "It's better than it was. It's going to take a long time to repair relationships between Comperr and Mountain Home, and undo the damage done by that fool Kaapo."

Ezren remembered his father complaining about Fiona's predecessor, but he didn't know much about him.

"So, when are you planning on going back?" Ezren asked innocently.

Fiona shrugged. "Honestly, I'm not sure yet. The king has instructed me to send a letter with some important messages, so we'll have to see how the response comes back. It could be as soon as a month, or as long as three months."

Now for the moment of truth.

"I was wondering...the next time you go, could Asteri and I go with you?" Ezren asked.

The reaction wasn't at all what he expected. His father spat out his drink in shock and Fiona's eyes went wide. Ezren felt his own eyes go wide in response, and they all simply stared at each other for a long moment. *What was so shocking about this request?!*

Then his father narrowed his eyes. "Wait, Ezren, are you talking about your *horse*? You and your *horse* going to Comperr?"

"Of course!" Ezren replied, even more confused. "Wait – did you think I was talking about *Princess* Asteri?"

Both of them visibly relaxed, looked at each, and broke out laughing.

"So he's not wanting to elope, then," Fiona laughed, speaking to his father.

"Elope?!" Ezren cried. "With *Asteri?!* We're just friends."

His father paused laughing long enough to tilt his head to the side and give him a look that said clearly to stop speaking nonsense. For his part, Ezren was genuinely confused. Asteri was...so young. She wasn't even in his age group at the Academy. Sure, she was only two years younger than him, and she was prettier than any of the girls his age, but he didn't have time for that sort of thing anyway.

Fiona was shaking her head. "You really need to rename your horse, Ezren."

His father chuckled, "In our defense, if you're going to Comperr, your *horse* is obviously going with you. It's no wonder we thought you were casually asking if we would aid and abet the kidnapping of the heir to the throne of Mountain Home."

Ezren didn't say anything. This conversation had really gotten away from him, and he had no idea how to recover it.

Fiona realigned the conversation for him. "So, you want to come along with the emissary on our next trip to Comperr."

Ezren nodded.

"Why?"

He was ready for this question. "Because Asteri, *my horse*," he added for clarity, "spends all her time cooped up in the stable. She hasn't been out of sight of the city walls since we moved into the castle, and she feels like she's spending all this time training and learning and waiting but doesn't ever actually get to do anything that matters."

They both looked at him thoughtfully. "Your horse feels this way, does she?" his father asked.

Ezren knew it was silly to keep pretending that this was all about the horse, but he couldn't help it; it was just easier to talk about it on Asteri's behalf instead of his own. He nodded.

His father leaned back and folded his arms. "Well, I'm not opposed to the idea, Ezren, but I don't know if you're ready for that."

Ezren sat up straighter. "I'm ready, da. I know I'll have to help keep watch at night and everything, and I'm ready to do that."

"But if you go, you can't just be a guest of Fiona's. You have to be a part of the emissary and fill a specific role. Would you be an archer? A spearman? A scout? What would you be?"

"I could be any of those, da. I'm definitely the best with polearms in my age group, and you know how good I am at shooting. I'm also good at riding and taking care of my horse so I could be a scout, too."

His father turned to the other adult at the table. "What do you think, Fiona? Anything you have need of on your next trip?"

She thought for a moment. "We can always use an extra scout, but it's a dangerous job. Being able to ride well is only a small part. You have to be able to eat in the saddle, fight well with a sword since you can't carry a spear or a lance, and move as quietly as possible while traveling off the road. I'm not sure I would want someone who has never been a scout before doing that job."

"Well, I'm not sure about that either," his father replied. "Scouting is possibly the most dangerous job he could have on the embassy. I was thinking maybe the rear guard or something."

"In the last year we've only been attacked once, and it was a group of bandits whose eyes were bigger than their stomachs," Fiona replied.

"Still..." his father said, thinking. "What would be your requirements for letting Ezren be one of your scouts on your next trip?"

"Well, for me, I would need him to have experience scouting. He would need to have gone on at least a few scouting trips under one of the Guards' best scouts," Fiona said, looking at Ezren.

His father nodded. "Quite reasonable. For me," he said, turning to Ezren, "I want to know that you can handle yourself against older, more experienced, and larger foes. If you want to go on the next trip to Comperr, I want you to rank in the top of your class in at least one of your fighting styles."

Ezren didn't know if it was possible for his heart to both leap and sink at the same time, but that's what it felt like at that moment. His da was saying he could go...but he had never been top of his class in anything that he knew of. Well, he probably was at polearms like he had claimed earlier, but they weren't tested in those. He was *close* to the top in everything, but the tournaments included everyone in the academy - including the older class of boys, and he always lost out to one of them.

Sword-fighting was a highly regarded skill, especially among the wealthy, most of whom favored it as a sport. As such, the boys in the academy were encouraged to excel in at least one of the styles. They learned the twin swords style, sword and shield, and two-handed sword.

Twin swords used two identical, single-edged medium-length swords and required a great deal of coordination and practice. Sword-and-shield combined a medium-length double-edged sword that could still be wielded with one hand along with a 'full' shield, or a shield that would comfortably cover from shoulder to groin when held straight out in front. Two-handed sword required using a sword the same height as the wielder and trying to utilize the extended reach of the blade to your advantage.

His best style was sword-and-shield, but had never been able to beat Introm, a boy two years his senior, son of the mayor of Gaia – the border city that has been contested during The Border War.

The academy had a tournament in the middle and end of every school year, so the next one wasn't for two months yet. That gave him two months...could he find a way to beat Introm in that time?

If that was his only chance, then he would do his best.

He nodded. "Alright, I agree. I will be the top of my class in the next tournament, and I can ask Ben Rider if I can go along with him on some of his assignments over the next two months. If I do those things, then I can go on the next trip to Comperr?"

Fiona and his father looked at each other, then back to him and both nodded. No mistaking it this time – his heart definitely leaped. He wanted to immediately go out and start practicing sword-and-shield, but he calmed himself, finished his dinner, then asked if he could go visit Raban. His father said yes, so he snatched his bow and quiver from the corner by the door, dashed out and went to go tell him the good news.

Down the stairs he went, then down a long hallway, and out

through a side door to the main castle courtyard. The castle was huge, and quite tall, but the barracks complex sprawled out before it and took up much more space. There was the Guards administration building -- where his father's office used to be -- the barracks them-selves -- where they used to live and eat – and all the different training grounds, buildings, armories, and narrow streets with small houses designed for Guards with families who were stationed on the wall.

Raban and his da lived in one of the barracks, a massive stone building with four stories. He climbed the stairs and walked down the hall to their apartment, knocking quickly.

Raban opened the door and smiled at seeing Ezren. Raban's hair was darker than most here in Novis Terram, but still not as dark as Ezren's, and his complexion was fairer as well. His hair had a feathery quality to it that Ezren's didn't have. Of a height, and of similar builds, their fathers often referred to them as the twins.

"Hey, Ezren, how are you?"

"Good, I wanted to see if you wanted to go hunt some rats," he said, holding up his bow.

"Coins, Ezren, I'd love to," Raban replied, then turned inside. "Oi! Sergeant! Can I go hunt rats with Ezren?"

Sergeant Kennard's voice came from in the apartment. "Don't shoot anyone by accident. Or on purpose."

Raban grabbed his bow and arrows and came out into the hallway with him. As they walked, Ezren filled him in on what had just happened.

"They're really going to let you go?!" Raban asked, his envy obvious.

"That's what they said, but I still have to find a way to beat Introm in sword-and-shield, and I need to talk to Ben to see if he'll let me go out with him a few times," Ezren replied.

Raban nodded. "I'll talk to Ben. You know he likes me more than he likes you."

Ezren looked incredulously at him. "He likes me fine."

"Exactly. He likes you fine and he likes me a lot more. I actually listen to him instead of just going off and doing my own thing."

Deciding to ignore that, Ezren let his thoughts go a different direction. "So do you think you'd be able to come with me when I go out with Ben? Would the Sergeant be alright with that?"

"I think so," Raban said, nodding.

Ezren raised a curious, almost mischievous, eyebrow at him as they went out the door and out into the street. "If he would let you go out with Ben…what about letting you go with the embassy to Comperr?"

Raban's eyebrows shot up. "I don't know about that, that's a long trip and pretty far away. Besides, would Fiona even allow it?"

Ezren shrugged. "I don't know, but I don't think it would hurt to ask."

Raban nodded pensively. "Alright, you ask Fiona and I'll ask the Sergeant. I would love to be able to go."

"So let it be written," Ezren replied with a smile. "Let's hunt some rats."

There was a bounty on rats in the barracks complex; they'd gotten terrible lately. Most hunters opted for traps, but there was no rule against shooting them with a bow. Ezren and Raban felt the added risk was worth the added entertainment. They had to be careful, though – hunting rats was no defense if they accidentally shot someone or broke a window.

As they hunted, they chatted about how Ezren could beat Introm. Their ideas ranged from the quite practical to the intentionally absurd.

Raban suggested he take time and go watch Introm train so he could learn more about how he fought and what his weaknesses were. It was a much better suggestion than his next one, which was to poison him with some Ne'refil root so he couldn't compete.

The conversation ceased when they spied some rats down a small alley. The rats were too busy digging through some kind of refuse to notice them as they stalked forward.

They could probably have taken their shots from further away, but they'd done this enough times to know that it wasn't worth the boost to their pride to try and take the shot from farther than necessary. Ezren waved at Raban to stop, and they lifted their bows. They each counted silently to three and released in perfect unison, each arrow thudding into a rat, causing a terrified shriek and thrashing by the hit rats, and a mad scramble from the rest of them.

The bounty certainly wasn't enough to pull adults away from their work, but it made good pocket money for boys their age, and by the end of the night they'd each bagged five rats and turned them in for five bronze coins.

They bid each other farewell, bronze clinking in their pockets, and Ezren headed back up to the castle complex. He opened the door to their apartment and was surprised to see his father and Fiona standing at the far end of the room, his father most definitely leaning in close to Fiona, who may have had her back to the wall but was most definitely leaning in towards his father as well.

They both jumped nearly out of their skins as Ezren came in. Fiona recovered more quickly, smiled at his father and said, "I told you so."

His father had a wry smile and looked from Ezren back to Fiona. "So you did."

She slipped out from between his father and the wall and went to grab her cloak where it was hanging by the door.

"It was great seeing you both. I'll be at the castle most days, so hopefully I'll be seeing you more over the next little while." Fiona went out the still-open door, waved once more, then pulled it shut behind her.

Ezren turned to look back at his father, who had his hands on his hips and was looking up at the ceiling.

"Um, da? Was that what I think it was?"

His father looked down at him. "Most likely, yes, depending on what you thought it was."

"So you and Fiona are...what exactly?"

His da chuckled. "We are...complicated, I suppose is the word. If you'd been home an hour later I would have a much clearer idea what we are."

Ezren didn't *know* what his father meant, but he could guess, and it wasn't something he really wanted to talk about right then. Thankfully, it seemed his father didn't really want to talk about it either. They both went to their rooms to bed. Each room had its own washbasin, which was another luxury that Ezren appreciated, so they each washed up and went to bed alone.

Ezren laid awake staring at the ceiling and out the window to the clouds passing in front of the stars. He wasn't sure how he felt about his father and Fiona becoming involved romantically. He would be happy to feel however he was *supposed* to feel about it, but he didn't know what that was. The deepest part of him was happy. His father had been alone for a long time, and it wasn't as if his prior marriage had been the most wonderful anyway. Ezren also loved Fiona dearly and appreciated her candid advice on topics he wasn't comfortable broaching with his father.

Shockingly, no clarity came with staring up at the stars through his window, so he rolled onto his side, closed his eyes, and went to sleep.

CHAPTER 2: A BROKEN ARMISTICE

L ord Perivon started in surprise when the door to the Map Room
flew open. Cleononia's wizard, Leir, stormed in, his bulk barely
allowing him to get through the door without having to turn sideways.
For that matter, he might be just as wide front-to-back as he was side-
to-side.

"They've broken the armistice!" Leir spat urgently. "Mhairi is under
assault!"

Perivon sighed. It had only been a matter of time, and as far as such
things went, now wasn't the worst time for it to happen. He immediately began writing out orders for Leir to deliver to his captains in the
field. Leir did not appreciate being used as a pigeon, as he called it, but
in war the speed of communication could make all the difference.

All told, he handed five slips of paper to Leir for the five different
Captains. The fat man snatched the papers out of hand and stomped
out of the room. With luck, things would play out much as Perivon had
predicted. Besides Radomir, he was the only living ruler in the West
that had seen war before Ambarta began snatching nations up.

War was easy enough to understand. Predict what your opponent
would do, ensure that you had more supplies than he did, and don't

take unnecessary losses. He smiled ruefully as he remembered a joke his father had often told when he was a boy: 'The pathway to victory was simple enough as long as you were intelligent beyond belief, wealthy beyond measure, and perfect in every way.'

He pulled the map of the area around Mhairi closer to him. Most likely Ambarta had come from Orjan or Corbina. The only point in having the army come down the glacier road would be to bypass Mhairi altogether and come straight for Dazbog. Since they had not done that, it was most likely they had taken advantage of the Northern Highway.

So hopefully…they had not scouted the barges on Lake Gabija set to take his garrison downriver once the fighting got serious. Facing those Virtesa boys directly was suicide.

His plan was simple enough. They had forced Ambarta into the initial armistice by blockading Redwood and stalling their army for too long on the Plains. When you couldn't fight your enemy head-on, you raided them until their army defeated itself.

Ezmith and the Lady Virtesa had certainly made precautions against those strategies, else they wouldn't have taken over two years to break the armistice, but he had a fairly good idea of what they planned.

They'd cobbled together a semblance of a navy to defend Redwood, but the Bahadir fleet alone should be able to handle it without significant losses and the port would be blockaded again.

Based on the reports he'd gotten from his spies, Ambarta had learned to be less reliant on those Folds of Ezmith's and would instead keep their armies marching along with their supply caravans. This would make them harder to raid, but no harder than what you'd normally expect from raiding an enemy army; indeed if that was all Ambarta had done differently this time around, then Perivon would almost be insulted.

For his part, he felt wonderfully prepared this time. With luck, the two wizards from Mountain Home would be here even before Ambarta's army, and certainly no more than a couple days after. More wizards from Comperr's Guild should arrive perhaps a couple tendays after that.

Yes, Perivon knew exactly how much damage Ambarta could and would do to Cleononia, and then they would be brought down to their knees and brought to account for bringing war to a region that had not known it for centuries.

He absentmindedly spun the ring on the middle finger of his left hand with his thumb. Most men would have stopped wearing the ring long since; it had been over a decade since he'd lost his wife, but wearing the ring reminded him to be the man she expected him to be. Cleononia was his to protect, the people here were his responsibility, and he could not let bitterness or anger distract him from his duty.

He was hungry, but he could eat anytime. He pulled a chair to the edge of the center table and sat, diagramming how his outriders could slow the Ambartan army's march between Mhairi and Dazbog.

～

Ezmith sat astride his great warhorse, a black gelding named Thunder, watching a hundred yards away from the wall of Mhairi as Eztas rampaged along the top. Predictably, the garrison had scattered, sounding the retreat almost as soon as Ezmith had cracked their wall like an egg. He kicked Thunder to a trot and called the advance.

He had Ambarta's entire army here, less the small garrisons left in the cities that might be targeted for a counterattack.

He rode behind the bulk of the army, some fifteen hundred infantry, armed with long spears as their primary weapon and wearing short swords and bucklers for fighting in close quarters or if they lost their spear. He had little cavalry; they weren't as practical for besieging a city as infantry and archers.

He had not had *any* cavalry until they had taken Disote. All of Disote's conscripted men fit the definition of cavalry, though they would be considered light rather than heavy. Disote used their forces to constantly patrol the highways and roads throughout the small nation, and it was joked that you could leave a sack of gold on the side of the road in Disote for a tenday and it would still be there when you came back for it.

As it was, he was mostly using Disote's forces as scouts, which only took a handful away from their home country at a time and left the bulk of them doing their patrols and protecting the ice trade that was shockingly lucrative.

Seeing that the taking of the city required no action on his part, he slowed Thunder to a walk and lazily made his way to the gate. Why *did* people buy so much ice? Any time Ezmith wanted his drink, or anything else for that matter, chilled, he simply chilled it with magic. Any wizard could turn water to ice with little effort, but apparently there were so few wizards that those with the means would pay incredible prices to have ice delivered to their palaces.

He watched the front lines of his force as it began to enter the city through the broken wall. They had their orders: Ezmith needed say nothing more than he already had. Even better: they had experience. This was hardly the first city they had taken.

Thinking of Disote's ice trade naturally moved his thoughts to the subject of his research on his last trip to Disote, specifically Glacies Castle. There was a centuries-long gap in historical records surrounding the War of the Intelligences. Historians called it Lost 500 Years. No one knew what life had been like before and during the War.

In fact, it was not perfectly clear what the War had even been fought about. He supposed there were probably some more informative histories somewhere far East in Admone, but the only historical records he'd found so far had been one volume in the Royal Library of Comperr which Ezrote had helped him find, and one in the library at Glacies Castle after they had taken Disote.

All he knew for certain was that prior to the War of the Intelligences, magic had apparently been much more ubiquitous. Creatures known as Moon Elves seemed to be the victors in the War, and all of the nations west of the Berg had been settled by refugees fleeing the conflict.

The lack of clear histories on something only a thousand years old bothered Ezmith greatly. He yanked Thunder around chunks of rock as he rode his horse into the city with no fear. He closed his eyes, drew in a little magic and created a sphere of protection around himself and his horse. If Perivon had ordered an archer to hide and attempt to assassinate him, the sphere would stop the arrow.

If Moon Elves had been the victors, then where were they now? How could a war of any kind make magic either more or less common? The magic was simply there, no amount of killing or combat could possibly affect who could touch magic and how much they could draw – could it? There were disturbing possibilities hiding in the missing histories.

Ezmith rode Thunder through the city all the way to the Western wall, where he dismounted and handed the reins to a soldier standing nearby. He climbed the stairs to the wall walk and gazed out to see if he could still see the dust trail of the retreating army. He could not. It wasn't the heat of summer yet, but it had been days since the last rainfall and the ground should have been dry enough to give clear sign of a retreating army.

There was nothing.

Ezmith furrowed his brows. This was troubling. The army had clearly retreated; the city was completely taken. But if they hadn't gone down the road…then where had they gone? His plan had been to catch them up on the Plains and either destroy or capture them before they could fall back to Dazbog.

He drummed his fingers on the top of the wall as he thought. There were only really two possibilities: they had fled some other direction or…they had not actually fled at all. Ezmith whipped around to the hundredman that was serving as his messenger today.

"Double the size of the squads! Search every building for enemy soldiers! Every squad is to report back to their hundredman every 15 minutes, no exceptions!"

The hundredman dashed off to relay his instructions. Beyond those instructions, the only thing Ezmith could do was stand a little readier than he had been a moment ago. He stayed on the wall walk but faced the inside of the city, looking around as if he would be able to see where the army was hiding from this vantage point.

If they were hiding here, chances are they would have already ambushed his army, or they would be any moment. If they *weren't*... Ezmith looked to his left, to the North, at the lake that Mhairi was built on the shores of. A small river perhaps thirty feet across in most places flowed from the lake down all the way to the coast and emptied into the ocean.

Could the army have escaped down the *river*? They'd have to have had barges prepared in advance. He turned and waved his hands deliberately in the air, drawing a box shape, then thrust his hand into it. The edges of the box suddenly glowed with brightness, and everything visible within the box became blurry and unfocused. No amount of adjusting his own eyes would sharpen what he could see. That was one of the many difficult things about scrying; for all intents and purposes the scry had its own eyes, and you had to control the eyes of the scry separately from your own.

He closed the fist of the arm he had thrust into the box, and it tightened on...something – no one knew what was in there or what substance it might be made of, but it essentially served as a handle for the wizard to move the scry to the desired position. He yanked the whatever-it-was to the right, and the image in the scry box flew past as if the eyes of the scry had launched forward at several times the speed of the fastest bird.

As the view was hurtling forward, Ezmith made a stroking motion with his left thumb and finger, bringing the image in the scry box into sharper focus. The view in the scry box found the flow of the water leaving the lake and turned sharply to the left to follow the river. Now that the view was in focus, the hurtling didn't seem as uncontrollably fast.

Ezmith followed the river for a few miles and, sure enough, a small fleet of barges started to come into view. The barges were large enough to fit about fifty soldiers comfortably, and they were in a single-file line about ten barges long. They would make good time on those craft; even being let out into the ocean a hundred miles north of Dazbog they'd likely still arrive in the city at about the same time they would if they'd ridden their horses to death on the Highway.

And they were virtually impossible to follow, let alone overtake. He considered for a moment whether to Fold his troops to somewhere along the coast, or even just create the Fold in the air above and they could rain arrows down on the barges.

But no...the soldiers were all equipped with full shields. All they'd have to do was hunker down and wait for the barges to float out of range. The barges were moving fast enough that archers Folded in place would have little time to be effective.

He could Fold himself there...no, Perivon surely had something prepared in case Ezmith showed up. The benefit wasn't worth the risk to his own safety.

Not for the first time, he wished he'd figured out how to Fold through solids or liquids. It would be deeply satisfying to suddenly drop a massive boulder or something from the sky onto the barges. Most of the time, he refused to Fold anywhere that he hadn't been before, because if he accidentally attempted to Fold through a solid object his Fold would rebound back into him with such force that he was useless for days.

Liquids were a little more forgiving, but opening a Fold through any amount of liquid required such focus and effort that the last time he'd tried he'd given himself a bloody nose and a headache that had lasted days.

Ezmith released the scry, the box disappearing just in time for him to slam his fist on the top of the parapet. Every time he thought he had anticipated Perivon's plans and accounted for them, the man pulled some move like this. The five hundred some-odd soldiers would be an added strength to the fortifications at Dazbog, but the information they carried is what would be most valuable. They would be able to tell Perivon with full certainty what numbers Ambarta's army came in, exactly how they had conducted the siege, and other details that Ezmith would much rather Perivon be left in the dark on.

Ezmith straightened and turn at the sound of running footsteps coming to tell him what he already knew.

"Sire, the city is empty of soldiers," the hundredman gasped between breaths. "Only citizens are here, and they are not resisting."

Ezmith nodded. While disappointing, the escape of the garrison did little to change his plans. "Send out the scouts. I want to know about every divot in the road between here and Orell, and I want the entire countryside between here and Disote covered. Also send scouts towards Dazbog. I want to know everything between us and the walls of the city."

The hundredman nodded. "Yes, sire," and took off running again. The man didn't need to run; it's not like Ezmith was going to hurt him if walked like a normal person.

Ezmith turned back to look out over the countryside and began some more scrying. Good scouts could gather much information that scrying could not, but the opposite was true as well, and scrying was wonderfully fast. He originated a new scry directly above the city of Dazbog. There were limits to scrying -- one could only scry a certain distance from oneself, and once materialized, a scry could only travel so far from the origination point before fading from existence.

He didn't scry long; just enough to verify that the outwardly visible defenses had not changed since the last time he had looked. He didn't have time for much more. His mother had instructed him to report as soon as the city was taken.

Leaving Eztas in charge now that the large man's battle rage had worn off, Ezmith created a Fold to the throne room in Redwood castle.

He stepped through his Fold to the cooler but wetter air of the Wood Coast. The sound of the rain pattering on the roof was a distinct reminder of his time in this country. He looked around, his lip curling somewhat in distaste at the familiar etched art style of the castle here. His mother loved Redwood and spent as much time here as possible. She said it reminded her of their first victory and their humble origins.

That's not what it reminded Ezmith of. It reminded him of all his failures, of how what was supposed to be a months-long siege had turned into a year-long siege. It was here that he had been first faced with his own...*incompetence* at being a military commander. He'd learned much since their time here, but going head-to-head with Lord Perivon had so far been just as discouraging as conquering the Wood Coast had been.

The throne room was empty, which was no surprise. Public audiences were held in the Map room, which, despite the name, was both larger and closer to the entrance of the castle. The throne room was reserved for smaller audiences and counseling with advisors. All the large rooms in the castle were decorated the same, as were the hallways.

The only decorations were paintings hanging on walls in hallways and the etchings, absurdly detailed and meticulous carvings in the wooden panels of the walls that depicted everything from sunsets to battles and campfires to hunting. The etchings weren't just cuts and grooves -- though many of the lines were done that way – the people of the Wood Coast also had a technique of heating the tips of different specialized knives to make burn marks along wherever they were cutting.

The combination was known across the world, and indeed Wood Coast etchings were something that his mother had seized on as a profitable export and another reason for merchant ships to dock at Redwood before Bahadir or Dazbog.

The art seemed fine enough, Ezmith supposed. He didn't know how such things were measured, and he did not care to learn. As he came to the doors at the end of the hallway, which led into the Map room, he took a deep breath and entered. The sound of women's laughter drew his eyes to the end of the long room, where his mother stood, holding a glass of wine, with Lady Aletheia, their vassal here in the Wood Coast, and several other women whom Ezmith did not recognize.

They were clearly discussing men in general, or perhaps a specific one. Ezmith felt his lip curl again before he could stop it. Why did his mother engage with this nonsense? Of course, Aletheia was the age where he supposed she *should* be looking for someone to marry, and he also supposed with the girl's parents dead that it would make the most sense for his mother to be helping that process along, but it was simply jarring to go from a battlefront to a...pillow party.

"Mother," he called, stopping while still several yards away. "I come with news."

His mother excused herself with a smile and walked over to Ezmith, her elaborately embroidered dress swishing with her steps.

"Is Mhairi ours?" she asked as soon as she got to his side.

He nodded.

She must have noticed something in his face, because she grabbed his shoulder. "Did something go wrong?"

"No, mother," he said, shaking his head and taking a deep breath. "The Cleononian garrison put up nothing more than a token resistance, and fled using barges on the Gabija river."

"Then what's wrong?" his mother asked, her face drawn in concern.

He was surprised she hadn't already seen it. Perhaps if she had been there herself along with him. "He knew. He knew we would come to Mhairi first, and he knew that we would try to chase down his fleeing garrison before it could reach Dazbog. By using the barges, he caused us to waste precious time searching every cellar and attic in the city for their forces, not to mention making the garrison impossible to follow or harry, even for me."

His mother nodded slowly. "You're worried about what else Perivon has predicted and what he may have in store."

Ezmith looked over to the other women still talking happily. They clearly weren't able to hear any of this conversation so he nodded. Looking down at the ground, he felt his anger rise. This whole situation was absurd – he was a *wizard*! Any fool with enough experience could lead an army, but *no one* could match his power with magic.

Even the scrying he had done to verify where the garrison had gone would have been beyond some wizards, and exhausted others to where they would need food and rest before performing more spells.

Perivon was *not* smarter than him; Ezmith knew and understood things that would have Perivon staring like a skick in torchlight. The only reason Perivon was a threat on the battlefield was because he had so much experience in battle. There was nothing special about him; he had no gifts or acumen, all he had was a stock of knowledge built up.

He felt his mother's hand rub his arm, and his eyes went to her hand.

"It's alright, Ezmith. So far, everything's gone according to plan. I'll go back to Mhairi with you in a few hours, and we'll go over our next moves." She looked to Aletheia and the other women. "Aletheia's interest has been caught by Ezrote," she said, smiling happily. "As long as he's not too opposed, we might end up having a strong connection here that need not be enforced by the sword."

She sighed fondly as she continued watching Aletheia. "This girl is strong enough of mind to be a threat if she ever becomes discontent, but once she's family then our interests will be her interests."

Ezmith eyed the girl doubtfully. *Ezrote?* How smart could she really be, then? His mother walked back to the circle and joined in the conversation as though she had never left. What could she possibly need a few hours for? Why couldn't they leave now?

He sighed, then took his leave to go to the castle library to see if Guillame was in. Guillame was a remarkably powerful wizard and scholar to boot. He also seemed to be the only person in the entire Wood Coast who frequented the library. Apparently reading was not high on the list of priorities for those who chopped trees and hunted for a living.

Guillame wouldn't have much of value to offer when it came to the war with Cleononia, but he was one of the few people Ezmith could discuss magic with and he was as knowledgeable as anyone about the Lost 500 and the War of the Intelligences. He walked down the hall towards the library, hoping to clear his mind for at least a few hours before Folding back to Mhairi, back to war.

∿

Ezren stood on the wall overlooking the training yard. Luckily this wall had a parapet on both sides so he could stand mostly hidden and still watch Introm train with Master Juildar. Introm favored the sword-and-shield, much like Ezren did, and it was the only form that Introm had won in the past.

Ezren watched as the two circled around the middle of the training yard. Introm was the taller, but only by a bit, so neither would give themselves an advantage by either closing the distance or making it larger. Ezren was shorter than both, which was something to keep in mind.

Sword-and-shield was a defensive style, easily the most defensive of the three. Twin swords was more aggressive and two-handed sword even more so. The two combatants circled each other, then Introm lunged forward with a long thrust. Even from the wall, Ezren could tell the thrust had no hope of success; Master Juildar did not even block or parry, he simply took a step back and was clear.

Ezren furrowed his brow. Master Juildar could have knocked Introm's sword down by the tip as he stepped back, digging it into the dirt long enough to come around to the back of Introm's sword-arm, miles away from Introm's shield and positioned such that Introm would either have to drop his sword to spin quickly enough to block or just accept the hit.

Maybe it would have made Master Juildar more vulnerable to a counter-attack. He continued to watch as Introm attempted an over-head swing, which the instructor blocked and countered with a straight thrust at Introm's chest. Introm barely managed bring his shield in front to parry the thrust, twisting his body so that the tip of the practice sword narrowly passed by his chest.

From this point on it seemed that Master Juildar was firmly in control. He had not over-extended with his thrust, so he was able to pull it back, raise his shield to stop any counter attacks by Introm, then stepped forward and swung the sword wide to come and strike Introm in the middle of his back.

It was hard to say exactly what Introm had done wrong, beyond either predicting incorrectly what Juildar was going to do or not predicting it at all. Besides just not being as good as Master Juildar, what exactly were Introm's weaknesses?

It was time to get serious about this. Ezren pulled out his notebook and his graphis and started to keep track of everything that happened in each bout as he continued to watch. He made a chart of every attack that was made by either Introm or Master Juildar, whether it was countered, and what attack or counter ended the match successfully, and who won.

They were at it for another hour and Ezren had an entire page of notes by the time they were finished. A lot of bouts could be completed in an hour and there was a lot of potential insight in what he had already recorded. Introm practiced frequently, so Ezren would have plenty more chances to get more information.

For now, though, he had to go find Ben Rider. Ben was supposed to be leaving for Comperr by the end of the day. One of Ben's odd quirks was that he always tried to leave with the sunset if he could. He refused to explain why, just that he liked to spend the first night on the road in view of the city.

He headed down the outside staircase and across the courtyard to the door that led down a long archway into the main courtyard of the castle complex. From there, he walked down through the barracks complex, past the administration buildings for the Guards, past the barracks buildings, and past the side roads that led up into the neighborhood of small houses for families of the guards.

Coming out of the barracks complex, the road crossed over the river then merged with the North road. Ezren took the other way down into the markets. There was a healthy amount of people in the streets bustling about buying whatever they needed for dinner.

Ezren went up into a quieter neighborhood with no shops and few vendors. Most of the men who had been in the guards for a while eventually moved out of the barracks complex and into the city, at least if that was where they were assigned, and Rider was no exception.

Just as Ezren was walking up the last part of the road to Ben's house, he saw Ben coming down, leading his horse Fengari, who was loaded down with full packsaddles.

When Ben saw Ezren, he smiled and rolled his eyes but did not stop. Ezren fell in beside him.

"I was wondering when I'd see you," Ben said. "Both your surrogate mother and your actual father gave me some warning."

That was unexpected. "What did they tell you?"

"Completely different things. Ambassador Bura instructed me in no uncertain terms that I was to let you accompany me on some check-up trips around Novis Terram, and Captain Kimorae instructed me in no uncertain terms that I should only let you come if you 'earned it'."

They walked in silence for a few steps. Ezren cleared his throat.

"Well, I need to get some training on how to be a scout so that I can go with Ambassador Bura on one of her trips to Comperr. I'm going to see the Royal Art House, and maybe even an elf!"

Ben quirked an eyebrow at him. "You've already seen an elf, kid. Probably more than one."

Ezren skipped a step. "What are you talking about – no I haven't!"

Ben chuckled, but he looked around carefully before speaking, and spoke more quietly. "Look, Ezren, it's one of their best-kept secrets. Elves look just like humans most of the time. Taller than average, and not a fat one among them, but winged elves have to transform before they can fly, and Moon elves don't glow or turn white unless they're doing magic."

Ezren stared at Ben, his jaw practically trailing along on the ground. Ben noticed and laughed good-naturedly.

"The main way you can tell is by their ears, and around here they'll always be wearing a hat, have their hood up, or just use their hair to hide them. Their merchants don't want to miss out on Mountain Home steel and all the other goods from West of the Berg any more than human merchants do."

Part of this revelation was exciting, but the greater part was disappointing. "I guess that means they don't actually ride unicorns the way we ride horses."

"No, they do not. I've only ever seen one unicorn myself, but I'm told they actually avoid elves, despite what the histories say."

Wait – Ben had *seen a unicorn?!* "How have you not told me this before?! Where did you see it?"

With yet another good-natured laugh, Ben replied, "I *have* told you this before, but you were too busy swinging your damn sword around to listen. I told you and the knife-thrower the entire story."

Ezren wasn't sure what to say to that. Maybe he *should* try harder to listen to Ben.

"Well, I still want to go to Comperr, and Ambassador Bura says that if I want to come then I have to be useful, so I need to learn how to be a good scout for the embassy. Can I go with you on a few scouting trips and have you teach me what to do?"

Ben pursed his lips thoughtfully. "I'm on my way out now, but I can definitely make it there within a tenday, possibly as quick as 8 days. I'll have to turn around and come right back, so I'll be back in probably just under two tendays. Let's talk then and we'll figure out when you can come with me on a jaunt or two. Would your father be coming along?"

Ezren looked up at him as they walked, "I don't think so. He didn't say anything about going and I don't think he'd be able to find the time."

Ben nodded thoughtfully. "What about Raban the knife-thrower? I suppose he wants to come too?"

They turned onto the main road in the city headed towards the East gate. "If you're alright with him coming, then absolutely. He would love to."

"I'm not just alright with it," Ben replied with his ready smile, "I *require* it, and if not Raban then someone else. The last thing I want is to be stuck alone with you in the woods."

"Coins," Ezren said with a smile. "Thanks, Ben! I'm excited about this."

Ben waved him away. "Don't forget to take good care of Asteri.

Don't push her further or faster than she's willing to go and pay attention while you're with her."

Ezren stopped as they reached a fork in the road. "I inspect my horse myself every day just like you taught me."

Ben continued walking and turned his head back and called to Ezren. "I wasn't talking about your horse."

Ezren froze. Did Ben mean…no…but wait…*what?!*

Ben turned his head and called back again, "And don't forget to rub her down afterwards!" and positively roared with laughter as he continued on his way.

Ezren stood there, mortified, for a long moment, occasionally getting jostled by the crowd that was beginning to thin as the dinner hour got closer and more people returned home.

He shook himself and headed back up to the castle complex. What in the Inferno did people think was going on between him and Asteri? They had great conversations and she knew more about history other interesting topics than anyone else he talked to, but there was so much she was ignorant of because of her sheltered life in the castle. When he was her age he had already survived off what he could snare in the woods, fought goblins, and rescued his father from certain death at the hands of a rogue tax collection brigade. Asteri had rarely even left the castle, and even more rarely done so without an escort of bodyguards and handlers.

But beyond his actual feelings for Asteri, there was a more important question that needed answering – why were all the adults in his life jumping to the conclusion that something was going on between them? If they were all under the impression that there was more to his relationship with Asteri than there actually was, could he be doing something to give them that impression? And if so, was he giving that impression to Asteri as well?

He felt the blood drain from his face – what about Asteri's *father*, the king of Mountain Home? He didn't know what the punishment was for a common Ambartan boy fraternizing with the princess of Mountain Home, but he doubted that the benevolence the king had showed them over the last years would continue if the king thought Ezren was...involved with the princess.

He had no idea what to do about all this, and despite thinking about it all the way back to the castle, he still had no ideas.

When he got to the castle complex, he went straight for the training yard that they used most often. He shook off his thoughts about Asteri and began to practice with sword-and-shield.

He hadn't scheduled any time with an instructor, so he faced off against a practice dummy and went through the moves. There weren't very many moves in this style, since there were only so many things that were practical to do when one arm held a shield in defense and the other wielded a medium-length sword, but he went through all of them, then went through them again.

There were three thrusts, and each could be targeted at three different regions – the torso, the legs, or the head. The three thrusts were a 'jab', which was mostly useful as a feint, a 'full thrust', intended for causing superficial wounds, and a 'long thrust', intended for ending a fight by running through your opponent.

He went through all nine possible combinations against the practice dummy, then began adding moves after the jabs that could take advantage of the feint.

Just like with thrusts, there were three different slashes, which could be done at three different areas of the opponent. Ezren performed a 'committed', overhead, slash as a follow-up to a jab at the legs. Theoretically, the opponent would drop the shield to block the sword, then be unable to defend quickly enough against the overhead slash.

A 'committed' slash was roughly equivalent to a full thrust; the idea was to injure your opponent, but not put enough of your body and power into it to end the fight right then and there. Any injury you could inflict on your opponent would slow or weaken them to some degree, so if you were able to injure them and avoid being injured yourself, you would eventually win.

The footing was quite different between the different slashes and thrusts, which was one of the reasons the distinctions between them was so important. In order to go from a 'committed' slash to a 'terminal' slash, you had to take an additional step forward, even further into your opponents swing radius. In other words, if you went for a terminal slash and failed, you were likely to die. A 'light' slash, however, often required no change of footing at all from whatever you had just done.

But thrusts and slashes only covered the sword arm. The shield arm could also be used for attack as well as defense. There was a standard defensive posture that paired with each of the different thrusts and slashes, but a significant part of each fight was predicting where your opponent would strike next and preparing your shield to intercept it in time.

When using the shield aggressively, there were really only two choices – a sweep or a bash. A sweep was much like a parry, the idea was to redirect your opponent's momentum and cause them to over-balance so you could then strike. A bash was when you brought your arm in tight and lunged forward with your shoulder to knock your opponent off balance.

Between the nine different thrusts, nine different slashes, and two different shield choices that could all be put in whatever order, there were thousands of different possible combinations of 3-move attacks.

Of those thousands, though, some weren't possible because of foot positioning, and many weren't practical in terms of effectiveness, so Ezren methodically went through the two hundred attack combinations they had been taught.

As he went through various combinations of thrusts, slashes, sweeps, bashes, blocks, and parries, he considered how he was going to beat Introm. He would have to schedule a lot more one-on-one time with the instructors, but he probably couldn't tell them that he was training to defeat a certain opponent, or they might be more hesitant to give him what could be considered an unfair advantage.

The key, though, as his father had said before about fighting, was to surprise your opponent. It was as true in a duel as it was on the battlefield, as true between two combatants as it was between twenty thousand.

It wasn't enough to just do the unexpected, however. After all, removing all your armor and trying to fight with your fists would be quite unexpected. It had to be both unexpected and effective. If you could make your opponent believe you were going to do one thing, then surprise them with something else, you could win.

One way or another, every fight ended because one side failed to either predict or properly prepare for what the other side would do.

Ezren took a break from training after a last high slash that brought the practice sword against the neck of the training dummy. The sun had nearly finished going down and stars were beginning to be visible in the sky to the East. He breathed heavily and felt the sweat soaking through the parts of his shirt where his armor was strapped on.

He held up the practice sword. The weight was remarkably close, though one might assume that the wood would be lighter than the steel of a real sword. He twisted the sword in his hand so that the blade pointed backwards parallel with his forearm. In twin swords, many of the moves called for twisting or spinning the sword in your hand such that you could angle the sword blade towards your opponent even when swinging backhanded.

With a double-edged sword like what was used for sword-and-shield, this was less important, and more difficult since the swords were longer and heavier. You also lost some strength when wielding a sword that extended back up the length of your arm instead of towards your opponent.

But…if his opponent wasn't *expecting* it…the timing of the hit would be slightly different. Maybe he could catch Introm off guard.

He raised the shield, did a jab at the legs of the dummy, then took a step forward, pivoting on his shield leg as he turned the sword handle in his hand and…promptly dropped the sword on the ground. He was right, though. A normal slash would hit at the same moment as his sword foot came down in front. Turning it as he had, it would not land until a beat after.

He idly practiced turning the sword frontwards and backwards as he considered the possibilities. It was a big risk. He tested the strength of his swing and grip against the practice dummy, and sure enough, having the sword backwards made it much harder to keep the sword under control; each impact threatened to yank the sword out of his grip, and the blade repeatedly came in contact with his forearm when it got stopped by the dummy's body.

The arm plates he wore did not fully encircle his forearms, and the practice sword was impacting his arm right at the edge of the plate. A real sword would slice him up if he tried to do what he was doing with this.

There was a way, though. He may not know what it was, but there was one. He stood in the training yard long after night had fallen, twisting and turning the sword and trying different slashes.

～

Timot waited up for Ezren, though he half-expected that he was at the training yard, which meat he wouldn't be home until late. He had seen Ezren headed that way as he himself left the office to come home for dinner. It wasn't uncommon for Ezren to forget to eat when he was focused on something. Sometimes he wondered if Ezren wasn't actually forgetting, but deliberately choosing not to eat just to keep himself 'tough'.

It wasn't the most irrational thing a boy might do when he was taken unexpectedly from a life of scraping by to a life of luxury and plenty. Frankly, while he wished Ezren would grow out of this phase more quickly, it was better than him leaning into all the trappings of palace life and becoming lazy or gluttonous.

Timot ate the food brought up from the kitchens and lounged, reading in his chair in the front room while he waited for Ezren to return home. He wasn't particularly worried about Ezren, but he wanted the boy to have a reminder that his father was paying attention.

At some point, the book fell to his lap and he gave in to his tiredness, falling asleep.

A pounding at the door caused him to jerk awake. He looked around blearily, unsure how long he had been asleep, and the pounding came again at the door. He got up quickly out of the chair, pulled his sword out of its sheath by the door, then pulled the door open just enough to look at who it was.

It was Werbal.

"You've been summoned Captain," he said in his usual fast-paced, breathless way. "Ambarta has broken the armistice."

Timot dropped the tip of the sword and opened the door the rest of the way. Thankfully, he was still dressed. He looked out the window in the kitchen as he grabbed his boots and went back to his chair to put them on. It was pitch dark outside.

"What time is it?" he asked.

"Sunrise will be in about an hour, Captain."

Timot stared at him for a moment, then pulled on his boots the rest of the way and marched directly to Ezren's room, opening the door quickly but quietly. Indeed, Ezren lay in his bed asleep, his head just visible over his blankets. Timot closed the door as quietly as he could, but annoyance caused him to shut it a little harder than he meant. The boy could have woken him when he got back. Maybe then he wouldn't have the ache in his lower back.

He motioned Werbal to lead the way and followed him out the door.

The halls were eerily quiet, the only sound being their own footsteps echoing from the walls and ceiling. They trekked all the way through the castle complex to the blue room, where only Wizard Paavali, a thin, spindly man who looked like he never saw sunlight, stood waiting, standing with his shoulders slightly hunched and wringing his hands. Paavali was a nervous fellow, as a rule, but he was a competent wizard.

"You've received word from Leir?" Timot asked as soon as he had entered.

Paavali nodded and opened his mouth, but before he could speak the door flew open and a rather unkempt Fiona came flowing in, followed immediately by an even more unkempt Captain Bagon.

"Leir has sent a message?" Fiona and Bagon both asked in unison.

Paavali nodded and opened his mouth for the second time, but the door flew open yet again to admit both King Radomir and Queen Oana. The room was a little crowded with this many, but everyone shuffled around to give the King and Queen more elbow room.

"Ambarta has broken the armistice?" King Radomir asked Paavali.

"Yes!" Paavali blurted quickly with an eye looking askance at the door. Sure enough, no sooner had Paavali answered than the door opened yet again and Mountain Home's other wizard, Mellion, entered. He was not an overly fat man, but with the build of someone who spent most of his waking hours sitting he made the room that much more crowded. His blonde hair was thin, but not with age, and cut fairly short.

Without giving Mellion a chance to ask the question, Queen Oana fixed her eyes on Paavali. "What is the message? Give it to us in full, exactly as it was given to you."

Paavali unfolded a piece of paper in his hand and began to read. "Ambarta has taken Mhairi. We are pulling our forces back to Dazbog, where we expect they will go next. Guillame appears to still be in the Wood Coast. Ezmith and Eztas are in Mhairi. Please send all wizards available to assist."

He folded the paper back up and looked to the king and queen. There was silence for a long moment as each person present internalized the magnitude of what had happened.

"Well," King Radomir shrugged, "we knew this was coming, and we knew what we would do when it did. Are there any changes we need to make to our plans?"

Captain Bagon shook his head. "I don't think so, though perhaps we should send Paavali and Mellion with a guard of a hundred men and have them travel off the Northern highway wherever possible. Now that Ambarta has moved on Mhairi, Perivon will have sent a ship North to pick them up at the border of Disote and Cleononia."

King Radomir looked to Fiona. "Ambassador, you will leave for Comperr with the sunrise. Rider will beat you there by a few days, but his message is still valid. Mellion, can you get a message to Vewen?"

Mellion nodded. "Most likely, yes. If not, a pigeon will be nearly as fast."

The king nodded. "Very well. Send the alert to Vewen and be gone with the sunrise as well." He looked around as if he could hear the pounding of their racing hearts. "Ambarta has brought war again, but with Ankon's blessing perhaps we can make this the last time. Go, all of you. You know what to do."

CHAPTER 3: RUMORS OF WAR

T he walls of Dazbog would certainly loom when one came close
enough, but Ezmith and his army were still far enough away that
the stone battlements looked small in the distance. Here the army had
stayed for almost two days while camp was made and the supply line
established.

Ezmith ground his teeth thinking of how long it took to get here.
Cleononian light cavalry had been raiding his supply wagons almost
endlessly since they had left Mhairi. There had to be 500 of them out
on the Plains! He couldn't be everywhere at once and had eventually
surrounded the supply caravan in a bubble of his forces, which meant
that half his army wasn't even marching on the road.

They'd had to stop earlier to set up their nightly defenses and leave
later because of everything that had to be taken down. It was only 200
some-odd miles from Mhairi to Dazbog, and it had taken his army an
entire *15 days* to travel the distance.

They had also suffered losses in essential supplies and even soldiers,
but those could be replaced – the time could not.

Now, though, he'd pulled several hundred patrolmen from Disote to
keep watch over the supply line from here to Mhairi, and another

hundred to watch it from Corbina and Orjan to Mhairi. Now, if Perivon wanted to raid their supply lines he'd have to send raiders all the way into Ambarta or Disote to do it.

Ezmith looked out at the walls, resisting the urge to scry to get a closer look. He knew what these walls looked like; he had been here before and had scried it many times. The wall was double-thick, meaning it would take even Eztas a while to break directly through it, and Ezmith would have to be within bowshot and vulnerable to knock it down with his magic.

That wasn't necessarily a problem, but even he had limits. It wouldn't just be arrows coming at him; Perivon's lapdog wizard Leir had middling abilities, and Dazbog also had several defensive siege weapons. Summoning enough Earth to break apart a wall that thick while holding a Shield that kept all dangers out would be...difficult. Perhaps impossible, though that was a word he was loath to use.

In this situation, his power was limited in much the same way as an offensive siege weapon would be, both in range and fragility.

Ezmith turned from the wall and ducked into his tent, which was large and circular, with a table in the middle that held a large and detailed map of Dazbog. The walls of the city extended all the way to the cliffs on either side, with the ocean coming right up against the cliffs as they sloped downward toward the harbor.

Ezmith stared at the map as though looking at an especially difficult puzzle. His mother was back in Mhairi, allegedly to assist in coordinating the supplies since Ezrote's duties were keeping him in Comperr, but Ezmith knew why she was really there. She was there to endear the people of Mhairi to her. She had done this everywhere they had conquered.

He couldn't deny the effectiveness of the strategy, but he didn't understand why it was necessary. People would eventually come to appreciate her rule because she was an effective ruler – she kept crime down to a minimum, made trade faster and easier, and charged only a little more in taxes and tariffs than the rulers who had been there before. She let the previous rulers of each nation maintain leadership as her vassals, and very few people in any of the conquered nations opposed her rule.

Still, he was glad she wasn't here with him. It was harder to think properly and act boldly when she was watching. He never knew when she would jump in and countermand him. The fact that every time she did so she had a strong reason that was impossible to argue with only made it worse.

He stared at the map, judging distances. Then a thought occurred to him...and he smiled. Yes, that would work very well.

The following morning, as the sun rose in the East, Ezmith marched out at the head of a hundred archers. The rest of the army followed, but at a distance, and they stopped just out of bowshot of the wall, while Ezmith and the archers continued forward. As they walked, Ezmith waved his arms, creating a loose Shield of air. Ten archers marched to either side of him, with four more rows behind.

The barrier wouldn't stop enemy arrows or other projectiles, but it would slow them down enough that they would not pierce even the lightest of armor and would do no more than draw a little blood even if they hit exposed skin. It was much, much easier to make a barrier of this nature, and since it was done by creating a headwind against incoming arrows, it would also provide a significant boost to the arrows being shot by his own men, at the cost of a little bit of accuracy.

With only a minimal amount of his focus and energy going into the protective barrier, and a hundred archers to return fire on the wall, he could put much more into breaking the wall down. Eztas was back in camp, enchanted with everything except the berserker, which would be saved until the wall was breached. Not only did the berserker wear off faster than the rest of the enchantments he placed on his brother, but once it was on there was no reasoning with the man. He was likely to run straight for the wall and begin punching it with no regard for the unfriendly wizard who may be able to dismantle every enchantment on him.

Ezmith held his hand up to stop the archers, double-checked his Shield, and began the next step: breaking down the wall. He raised his hands in front of him, feeling the Earth in the thick rock of the wall. The top of the wall was filled with archers, as far as his eyes could see. In the middle, though, he saw the distant figure of an incredibly fat man he knew to be Leir, and two others who did not carry bows or other weapons.

He was just asking himself who these two were and whether they might be other wizards, when enemy arrows began to rain down on them. His barrier was doing its work, though, and while his own archers flinched instinctively when arrows bounced off of them, they held their ground and returned fire as Ezmith continued his work.

No sooner had he Discerned a slightly weaker spot in the wall to put his focus, however, than he felt his Shield pushed on.

Leir was fighting back.

No matter, he could handle Leir easily enough. But then...the pressure on the Shield doubled, then tripled, and before he could redirect his energy to maintaining it, the Shield had broken apart, and enemy arrows were thudding into his tiny contingent with devastating force. He held onto his attack on the wall and quickly made a small Shield around his own person.

Immediately he felt swipes coming at it from what must have been at least two wizards, while a competing wave of Earth worked to strengthen and stabilize the wall that he was attempting to crack.

Ezmith's hands began to shake from the exertion. It was easier for the defending wizards to maintain the wall than it was for him to change it, and even if he had still had the time, he may not have been able to ever break the wall against the three wizards fighting back. Frustration poured out of him along with the sweat on his face.

There were ten times the number of archers firing from the walls as he had with him, and his men were getting cut down with terrifying speed.

Ezmith roared, his frustration boiling over. He released Earth and instead conjured fire with the speed and power only he was capable of and hurled a massive fireball at the top of the wall. Just as he released it, he felt a thump in his left side. He looked down and saw an arrow sticking out of him. As if the pain had been waiting for him to see the arrow, it came in a wave that caused his vision to waver.

"Retreat!" he croaked as loudly as he could before beginning to fall down in agony. Two archers grabbed him under each arm and pulled him away as they all ran, fleeing from the rain of arrows. Ezmith looked up blearily at the wall and saw the smoldering circular cut-out his fireball had made at the top of the wall. He managed a weak smile just as one of the archers hiked his left arm to get a better grip and the surge of pain caused him to black out.

"...would not be here in time to make a difference," a man's voice said apologetically.

"I don't care!" a woman that sounded just like his mother replied. "You say he'll be fine, but he's not even awake yet!"

"He *will* be fine," the man said, less apologetically and more defensively. "Many people lose consciousness when they experience sudden and intense pain. We were able to remove the arrow without losing any splinters and he's all sewn up. He won't be dancing any jigs for awhile but I expect he'll wake up any time now."

Ezmith slowly opened his eyes, more in an attempt to stop the spinning sensation than anything else. Having his eyes open did lessen the feeling of whirling around but did not help at all in getting his bearings. He was seeing the ceiling of his tent, or at least he thought he was. Suddenly his mother's face shot into his view, nearly filling it with how close she was. He jerked back in startlement.

"How are you feeling, Ezmith? Does it still hurt?" She asked.

He thought for a moment. "It was a delaying tactic," he said simply.

His mother's face suddenly got smaller as she twitched her head back in confusion. "What are you talking about?"

"All the raids on our supply wagons. It was just to slow us down enough so that the wizards could travel from Mountain Home and get here before us."

His mother sat on the edge of the bed next to him. "Ezmith," she began. "You were shot. The surgeon says you're going to be fine, but that you'll have to stay in bed for a few days."

"We knew Mountain Home was going to send their wizards, but we thought we could take Dazbog before they arrived," Ezmith said, staring hard at the ceiling. "How long have I been asleep?"

"Three days," the man, who must have been the surgeon, replied.

"I came from Mhairi as soon as I received the message," his mother said. "They say you've been in and out, but that you last lost consciousness while they were removing the arrow and haven't been awake since."

Three days?! They'd lost another three days during this siege! Were his soldiers even stopping trade from going in and out of the city?! Had his captains made another attempt at the wall?! Had *anything* been done while he was unconscious?! He felt his hands shaking with rage, though his mother would likely take it to be from pain or weakness from his recovery. He gripped his bedsheets as hard as he could. As he spoke, his words came out clipped and deliberate. He was not sure how much of his anger showed through.

"Captain!" he called through gritted teeth, assuming that his First Captain, Captain Beaumont, was in the tent. Sure enough, he heard the man step forward.

"Yes, sir?"

"Order the siege engineers to begin building a catapult that can hurl a boulder into that wall from out of bowshot. I want it completed within *one tenday*. If they fail to deliver, execute them and find more."

"Sir?" came the cautious reply.

"Do it!" Ezmith yelled, then winced at the pain in his side. "Also, send a battalion back to Mhairi, gather up a hundred citizens including women and children and bring them back here."

"Hold, Captain," his mother said, then turned back to Ezmith. "Why? Why are you bringing them here?"

He looked at her, his already elevated fury rising higher. "We are playing by Perivon's rules: it's no wonder he's winning! I *will* beat him, and we *will* conquer Cleononia. Once the citizens are here, we will send a message to Perivon that we will hang ten of his citizens at random every day that he does not surrender the city of Dazbog!"

His mother's eyes widened. "Ezmith, yo – we can't do that. It would turn every citizen of Cleononia against us. We wouldn't just have to worry about raids from Perivon's army, we'd have to worry about them from every Cleononian old enough to carry a spear."

He glared at her. "By the time those people have learned about what we're doing, Perivon will have surrendered Dazbog to us. We will hang them within view of the city walls, so he will know for certain that we mean what we say."

"Ezmith," she said slowly, "think of how Mountain Home will respond. So far they've stayed mostly out of the conflict. They may be concerned about Comperr, but if they hear we are hanging innocent citizens at random, they could have ten thousand soldiers here in a tenday."

"Then we will deal with them when they get here!" Ezmith yelled, ignoring the pain that continued to flare up in his side. "No army can stand against Eztas and I, and Mountain Home wouldn't even have their wizards with them! We could break them where they stood!"

His mother squeezed her eyes shut and brought a hand to her face. Her voice remained perfectly calm, however. "You are not thinking past your anger right now, Ezmith. You would sacrifice the whole flock for the sake of one sheep."

She brought her hand down on Ezmith's. "Rest. Heal. Once you're back on your feet and the fire has had time to leave your blood, we can talk about the best way to take Dazbog." She turned to Captain Beaumont.

"Proceed with the orders to have a catapult built, but for the time being there is no need to threaten the lives of the siege engineers. Let them know that failure will bring consequences, but do not say what."

"Yes, Highness," Captain Beaumont replied.

Ezmith continued to glare at his mother. How *dare* she counter-mand him in this manner? The army was his to control, not hers. He conquered, and she ruled the conquered lands.

She either did not notice his glare or chose to ignore it. She turned to the surgeon.

"Is there something we can give him to help ease his pain? Or perhaps even help him sleep?"

"Yes," the surgeon replied. "A tincture of Wellflower will do both. I had some prepared already."

The surgeon handed a small cup to his mother, who held it to Ezmith's lips. He tried to struggle for a moment but realized he could barely lift his arms. Rather than embarrass himself by trying to resist, he lifted his head a trifle, glared into his mother's eyes, and drank the tincture.

He laid back, continuing to glare, as she sat there gently stroking his hand.

He would not forget this.

He would not for…

He wou…

Darkness took him.

~

Master Stark watched Ezren over the top of his shield as they circled each other.

He's doing it again, Ezren thought, his heart beating rapidly. *He's deliberately waiting to strike instead of finishing off the fight.* He'd noticed this about his instructors, and his working theory was that it was a teaching strategy either to give the student opportunities to strike or just to present a challenge appropriate for the skill level of the student.

He may not like that Master Stark was holding back – how was he ever going to get better if his instructors didn't press him? – but he could try to use it to his advantage. He aimed a light slash at Master Stark's middle, which was easily blocked by the shield, but then he did another light slash at Stark's feet, which caused him to bring the shield down low.

Master Stark didn't step back during the drop, so Ezren kept turning with the momentum of the slash until his right side was facing Master Stark and executed a full thrust right at his now-exposed middle. Master Stark's sword came swiping over to intercept it, but it came too late, after the end of Ezren's practice sword had impacted the breastplate with a definite "thunk".

Tournament rules were different from real fights; here Ezren's move counted as a victory though even a razor-sharp sword wouldn't have penetrated the armor with a thrust like that. However, in real combat it could not be predicted how much armor your opponent would have on; many foot soldiers got by with leather armor, and many bandits, brigands, and other threats may not have any armor at all.

So while Ezren's winning move here may not have made much sense given the plate mail worn by his opponent, there were many real-life situations in which it would have worked phenomenally.

Ezren stood up straight, blinking the sweat away from his eyes as Master Stark removed his helmet with a smile.

"Well done, Ezren! Very well done! The reason that finishing move worked so well was because you committed exactly the right amount, then took a risk you were confident would pay off. That's the hard part – taking enough of a risk that you surprise your opponent but not enough of a risk that you end up getting run through instead of him."

Over the last two tendays, Ezren had gotten much closer with both instructors that taught the sword-and-shield, Masters Juildar and Stark. They weren't available for one-on-one instruction as often as Ezren would like, but he'd still made much progress in that time. Not only that, but because of their help and feedback, the times he spent training on his own were more productive as well. He had even roped Raban into coming up a few times to train with him. Raban may not have had as much practice, but he seemed to have the speed of a snake and a natural talent for it.

Master Stark put his helmet back on.

"Alright, this time we're going to work on defense and countering. I'm going to keep the pressure up, and you're going to do everything you can to take control of the fight. You cannot win if your opponent is controlling the fight, so you must find ways to turn your opponent's aggressiveness to your favor."

Ezren took a moment to breathe deeply, trying to catch his breath. He'd been out here for hours; before training with Master Stark he had gone through hundreds of moves on the practice dummy. Now, after fighting a real opponent that required him to hold his shield up against actual counterattacks, his arms felt like they wanted to fall right off.

Even so, he assumed the basic ready stance, the top of the shield roughly level with his chin and his sword held at shoulder height, pointed directly at his opponent.

The moment he was in position, Master Stark launched into action. A thrust came directly for Ezren's face, which he parried just in time by lifting his shield up and stepping back hastily, almost stumbling. The thrust was immediately followed by Stark's shield slamming into his own, taking advantage of his poor footing compromised by his hasty step back. Ezren stumbled backwards, only just keeping his feet as the onslaught continued.

A slash came first at his head, then his feet, and only his reflexes saved him – the shield came up just in time to block the first slash, and he jumped straight up to avoid being hit in the legs.

Jumping proved to be a terrible response, however, because no sooner had his feet left the ground than his instructor's shield slammed into his own again, sending Ezren sprawling to the ground, landing hard on his right shoulder.

Master Stark lowered his sword and shield and walked over to Ezren as he struggled to get up to a sitting position.

"That should never have happened," Master Stark said with a rueful smile, looking down at Ezren. "You should have easily been able to get your shield down fast enough to block that second slash. Jumping was a panicked move, but it was easy to see that's what you were about to do. It seems like you're tired, Ezren."

Ezren finally stopped struggling and just put the sword and shield on the ground, then got shakily to his feet. Master Stark looked at him inquisitively.

"We haven't been at this for very long, Ezren. How are your arms and legs feeling?"

Ezren shook his head. "They feel like they're made of lead. I went through all the moves by myself before we started."

Master Stark nodded. "That would account for it, I suppose, but the most dangerous thing for a fighter is fatigue. Fatigue will kill you quicker than incompetence or stupidity. You can only rely on hot blood for so long."

Ezren shrugged. "There doesn't seem to be much I can do besides continuing to practice."

Shaking his head, Master Stark began to walk towards the weapon racks and gestured for Ezren to follow. "Has your father never talked to you about his guard training?"

Ezren didn't remember his father talking about his guard training at all – that was a dark time for both of them, what with their home having been burnt down just after they'd completed building it. Neither of them had talked much for months.

"No, sir, not really," he replied to Master Stark.

With a sigh, his instructor began to remove his armor and put it on the rack. "Well, guards undergo training specifically to make themselves stronger and faster. Haven't you ever wondered what all this is for?" He asked, gesturing to a series of bars set up at different heights above the ground, then pointing to a rack of practice swords that had various sizes of round disks attached at different places along the blades.

Ezren had never really paid attention to these. There was also a number of metal...things...that resembled miniature, skinny tables with four legs that would come down snugly on a shield. As he looked closer, he saw there was a stopper in the top of each of them.

"Honestly, sir, I have not thought much about them. What are they for?" He asked.

Master Stark pulled one of the practice swords with just one disk on it about a third of the way up the blade and handed it to Ezren.

Ezren gave it a swing or two. The sword was noticeably heavier than a normal practice sword.

"These are for strength training," Stark told him. "Don't practice too much with them, because if your arms are too used to a heavier sword then you'll be off-balance in a real fight, but they'll help your arms and shoulders gain strength much faster – Juildar has an entire set of moves he only practices with weighted swords so he can train with them every day without affecting his fighting. If you want your arms and shoulders to get stronger faster, these are essential."

Swinging it a few more times, Ezren had no doubt about that. He lowered the point to the ground and pointed to the miniature metal tables.

"What are those for?" he asked.

Master Stark grinned. "Those are for shields. They slide on top to make the shield heavier and do the same thing for your shield arm as the weighted sword does for your sword arm. They're not perfect; they make the shield more top heavy and don't work your arm in quite the same way, but they do well enough."

"But while we're talking about it, we should go over the rest as well." Master Stark walked over to the horizontal bars above the ground. To Ezren's surprise, he jumped up, grabbed the tallest bar, and began lifting himself up and letting himself down repeatedly, looking down at Ezren as he did so.

"There's more to strength than just being able to swing a sword for a long time. What if you find yourself needing to scale a cliff? Or a fortress wall?" He hopped down and let himself fall face-down onto the ground, only just catching himself with his hands, then repeatedly pushing himself up off the ground.

"What if you find yourself pinned by a fallen tree, or some other debris, and no one is there to save you?" Master Stark hopped to his feet.

"When was the last time you ran, Ezren?"

Ezren was taken aback. "Ran?" he shrugged. "I run all the time. I run to class, I run down to the barracks to meet my friend, and we go out to the woods and run sometimes."

"I want you to start running for no other reason than to make yourself out of breath. The more you work yourself so hard that you can feel your heart pounding in your head and like you're about to black out, the harder you'll have to work yourself to get to that point."

Ezren nodded. "And that's how I can stop fatigue from killing me? By letting it *almost* kill me over and over?"

"Essentially, yes," Master Stark replied.

That sounded pretty awful, but Ezren was prepared to do what he needed to do to go to Comperr. They continued the conversation, and Ezren got more details on exactly how he should go about training for the next while. Weighted sword and shield at least a few times each tenday. The other exercises and running as often as every other day if he felt like he could handle it. He still had a little over a month before the tournament, and Master Stark seemed confident that was enough time to make a noticeable difference.

As Ezren shed his armor and replaced his practice sword and shield on the racks, Raban came running in. It was typically frowned upon for youth that weren't students of the Academy to come up here unattended, but the instructors all liked Raban. In fact, they usually seemed happier to see Raban than they were to see Ezren.

Raban looked around, spotted Ezren, and came running over.

"Ben's back!" he declared with a grin and glint of excitement in his eyes.

No more needed to be said. Ezren launched into putting his equipment away as quickly as he could get his arms to move. In under a minute they were both bidding Master Stark a hasty goodbye and running out of the training yard, down through the castle complex, through the barracks complex, and onto the main road that would take them to Ben's home.

They arrived and knocked on the door, but there was no answer. They knocked again, even less patiently, and then they heard a voice behind them, making them jump.

"By Ankon, boys, can't a man have some rest after traveling a thousand miles in less than two tendays?"

They whirled around, and there stood Ben, still taking off his riding gloves. He smiled his long-suffering smile and motioned them to move aside, stepping past to open the door. Once inside, he left it open for them to follow.

"Not like it matters, though, I got a summons to the castle before I'd even stabled my horse. King Radomir wants a lot more scouting done on the borders with Robinton and Ambarta. I'll know more after the meeting but I would suspect I'll be leaving in the next couple days. Can you two be ready?"

Barely waiting for them to nod, he gestured for them to leave. "Very good, now get out. I've got to make myself pretty for the king and queen."

Ezren and Raban went out and stood on the street outside Ben's house. They looked at each other with wide eyes and even wider smiles.

"This is going to be absolute coins!" Raban declared.

Ezren nodded. "You've got a horse, right?"

"Yes, sort of. I can get one." Raban responded excitedly.

"We're going scouting!" Ezren yelled.

They both jumped up and down for a moment, then realized what they were doing and stopped, looking around to see if anyone was looking at them. They weren't kids anymore.

As such, in the most dignified manner possible, they took off running at full speed to head back to their homes to talk to their fathers.

~

Timot walked, somewhat bleary-eyed, past Werbal's desk and into his own office. He hadn't slept well the night before. Ezren had come home fizzling like a lit Skyfire, saying that Ben Rider was back, which Timot had already known, and that he was going to scout the border with Robinton and Ambarta, which Timot had also already known.

What had led to a long discussion was Ezren's expectation that he would be going with Ben. Granted, that had been their agreement, but that was before Rider had been assigned to scout a border with a hostile and unpredictable enemy. All of their information said that Ambarta was devoting their full attention to Cleononia, but Ezmith was no fool, and would know that Mountain Home was not occupied by a war with Comperr this time.

He would have gotten to bed late just due to that conversation, but that hadn't been the end of it. An urgent knocking had come at the door just as Timot had finally agreed to let Ezren go, trusting that Ben would do his best to keep them out of danger. At the door had been one of the pigeon caretakers, who handed him a message that had just come from Fiona in Comperr.

The message had been short and simple, as all messages sent via pigeon had to be, but it packed enough information into a few words to keep him up most of the rest of the night:

"Raanan irate at Rider's message. Threatened new war. Metnal obstinate, Vewen has left for Cleononia."

A lot of information, to be sure, and yet not nearly enough. King Raanan was a blustering fool who went from jolly to spitting mad at the drop of a hat, but was his threat of a new war just bluster or was it real? How long ago had Vewen left? Fiona had been there for days now, why had she just now sent the pigeon? How was she going to address the issues? Was there any good news?

He had decided to have Captain Bagon woken before waking the king, and the two of them had discussed the message to an exhaustive degree, then agreed that the king could be informed first thing in the morning.

Now, having only had a couple hours of sleep, he lumbered into his office. On his desk was a new stack of papers that he would have to find time to deal with around all the meetings and discussions over Fiona's message. It was going to be a long day.

No sooner had he sat down than there was a knock at the door and Werbal poked his head in.

"You've been summoned to the blue room, sir," he said. Then, looking at Timot for a moment, he paused. "Are you alright, sir?"

Timot nodded and stood up with the assistance of his hands. "I'm fine, Werbal, just didn't get much sleep last night."

He walked the familiar route to the Chordus Chamber, and found Captain Bagon there waiting. Somehow, Bagon looked like he'd gotten a perfect night's sleep. The bags under his eyes were no bigger than normal, he stood as straight as he always did, and his uniform was perfectly pressed. Come to think of it, maybe Bagon looked the same as always because he never got much more sleep than he had the night before.

He looked around the Chordus Chamber and sighed. It wasn't that he missed commanding troops on a battlefield, but he did get tired of standing around in a castle and talking all the time.

King Radomir entered and they immediately launched into telling him about Fiona's message, as well as the conclusions they had reached in their conversations the night before. The king listened attentively, his brow furrowed.

"That is why it is our recommendation that we keep our armies here instead of sending them to Cleononia's aid," Timot finished, holding his breath for the king's response.

The king nodded slowly, staring off to the side in deep thought.

"Would you recommend moving forward on our threat to Raanan? Sending our troops in as glorified merchant's guards and building outposts along the Northern Highway in Comperr's land?"

Timot and Bagon shared a look. "No, sire," Bagon replied. "Comperr isn't precisely friendly with Admone or Meand, but such a move could be easily construed as an act of aggression. With Raanan already threatening a second war, he may very well look to them as a means of achieving a different outcome this time."

"Not only that," Timot added, letting out his breath, "But we could never match Comperr's numbers on an open field. We held and defeated them here largely because of our defensive advantage, and while we may have been able to press that advantage right when they initially retreated, they've now had years to build their forces back up. Comperr is no stranger to war, and the Northern Highway is too important for them to lose control of it."

King Radomir turned pensively to the maps on the table in the center of the room. One of them, the largest, showed as far east as Aland and the Seren Ocean. Admone was dead center in between the Berg and the Seren, and by itself covered a land mass as large as all the nations west of the Berg combined. If and when Ambarta succeeded in conquering Cleononia, they would come close to rivaling Admone in land mass but would be nowhere close to the population or military strength.

The king looked at the map for so long that Timot unconsciously began holding his breath again. But then the king looked up from the map, looking back and forth between him and Bagon, his eyes piercing and strong.

"Whether he's right or wrong, Perivon insists that he does not need our soldiers, just all the wizards we can find. We will not send any of our soldiers to Cleononia's aid."

Timot nodded, letting out a breath he had forgotten he was holding. But the king wasn't finished yet.

"We will then send messages to Admone and Meand, explaining why we are having our soldiers patrol the Northern Highway and that they will enjoy the benefits of the increased security as well. Make it clear that our forces will yield to Comperr soldiers sent to perform the same function. Then dispatch five battalions of cavalry to patrol the Northern Highway throughout Comperr."

Timot closed his eyes. He had been afraid of this. If King Radomir were to be said to have a flaw, it would be stubbornness. He said he would send troops to cover the Northern Highway, so he would do so, and consequences be damned.

The king clearly noticed their consternation.

"You are worried that we are crossing a line by sending our troops in. I disagree. That line has already been crossed. It was crossed when Raanan continued to refuse to ensure the safety of merchants within his kingdom. One of the only things of real value that rulers do for their subjects is protect them in their lives and property, and Raanan refuses to do so. I believe the rulers of the other nations know Raanan well enough to know that our messengers speak truth, and they will allow this to be resolved between us. As far as Comperr's military strength...let them come. Let them gather their strength and push our forces back. We will retreat with as little blood shed as possible, because Raanan will be doing nothing but setting the noose for his own neck. If they follow us to our borders, we will beat them back as we did two years ago. Either way, they will only prove what we've been telling their neighbors all along."

The king's shrewdness was difficult to dispute, but there were an awful lot of assumptions baked into his bread, and Timot wasn't sure how comfortable he was with courting another war with Comperr. He wasn't sure he would ever court another war.

Then it struck him – perhaps that was the very reason why it was important for someone who had not personally tasted the horror of war to make the final decision on whether war was to be pursued, so long as he was advised by those who had. Someone like himself or Bagon would likely let atrocities go unanswered simply to avoid the cost and toll responding properly would take on the families of those he cared about. Radomir knew those costs but had not experienced them personally. Perhaps that was how the best decisions were made. A balance between caution and aggression.

"What of Vewen? Did Ambassador Bura's message say when he left?" The king asked.

Timot shook his head. "No, sire."

"How long will it take them to get to Dazbog?"

Timot looked at Bagon, who gestured for him to continue answering. This was another thing they had discussed last night. "From what Mellion told us before, magic can be used on horses to allow them to travel further and faster than they could normally. Theoretically they could travel a hundred miles each day for several days in a row. Not even Rider could keep a horse alive at that pace for more than a single day."

"However," Bagon interjected, "Mellion also told us that this takes a toll on the horse as well. A horse taken at that pace would take much longer to rest afterward, and the further the horse is pushed with the magic, the longer it would need to rest. If they tried that magic to travel from Comperr to Dazbog, the horses would collapse halfway there and require a month to rest before continuing."

King Radomir shook his head. "Get to the center of it, Captains, how long will it take? I don't need a secondhand lesson in magic and horses."

Timot answered, "Most likely about two and a half tendays. Could be as long as three, if the weather turns."

"25 days..." the king said thoughtfully. "Perivon's last letter said that with Mellion and Paavali they should be able to hold Dazbog until Vewen and the others arrive, at which point they would start to push Ambarta out."

Bagon shook his head. "The Guild wizards will be obstinate about not pursuing any specific outcome in the war. They are going to subdue a rogue wizard, nothing more. Likely, apprehending Ezmith would end the war in Cleononia's favor, but even if that does not end up being the case, Vewen and his wizards will refuse to intervene further."

King Radomir raised an eyebrow. "That could be a distinction without a difference, Captain. It will likely amount to exactly the same thing."

Bagon nodded in agreement.

The king looked back and forth between them.

"Is that all? Anything else to report as of now?"

Timot looked at Bagon, then back to the king and shook his head.

"Very good," King Radomir replied. "Do as I instructed in regards to Comperr. Then…I suppose we wait. Wait for word from Cleononia, wait for Vewen to reach Dazbog, and wait for more word from Ambassador Bura."

The king exited, with Bagon following immediately. Timot spent the long walk back to his office pondering the implications of the decisions that had been made this day. He began reviewing in his mind the city's defense plans and how he would prevent the castle from being overrun if it came to it. There were a few ways out of the castle he could send Ezren and the rest of the children through…Ezren could at least keep them alive in the wild.

He stopped at a painting in the hallway. True to Mountain Home's philosophy of finding balance, a good portion of the paintings in the castle depicted unfortunate events in their history – defeats, losses, and times when hindsight had shown them to be on the wrong side. This particular painting seemed almost too on-the-nose for how Timot was feeling at the moment.

It depicted the Exodus – when thousands of families had been forced to flee the border with the Berg because Mountain Home's army had gone deep within to attempt to root the goblins out and been handed a devastating defeat. The goblins had pursued the defeated and haggard army past the border and sacked the sizable towns there so completely that not even ruins remained. The families had walked with no supplies from those cities to Wilhelm, or Wil'alla as it had been called then.

Thousands of lives lost because of Mountain Home's hubris. It was a chilling warning of where the king's decisions this day might take them.

He continued his walk to his office. He didn't think it was hubris that provoked the King's decisions this day, but it certainly wasn't humility.

CHAPTER 4: WELL, STERCORE

I t felt wonderful to be back in these forests again. Ezren held Asteri's reins with one hand, guiding her with his legs as much as the reins while his other hand held his bow with an arrow already nocked. Far to his left, he could occasionally hear the crunch of Raban's horse, which actually belonged to The Sergeant, stepping on leaves and other dead-fall. The horse, which was named Thumb of all things, was a grey gelding of middling height, only a hand or so taller than Asteri.

To his right, he occasionally saw glimpses of Ben on his horse Fengari through the dense trees, but heard nothing. Ben had never said anything about training horses to walk quietly in the woods, but somehow Fengari must be avoiding more of the dry leaves and twigs than either Asteri or Thumb, because he rarely heard anything from that direction.

They were both somewhat behind him on either side. This part of the forest was just north of Salimelish, almost directly West of Berengaria, and moving closer to the border with Robinton, which was only about ten miles away now.

They'd been out of Novis Terram for three days, and Raban and he had already learned more about scouting than they thought there could be to learn, and it seemed this was just the beginning. For example, he was riding in the Point position. It was his job to keep his eyes forward, to see any threats from as far off as possible.

Ben and Raban had strung their bows but left them hanging on their saddles. It would fall on Ezren to reinforce either of them if they were ambushed from a flank.

They didn't expect to find anything; Ezmith and his mother likely felt they had nothing to fear from Mountain Home for the time being, but it was this scouting party's job to find out exactly what, if anything, had been placed at the border in defense.

A 'simple matter' Ben had called it, but Ezren was still on edge. The only danger they had encountered so far had been a Phoenix defending her nest, but that didn't mean there wasn't danger ahead. Ben had nearly shot the thing out of principle, but it wouldn't have done any good unless they were willing to stick around long enough to scatter the ashes. A 'waste of a good arrow', he had claimed.

Springtime was starting to truly take hold, even this far north, and the lush greenery shone with melted frost that became dew almost as soon as the sun came up. This was one of the densest forests in all of Mountain Home, and it wasn't particularly large, certainly not compared to the Wood Coast.

According to Ben, the forest would begin to thin in about a mile, but it wouldn't end completely for another 25 miles after the border, well into the Heran Hills.

The border with Robinton was remarkably well-established – posts marking the border were placed every hundred or so yards, all along the roughly 80 miles from the base of the mountains to the Northern Highway. Ezren had learned that from Professor Verna even before Rider had told them about it.

Professor Verna had taught them all about Robinton and how it came to be. After the death of Oberon, some hundred years after he established Mountain Home, his son took the throne. There was a small but passionate part of the population that was opposed to leadership being passed down through lineage, and instead wanted each king to be chosen by a ruling council of the mayors of each city.

The situation almost escalated into a civil war, but the leaders of the dissenters instead moved West to establish Robinton, clearly and inescapably marking the border as they went. According to Professor Verna, such a thing had not happened at any other time in recorded history. When nations disagreed, they fought. When a single nation disagreed within itself, it fought within itself until one side was subjugated to the other. A peaceful separation was "unheard of". Professor Verna seemed to have a somewhat bleak view of humanity.

Bringing his focus back to his surroundings, Ezren looked and listened. All was quiet, except for the sound of a woodpecker up ahead.

The plan was to take the rest of the day to ride the next ten miles to the border. That seemed slow to Ezren, but Ben said that scouting properly could not be done quickly, and taking long enough to get good, accurate information was far better than delivering bad information.

To his right he heard the call of a whitebird, their agreed-upon signal that enemies had been sighted. He jerked his head around and saw Rider looking right at him. Ben lifted his hand up, then made a gesture, angling his hand downward several times to make sure Ezren saw.

'Dismount and hide', the gesture meant.

Ezren nodded, then looked to Raban, who should be looking to him for the same signal. He gave Raban the gesture, and they each dismounted quietly. Speed was important, yes, but silence was crucial.

Ezren looked around his immediate area for how the three of them could be positioned most defensibly. There was a small dip in the ground back about ten feet that should be large enough to hide them if they could get the horses to lay down. Fengari would likely not hesitate, and Asteri had done it enough times that she *should* go down without a problem. Who knew about 'Thumb' though. What a ridiculous name for a horse. A horse should have an Ankonite name. Everyone knew that.

He carefully led Asteri back to the dip and coaxed her into laying down as Ben and Raban joined him. Fengari laid down as soon as Ben pulled on the reins, but Thumb steadfastly refused. Eventually, Raban just moved him behind two trees growing right next to each other, tied him to the tree, and told him to hold still.

They all crouched in the dip watching in the direction that Ben had come from. For a while, Ezren could not see anything. Then, as he watched, he caught glimpses of shining armor and large moving shapes about 50 yards off, running parallel to their position.

"What is it?" he whispered to Ben.

"Ambartan patrol," Ben whispered back.

"A patrol? Why are they patrolling out here?" Raban asked.

"For the same reason we are," Ben replied, still in a whisper.

"Well, why can't we just keep going? If we're all just checking to make sure the other is not attacking us, can't we all just go on our merry way?" Raban whispered back.

Ben looked at him patiently. "Firstly, we don't want to let them know we are scouting the border; it could make them nervous if they're worried about an attack and give them more information than they need even if they're not. Secondly, there are more of them than there are of us, and soldiers on enemy land don't always ask questions before they start shooting. Thirdly, there is always the chance they're an advance group for a larger army."

Ezren grinned, but still whispered in reply. "In other words, Raban, it's a bad idea."

They watched as the group came even with them and then went further into Mountain Home. Once they were out of sight, Raban took up the questioning again.

"So how long do we stay here?"

"Oh, we'll be here the rest of the day, boys. We're not moving from this spot until tomorrow. And don't move, either, unless you have to. Hopefully we'll see when that group comes back, but even if we don't, we'll risk leaving in the morning."

"The whole day?!" Raban whispered incredulously, somehow

managing to be just as loud as if he wasn't whispering. "What are we supposed to do in this dip for the whole day?"

Ben sighed and touched two of his fingertips to his own forehead as though asking for patience. "Practice holding your breath," he finally replied.

"What?" Ezren asked.

"Practice holding your breath. You'd be surprised how often it can come in handy. Sometimes an enemy will pass by so close that they'll hear you breathe, or there will be a wild animal with much better hearing than a person, or the only place to hide is underwater, and being able to hold your breath for long enough could be the difference between making it home alive and not."

"Is that what you do?" Raban asked.

Ben shrugged. "Not as much anymore, but I used to do it all the time."

They shifted, trying to get as comfortable as they could. There was only so much they could do when standing wasn't an option and they couldn't risk the noise it would require to shift rocks around. Ezren stared up at the sky, watching wisps of cloud float by for what seemed like forever.

Maybe holding his breath wasn't such a bad idea. He breathed in deeply, held his breath, and counted the seconds. He held as long as he could, until he felt like his face would burst, then let it out and started catching his breath. He had lasted 55 seconds. That didn't seem half bad, but now he was gasping for air so loudly that Ben looked at him and hit him softly in the leg to remind him to quiet down.

He caught his breath for a couple minutes, then gave it another try. He hadn't believed it would work, but the day seemed to fly by as he timed himself holding his breath, then started timing his breaks, and continued. Raban tried it a few times but tired of it quickly and began trying to build a pyramid out of little sticks on the ground.

They saw no sign of more Ambartan soldiers until the sun was low in the sky and the patrol they had first seen passed on their way back towards the border. After they passed by, Ben relaxed but still insisted they spend the night in the dip.

Horses had to be picketed, not hobbled, to prevent any chance of them wandering off and being seen, and they didn't make a fire that night.

Fires were rare on scouting trips, Ben told them. For the most part you packed food that didn't need cooking and you carried enough clothes and blanket that you didn't need the warmth. Scouting properly did not always require you to remain undiscovered, but it usually did and even the times when it wasn't required it was still advantageous.

Ezren started to wonder if Ben wasn't just a little bit paranoid.

Night came on slowly and they weren't allowed to speak. This wasn't as exciting as he had expected, but Ezren was just grateful to be out of the city. He *still* felt more comfortable out here than in those narrow streets, despite having lived in Novis Terram for years. He was seeing a part of the world he had not seen before, and doing this was going to allow him to see even more interesting things.

Raban casually tossed a rock onto his little twig-tent, knocking it down. He was clearly bored. Ben sat cross-legged for a while, his eyes closed and his back to a tree. He was too erect to be sleeping, so Ezren wasn't sure what the scout was doing.

The sun went down and the stars came out. For some reason, so many more stars were visible out here in the woods than in the city. The entire sky seemed alight, so much that it almost seemed there was more light than darkness up there. Ben took the first watch, as he usually did, but Ezren laid awake for a time just staring up at the stars.

They were yet another mystery, something that no one truly understood. What were they? Why were they only in the sky at night? He had searched the castle library on multiple occasions and was beginning to wonder if he was the only one in the world curious about them. Sure, people had observed them, tracked their movement across nights and months and years, and there were countless constellations that people had named, but that seemed to be the extent of anyone's curiosity.

Slowly, his tiredness took him and he drifted off to sleep.

~

This contraption was enormous. It was taller than their castle at Lugos, and almost as wide as it was tall. Ezmith felt his eyebrows raise as he examined it, the engineers dry-washing their hands as they followed him.

They were miles away from Dazbog on an open plain, hopefully far enough that Perivon's scouts would not discover what they were doing here.

At the moment, the throwing arm was pointed straight up, but when it was being prepared to fire it would be brought down to one side, with the incredible counterweight on the bottom being propped up. The counterweight was an enormous wooden basket that was filled with rocks. The basket was the size of a small cottage, and Ezmith could only imagine how much weight was contained within it.

To one side, there was a row of five granite boulders, all chiseled down to nearly perfect spherical shapes. Each seemed to be about 18 inches wide. They certainly didn't look big enough to cause much devastation to the fortified walls of Dazbog.

"You say this will be the first test?" he asked the engineers.

The head engineer stepped forward. His name was...Daveed, Dareno, something like that. Names of people like him were not important. Indeed, in many ways it might be better to simply assign them numbers.

"Yes, sir, for this version. With the payloads-" he began.

"The what?" Ezmith interrupted.

"The payloads, sir, that is what we call the boulders." The man even pointed to the row of boulders as though to clarify which boulders he meant.

"Very well," he said through only slightly gritted teeth. "Go on."

"Yes sir. With the payloads cut down to the same size, we can more effectively aim the slinger-"

"The what?" Ezmith interjected again, losing more of his patience.

"The siege weapon, my Lord. It does not operate as a normal cata-pult, so we came up with a new name for it."

"Continue, but I expect you to define any of your made-up words as you go. I have no desire to keep asking after their meanings."

"As you say, sir," the man said with a bow. "If we know how much the payload weighs, we can predict where it will land, and make adjust-ments to the slinger to ensure that it hits where we want. All told, sir, we expect it to be able to launch the payload about 300 yards."

Ezmith looked over at the boulders, considering. A chunk of granite that size probably weighed almost three hundred pounds. It would likely take three men or one Eztas to carry each one over to the...slinger.

"Well? Show me."

The engineers jumped into action. Four of them ran to two large cranks on either side that turned gears. The gears were attached to a rod that had turned while they turned the cranks, pulling tight four different arm-thick ropes that were themselves attached to the top of the throwing arm. The engineers cranked and cranked, and slowly but surely the throwing arm came down and the counterweight went up.

Once the tip of the throwing arm reached the base of the slinger, an engineer inserted a thick steel rod connected to a much thinner rope. The rod held the throwing arm in place as the engineers finagled a sling that was almost as long as the throwing arm itself was. They stretched it out on the base of the slinger between the two supporting trusses that held it all up on either side.

One of the engineers rolled a payload over until it was right next to the slinger, then three of them hefted it together, set it down on the base, then rolled it down into the sling. An engineer checked the tip of the throwing arm to make sure the sling was connected on both ends, but to Ezmith it looked like one of them was just loosely looped onto a metal rod.

There was a patch of trees off to the right of the slinger, but other-wise it was empty plains in all directions. Some three hundred yards away, some workmen had built a chunk of rock wall perhaps ten feet wide. Ezmith did not know how thick it was, but he would go inspect it after the demonstration and find out.

The engineers consulted with each other for a moment, all seeming to talk at once, then after a minute of discussion one of them came to another crank that was sticking up vertically at the front of the slinger, opposite the tip of the throwing arm. He turned the crank around quickly about five times, and the slinger spun a tiny amount, angling ever so slightly so that by Ezmith's eyes, it was aimed dead center at the wall.

The head engineer stood tall with pride and anticipation and looked for a moment as though he were going to give some kind of speech, but after a glance at Ezmith, simply gave the order for two of his men to fire the slinger. The two men grabbed the thinner rope attached to the end of the metal rod, counted off, then yanked together on the rope.

The rod popped out, and the throwing arm immediately lurched upwards, yanked that way by the counterweight falling. Despite how quickly it was certainly moving, it seemed to arc majestically, and as it rose, one end of the sling slipped off the end of the throwing arm, opening the sling wide to release the payload hurtling across the space. Ezmith watched eagerly as the boulder flew through the air and slammed mercilessly into the rock wall that had been built.

His eyes widened in shock as the entire wall seemed to explode with the impact. A moment after he saw the impact, he heard it, and it was a loud smashing and crunching sound. Eyes still wide, staring at where the wall had been, he began walking towards the wall. The engineers had begun cheering as soon as the boulder had hit the wall and were still celebrating as Ezmith walked.

That was fine; what he had just witnessed shocked him and he wanted a moment to process it. This...slinger...was, in its own way, more powerful than magic. He was the most powerful wizard, potentially in the entire world, and he could never wreak so much damage from so far away.

The wall was well and truly destroyed. Only the very bottom remained to tell him how thick it had been. As he had guessed, it had only been a couple feet thick, and made recently enough that the cement had not had enough time to properly solidify. Even so, it was an impressive accomplishment. With just one of these, he should be able to take down the wall at Dazbog and flood the city with his troops.

He heard the footsteps of an engineer behind him. Without looking, Ezmith called out instructions. They had to get the slinger and its payloads to Dazbog as quickly as possible.

Only a few days later, Ezmith sat astride Thunder next to the slinger, well out of the effective range of the Cleononian archers. At three hundred yards, they would be almost out of the range of even Enderian Rangers.

Next to him stood Eztas, breathing loudly with the effects of most of the enchantments on him. Behind them waited their archers and infantry. They'd been instructed to stay in groups of fifty once they were through the wall and immediately fan out, killing all Cleononian soldiers without quarter.

Civilians were not to be harmed, per his mother's order.

The slinger was loaded, and two engineers stood holding the rope attached to the metal rod that would launch it into action. All was ready. Ezmith smiled.

"Fire," he said calmly. The engineers pulled the rope, sending the throwing arm up, followed by the payload. Everyone watched in awe as the arm arced upward, throwing the boulder through the air, hurtling at terrifying speed directly at the walls of Dazbog. The boulder impacted just above the middle of the wall, to the left of the gate. It punched a hole in the wall and sent all the rocks that comprised the front half of the wall above the point of impact tumbling down.

"Fire again," he said. "Target the same spot."

After the engineers had the end of the throwing arm almost all the way back down, he raised his voice, calling out to his army. "Advance!" Ezmith moved Thunder forward at a walk, knowing that it would take the engineers about another minute to finish preparing the slinger for another volley.

He rode forward resolutely, hearing the marching steps of the army behind him. He had brought unparalleled power to Dazbog. They would pay for the wound he had taken. They would pay for the time they had cost him. They would pay for defying him. And they would pay today.

As the second boulder flew past overhead, Ezmith bellowed the next command.

"Attack!"

Even as the battle cries and wordless roars erupted behind him, even as he kicked Thunder to a run, he wove the final enchantment onto Eztas – the battle rage. It overtook his brother immediately, and he tore off running faster than any normal man could, swinging his massive war hammer and shield as he ran. Ezmith slowed Thunder to a trot, allowing his army to overtake him and reach the walls first.

He just needed to be close enough to provide magical cover for his troops in case the wizards joined the fight, and only a fool would ride at the front of the army. Indeed, even as he had the thought, he saw Fireballs arcing towards his troops.

Creating Shields of air and water, he neutralized the fireballs with a loud hiss. He looked around to try and see where the wizards were; he'd like to kill them if possible. Not seeing them, he instead began to use Arrows of Air en masse to strike at clumps of soldiers on top of the wall. The second payload from the slinger had indeed struck the same position and knocked down the back portion of the wall, leaving a gap two people wide and just low enough that his soldiers could clamber up into the gap.

Eztas reached the wall and leaped in fearlessly. He had little reason for fear even if the Battle Rage had allowed it; the other enchantments on him made him nearly indestructible, and ferocious besides. Of course, it was up to Ezmith to make sure that the enemy wizards were too occupied to attempt to unravel his brother's enchantments.

He continued to deflect and counter the other wizards' attacks as the rest of his army reached the broken wall and began climbing up into the city.

He smiled as his heart pounded, and it felt like there was fire in his blood. It was far more common for him to stand back and watch battles so that he could put his efforts and magic where they were most needed. This time, though...the gap in the wall beckoned to him.

Even better, though...he could try an idea he'd had as he'd been bedridden from his arrow wound.

He dismounted, then ran straight at the unbroken wall on the other side of the gate, waving his hands in a spiral motion in front of him. He bumped past soldiers angling for the gap. He felt the air around him swirling faster and faster, but it was the air underneath him that mattered. As he completed the spell he jumped, sprawling as though to land chest-first on the ground, but his spell of Rushing Air caught him. He flexed his wrist, and the air pushed upward at an angle, launching him to just the right height to come up onto the top of the wall, and another quick Rushing Air pushed him upright so he didn't land flat on his face.

The soldiers all around him stared in shock, but only for a moment as he sent a slice of fire out in a circular wave, cutting the soldiers all around him cleanly in half. Taking in the cries of pain and the thuds of the pieces of their bodies hitting the wall walk, Ezmith looked around, more excited than he had been in years...since he had snuck into the rooms of the former Lord and Lady of the Wood Coast and hung them with their own bedsheets.

He still could not see the wizards, but he sensed magic in the marketplace near the front of the city, and he saw the flailing, flaming bodies of Ambartan soldiers who were as good as dead.

It was simple: keep the enemy wizards on the back foot, and kill more of Perivon's men than those wizards killed of his. A wide grin grew on his face. He accepted this challenge, and he *would* win.

～

Less than an hour after the wall was breached, Perivon called the retreat. It was unlikely that Ezmith would predict that they would be prepared to go out to sea. Most likely he assumed that taking Dazbog would amount to taking all of Cleononia.

The massive siege weapon had surprised them, but in the end it hadn't changed much. They had known that Ambarta would eventually take Dazbog, and they had stored plenty of supplies in the ships that would take his garrison out to sea until one of Perivon's other plans came to fruition.

Perivon watched out the window of the map room with a spyglass, looking for signs that the call to retreat had reached his men. His eye found Ezmith, still on the wall, hurling magic and death into the backs of his retreating soldiers. By Clayara, the man seemed to be *laughing*.

The pain of who-knew how many losses was already reaching his heart, but Ambarta had undoubtedly suffered more losses than they had expected once they breached the walls, and this was a temporary fallback until they could retake the city.

Perivon snapped the spyglass shut and put it in his coat pocket, leaving the room and heading to the docks. He did not feel the need to rush – even if the city were empty it would take any Ambartan soldiers some time to reach this room – but his frustration and anger at Ambarta's ambition sped his steps.

He walked briskly down the hallways and flights of stairs that led him out the back way towards the docks, then continued his brisk walk, now surrounded by his coterie, down the cobblestone roads that took him the rest of the way down. He stood on the dock as thousands of his soldiers passed by to board the ships he had waiting.

He looked South, towards Redwood, wondering how close his naval force there was to taking the city. He looked East, towards Comperr, where the Guild wizards should be en route from. Unless Ezmith had in his magical repertoire the ability to read minds or see the future, he could not manage to stop both of those wheels from turning.

As he saw Ambartan soldiers beginning to appear far up the roads, he turned on his heel and boarded his ship, bidding a temporary farewell to Dazbog, and a solemn prayer of gratitude to the soldiers who had volunteered to be the rear guard, holding off Ambarta long enough for the rest to make the retreat.

~

What was Perivon thinking? Ezmith wondered an hour later, looking out to sea from the shoreline. The entire Dazbog fleet was out there anchored like some strange floating city, out of range but not out of sight.

He didn't like things he didn't understand. He couldn't simply shrug and leave Perivon to rot while they consolidated their control because he did not know *why* Perivon would choose to go out there. An itch in the back of his mind was telling him that something was going to come falling out of the sky and strike him unawares.

He folded his arms and narrowed his eyes as he often did when thinking hard. The only reason to evacuate the garrison rather than surrender was to eventually strike back, but they could not hope to do so while Ambarta occupied the city.

With all three of their wizards on the ships, they had no way of receiving messages from the city unless they had trained pigeons to consider one of the ships their home. That seemed unlikely, but it may be worth putting locks on all the pigeon cotes in the city just in case. Were any of their three wizards strong enough to scry? Leir might be.

He turned on his heel, giving the order to his captains to have locks put on all the pigeon cotes, then strode up the sloping cobblestone street to the keep. Now that the siege was over it was time to focus on other matters.

He had not heard from Guillame in the Wood Coast for some time, not since he had reported that the Bahadir fleet had arrived and fighting on the sea had commenced. Surely Guillame would have let him know if the battles had gone ill.

He arrived in Perivon's map room, a room with so little decoration that the lack seemed, of itself, a decorative statement. He considered reaching out to Guillame himself, but he had enough to do before his mother arrived that he put it out of his mind. Guillame would reach out when there was something worth communicating.

The hours passed at once quickly and excruciatingly slow. His side where he'd been shot was aching dully, likely from his exertion in the battle earlier. His orders for soldiers to clear the rubble and begin repairing the breach in the wall went out alongside orders to inventory the city's stock of goods. He sent out a statement to be promulgated that all merchants would now be allowed to leave the city and continue to conduct trade as they had before the siege only minutes before sending an order offering a bounty for any Cleononian soldiers hiding in the city.

There were many things that needed to be done immediately after taking a city, but he was well-practiced at it by now and went methodically through his list as the hours passed by. It would take his mother a few days, perhaps four, to travel from Mhairi, and he always made it his goal to have things moving well before she arrived. He had offered to Fold her to and from each city as they conquered, but she preferred to travel the landscape and be seen by her "new subjects".

The sun was just beginning to set when he felt a tickling sensation in his mind. Guillame was trying to reach him. Long distance communication was only possible between wizards and was a distinctly unpleasant process. He pushed the papers out of his way and pulled a single blank paper in front of him and held the graphis over it. Now for the unpleasant part.

He closed his eyes and...yielded his mind and body to the tickling sensation. He felt his hand begin to move, as if by its own accord. Some wizards could do this with their eyes open, but Ezmith found it far too disconcerting to maintain his focus. His hand continued to write and the tickling sensation enveloped his mind so completely that it took all his discipline to continue yielding control of his hands. They wanted to leap to his head and scratch all the way to his brain.

It seemed to go on for a long time, and indeed when the tickling finally subsided and he opened his eyes, the paper was nearly filled with the message. Brevity was not one of Guillame's strength. The man refused to accept the utility of abandoning complete sentences when communicating in this manner.

Ezmith's eyes widened as he read the letter written perfectly in Guillame's hand, and his heart began to pound. Something had indeed fallen from the sky to strike him.

Ezmith,

This is Guillame from the Wood Coast. Much has happened since my last message to you, and I regret that I was not able to alert you sooner. I do not know how or why, but not one of our ships returned from battle with the Bahadir fleet. As I had no hint as to whether that indicated the battle was going well or ill for us, I delayed informing you of the oddity.

It has since become clear that the battle went very ill indeed, for Bahadir ships sailed deep into the port and soldiers began pouring into the city via rowboats. I could not count them, but the number was certainly greater than a thousand. They quickly overwhelmed the Redwood garrison and took Aletheia and myself hostage.

Despite my reservations, I did use magic to defend myself as we discussed, but it proved fruitless in the end. I am now held in one of the deep cells, kept in pitch blackness and, most recently, in complete isolation. I do not know how long I have been here, but this is the first time I have been unsupervised, and as you know, I would have been immediately stopped and punished had I been caught communicating with you.

As of now they are keeping me fed well enough, and I imagine Aletheia is getting better treatment. I have no idea what is going on in the rest of the city. For all I know the army has left for Bahadir and left us imprisoned as some dark joke.

Regardless, rescue would be appreciated and no doubt strategically beneficial, as I understand Etchings and other Wood Coast products have become an important part of your war fund.

Thank you for your time,

Best Wishes,

Wizard Guillame De Igleso Mahn Demnefacado

Ezmith felt himself breathing hard. He calmly set the paper down on the table, then flexed his fingers, enchanting his fists to make them hard as granite and flame-covered besides.

He let a primal roar escape from his mouth as he laid about himself, smashing the heavy chairs with single punches, and snapping the thick oak table into two pieces, leaving dark scorch marks on everything he hit.

His plans *never* went this wrong. He was a *genius*! Unparalleled in everything that mattered! Perivon was just a man!

He raised his hands, breathing heavily, looking at the beautifully altered skin emanating eternal flames. Oh, how he wished he could enchant every one of his soldiers in this manner! Give them strength and power such that no weapon, wall, or man could stand against them!

He finished destroying all twelve of the chairs in the room.

Alas, these enchantments only worked on a select few. Other wizards, and, as far as he knew, only his brothers.

He had his theories on this, but none of them made complete sense. Whatever had happened a thousand years ago during the War of the Intelligences that had limited magic must have had some order or structure to it, and those that could still touch magic must have something in common with one another. Once his mother had finally confessed to him how he and his brothers had received their powers, Ezmith had surmised that whatever the old wizard Galdrach had done, it had given them that something, which was why he could enchant Eztas. He had tried enchanting other people before, and it worked as long as he actively maintained the enchantment, but as soon as he let go it dissipated almost instantly.

His rage somewhat satiated, he allowed the enchantments to fade and wondered idly if that meant that he could communicate with his brothers the way he could with wizards. Eztas may be problematic, slow as he was, but Ezrote would likely pick it up quickly.

He was avoiding the problem at hand. He forced himself to refocus and concentrate.

It was simple: he had to retake Redwood. Guillame was not wrong – the taxes they gleaned from the Etching and lumber trades were second only to Disote ice in funding their war chest.

All told, they had around three thousand soldiers here in Dazbog now. A significant force. If he took a thousand of them with him to clear out Redwood and left Eztas here...Eztas' unnatural strength was a force to be reckoned with even without the ancillary enchantments... Ezmith could clear Redwood of Cleononian soldiers within a day or two and possibly strike a significant blow to their navy if it was still in port.

He had no time for more thought. He immediately called to Captain Beaumont to assemble two battalions, one of infantry and one of archers to meet him in the Land Market within the hour.

Darkness had settled fully over the city by the time they were all assembled, but Ezmith was committed to getting to Redwood this night and expelling the invaders as quickly as possible. It would be satisfying to report to his mother what he had accomplished in the time it took her merely to travel from one city to another.

A brief Scry had told him that the throne room of Redwood Castle was abandoned, so he created a Fold there. He stood ready as the Fold materialized, a Shield created and a Fireball prepared, burning endlessly in his palm, but there appeared to be no ambush waiting. He entered cautiously, then signaled his soldiers to move through as well.

Their instructions were clear and simple: take the castle, quietly, if possible, but speed was more important than stealth. The soldiers moved through, and the combined sound of hundreds of them all moving through at once was anything but quiet. It would have to do.

Ezmith moved down the hallway behind the last of the soldiers and made his way down to the cells to free Guillame and search for Aletheia. He occasionally heard fighting, but not nearly as much as he had expected. Had Guillame somehow grossly overestimated how many Redwood soldiers were here? Or, even less likely, had most of them already left? There didn't seem much sense in taking an enemy city in this way and then simply abandoning it. Even if his defenses had crumbled within hours, Cleononia should have left an occupying force large enough to prevent uprisings and restrict trade.

He looked out to the bay through a window in a hallway and saw that there were only two Cleononian ships in the harbor. Perhaps they really did flee.

He continued down and created another ball of fire to provide light as he entered the dungeons.

"Guillame?" he called out.

He heard a throat clear before a somewhat croaky response came, "I'm here, Ezmith."

Ezmith followed the sound of the voice to a cell where he saw a much-battered Guillame sitting on a hay-covered floor with his back to the wall. Ezmith had not thought of bringing the keys, but he didn't need them. He focused on the lock for a moment, shifting the metal to allow it to click open.

So far, freeing Guillame had been simple enough that Ezmith had to wonder why the old wizard had not simply freed himself. He was squeamish about using magic against people, and likely feared he would be forced to do so if he freed himself. Besides, if the castle had actually had the thousand some-odd enemy soldiers Guillame thought it did, a single aging wizard likely wouldn't survive an escape attempt.

Guillame got to his feet as Ezmith held the door open.

"That was much faster than I had expected," he said, rubbing his arms to ward off the chill.

"Even so, the castle seems almost empty of Cleononian soldiers, Guillame. Is it possible that you overestimated how many had come?"

To his surprise, Guillame shook his head firmly. The man was normally full of self-doubt. "It was simple math; I counted how many were in one rowboat, then counted how many full rowboats there were. I suppose I could be off by a hundred or so, but there were at least a thousand soldiers that invaded the city."

Where are they hiding, then? Could it be that they really had left? The very idea seemed ridiculous. He and Guillame walked up in the dim, torchlit castle back to the throne room, where Lieutenant Suntly was waiting for Ezmith.

"The castle is ours, my Lord," Suntly reported.

"Very good, Lieutenant," Ezmith replied. "How many soldiers had to be cleared out?"

"A handful, my Lord. No significant amount. Certainly not enough to have overwhelmed the garrison that was left here."

Ezmith nodded. He was missing something, and he knew it.

A bright flare of light came through the window that looked south over most of the city. The three men walked together to the window and saw that a building had caught fire. It looked to be a warehouse based on its size.

"Son of a motherless goat," Guillame whispered.

"The rest of the army is hiding in the city," Ezmith declared confidently. "They intend to harry and hamper our trade through here. Send the battalions out immediately and clear them away street by street," he ordered, looking at Lieutenant Suntly.

It wasn't as simple as that, of course. The army hunted throughout the city all during the night, and while they killed some and apprehended more, the vast majority of the enemy army seemed to escape their notice. Ezmith gave the order to begin taking shifts and continuing to patrol the streets in force.

The enemy soldiers did not seem properly deterred by this strategy, however. Buildings continued to erupt in flame throughout the night and patrols were ambushed by large groups. Ezmith couldn't be everywhere at once, and while he could use scrying to some effect, there were simply too many places to hide, and the Cleononians never seemed to rest or sleep, or they did so somewhere he could not find.

A day passed, then another, and a third, as his numbers were whittled down even faster than the enemy's were. Finally, Ezmith took to the streets himself, disguised as a Sergeant with a small battalion. This tactic seemed to work well enough, as his small battalion made an enticing target for enemy troops, and he was able to cut them to shreds before they could kill many of his men.

Even so, it was slow going, and the damage to the city began to add up. Countless works of etching and milled lumber went up in flames throughout the city over the course of the tenday it took to clear out all of the enemy soldiers. He also managed to sink the two Cleononian ships in the harbor, though he suspected they had only been left in case the entrenched soldiers were able to escape that way.

He had tried out his theory of communication with Eztas, and got a simple message through that they were fighting in Redwood and he was clearing them out, but he had no desire to Fold back to Dazbog until he could say that the job here was done. Nothing should be happening up there that couldn't be handled by Captain Beaumont, Eztas, or his mother.

~

Perivon watched as Leir moved and twisted his hands, apparently looking at nothing. Mellion and Paavali stood on either side, looking over his shoulder at the same nothing. Leir was scrying the Redwood castle to see whether Ezmith had arrived there yet.

The boy was impetuous and still young enough to feel like he had to do everything himself, so Perivon had little doubt that he would show up, and he would be kept busy long enough for them to retake Dazbog. Hopefully he'd be busy long enough that the Guild wizards would be here and could just apprehend him the moment he showed his face again.

Leir's eyes suddenly went wide and all three of the wizards smiled triumphantly. They must have seen Ezmith. They looked to him as one and nodded.

"Ezmith is in Redwood," Leir confirmed.

Despite the good news, a smile was far from Perivon's face. Death was filling the streets of Redwood, and more death loomed on the horizon. "Give the order," he said, turning his head to General Ossam.

Ossam gave a short bow and left the cabin to go on deck. In a few short minutes, they all felt the lurch of the first run of the sweeps that would take them quickly and silently back to the harbor of Dazbog... back home.

∼

The rough tally that they had kept throughout the fighting of enemy soldiers they'd killed was nearing a thousand, and after a day and a half of silence it seemed that the rest had either given it up or fled the city. Ezmith stood in the throne room, trying to focus on the mental exercises he tried to do each day to continue honing his magical abilities, but he was having difficulty getting past the frustration and anger.

This was a sort of victory, he supposed, but simply being forced to fight this battle had been a defeat. Victory in such a battle was no victory at all, and he suspected that was exactly what had been intended. Sure, Perivon had probably hoped for his soldiers to survive, or had at least provided a way for it to happen should luck shine upon them, but all the losses Ezmith had taken in men, goods, and time combined certainly dwarfed Perivon's.

He shook away those thoughts. It was time to return to Dazbog and face his mother. She would demand details, may even insist on visiting Redwood herself, though Aletheia had been found sequestered in her apartments and had already resumed governing the city. He would be forced to relive every humiliating moment and justify every decision merely to satisfy her need to know *everything*.

Of the thousand he had brought here, only four hundred remained, and he had ordered them to stay here and hold the city against another incursion. They had never found a remnant of the garrison that had been stationed in Redwood originally.

Without Ezmith, even the soldiers he'd brought would probably have all died to the guerrilla tactics of the Cleononians. The Bahadir fleet was still blockading the port about a mile out on the ocean, but there was nothing he could do about that for the time being. He only hoped the Ambartan coffers held enough to continue their push to make Perivon yield.

Reluctantly, he opened a Fold to the map room in Dazbog, stepped through, and allowed the Fold to close. The room was empty, which was unexpected, but not alarming. He took a step forward, but the door flew open and a man dashed inside, already hurling a massive fireball straight at him! Paavali! Only Ezmith's instincts, honed in years of battle, saved him – he threw up a Shield just in time to catch the flames and heat of the Fireball, but the force of the blast still knocked him onto his back and sent him sliding several feet.

Enraged, he prepared to strike back, but Leir and Mellion both entered behind and the three of them kept up a constant barrage of Fireballs, Hand Lightning, and Shockwaves. It was all he could do to get up and maintain a shield strong enough to protect himself. He leaned forward, both hands pressed forward to hold the shield, and felt his feet sliding backwards on the floor. Summoning every last drop of his strength, he held the shield with his right hand and used his left hand to blindly create a Fold to just outside the city, so small that he had to dive through it, which he did as his shield crumbled behind him.

He tumbled on the grass, rocks digging into his skin as he rolled. The bottom of his robe was smoking, singed from the last Fireball that had come at him just as his shield was crumbling. He got to his feet, fuming, and smacked the tiny embers off his robe.

"Cowards!" he yelled towards the city. They *were* cowards, lying in wait and coming on him in secrecy. If he hadn't been ambushed, he could have taken all three at once. Of course he could have.

Lingering here was not an option; it seemed that Cleononia had retaken the city and he was within bowshot of the wall. He made a shield behind him to stop any arrows and stalked away from the city, fuming as he made a scry box to try and find where his army had gone. The scry hurtled over the ground much faster than he walked and discovered his army less than a mile down the road, still close enough to exert some influence on Dazbog's trade.

He had been there before when they traveled here, so he made a

Fold to right outside the camp and went through without missing a step. He stormed into the camp and headed for the command tent, which would be pitched in the very center. He was no longer worried about losing face over the events in Redwood; Captain Beaumont and his mother had let everything go to stercore in his absence.

The only way to get something done right was to do it yourself.

He swiped the tent flap aside as though he were backhanding someone and stomped in. His mother and Beaumont stood at the round table in the center reminiscent of every Map Room he had ever seen.

They looked up as he entered, both sets of eyebrows rising, likely due to the combination of his tousled appearance and the look of pure rage on his face.

"You let them take back Dazbog?!" He yelled. "I was only gone for a tenday and you couldn't hold the city against a defeated rabble?!"

Beaumont's face had gone white and he looked terrified. Why? Ezmith couldn't kill him over this – how would he find a good replacement if everyone knew he had killed the predecessor?

His mother's face also went white, but she stood straighter and clearly prepared herself for battle – squaring her shoulders and widening her feet. He half-expected her to put her hands on her hips like she had when he was young.

"That was their plan all along, Ezmith. Perivon played *us all* like a dulcimer. Their fleet had been stocked in advance with rations, weapons, everything they needed to wait us out. The night after you left for Redwood, the ships docked and the entire Dazbog garrison came pouring out, ready to fight."

Ezmith opened his mouth to speak but she ignored him, continuing:

"Captain Beaumont had positioned our troops brilliantly in chokepoints to stop them from overwhelming us with their numbers until you could return, but you never did. Days passed, and Perivon must have become impatient, because then their wizards joined the fight."

"The chokepoints went from our salvation to our doom in a single moment." She paused to swallow and gather herself. She always took the loss of soldiers personally. "At that point there was nothing left for us to do but flee and keep as many of our soldiers alive as possible."

"How many survived? How many do we have left?"

His mother and Beaumont looked at each other, and his mother nodded. Was she giving Beaumont *permission* to answer his question?!

Beaumont looked to Ezmith. "Not counting what you took to Redwood, we have 1,776 soldiers remaining."

Oh. Well, that wasn't so bad. He had only left 2,000 here when he went to Redwood, so losses seemed to have been minimal somehow.

"How is that possible? You lost fewer than 300 men?" His anger rose again as he processed this information. "Did you even bother fighting for the city?!"

"Of course we did, Ezmith!" His mother replied. "The chokepoints on the roads leading up from the docks stalled out the attack and minimized losses on both sides. Until the wizards involved themselves. We don't know for sure, but we expect most of our losses came when the wizards attacked. As soon as that happened, the only intelligent thing to do was flee. Eztas by himself could not make up for three enemy wizards, and we had no way of informing you of our predicament."

Ezmith considered bitterly how effective the doggedness of the Cleononian soldiers in Redwood had been and compared it to his own soldiers. At the first sign of trouble the Ambartans abandoned everything they'd been working towards. They probably just *assumed* Ezmith would come back and fix everything. Why risk *their* lives when *Ezmith* could just magic their way in and Eztas could take on armies single-handedly?

"Where is Eztas?" He asked. His fury was beginning to ebb, but he still wanted to give his brother a piece of his mind.

His mother shrugged, though a look of concern painted her face. "Out wandering the woods, as he has lately. He doesn't seem to like being with the army."

Ezmith snorted. Eztas *hated* being with the army. He had spent the last two years during the armistice at their home in Lugos almost constantly reading. Nothing interesting; Eztas enjoyed children's tales.

He appeared no sooner than the moment he was told to and disappeared as soon as the battle rage wore off.

They continued their discussion about the current situation. Ezmith told them what had transpired at Redwood and why he had left the army there. Their army was still in an effective position to halt trade in and out of Dazbog – they were camped on the only main road to the city, and they had a few hundred troops camped about 20 miles to either side to make sure that no caravans slipped by.

The real question was how to retake Dazbog now? They could try building another slinger, but the original had been packed up and taken into the city, which meant that it had fallen into the hands of the Cleononians. It was entirely possible that their engineers could figure out how to set it up, especially now that they'd seen it used. If Ezmith set his engineers to building a new one, it may just get destroyed with a payload lobbed by the original in Dazbog as soon as they set it up within range of the city wall.

He could try to Fold his army somewhere into the city but it seemed that the enemy wizards had found a way to detect his Folds and he couldn't be sure the element of surprise would be with them and not against them.

There were other options…they could build a slinger in secret and set it up in the dead of night; it only took two volleys to break a hole in the wall, after all. But Perivon would certainly have devised some method of dealing with a breach, so they may have to make two breaches, requiring more volleys and giving Dazbog more time to send a payload their way as well. It would only take one volley to destroy a slinger.

They could also make more than one. The right lumber could be found, if not quickly, and it would further delay the siege. Or perhaps the engineers could come up with some way to make their design even better so that it could launch from out of range of the original.

All this would take time. So *much* time. Nearly a month had passed since they had taken Mhairi. This conquest was shaping up to take as

long as the first conquest they had embarked on – the Wood Coast --
when they had made countless ignorant mistakes and missteps.

Of course, if they pursued either of those ideas, Perivon could just
open the gates and let his numbers advantage and competitive magic
wash over Ezmith's forces like a flood.

As though the thought was a prophecy, no sooner had he finished it
than horns blared, signaling that an enemy army was approaching.

Ezmith closed his eyes. Of course. That same numbers advantage
could be leveraged right now. Unless...could he keep the three wizards
busy while Eztas evened out those numbers? His eyes popped open and
he ordered Beaumont to find his brother and send him to the front
ready for battle. Ezmith stepped out of the tent.

"To arms! We stand and fight!"

The call was repeated and there was a clamor as soldiers strapped
on armor, grabbed weapons, and marched for the front of the camp.
Ezmith was the first there, and he stood tall and proud, his robe waving
behind him in the breeze coming off the ocean in the warm Spring
weather.

He heard and sensed the army forming ranks behind him as he
watched Cleononia approach. From where he stood, he could not see
high enough to get a sense of how many soldiers had come out, but he
could see riders at the back of the army. There appeared to be nine of
them. Perivon may have ridden out, and three of the riders were most
certainly the wizards based on their robes. The other five...sunlight
glinted off the armor they were wearing, so they were likely officers in
Perivon's army.

It was of no consequence. There was also no point in waiting. He
reared back his hands, then thrust them forward, sending a hundred
fist-sized Fireballs at the approaching army. At that size and in that
quantity, the Fireballs would dissipate as soon as they hit the soldiers'
armor, and even if they hit skin they would only leave a minor burn,
but displays of magic had a way of frightening simple men, which most
soldiers were.

The Fireballs hurtled towards the approaching line, but all of them puffed out of existence long before reaching it, seemingly impacting on a Shield. He smiled. All three of the wizards must be working together to make a Shield that large. That meant he most likely could not penetrate it, at least not without concerted effort, but they probably weren't also protecting themselves from above.

He summoned Lightning and sent it slamming down right on top of one of the riders. Just before it hit, however, the bolt was slashed. Ezmith frowned. None of the three wizards there were capable of holding a Shield as large as they were *and* slashing a lightning bolt.

The army had formed up behind him but he was no longer confident that this was a good idea. Did Perivon have a fourth wizard up his sleeve?

Despite being within bowshot, no arrows had come from the Cleononians, which made sense as they were still marching forward. The archers would want to close a little more before halting and getting set up to fire.

His own archers were waiting for a command to fire, but it would be pointless to do so with the Shield in place.

Ezmith stared hard at the riders behind the army as they came closer. He quickly created a scry box and placed it in front of them. They might sense it, but he only needed to see for a moment.

The riders leapt into view in the box and the blood drained from his face. Perivon was indeed there, as were Leir and Mellion and Paavali and two men Ezmith recognized as Perivon's captains. Of the other three armored riders, Ezmith only recognized one, but knew immediately who all three of them were. It was Vewen, a wizard from Comperr and a devotee of the Wizard's Guild, which prided itself on putting down wizards who used their magic for conquest. That meant the other two were also Guild wizards. They were disguised as Cleononian officers.

Six wizards.

Working together, they could put him at their mercy.

Fear was quickly replaced by anger. He would be paying Metnal a visit soon, to be sure.

"Fall back!" he yelled. The tents would have to be abandoned, but he could Fold the army directly to Mhairi where other accommodations could be made. His soldiers looked at him, confused.

"Gather what you can carry and run to the rear of the camp!" He barked out, hearing the command repeated further and further away as the troops reacted.

No sooner had he and his soldiers turned than the call to charge must have been given to the Cleononian infantry, because a wordless roar rose behind him and Ezmith felt magical attacks begin to form around him. Some were visible like the Fireballs and Lightnings that he could slash, block, or dodge, but others he could only sense, like a spell to hold him in one place or to block his ability to reach magic.

He could have overpowered the original three wizards under the right circumstances, but with six wizards focusing on him at once, it was all he could do to fend off the attacks. He dived behind a tent, knowing that the Guild wizards, at least, would be more hesitant if they could not actually see him, and the attacks from all the wizards would become less effective when they didn't know where he was.

He ran in a crouch past tents and horselines that would have to be abandoned, forges and fletching stands that would have to be left behind, and soldiers that didn't seem to understand the urgency of the retreat. They may have to be left behind as well. He would not be taken by these wizards. Death would be the best outcome he could hope for if such a thing were to happen.

He continued his run through all the way to the rear of the camp, where a hasty estimate told him that around a thousand of his soldiers had gathered. He threw his hand forward as he ran, creating the Fold as large as he could and running through it first, followed closely by his mother, Captain Beaumont, and Eztas. Then the soldiers began to pour through carrying swords, shields, bows, and occasionally a blanket, coat, extra bundle of arrows, or some other odd or end that they felt was worth grabbing.

Ezmith watched around the Fold edge as more of his soldiers went from jogging to a full sprint. He watched as many of his men were cut down by swords or arrows as they attempted to flee. Every time one went down, Ezmith winced. Every loss would make it that much harder to push Cleononia back. Every loss was one fewer body between him and the six wizards coming for his head.

Ezmith held the Fold open until arrows started to fly through it, then let it close. They were in the East Market in Mhairi, safely within its walls. It would take Perivon's army at least six days to close the distance, longer if they stayed with the supply wagons.

Six days felt like no time at all, but Ezmith was already forming plans. He gathered Beaumont, his mother, and Eztas around him right there in the courtyard.

"We need to send riders out immediately to every land we control. Every able-bodied man to report to their capital with any weapons they have access to. In six days from now, I will create a Fold to each capital and bring all the gathered men here. Get riders together, and I'll Fold them wherever will be fastest."

"*Every* able-bodied man?" Captain Beaumont questioned uncertainly. "Sire, even if most do not heed the command, we could have tens of thousands of men here, untrained, with whatever weapons they had to hand. The city could not come close to holding them all, and chaos would ensue. If *all* heed the command, we would have no way to even keep them fed, let alone equipped."

Ezmith ground his teeth. He had been thinking of the decree they had sent through Ambarta when they were preparing to move against the Wood Coast, but that decree *had* been very specific that only young men between the ages of 21 and 24 were required to train with the guards, and only about five hundred had come with any consistency.

Every able-bodied man would include anyone from age 17 all the way until perhaps 100 or even older who could still move spryly enough for military service. Even with just Ambarta, the least populous of all the provinces, men who fit that description likely numbered more than ten thousand.

These were *details*! Why must he decide *everything*?! Couldn't Beaumont have understood his intent and executed it in an intelligent way?!

He kept himself from yelling aloud, but only just. When he replied, his words were venomous and icy.

"Let us be more specific, then," he began. Calm, careful, clear. The people around him were too stupid to understand what needed to be done, otherwise. "All able-bodied men between the ages of 20 and 40 are *required* to report to their capital six days from now with whatever weapons they have, including bows. We will form up a camp on the East side of the city and reassign our professional soldiers as officers over the new recruits." He looked hard at Beaumont. "Will that sufficiently cover your concerns?"

Beaumont couldn't reassure him fast enough. "Yes, sire, of course, I will have copies made and prepare riders."

It only took about fifteen minutes for the copies of the proclamation to be made and horses saddled, but it seemed interminable. His mother waited next to him in silence.

"I thought you would have told me how many different ways in which my plan was foolish by now," he said gruffly to her.

She put her hand on his shoulder for some reason. "You are wise, Ezmith. In the ways of war you are wiser than I. I believe you are doing the right thing. The only way we will take Cleononia now is if we bring the largest hammer they have ever seen."

He turned to look at her. "I am also going to Fold to Novis Terram and try to convince Radomir to bring his wizards home."

She nodded slowly. He expected her to ask to go with him, but all she said was, "Be diplomatic, Ezmith. Radomir will not respond well to threats, and he may ask for some concessions. Still, I do not expect he will comply."

It was Ezmith's turn to nod. "I know. As soon as I am done there, I will retrieve Guillame from Redwood and Flimbast from Orjan. I will also check to see if Galdrach is at his tower in Robinton, though he rarely seems to be. Then I'll pay Metnal a visit and discuss this treachery."

His mother put a hand on his arm. "You know Vewen, Ezmith. It's entirely possible he's come here of his own accord, perhaps even in defiance of Metnal's direct order. I know it's tempting to seek revenge, but the last thing we need right now is to make an enemy of Comperr."

Ezmith ground his teeth, but his mother was speaking sense. In all likelihood, Metnal was still properly cowed.

Since they were still waiting, he continued to confide his thought process in his mother. "Guillame is capable enough he may be able to handle two of the weaker Guild wizards, and Flimbast can occupy Vewen. That leaves Leir, Mellion, and Paavali for me. We will at least be able to hold, though I do not know if we will have the strength to push until the reinforcements are assembled and given at least a semblance of training."

He had nothing else to say, and it seemed his mother had no more either. They waited together in silence, Ezmith rehearsing in his mind what he would present to Lord Radomir, the unofficial "King" of the Western Region.

CHAPTER 5: THE TOURNAMENT

Back in Novis Terram, Ezren sat and watched the fight, almost overcome by nervousness. His legs bounced up and down and he tried to steady his breath. The winner of this fight would face the winner of Ezren's next match. The two boys, Dakstra and Herke, were both passable fighters, but only half of the boys in the class had been eliminated so far, and neither of them had the skill to make it much further in the tournament.

Ezren closed his eyes, attempting to calm his nerves. He *was* prepared. He *did* have the skills. He had already been second only to Introm in sword-and-shield, and he had spent the last two months doing little else besides training. His instructors said that he had come leaps and bounds, and even his father's two lieutenants had commented on how much he had improved.

He rubbed his thumbs along the calluses of his hands. The calluses were larger and more plentiful on his right hand, of course, since that was his sword hand, but part of a well-rounded sword-and-shield training was switching hands and reaching a certain level of competence with your off-hand.

He had expected that with all his focus on this training, that other areas in his life would suffer, but that had not seemed to happen. His daily exercises with Asteri had gotten shorter, sure, but he still made time for them, and he was still achieving top marks in all of his academic studies, though he was not delving nearly as deeply into the subject matter as he used to.

Further, his intense training had given him and his father even more to talk about and do together. They'd spent more time together in the last months than they had in the year prior, practicing or discussing combat.

His nerves had still not calmed, so he began an exercise that Fiona had taught him. He flexed his toes over and over, then relaxed them, and tried to relax his toes as deeply as they had ever been relaxed. Then he moved up to his calves, and flexed them over and over, relaxing them as deeply as he could.

He went through all the muscles in his body, feeling how much stronger they felt after his efforts over just the last month. Swinging the weighted sword and holding the weighted shield had tired him out much faster than he had hoped at first, so he had dedicated a significant amount of his training time to increasing his strength and endurance.

The flexing exercise somehow calmed his nerves. He shouldn't have been surprised – everything Fiona suggested worked exactly as it should. She was here, sitting in the rows of benches that had been set up for spectators. This was the third match she had made it to, and though he would not have admitted it out loud, seeing her there brought him comfort.

His father would have been here if he could, but they had agreed that these matches were almost guaranteed to go in Ezren's favor, and his father had much to do after the news that Fiona had brought back from Comperr.

He tilted his head from side to side, trying to stretch the tension out of his neck and refocus. His next opponent was Cluman, the only boy here from Comperr. His parents were a Lord and Lady, but of an area only about ten square miles, which seemed bizarre to Ezren. Cluman said that there were lots of Lords and Ladies in Comperr, and you had to be nobility to even own land in the first place, so there were lords and ladies who owned only the land their home stood on and an acre or so all around.

By that criteria, his father would be a Lord based on the land they owned in Berengaria. They hadn't lived there since the cabin had been burned down, and had only visited a few times, but it was still theirs and was just waiting for them to do something with it.

Cluman was nice enough, a year older than him, but he was another boy who would not be expected to pass this round even if he hadn't been against Ezren.

Scattered cheers broke out as the last fight ended. Ezren jerked his head up to see who had won. It appeared to be Dakstra, who had his arms up in triumph like some hero out of legend. Ezren scoffed before he could stop himself. Boasting over defeating Herke was much like boasting after successfully tugging on your boots in the morning. Not to mention disrespectful to Herke himself. It was unsporting to gloat over your opponent after victory.

Wasting no time, Master Juildar blew a small horn that announced it was time for the next match. Ezren's match. There was no need to be nervous, he reminded himself. He had never lost to Cluman in practice or previous tournaments, and with all the extra training he had done over the last two months, he should be confident.

He looked up at Fiona, who gave him an encouraging wave. He smiled back and got to his feet, hopping up and down before putting his helmet on and moving to the large circle that marked the combat area.

He met Cluman in the middle and they greeted each other respectfully by hitting the other's shield lightly with their sword.

Master Juildar went through the scoring and instructions as he was required to do prior to each match.

"...one hit to the head, two hits to the body, or three hits to the arms and legs. No mixed combination of hits will bring victory. You will fight up to three bouts, until one of you has bested the other twice. Do you understand?"

Ezren and Cluman spoke in unison, "Yes, Master Juildar."

"Very well," he said, stepping back and holding a silver coin in the air. "You will begin when the coin first hits the ground."

He tossed the coin high into the air, and Ezren and Cluman readied themselves, looking directly at each other instead of at the coin. Their ears would tell them when the coin landed. Ezren's heart pounded, his nerves welling up so much he felt nauseated.

No sooner had Ezren heard the 'clink' of the coin hitting the ground than Cluman came at him in a fury and his nerves disappeared in an instant. The tactic was a good one; when you felt overmatched by your opponent, you could sometimes make up for the difference in skill by added ferocity.

Unfortunately for Cluman, Raban had done this very thing to Ezren many times over the last two months, and he had learned how to deal with it. You couldn't stand still and you couldn't back away quickly; you had to step back deliberately, just enough to keep your legs clear of any slashes, once, twice, sometimes a third step.

The push would be slowed down, and all the opponent's ferocity would have to go into simply moving their sword and shield faster and faster, which made them overcommit on slashes and thrusts. Sure enough, after Ezren had taken two steps back, Cluman did a long thrust directly at Ezren's torso.

Cluman's aim was true, but Ezren was too far away – he had time to react. He swung his shield around to sweep the blade, then took the time to spin almost a full circle to swing his sword backhanded and hit Cluman's helmet just behind the ear. He knew he had time for the spin because Cluman could not have come out of the thrust fast enough to strike again.

Cluman tumbled over and Master Juildar blew his horn, signaling the end of the first bout. Ezren reached his hand out to help Cluman up and Cluman took it, a wry smile on his face as he let Ezren help him to his feet.

"So much for that idea," he said ruefully.

"Don't worry about it," Ezren replied. "You just overcommitted on the thrust, that's all. One mistake. I may not have been retreating as fast as you wanted but I *was* retreating, and I didn't have any time to counter."

Cluman nodded thoughtfully, then looked up quizzically at Ezren. "You know, it's probably not the best idea to give your opponent advice while he still has the chance to use it against you."

Ezren laughed and nodded. "I suppose you're right about that."

They got back into position at the center of the circle and waited for Master Juildar to throw the coin in the air again.

At the 'clink' of the coin landing on the ground, Cluman immediately began quick attacks, but it was all jabs and weak slashes. Either he was afraid of committing too much to one move based on what had just happened, or he was trying to lull Ezren into something.

Either way, jabs and weak slashes were not enough to control the fight, and after a quick-step back, Ezren seized control by stepping forward and sweeping his shield in almost a full-circle in front of him. This knocked aside Cluman's latest jab and caused him to hesitate, unable to see clearly what Ezren might be positioning his feet and shoulders to do next.

From that point on, Ezren had control of the fight.

He did two weak slashes, one at Cluman's shins, then another much higher up at his shoulder. Cluman's shield blocked both strikes, but Ezren shifted to several committed slashes aimed at Cluman's head, which were strong enough that Cluman needed to bring the shield higher to block properly.

The further a strike hit from the center of the shield, the harder it was to prevent the shield from twisting, so Cluman had to lift the shield so that Ezren was hitting was directly on the center.

In the meantime, Cluman was unable to counter effectively because of the way his body was contorted holding the shield. Ezren's shield blocked the attempts easily, and after Cluman had his shield up high for several hits, Ezren swung his right foot out with all the strength he had and kicked the side of Cluman's shin. The plate of armor covering his shin contacted just behind where Cluman's stopped, but causing pain was not the intent of this move – it was to knock Cluman's feet out from under him, which it did successfully.

Cluman threw his arms out to catch himself, landing hard on his shield. His sword came out of his hand as he sprawled, landing a few feet away, and he lunged for it as Ezren did two full thrusts at his torso, winning the match before Cluman could retrieve his sword.

Master Juildar blew the horn, and Cluman got to his feet. Ezren offered a hand, but Cluman did not see it.

They went back to the center of the circle and hit swords and shields again. Cluman congratulated Ezren and wished him luck in the next rounds, but his eyes were set with anger. Ezren didn't understand why he would be angry. He walked off the circle with Cluman.

"We were never taught that move," Cluman said angrily.

"It's a really difficult move to predict," Ezren started, trying to commiserate. "Master Stark has done it to me more times than I can count, and the only real way to stop it is if you know it's coming."

Cluman looked over at him, the anger on his face undiminished. "Master Stark? So that's it – you're getting private lessons. No wonder you're so good! How is that fair? The son of the Captain of the Castle Guard gets private lessons and special treatment and then gets to win tournaments."

Ezren was shocked – the change that Cluman had undergone between his reaction to losing the first bout to losing the second made no sense.

"They weren't just *giving* me lessons, Cluman. I *asked* them to, and you could have asked too. I've worked really hard to get better at this. If you want to get better, you just have to work really hard too."

Cluman stopped, then glared at Ezren incredulously. "Go chop an ironwood tree, Ezren." He stormed off, shaking his head. Ezren did not follow, but watched him go for a moment, baffled, before walking over to where Fiona was still sitting on the benches, and she smiled wide and hugged him when he came close.

"You did wonderfully, Ezren! Great job!" She said, and without missing a beat, asked, "Now, what's wrong? Was Cluman upset about losing?"

"Yes," Ezren started. "He seemed fine after the first bout, but was really angry after the second one."

"What did you say to him?" She asked.

Ezren walked her through the conversation, and after he finished, much to his continued surprise, she closed her eyes and shook her head.

"Oh, Ezren. You really have no idea, do you?"

Ezren shook his head hopelessly and shrugged.

"I would have thought you of all people would see it immediately. Cluman is from *Comperr*. You know, the country we were recently at war with? And the country that we are getting very close to going to war against again?"

Ezren looked over at Cluman, considering. "So people are probably treating him...like they used to treat me."

"If not worse," Fiona said, nodding.

Revelations hit Ezren like a flood. "So he was hoping to do well in this tournament to try and earn some respect," he hesitated, thinking back to his own feelings. "But more than anyone else's respect, he just wanted to be able to respect himself. He wanted to find a reason to ignore what everyone around him was telling him. A reason to believe that they were wrong."

Fiona smiled, a mixture of sadness and pride.

He continued, "When he came up against me, he knew he was going to lose, and when he lost the first bout he could pinpoint exactly why and how, so it was easy to understand. But when I beat him the second time...it's because I tricked him and did something he didn't even know was a possibility. He felt cheated and humiliated."

Fiona nodded in agreement. But Ezren frowned. That explained most of it, but...

"Why did he get so upset when I said he just had to practice more?"

Ezren jumped and stared as Fiona laughed out loud. "Well that, Ezren, that's just Cluman being a normal person. *No one* reacts well when you point out the obvious thing they 'should' have done. That's the kind of response he might be open to a few days from now, but when the pain and embarrassment is still fresh, of course it made him angrier."

"But Cluman's my friend," Ezren replied, somewhat annoyed that she was taking this so casually. "What if he doesn't want to be friends anymore after this?"

Fiona waved her hand dismissively. "You won't let that happen, not now that you understand how he's feeling. Besides, you're both teenage boys. If it comes to it you'll roll around in the dirt for a bit and then be even better friends than you were before."

Ezren turned his eyes forward to watch the match that was going on next. It was the last match in this round, after which four of the sixteen boys in the class would move on. He wasn't nervous about his next match, though he knew he would be right before. Not only would Dakstra be an easy opponent – easier than Cluman, most likely, but after seeing Dakstra boast over his last victory he was determined to win...decisively.

The winner of the current match would face Introm in the next round. The two boys were both quite skilled, and as Ezren watched he wondered if either of them might give Introm a tough time, or possibly even defeat him. The match went to three bouts, and lasted longer than any match prior to it, but eventually Tristan emerged victorious and Memb was knocked out of the tournament.

There was a short break between each round, and Ezren used the time to shake off some of the nerves that were beginning to rise again.

Before long the break was over and Ezren was back in the circle, facing Dakstra. The matches in this round were up to 5, the winner being the first to take three bouts. The match indeed went smoothly, Ezren winning the first two bouts, each over within a matter of seconds by a successful hit to the head.

Dakstra was even angrier at Ezren than Cluman had been, but this time Ezren didn't care. Dakstra was a real tool and deserved the humbling after how he had treated Herke. For Ezren's part, he was careful not to even smile after winning. Anyone watching knew that only luck of the draw had gotten Dakstra this far into the tournament, so him being soundly thumped in this round was no surprise, and certainly no cause for pride for the one who did the thumping.

The match between Introm and Tristan took almost as long as the one between Tristan and Memb had, and went to three bouts, but Introm took the victory and moved on to face Ezren in the final match of the tournament.

As was typical, more and more people had showed up to watch as the tournament wore on. Part of that was simply that the matches got more interesting as the fighters were more skilled and their skills were more evenly-matched. The other part was that this was Introm's last tournament and he was hoping to enter the Guards immediately upon graduation despite his father's wishes.

The Sergeant-in-Charge, who headed up the training for new recruits, was there, along with many of the high-ranking officers in the city. Introm's parents were even visiting from Gaia. Ezren had heard Introm say that his father and mother wanted him to stay in Gaia and take over the peacekeeping brigade that they maintained in addition to the Guards stationed there, but Introm wanted to join the Guards and travel the world much like Ezren did.

Come to think of it, Introm might be on to something there. If Ezren really wanted to see the world, and he did, what better way to do it than becoming a scout like Ben Rider? He had only been out one more time since they had gone to the border with Robinton, but they were planning on going out in the next couple days again. This time they'd be patrolling up around Novis Spring to make sure no bandits had made camp in the area.

There was a short break between Introm's last match and the final match to give him time to rest.

Standing next to the bench on his side of the circle, Ezren bounced up on the balls of his feet and swung his arms, getting a sense for how tired his muscles were. To his surprise, he wasn't really feeling any tiredness at all. Granted, his path to the final match had not been particularly challenging, but he'd been fighting all day and was doing just fine.

During the break, the benches filled up, then the wall walk all around the training yard filled up, and people were even visible trying to watch through the arrow slits. Ezren felt his nervousness rise. There had not been nearly so many people at the previous tournament when he had faced Introm last. He looked to where Fiona was sitting on the benches and saw that his father had sat next to her, still in his uniform. He must have come here straight from his office.

His father held up a fist in encouragement with a smile and a nod, and Ezren nodded back, though he couldn't bring himself to return the smile – he was too apprehensive. A lot rested on this fight for him; if he lost he wouldn't be allowed to go to Comperr with Fiona. He'd continue to be stuck here, forever learning, forever training, never actually *doing* anything.

He continued looking around but regretted doing so when he noticed Asteri up on the wall walk. She was flanked on either side by Guards who were either the largest men he'd ever seen or simply appeared that way standing next to a petite 14-year-old girl. Seeing Asteri was nice, but his heart leapt and his nerves lurched right alongside it upon knowing that she was watching. She noticed him looking up at her and waved encouragingly. He forced a smile and waved back, then turned to look the opposite direction.

He set his jaw and checked the straps on his armor, making sure it was snug but not tight. He snuck a look over at Introm, who was mirroring him. Remembering what Fiona had said about Cluman, Ezren tried to think through what Introm might be feeling.

Introm was assured a place in the Guards whatever happened here today, but perhaps he wanted to be one of the rare few who became Sergeants within the first year of service. Perhaps he wanted to be able to have some say in where he went first and winning here would make the Guards want him badly enough to grant him that concession. He watched as Introm looked to the benches and waved, a timid smile on his face.

Ezren followed his eyes to Introm's mother and father. His mother smiled and waved back, but his father's face remained a stone. Perhaps *that* was why Introm trained as hard as he did. Ezren remembered the years spent striving futilely for his mother's affection. That realization made it all crash home like ocean waves were said to crash against the Western cliffs.

Introm wasn't thinking about the Guards – he wanted, no he *needed* to win this to show his father that he was worth loving. Ezren sighed sadly. Should he lose, then? Introm's cause was surely nobler than his own. But he knew from experience that if Introm's father did not love him before the match then no outcome here would change anything.

Not only that, but how could he lose on purpose without being obvious that he was doing so? He might lose even trying his hardest to win. Besides, Introm deserved more respect than that. Introm was always quiet, studious, and polite. They had never had a conversation nor spent any time together outside of school, but neither had Introm ever been rude or mean to him, even when Ezren first arrived and most of the other boys had made him the primary subject of their jests.

All that aside, Introm was an incredible fighter. Ezren had heard the Sergeant-in-Charge comment that Introm could likely defeat most of the men in the Guards who hadn't yet seen combat.

Ezren's jaw relaxed as his resolve strengthened. Introm had his reasons for wanting to win here today, but Ezren had his own reasons for wanting to win as well, and both of them deserved the chance to earn it. He would give his all trying to achieve victory, and he knew Introm would do the same.

Sooner than he expected, Master Juildar blew the horn to signal the combatants to come to the middle of the circle to begin the match. Ezren checked his helmet and retrieved his sword and shield.

Introm met him in the middle and they hit swords and shield in respect. They locked eyes as Master Juildar explained the rules in a loud voice, more for the audience's benefit than for their own. As this was the final match, it would go until one of the combatants had won three bouts instead of only two.

Juildar threw the coin in the air, and time seemed to slow for Ezren. He breathed in deeply, noticed every detail of Introm's face, and watched to see if his eyes would flick, giving away the direction he would move first. They did not.

'Clink'

Introm launched into action, doing a long thrust that made Ezren leap to the side in surprise. By the time Ezren could counter, Introm had reset his footing and easily blocked the slash with his shield. Introm continued to press him – a weak slash at Ezren's shoulder, easily blocked by Ezren's shield, then a jab at his stomach, which Ezren parried with his shield, and then a committed slash at Ezren's shins, which Ezren had to leap over.

He realized too late what Introm was doing, and, sure enough, no sooner had Ezren's feet left the ground than Introm himself leaped straight at Ezren, shield leading the way, and bashed him with incredible force, sending Ezren flying backwards, helpless as a bird with no wings, to crash onto the ground.

Even as the wind was knocked out of him and his joints rang with pain, he seized one thought – *the bout isn't over yet. Introm hasn't scored.* He rolled away as Introm came with a slash down at him, then held his shield up and to the side to stop Introm's backhanded slash. He had a chance, a moment, and he took it. He sat up and swung his sword over in one smooth motion, hitting Introm solidly in his left calf.

The horn blew one short note and a small flag was inserted into a board that counted how many hits each fighter had gotten. There was no break, however, because no one had won the bout yet, and Ezren realized, once again too late, that he had sacrificed his chance to gain his feet in order to get that hit.

Sword, shield, and feet rained down on him, and he fended them off as best he could, trying to push himself backwards on the ground with his own feet. Introm's strong kick to his shield rolled him over and he felt Introm's sword thwack against his back plate. One more and he would lose the bout.

He continued his roll and flailed his sword at Introm to keep him at bay until he could stand to his feet.

He got to his feet just in time for Introm's next rush, but he didn't have his footing set properly. Introm's full thrust nearly got past, and getting his sword over in time to parry it knocked him even more off balance. That said, he had managed to parry Introm's sword to where it was lodged between Ezren's sword and shield, pinning him somewhat.

In the split second it took Ezren to decide what to do next, Introm spun, the changing angle allowing him to pull his sword free and continue the swing all the way around and hit Ezren's back just as Ezren was trying to dash away.

Master Juildar blew the horn to signal the end of the bout.

Ezren hit his shield with his sword in frustration. He was better than this! He knew how to set his footing properly! Master Stark had *taught* him not to jump over a slash! He forced himself to take deep breaths; Master Stark had also taught him that letting anger control you was the second-fastest way to lose a fight.

What could he do differently in this next bout? The real problems seemed to come when he let Introm have control over the fight. Ezren needed to fight harder for control over the fight rather than simply reacting and defending.

He faced Introm at the center of the circle, this time with a strategy of how he was going to seize control immediately.

'Clink'

Ezren squatted down behind his shield as Introm's slash whooshed over his head. Lucky, that; he had been planning on squatting down anyway but now it would look like a quick reaction. The moment he was down far enough, he leaped forward in what Master Juildar would no doubt consider a terminal bash and slammed right into Introm's shield, knocking him backwards.

Introm was larger than he was, though not by much, and while he didn't go as far as Ezren would have had their roles been reversed, he stumbled back a ways and was clearly imbalanced. Ezren pressed his advantage home much as Introm had, using a short series of jabs and weak slashes to keep Introm's hands busy.

A jab towards Introm's shins brought his opponent's sword down low, which was a mistake! Introm should have used his shield, and now his sword was out of position! Keeping his shield in front of him, Ezren was able to pull his sword out of his jab much faster than his opponent was able to reverse his momentum. A committed slash at an angle contacted with the right side of Introm's helmet.

He'd won the bout! The score was now tied, 1-1. The horn blew and he turned to walk back to the center of the circle.

Introm showed little emotion on his face at having lost a bout, but his eyes showed the same determined resolve he always seemed to have.

'Clink'

A strange thing happened. As both he and Introm sprung into motion, they each mirrored the other in synchronicity. As Ezren slashed at Introm's shield, he felt the same impact on his own. Their swords connected right between them as they came for each other's shins. They each twisted to their left to avoid a thrust while thrusting themselves.

The phenomenon only lasted for a few moves, but it transformed into a...dance was the wrong word, but it was closer than he would have expected. Both he and Introm moved quickly and fluidly, the rattle of practice swords and shields seeming never-ending. As he ducked, dodged, countered, thrust, parried, bashed, and even kicked, Ezren felt something rather unexpected:

This was the most fun he had *ever* had.

Sweat soon began to pour down his helmeted face and his breathing deepened, but he was not only keeping Introm at bay, he was forcing Introm to keep *him* at bay. The bout lasted longer than either of the previous two, but it seemed to fly by much faster as the two combatants did their best to strike at one another.

Here and there a sword did get through defenses – Introm scored a hit on Ezren's shoulder, then Ezren scored a hit on Introm's thigh, but the bout continued even as Ezren felt himself beginning to slow, though he could see that Introm was slowing as well.

He found that he could predict where Introm was going, though it seemed his opponent could also predict where Ezren would strike next. The bout came to a sudden end as Introm suddenly lunged forward with a well-aimed thrust at Ezren's face. Ezren was barely able to turn his head fast enough for the end of the sword to impact the side of his helmet instead.

The horn blew the end of the bout, barely audible over the cheering of the crowd. Taking the bout put Introm only one point away from winning.

But unlike after the first bout, Ezren wasn't angry. In fact, he was excited. This was unlike anything he had ever experienced. The cheering from the crowd, the speed of the fights, and the thrill of knowing he would have to draw on every ounce of his talent and abilities to have a hope of winning was...euphoric. And his respect for Introm...the only thing he wanted more than for Introm to win this match was for himself to win this match. No matter what came next, Introm had his respect and admiration. Ezren had studied and practiced diligently for years before spending the last months doing little else, and he knew that Introm must have done the same to achieve the level of proficiency he had.

There was no resentment against Introm for winning the bout, and would be none were the older boy to win the match. Introm had *earned* this victory, and the only thing stopping Ezren from dropping his sword in forfeit was that he had earned it too. Both of them deserved the victory, which made the battle for it all the more intense.

'Clink'

Once again, they fought for control of the battle, and while the mirroring that had happened in the previous bout did not happen again, they once again fought ferociously and with all the skill they could muster. For several minutes, Ezren was unwilling to take any significant risks, always choosing a committed thrust or a jab over a full thrust and choosing body strikes instead of head strikes because he knew that if he took too big of a risk, Introm would punish him for it.

Whether Introm shared his philosophy, Ezren did not know, but his opponent was also choosing not to attempt more risky strikes. As the bout continued, an idea entered Ezren's mind. He had experimented with turning the blade in his hand to strike overhand like one might do with a knife, but he had never found a good way to do it.

He wasn't consciously thinking of it now; the bout required every ounce of his thought, but something about the way Introm had twisted his sword *behind* his shield gave an Ezren an idea.

~

Timot didn't realize his mouth was hanging open until Fiona rapped the bottom of his chin, clicking his mouth shut. Looking over at her, he saw she was smiling. She knew exactly why he was in awe.

He knew Ezren was good at sword-and-shield, had practiced with him enough times over the last month to get a sense for how capable he had become, but this...it was like seeing Ezren *unleashed*. He was watching two teenage boys fight with skill and ferocity that many professional soldiers would not have been able to match.

The bout didn't show any sign of ending soon, so he looked around at all the people watching. Many were here because of Introm – his parents were influential in the court and Introm was highly regarded as one to keep an eye on.

But...some of these people were here for his son. He noted his two lieutenants, and Werbal, of course. He saw Ben Rider leaning on the rampart on the wall walk, and Princess Asteri flanked by Gemo and Leen. Raban and Sergeant Kennard had arrived soon enough to be sitting only a few benches behind Fiona and him.

He watched the crowd, hearing many of them cheering for Ezren, and felt a lump rise in his throat. His eyes began to water, and he cleared his throat, looking forward at the ongoing battle.

No matter what happened, he decided right then and there that he would allow Ezren to go to Comperr if Fiona allowed it. Looking back to her watching Ezren and seeing the smile of pride on her face, he had little doubt that she would agree.

He turned back to continue watching the fight. One of Ezren's defining traits over the years had been his ability to focus and discipline himself to whatever he felt was worth setting his mind to, but now Timot felt like he was seeing the potential that came from that discipline.

Normal folks, and especially the wealthy in the castle, talked about all the things they would love to learn or do, then went about their lives as usual, choosing to relax with a book or a game of foxes after a day at work. He himself was guilty of it. Ezren showed clearly the result when one did not allow themselves excuses.

Smiling contentedly, a deep and abiding pride filling him, Timot watched Ezren excel.

~

Ezren had him – he didn't know how he knew, but somehow he knew that if he spread his feet wide and held his shield ever so slightly further to his left than normal then...yes, Introm struck like a viper, but Ezren parried, not to the side, but up so the thrust went past his head, so close he felt the wind on his face. While Introm's sword was uselessly high, he flicked up his sword and rapped the side of Introm's helmet.

An audible gasp from the crowd preceded the blast on the horn, followed by the cheers of the crowd. Whether in support of Ezren or simply from enjoyment, he didn't know.

As Ezren walked back to where he would stand at the center of the circle, he saw that Introm was laughing softly and shaking his head. He noticed Ezren watching, and said, "You've gotten better, Ezren. You've gotten a lot better. You might actually beat me today."

Ezren shook his head slightly. "I don't know about that. I've gotten lucky a couple times but I'm just trying to keep up."

The two boys took their positions for what would be the final bout, one way or another. Ezren had evened up the score on the last one, but so far they'd been trading back and forth. If the pattern held then Introm would take this bout. How could Ezren break the pattern?

'Clink'.

Ezren tensed up, waiting for Introm to strike, then noticed that Introm had done the same thing. He expected to hear more laughter from the audience, or perhaps jeers, but there was complete silence. He took a step to his right, and Introm mirrored him. They walked a half-circle, switching places, before suddenly Introm struck – a full thrust at Ezren's torso that he parried with his shield.

But Introm had stepped forward with his left foot during the lunge, so he was able to take a wide step to the right and terminally slash with all his strength at Ezren's shield and knock it even further to the side. Thinking Introm would go for his head, Ezren raised his shield high in defense, but the second slash instead impacted on his back, knocking him forward.

Knowing that Introm would try to press forward his advantage to get another strike, Ezren rolled only once, then came up on one knee, holding his shield to block Introm's slash while thrusting with his sword, catching Introm right in the chest.

Introm leaped back, but too late: the score was 1-1 torso hits. It would only take one more hit for either to win as long as they struck either the head or the torso. If they struck limbs, it could take as many as three more hits to end the bout *and* the match.

Ezren got to his feet as Introm settled back. He could almost see the thoughts whirling in Introm's head just as they were in his own. He needed a way to surprise Introm. If he kept on as he had, he felt like his opponent would likely score the next hit, and that might be the end of it.

Introm must have come to the same conclusion because he came forward much the same as he had the previous two bouts, though with more measured strikes, and Ezren found himself primarily occupied with fighting the match. He was being forced back, step by step, and he knew it was only a matter of time before he felt the impact of Introm's sword somewhere.

The problem was that every time Ezren tried to position Introm's shield out of the way of his next strike, Introm was able to bring the shield right back or parry with his sword. Ezren was fast, but Introm was just as fast. The only way he would be able to get to Introm's torso would be to strike faster than he seemed to be able to...or from a different direction.

Then something in his brain connected, and he thought of a way to do exactly that. But...he had never done it before, and Master Stark had told him directly that it was usually a bad idea to try something for the first time while in a real fight.

Well, if he kept on as he was he knew he was going to lose. The worst thing that could happen if he tried something strange and it didn't work was that he lost, so really there was no reason *not* to try it.

Introm was coming in with a thrust, his right foot forward, so Ezren parried with the shield and stepped forward with his left foot. Introm hadn't expected that -- normally you would step backward away from a thrust – but when Ezren slashed at Introm's shoulder, Introm got his shield up to block in time.

Then Ezren extended his shield arm, creating enough space between his body and his shield for him to bring his sword in between, flipping it in his hand as he did. Then, his hand and sword coming out from behind the other side of his shield, he jabbed backhanded, which would have been impossible with a standard grip. Introm was raising his sword in an overhead slash that would come down right on Ezren's undefended head.

He felt the thud of the practice sword contacting...Introm's torso.

Ezren froze.

Introm looked at him in shock.

The crowd erupted.

The rest of the day passed in a euphoric fog. His father and Fiona rushed over to him, beating Raban and Sergeant Kennard by only a few moments. He looked up, searching for Asteri on the wall walk and she was there, jumping up and down and clapping her hands.

Master Juildar presented him with a bronze-cast trophy that was about a foot tall. It had been cast in the figure of a soldier standing at ready with shield raised and sword poised. Introm came and shook his hand, and that was the end of formalities.

Dinner was in their apartments as usual, but Fiona and the Kennards joined them and the kitchen sent up what they said was their finest cuts, courtesy of the King and Queen. The beef tasted the same as any other Ezren had tasted, but all of the adults seemed to disagree, moaning with enjoyment as they took their first bites.

They played foxes, told stories, and joked around until long after Ezren was normally in bed. When the celebration finally came to an end, Raban and Sergeant Kennard were first out the door. As Fiona was leaving, his father took her arm gently and said, "Thank you for being there today."

His father kissed her cheek, her face got red, then she left.

Ezren smiled, but couldn't summon the energy to rib his father. They bade each other goodnight, and each closed the doors to their rooms.

CHAPTER 6: TROMOS

Two days after Ezren's incredible win, Timot ate his breakfast quickly. He was expecting news from Cleononia any day now, ever since Vewen had sent a pigeon alerting them that the wizard's party had arrived in Dazbog.

Ezren was up with the sun as well, like usual, but he was packing saddlebags to be out with Ben Rider again for a few days. Raban was going with them, as he had on their previous two trips, which Timot was glad of. He trusted Rider, of course, but he knew that if Rider were truly forced to choose between protecting Ezren or returning to give word of an imminent threat, he would choose to return to provide warning and leave Ezren to his fate. This way, Ezren wouldn't be alone if Rider had to ride ahead to fulfill his duties.

That wasn't a character flaw or a criticism -- that was Rider's *job*. Any good scout would do the same and if it was anyone besides Timot's own son, he would wholeheartedly support the decision.

King Radomir had asked Fiona to head back to Comperr a tenday from now, so at that point Ezren would get his wish – he'd get to travel to Comperr city and see all the sights to his heart's content.

Maybe between this trip with Rider and leaving for Comperr,

Timot and Ezren could take some time to go visit their cabin in Berengaria. They had yet to do anything with the plot and the charred, blackened remains of their cabin still stood there. They could go spend a couple nights and make some decisions, perhaps even clear out the old burned wood and make space for a new, better cabin.

He had tested the idea with Ezren, and his son seemed excited at the prospect. Granted, that boy would be excited about anything as long as it got him out of the city, but Timot was excited about the idea as well. The last two months of spending more time with Ezren had brought to his realization how little time they'd been spending together before that. He was ready for that to change.

Getting up from the table, he wished Ezren good luck on the scouting trip and bade him farewell, then left their apartments to go see if a message had arrived in his office yet. From here, it was fastest to go along the wall past the academy training grounds, but the clouds outside threatened rain, so he took the slightly longer route through the entrance hall.

He was looking down to wipe the crumbs from his breakfast biscuit off his uniform, so he did not see the person in front of him until he almost crashed into him. He stepped back quickly as boots came into his vision and looked up.

It took a brief moment, but Timot quickly knew exactly who he faced. The hard features, somewhat filled out over the years since he had last seen them, the straight posture with his hands clasped behind his back, and the dark green velvet robe he wore, all slammed themselves home in Timot's memory. He would never forget this face.

It was Ezmith.

His eldest son. The last time Timot had seen him, the young man had mercilessly decapitated one of their servants with little justification, then was about to kill Ezren and him before Timot's other two sons intervened.

With Ambarta's ambitions, it had only been a matter of time before Timot confronted his estranged family again, but seeing Ezmith suddenly standing there with no warning, seven years older and a small but smug smile on his face, Timot only just held onto his calm.

"Are you here to kill me?" He asked, his voice even and steady.

Ezmith raised one eyebrow in surprise, though why the question should surprise him was beyond Timot. "No," he replied. "The Lady Virtesa has determined that now would be an...inopportune...time to take your lives."

"Have you harmed Eztas or Ezrote?" Timot asked, still not moving.

Ezmith sneered. "Ezrote is back in Comperr and will be until our conquests are completed. Eztas is now no more than any other common soldier. Both were punished, but both are unharmed despite their betrayal in sparing your and Ezren's lives." He looked around idly. "Where is the boy? He would be what, sixteen now?"

"He's out of the city," Timot replied evenly. "He's been training with Guard scouts."

"Out of the city," Ezmith repeated as though he knew Timot was lying. "I suppose we won't be having the family reunion I was hoping for."

"Why are you here, Ezmith?"

"I'm an emissary, of course," he replied smoothly, even adding a bow ruined by his smirk. "I'm here to negotiate with Lord Radomir about bringing his wizards home where they belong."

"Then why aren't you with him already?"

"I've only just arrived," Ezmith replied with that same small, smug smile. "However, I have come a great distance, so perhaps you could let Radomir know that I'm here?"

Timot almost refused outright. Ezmith was incredibly dangerous, and he may actually be here to assassinate Radomir in order to throw Mountain Home into chaos.

As he thought it through, however, if assassination was Ezmith's purpose he would just march nonchalantly through the castle, murdering everyone he saw to ensure there were no witnesses. Besides, Radomir would *want* a chance to talk directly with Ezmith if he could, though Timot could tell him how pointless it would be.

"Come," Timot said to his son. "*King* Radomir often entertains foreign dignitaries in the Jucundus Chamber. I'll take you there, then send word to the King."

Timot turned and began walking, hearing Ezmith's footsteps behind him. He left him under guard in the Jucundus Chamber and told a servant off to get refreshments, then went straight to the royal family's apartments and knocked.

One of their personal servants, Delogera, opened the door with an affronted look on her face.

"Please inform King Radomir that Ezmith Virtesa from Ambarta is here and awaits him in the Jucundus Chamber," Timot said before Delogera could reprimand him for bothering the royal family this early in the day.

"What?!" came Radomir's voice from inside before he was pushing past Delogera, already fully dressed.

"Ezmith, sir, he's here. And he's asking to meet with you," Timot explained.

Radomir paused for a moment. "Are you alright, Captain? Would you like to go back to your office while I meet with him?"

Timot shook his head. "No, sir. I would like to be there with you if you'll allow it."

"Do you think he's here to kill me?"

Timot shook his head again.

Radomir snorted. "I suppose if that's what he's here for there's not much we could do about it anyway."

He came the rest of the way out into the hallway and immediately began walking briskly towards the Jucundus Chamber.

"Did he say what he *does* want?" He asked as they strode quickly through the halls.

"He says he's here to negotiate Mellion and Paavali returning to Mountain Home," Timot replied.

"Have they been captured?!" Radomir asked, alarmed.

Timot hesitated for a moment, then spoke slowly: "That is not what it sounded like, but perhaps."

They reached the Jucundus Chamber and without pausing even for a moment, Radomir pushed the door open and strode through.

"I'll admit I did not expect this," he said upon entering.

A servant with refreshments was just placing a platter of wine and cheese on one of the small tables. The servant bowed quickly and made a beeline for the door.

Timot closed the door behind her as she left. He turned, taking a few steps to Radomir's side to get a clear view of Ezmith. The Jucundus Chamber was larger than the Chordus, and with no table in the center. Instead, there were groupings of soft chairs and couches throughout the room that could be rearranged depending on the size of the group. The room was decorated with depictions of landscapes and wildlife, all emphasizing peace and serenity. The peaceful décor clearly stated that the purpose of the room was to host wartime negotiations.

"Why are you here?" The king asked.

Ezmith somehow kept his smile constant without making it look fixed. Before answering, he took a goblet from the platter and took a sip.

"I want you to command your wizards to return here. It is in your best interest for Cleononia to be under Ambartan control."

Radomir snorted. "Please explain why."

"Has trade from Disote, Robinton, and the Wood Coast not run more smoothly since we conquered them? By consolidating power under the Lady Virtesa and myself, we've been able to make the lives of everyone under our rule better and more prosperous. Mountain Home has benefitted from this, and now we ask that you allow us to do the same with Cleononia."

It was an interesting point, and something that Timot had thought about on many occasions. He had spoken with many merchants passing through the city from those regions, and the only consistent complaint was that taxes were higher. Patrols were more reliable throughout all the regions, roads were kept in better repair and even being widened, and apparently there was an undertaking to clear the rapids in the Novis river to allow at least shallow-drafted riverboats to take advantage of a much faster route from Novis Terram to Bahadir.

By all reports, his former wife Kimaya, who was now known to the world as the Lady Virtesa, was a competent, caring, and benevolent ruler.

Of course, one had to wonder what lurked beneath the surface, and how many dissenters or non-compliant citizens had simply and conveniently disappeared.

King Radomir shared a look with him. They had discussed all this before, and Timot had explained that more than anything, Kimaya simply wanted to be revered. She wanted to be adored and respected. Frankly, she wanted to be worshipped. Most of the time, this incentivized her to be empathetic to the needs of her people and do her best to make their lives better. Sometimes, though, no amount of empathy would change a person's mind, and that's when she would justify solving the problem in a...different...way.

The king looked back to Ezmith. "Whatever benefits you claim to be offering, Lord Perivon and the rest of the Cleononians seem to be willing to fight to the death to keep them from materializing. I've never known Lord Perivon to toss the lives of his men's aside wantonly, so if he judges this fight to be worth fighting, I defer to him."

Ezmith's smile began to slip. So, he hadn't *actually* gotten more self-assured, he had just gotten better at pretending he was. Ezmith was harder to understand than Kimaya was, but thankfully Timot had the benefit of having raised him into adulthood. Where Kimaya had the very human ability to only apply empathy to others when it was convenient, Ezmith lacked any empathy whatsoever. It was the piece of him that seemed to have been traded for his exceptional wizardly powers. For the thousandth time, Timot cursed Galdrach for not informing Kimaya and him about the cost of his potion.

But there was more to Ezmith than his lack of empathy. He was supremely confident in his magical abilities, and yet he lived in fear that those around him would discount him or think little of him. Not all that dissimilar from his mother, he supposed, but it came with a raw, sharp edge that made him far less predictable and more dangerous.

Ezmith swirled the goblet in his hand, looking down at it for a moment.

"Surely you have felt your diminished influence these past years," Ezmith said to the King, staying calm. "Does it not chafe to know that the other rulers who would once leap to obey your summons must first gain our approval before even replying to a letter?"

He set the goblet down, clearly having decided his direction with this argument. "How many more men of Mountain Home lost their lives in the war with Comperr because none of the Western nations could or would come to your aid? Do you look forward giving your daughter an island throne ensconced between two great powers one treaty away from dividing that island amongst themselves?"

Ezmith continued, shaking his head. "No, Mountain Home was only considered a great power because of the alliance of nations it had behind it. Now, with relations between Ambarta and Comperr the strongest they've ever been thanks to the flood of trade we've been able to provide them, where will Mountain Home fit in this new world a year from now? Ten years from now? A hundred?"

The king chuckled in response. He *chuckled*. Timot had told him everything about Ezmith, and how his temper could make him do horrific things, then when Ezmith threatened him with complete annihilation of his entire country, Radomir...chuckled.

Timot tried to school his face, but he knew his eyebrows were in danger of disappearing into his hair.

"How convenient it is to be young, to still be able to see things so black and white, isn't it Ezmith?" the king asked. "You do not even realize how many assumptions your threats are based on, do you? Comperr has good relations with *everyone* right up until the first arrow is fired, and they've never been afraid of losing a little trade to fight a war: with a friend like Comperr you don't need any enemies. Take them away and what do you have to threaten us? Even after taking Cleononia you could not match our armies, and you have seen quite recently how the Guild of wizards will take action even when King Raanan of Comperr is unwilling to."

No doubt about it now, Ezmith's smile was definitely gone and replaced with a snarl.

"Then let me make this perfectly clear, Radomir," he said, taking a deliberate step forward. "I could snuff your life out on a whim. I could kill both of you without making a sound, then march my way through your impenetrable castle to the queen and princess. By then, I'll have killed enough of your guards that it won't matter if we make a little noise, so I can take my time with them, keeping them alive long enough to feel more pain than you would think the human body could handle. I can decapitate, both literally and figuratively, the entire leadership of Mountain Home and throw your nation into chaos. And I can do that in a single afternoon without even breaking a sweat."

He paused, having taken several more steps forward and was now nearly nose-to-nose with King Radomir.

"I will do exactly that if you do not send your fastest rider to Cleononia to retrieve your wizards immediately."

Throughout Ezmith's speech, Timot had watched the King's face, and the moment Ezmith mentioned Oana and Asteri, he could tell that all possibility of diplomatic resolution was gone. Not only that, but there was a decent chance that half of Mountain Home's army would be on its way to crush Ambarta's as fast as Ezmith wanted the messenger to be sent.

"Then *do* it," King Radomir said, to the widening of Timot's eyes.

The King stared directly into Ezmith's eyes, the challenge in his voice matched by his body. "*Do* it, boy. Cement yourself as a fugitive and a vagabond for the rest of your life. You are already on the run – that is the entire reason you are here, isn't it?"

Without giving Ezmith a chance to respond, Radomir continued, "As of right now, surrender and retreat *might* convince the Guild to call back its hounds. You *might* be able to sit somewhat comfortably on the usurper's throne you've carved for yourself, but imagine for a moment what the rest of your life would entail should you commit even a single one of the atrocities you just threatened against me. Would your own mother even stand for you? The meanest peasant would deny you a hayloft to sleep the night and would likely run to find the guards the moment he convinced you to spare his life."

An almost evil smile crept onto the King's face as he broke eye contact long enough to look Ezmith up and down insultingly. "You pretend you have so much power, like a child at play. Power is not, and never has been, a basis for authority, but rather the result of it. With a flick of your hand you could end me, but with a flick of mine I could scorch every inch of the earth under Ambarta's rein. For nearly a millennium the rulers of Mountain Home have had the strength of arms to conquer the rest of the Western nations, but never have. Do you know why? Because power alone does not loyalty breed. Your 'power' is like a mountain of pine needles. All it takes is one hot coal for it to all erupt in flame."

Simply the fact that Ezmith allowed the king to speak for so long was evidence of his recognition that Radomir was right. That Ezmith continued to say nothing after the king had ceased speaking was proof. After giving Ezmith a moment to respond, Radomir ended the meeting.

"Now, boy, go back to your mountain, and stop pretending you have either the power or the authority to follow through on your threats."

Turning on his heel, King Radomir left the chamber, throwing the doors open as he went.

Part of Timot wanted to follow him, wanted to sprint as quickly from the room as he could and go find some covers to hide under. Ezmith's threats, though...his eldest son had certainly changed for the worse. Despite his fear, he stayed. Perhaps he could help Ezmith in some small way in this moment.

Ezmith spoke first: "*That* is the man who commands your loyalty? You abandoned your own family but that bloated, brazen, conceited pig is enough for you?"

It wasn't shocking that Ezmith might have an unfavorable view of Radomir in that moment, but for Timot's part, he thought Radomir's handling of the situation had been astonishingly apt.

"It seems you rewrite history to suit your desires, Ezmith. I abandoned no one; I was sentenced to death, if you recall. A sentence you were moments away from carrying out before your brothers had compassion on us."

"You abandoned us before that, *father*. It was your abandoning of our cause that led to your death sentence."

Timot shook his head. It never ceased to amaze him how one's perspective could cloud their interpretation of events.

"Ezmith…how are you? Really."

Nothing Radomir said had caused nearly as obvious a reaction as that simple question. Ezmith looked at him as though he'd grown a second head.

"I'm…I'm fine, Father," he stammered out, looking bewildered.

"Are you happy?" Timot asked, almost surprised at his own sincere desire to know the answer. "Everything you've done up to this point… has it given you what you were looking for?"

Ezmith continued to stare at him, nonplussed.

"I-I…no, I wouldn't say I'm happy, but…yes, in certain ways I have gotten what I was looking for."

Timot nodded sadly, both at Ezmith's admission and his obvious shock at being asked such a simple question. Kimaya and he had most certainly failed as parents, at least with Ezmith.

He looked down at his feet, hands on his hips, uncertain of the best way to proceed. "Well, I cannot say that I wish you success, but I do wish you happiness, Ezmith. I truly do. I don't know how long you all have known that Ezren and I were alive, but thank you for leaving us be. I understand the threat you perceive Ezren to be and am grateful that you have not attempted to remove either of us."

Recovering himself, Ezmith scoffed. "Ezren is hardly a threat now. There's not a province in our nation that cares one whit for the prophecy either way, and nothing he could do would make Cleononia *less* amenable to us. The prophecy was a convenient excuse at a time when we still needed one, nothing more."

"So you know the truth of the prophecy, then? When did Kimaya tell you?"

"Two, perhaps three years ago. I do not remember exactly, but I had known long before that. I believe Ezrote has come to the same conclusion, but I doubt Eztas has."

Timot shrugged. "As far as I can tell the prophecy was real, or at least done long before Kimaya made her plans. For all we know, her actions truly were fulfillment of it. There are four of you, after all."

"*Three* of us," Ezmith corrected. "Ezren's impotence truly does invalidate the idea that we are the ones." He shook his head and scoffed. "Worthless boy."

Timot stood up straighter. Ezmith was his son. Timot had helped raise him from birth to even older than Ezren was now, but their choices had driven them apart and turned Ezmith into a man that Timot did not know. Ezren, on the other hand, was a kindred spirit and a wonderful boy turning into a man who would be a force to be reckoned with in the world. Timot locked eyes with Ezmith and drew back his shoulders.

"If, in all the days of your life, Ezmith, you could attain even half of the worth of that boy, you could call yourself a success. Ezren has shown himself to be more a man than you have ever managed. He protects those he loves, goes out of his way to help anyone he sees that needs it, and disciplines himself to spend every hour of every day either training or doing. Ezren wouldn't know play if it bit him on the ankle."

Ezmith's snarl returned in a flash. The man truly was fragile. "Have a care with your words, Captain. Despite Radomir's threats, I could kill you and be gone too fast for anyone to prove it was me."

Perhaps it was still the shock of seeing Ezmith face to face again after so many years, but Ezmith's words did not strike fear into him. Ezmith might hurt him, but what he needed to say was more important.

He sighed. "Ezmith, you say that I abandoned you. For six years I have been off living a completely separate life while you've grown and changed and become a different person. You never had much respect for me even before I left with Ezren, and I doubt you'd have much respect for what I've been up to since, so why should my words have such an effect on you?"

Ezmith's eyebrows drew down. He didn't seem to understand Timot's point.

"Why are your emotions so easily manipulated? If you truly perceived me the way you claim to, then none of my words, no matter how cutting, would have any effect on you. The truth is, Ezmith, you have always believed, thanks to your mother, that your powers made you inherently special, made you better than those around you. Yet you see how Lord Perivon, someone you no doubt look down upon, has stolen your goats over and over in your war against him. You see evidence all around that you are not that special; *everyone* has gifts, everyone has talents, and while yours may be among the greatest, no amount of inborn gift or talent can make a person command the respect of those around them."

"You take this contradiction between what you have been taught and what you see with your own eyes and conclude that you are somehow to blame for the discrepancy – if you were as smart, as strong, as wise as you were supposed to be, then people *would* see you as their better."

Ezmith's face was impassive, but his eyes bored into Timot's, taking in every word.

"But you're wrong, son. You're wrong. You forgot to consider the possibility that your mother believed a lie, and passed that lie on to you."

Instinctually, Timot raised a hand and put it on Ezmith's shoulder. Surprisingly, Ezmith did not brush it off.

"You are *not* better than everyone else. You are special, unique even, but then, all people are. Your strength and confidence needs to come from within, not from the approval of a man who you once called father. Rely on others to tell you when you misstep, but keep confidence inside you that your worth as a person is not in doubt simply because you made a mistake."

Ezmith's eyes were watering, but his voice was strong and clear in his reply.

"Why are you telling me this?"

Timot let his hand fall from Ezmith's shoulder. "I believe this may be the last time we have an opportunity to speak one on one, alone. You are on a far different path, and though you would always be welcome, I do not believe you would join Ezren and me on ours. Most likely, the next time we see each other will be on opposite ends of a battlefield."

Ezmith nodded, cleared his throat, and stood up a little straighter.

"I need to return to Mhairi. Mother will be awaiting my report on Radomir's response. We will no doubt turn our spears toward Mountain Home once Cleononia is ours."

Timot nodded. "Fare well, Ezmith."

Ezmith looked as if he were about to reply in kind, but instead turned and created a Fold. On the other side, Timot could see the inside of a study with the edge of a table just visible on the side. He could not tell where it was. Ezmith stepped through the Fold and closed it without another word.

~

Stepping through the Fold and closing it behind him, Ezmith struggled with himself. Who was that man and where had he been when Ezmith was younger? The Timot Kimorae that had left them six years ago had been an apathetic, lazy waste of a human being. Despite the passed time, his father had looked younger, sharper, and more fit than Ezmith remembered him.

But more than that...it was not possible that his father truly cared for him, was it? Surely this was some elaborate trick to gain advantage.

Ezmith nodded and sighed as he figured it out – the man was simply trying to drive a rift between him and his mother. Why else would he say that his mother had lied to him? What could Timot possibly gain by trying to convince Ezmith that the man cared?

Anger began to rise inside him. He understood what was happening here...He had always known that his father was worthless, but had never known he was treacherous and cold enough to take an attempt to drive a wedge between Ezmith and the only person who had ever really cared for him – his mother -- and wrap it in an avalanche of seemingly heartfelt exhortations to a live a better life.

What did his father know of what made a better life? He was blind to all that he could not see with his own eyes. Ezmith saw and understood things that would break his father's mind, and yet the man had the unmitigated gall to lecture *him* on not being, what, *special?* Special didn't even begin to cover him!

And the thought that *Ezren* was more of a man than he? Ezmith felt his fists clenching and unclenching as he shook with pure rage. He looked at the map, showing the distance from where they had camped outside Dazbog and where they were now here in Mhairi.

He shouted a command to the guard outside the study to let no one enter until he allowed it. None were to come in.

Satisfied that he would be left alone, Ezmith balled a fist in his right hand and struck himself in his right cheek. As hard as he could force himself to swing, it did not carry the same strength as an enemy's fist would have. Ezmith made up for the difference by continuing to hit himself. He bloodied his own nose, bruised his own cheeks, and swung his fists against his chest and stomach as hard as he could bring himself to do so.

He wasn't just *special*! He was *everything*! He was supposed to be the child of prophecy! He was supposed to lead the four winds to bring prosperity to all!

Unable to breath properly after the pummeling to his sides and chest, he dropped to his knees, then continued to hit himself in his thighs as hard as he could bring himself to do.

Eventually, he stopped, and fell to his side on the floor, curled up, whimpering in pain much as he used to do as a child.

There was one thing that his father had said that was correct – Ezmith should have no care for what he said. His father was a worthless man, and his words were the impotent flailing of an inferior being trying vainly to stand against a greater power.

Bringing himself shakily to his feet, Ezmith took stock of his injuries and cast a spell that would return his body to its optimal state. Though he'd used the spell many times, mostly while growing up, he had never come up with a name for it.

He shivered inexplicably as waves of heat moved through his body and beads of sweat immediately appeared on his forehead. Within just a few moments, he felt the swelling on his face and the lingering pain on the rest of his body fade away.

Not even a bruise would remain to tell his secret. He wiped away the last traces of his tears and set to making further plans. He knew what he had to do. There were days yet before anything of note would be needed for his army, though he supposed he could set his people to work fortifying Mhairi.

Sneaking away would be simple enough. He could spare the time… yes…tonight. He would do it tonight.

∾

That conversation had gone far better than Timot had expected. Granted, it had been rather spur-of-the-moment, but even as the words were leaving his mouth he had been afraid of how they would be received. The truth of it was, though, that he cared about Ezmith and wanted him to find some measure of fulfillment and happiness in his life, despite how his story might end.

After Ezmith disappeared through his Fold, Timot went to find King Radomir to discuss the meeting and its implications. To his surprise, the king had no intention of sending an army to wipe Ezmith off the face of the earth. No, Ezmith was all bluster and Perivon would continue to run circles around the boy until Ambarta gave up all hope of conquest.

Once Perivon had driven them out of Cleononia, Radomir would send an envoy to Cleononia to meet and discuss how to restore each of the nations to their former ruling arrangements. The Wood Coast would be the most difficult, with the previous Lord and Lady dead and their daughter Aletheia seeming to be firmly entrenched with the Virtesas.

Raanan in Comperr was still the greater threat by far and Timot should keep focused on that. His duties as Captain of the Castle Guard were unlikely to lead him to direct engagement with any Comperr forces but assassination attempts or other infiltrations were not uncommon for countries on the other side of the Berg. He needed to be constantly evaluating the castle's defenses and making sure that a bodyguard accompanied not only all members of the royal family, but all critical leaders and decision-makers while they were in the castle.

There never seemed to be a shortage of things to discuss with the king, so the conversation ran long, but he got out just in time to catch Fiona on her way somewhere. He grabbed her arm just as she was passing in an intersecting hallway.

"Ambassador Bura," he began softly. "Perhaps you would be willing to spend some time this evening discussing...our plans for dealing with Comperr."

She eyed him suspiciously. "I suppose I would."

"Excellent," he said with a twinkle in his eye. "There is an inn down in the city that has a most excellent means of preparing steak."

She smiled, her suspicions confirmed. "Yes, I can see how extravagant food might help us discuss our plans. They have wine as well, I imagine?"

He smiled back. "It is an inn, after all."

He gave her the name of the inn and directions. She still had some work to do before she could leave, and Timot needed to wrap a few things up as well. He went back to his office, listened as Werbal rattled through his notes, read the report on the last physical readiness test that the Guards under his command had undergone, and made some changes to the squad assignments. He liked keeping Guards together who worked well together, but making changes without warning was a good way to lower the possibility of any kind of conspiracy forming.

Knowing what awaited him this evening made the time pass interminably slow, but eventually it was time for everyone to go home. Timot pulled on his formal coat against the chill and marched out, the sun low enough in the sky that it was beginning to be dim outside. The lamplighters would be out in force in just a short while, possibly even before he arrived at the inn, which was across town.

He had chosen that inn not only for their steak, which really was quite good, but also because it was unlikely that he and Fiona would be spotted by someone they knew from the castle.

As he walked out of the castle complex and into the barracks complex, he had the feeling that he was being followed. This instinct had saved him in the past, and he had learned that it was right far more often than it was wrong, so he paid special attention to what he could hear around him as he took several unnecessary turns.

The normal hustle and bustle of the barracks complex at this time of day made it hard to discern anything, and he certainly did not hear any noises that might give away a potential shadow. He adjusted the sword on his belt and checked the knife on the other side. He had left his shield at his office but was quite capable with just the sword and knife if it came to it.

He made a show of stopping outside an alley, checking his sword again, squaring his shoulders, then stepping into the alley. After going about halfway in, where the shadows were quite deep, he turned and waited. Hopefully he would see a face poke around the corner, then his shadow would know that they'd been spotted and flee. Normally, he would prefer the shadow make an attempt at whatever he was after, but Fiona might already be waiting for him and he wanted the quickest possible resolution to this.

After a moment, as Timot had second thoughts about his choice of alley – it was dark as night already in here – a cloaked figure turned and walked briskly into the alley. If this was his shadow then there was no doubt that the man was here to kill him. Timot drew his sword and knife, annoyed that this would likely put a stop to his plans for the evening. Fiona would understand, of course, but Ezren may only be gone for a few nights, so they did not have many opportunities for this.

The cloaked figure slowed as it got closer, then stopped just far enough that Timot could not reach him with a lunge. The man pulled off the hood of his cloak, revealing Ezmith, his face a stone.

Timot lowered his sword slowly as he processed exactly what was going to happen here.

Ezmith said nothing, merely stared at him. He likely wanted Timot to beg, to seize that as evidence that he was a groveling worm, both deserving of Ezmith's scorn and unworthy of his regret. The truth was, though, that Timot wanted to beg. Not for himself, but for Ezren.

Ezren was growing into an amazing man, but the one thing that worried Timot was that Ezren seemed to rest his entire value, his sense of self-worth, and indeed his sense of self entirely, on Timot. One of Ezren's professors before they had moved to the castle had originally pointed it out to him, and he had observed the depth to which she had been right over the last few years.

Losing Timot now, like this...he was truly afraid for what might become of Ezren, and how he might react.

His eyes welled up with tears as he looked into Ezmith's cold eyes. "Please," he said, his voice cracking slightly. "Don't do this, Ezmith. If there is even a part of you that cares for your younger brother and wants him to find happiness, please do not do this."

Nothing in Ezmith's face gave a hint as to whether that plea fulfilled his hopes of Timot begging, nor whether it had any effect on him. He was silent for long enough that Timot considered speaking more, but no, he had said the only thing of value that he could say in this moment.

Ezmith stared hard at him, and Timot could see him ramping up his anger, likely to bring himself up to the point where he could do what he came here to do.

Timot nodded, understanding, wishing for some other outcome, wishing for his son to make a different choice, but knowing that this was indeed the son he had failed to raise properly. Perhaps this was justice; he'd been on borrowed time for six years, had been blessed with the greatest gift a man could receive during that time – a close and abiding relationship with Ezren – and now he would get his just desserts for his failures with his other three sons.

He sheathed his sword and knife and held his arms out wide, the tears in his eyes giving way to the peace he found in this moment.

Ezmith did not move. He did not even blink. But Timot felt the sharp, shocking, intrusion of what felt like a knife blade in his stomach. Looking down, there was nothing there, but he felt the knife slide out, then back in at a slightly different spot, then again, and again, and he fell to his knees, his blood pouring out onto the ground, forcing his eyes to focus on Ezmith's face as he fell.

As the darkness closed in around him, Timot made one final wish to Clayara: let his sons find happiness and live a better life than he had taught them to live.

CHAPTER 7: A BROKEN SON

Fiona Bura sat at her table at the inn long after Timot should have arrived. The inn had no clock, so she had no way of knowing exactly what time it was or how late Timot was, but it was unlike him to be late at all. Despite all the requirements of his position, he had a remarkable ability to never make arrangements that he could not keep.

There was a very small part of her that worried that his absence might have something to do with her, but she knew that for the absurdity that it was. A much larger part of her felt a growing sense of dread. Though something terrible befalling Timot was much less likely than simply that some issue had needed to be addressed, the sense of dread was far more difficult to stamp out and seemed to grow in spite of her efforts to assuage her own fears.

She turned over a small wooden ring with a steel inner lining in her fingers. With the right wood, the steel on the inside would have been unnecessary, but her father had made the ring for her mother before they got married, and neither of them had access to the best materials. Despite having not seen her father since she was twelve, and remembering why she and her mother had fled, she kept the ring at her mother's behest.

Over the years, it had become a way for her to remember who her father had been before life had stolen his hope.

Had it really been thirty years since her mother had given her that ring? The effect that her mother had no doubt wished it would have on her made much more sense for a teenager.

She pocketed the ring and stood up. Whatever had kept Timot, it had kept him long enough that he would likely not expect to still find her here. She left the inn, resolving to go back to her apartments in the castle and wait for Timot to find her in the morning. Leaving the inn, she walked the nearly empty streets. The darkness was broken only by the street lamps flickering every so often.

She walked with little fear. Though footpads and cutpurses existed in Novis Terram, compared to Comperr a person walking these streets at night was as safe as a babe in swaddling.

She moved up through the city and walked the marketplace plaza where almost all the shops were tied down for the night. A handful of shops were hosting some kind of event, and a ring of torches lit up a small crowd of people dancing to the music of a dittern and a flute.

She walked past, not paying much attention to them, and continued up through the plaza and up the road that would go through the barracks complex to the castle. The walk was uphill, though slight, and as she climbed up she saw another ring of torches.

It wasn't another set of shops. A few more steps brought her close enough to see that these torches weren't on stands – they were being held by Guards. They were standing outside an alley. As she approached, a voice commanded loudly.

"Alert King Radomir and Captain Bagon immediately!"

A guard not holding a torch sprinted away up towards the castle. Fiona's sense of dread rose up and she quickened her step towards the ring of guards. As she approached, a guard who did not recognize her held out his hand.

"Sorry, Ma'am, we're not letting anyone in right now."

She looked past the guard and saw Lieutenant Kindo walk out of the alley carrying a torch.

"Lieutenant!" She called, getting his attention.

The look of pain on Kindo's soft face tied her stomach in knots, but he waved her forward and the Guards parted to let her come through.

"Ambassador..." he began. "I don't know how to tell you this."

No. This wasn't possible. "Show me," she replied hesitantly.

He nodded and turned, leading the way deeper into the alley. The light from his torch brought the body on the ground into sharp relief.

It was Timot.

In an instant she had fallen to her knees and covered her mouth with her hands. Timot did not look dead – his face looked as though it was sleeping, and the warm light from the torch made his skin appear healthy instead of pale as the puddle of blood around him would predict. The blood had long ceased running, but it had flowed to the downslope side of the alley and pooled up against the base of the building there. Probably a house.

The wounds were impossible to miss. What looked like five separate stab wounds peppered his torso.

She knelt there, fighting to keep the tears back, until she felt Lieutenant Kindo's hand on her shoulder, placed there to comfort her. That was too much: she sat back on her heels and shook with her sobs. She put her face in her hands and cried. She usually tried very hard to avoid displays of emotion where anyone could see, especially those with whom she worked, but in the face of this tragedy she simply could not care less.

She didn't know how long she sobbed, but Kindo's hand did not leave her shoulder until she heard the familiar voice of Captain Bagon demand to know what had happened.

"Was it a cutpurse?" he asked roughly, angrily.

"As to that, Captain," Kindo replied. "I don't really know. Captain Kimorae never carried more coin than he could fit in a pocket, so there was no purse to be cut. And I'm not sure how he ended up in this alley, either. Doesn't look like he was dragged here after the fact."

Fiona dried her eyes on the cuffs of her sleeves so she could see around her more clearly. Kindo was right, she decided. Timot had most certainly died here. She looked up at the buildings to either side. The one on the West side was tall enough to block the sun long before it set, and the other building was tall enough to prevent most reflected light from entering the alley either.

"I think this spot would be as dark as it is now even before the sun had finished setting," she said, standing.

Captain Bagon came forward and placed both his hands on her shoulders. "Are you alright, Fiona? I know you two were close."

Was he serious? Was she *alright?!* Of course she was not alright!

"I am devastated, Captain. Broken inside, and if I allow myself to think on it I will be useless. Now, I happen to know that Timot was most likely on his way to meet me, which means he should have been here sometime around sunset, likely a little before."

A little voice inside told her that she had some blame in this – if he hadn't been going to meet her, this never would have happened.

She pushed away the thought instantly, knowing that it was something she'd have to deal with at some point, but not now, and certainly not before knowing exactly what happened to Timot. He had told her what a good portion of his job entailed. Catching wrongdoers posing as rightdoers was a sure way to make violent enemies.

All these thoughts went through her mind in the time it took Bagon and Kindo to nod uncertainly.

Kindo spoke. "So if he entered this alley by choice it was because he wanted the darkness."

Fiona nodded as Bagon squatted down next to Timot's body. To her surprise, he reached out a hand and rested it on the side of Timot's head.

"*Vale paliós filos. Eíthe i fengarólousti vólta sas na eínai sýntomi kai i Clayara in reditu tuo te amplectatur.*" Bagon recited. Translated, it meant, "Fare well, old friend. May your moonlit walk be short and Clayara embrace you upon your return."

She put a hand on Bagon's shoulder as Kindo had done for her, and Bagon placed his hand on top of hers. He kept his face turned away for a moment, then cleared his throat, stood, and turned to look at them. His eyes were rimmed with red.

"Lieutenant, has word been sent to the king?" Bagon asked.

Kindo nodded. "Yes, sir."

"Very good. Go intercept the king and request permission to send one of Dazbog's pigeons back with a message for Mellion to return at once. I want to know who killed one of the greatest men I've ever worked with."

Kindo gave a short bow with his hand to his chest and left the alley at a jog.

Bagon watched as Kindo ran out of the alley, then turned to Fiona, seeming at a loss for words.

"Ambassador, Fiona, I- I'm so sorry," he said, his voice cracking.

Partly from Bagon's uncharacteristic vulnerability, and partly from the removal of distractions as they waited for either the king or Kindo, Fiona felt the tears welling up in her eyes again. She pulled the big man into an embrace and cried into his chest. He rested his head on top of hers and squeezed her tightly. She felt the drops of his tears as they landed in her hair.

～

When the rider came from the direction of Dazbog at a full gallop, Mellion didn't think much of it; it was most likely some urgent matter of state for Perivon to deal with while simultaneously winning a war.

He was quite surprised when the message turned out to be for him, and even more surprised when it was a summons to return to Novis Terram with all speed. Captain Kimorae had been murdered, and they wanted him to employ every magical method possible to ascertain the who and the why. The how was apparent – five stabs to the chest and stomach.

A pang of sadness hit Mellion; he knew the man, after all, but he was too far from Novis Terram to be of much service in the investigation. People left traces, in both physical and magical forms, and he could detect those traces, but they faded with time. Within a day or so of the event, he could have discerned everything from what the murderer was wearing to whether magic had been involved in the attack.

As it was, by the time he got there, even if he rode horses to death with enchantments, everything including the emotional residues would likely have faded. Even now, with the time it had taken for the message to reach him, much of what he could have gleaned was lost.

Not only that, but he had duties here. Now that the Guild wizards were here they could likely still hold, but leaving was not something that he could do without consulting the others.

He brought all the wizards and Lord Perivon together and discussed the best way to proceed. To his surprise, Vewen suggested that they meet with Ezmith under a white flag and offer a trade. Provide a Fold for Mellion to travel to Novis Terram instantly with their promise that he would not return for at least a month. If Ezmith refused, Mellion could be there and back in just over half that time.

Everyone agreed to the plan, and Ezmith agreed to their proposal. Mellion was nervous as he stepped through the Fold, worried that Ezmith might send him to the wrong place, or perhaps even close the Fold while he was stepping through, and who knows what would happen then?

Despite his fears, he could see that the Fold had opened in a corner of the entrance hall of the castle at Novis Terram and he stepped through with no issue. The Fold closed behind him. He strode swiftly to Captain Bagon's office. Two days since the murder. There was no time to waste if he was to get any information at all.

Ezren rode into the city with the fire of a phoenix in his heart. This last trip had been incredible – they had gone all around the entire area surrounding the Novis Spring. They had spent days, passing all sorts of ancient ruins, the youngest of which were a thousand years old. Ben had told them some of the histories of the ruins, though he admitted no one knew the origin of the strange pillars sticking out of the ground all around the shore of the Spring.

Even better, they had found a small group of bandits that Ben had recognized. They were the last three bandits in a large band that had been apprehended by Guards out in Wilhelm nearly a month gone. Those three had been the only ones unaccounted for. With his ready smile, Ben had suggested that they go ahead and try to take them.

Ezren and Raban had been nervous, but ready for some action. Bandits were rarely trained swordsmen, so the two boys with their proper training could subdue them, and Ben would focus on the leader.

The plan had gone off without a hitch, and now the three bandits rode bound on horses tied to their own. Ezren, Raban, and Ben rode in under the gate triumphantly. The boys broke off from Ben just inside the gate, as he needed to take the bandits to the dungeons and Ezren and Raban both wanted to go home.

Ezren couldn't wait to tell his father and Fiona about the trip. He thought going out with Rider would tide him over until he could go to Comperr, but instead it had made him even more anxious to get out there. Fiona's next trip was only a few days away, but Ezren already knew that it would feel like forever.

He rode Asteri to the castle stable, rubbed her down and inspected her just like Ben had taught him. The stable was part of the castle complex, so the walk to the castle proper was short. Early on in his walk, one of the serving men had looked at him, then turned around and ran the other way. He had probably just forgotten something.

As he continued it seemed like people were looking at him more than usual. Often, when he caught someone looking at him, their face was sad or had a pained look. Strange. Had something happened? He almost asked one of them, but instead resolved that after taking his things to their apartments, he'd go visit his father's office and just ask him.

He walked down hallways, climbed stairs, then walked down another hallway to his apartments. Maybe he should wash up before going to find his father as well. Now that he was back home, he was feeling the dust and grime from the miles on the road.

As he opened the door to his apartment, he was surprised to see Fiona sitting in one of the chairs facing the door. She stood up as he entered, and he stopped at the look on her face. Something was not right.

"Hello, Fiona," he said uncertainly. "What's wrong?"

Tears welled up in her eyes and she patted the seat next to her. "Please, Ezren, come sit."

Something constricted the muscles in his legs and he found himself unable to move, standing with the door still open.

"What's happened?" He demanded without moving, unwilling to entertain certain possibilities.

She looked at him for a long moment, a tear occasionally running down her cheek. "Ezren...your father...there was an attack..." her voice cracked. "Your father is dead."

The rest of the muscles in his body followed the lead of his legs and he froze, unable to move. No, that wasn't possible. He refused to believe that this was real. This was some terrible joke.

"Wha- no, he's not, he can't be. Someone would have told me. Why would you joke about that?"

The tears flowed more freely from Fiona's eyes and her body shook slightly.

"I'm so sorry, Ezren. Timot is dead. He was murdered three nights ago in the city..."

His body felt strange; like the heat from the hottest day rose up through his body from his toes to his head, and then the coldest cold he had ever felt followed, never quite reaching his head, but settling on his chest. He realized he was breathing as fast as though he had just run all the way through the city, but his body felt like he was holding his breath.

Fiona wasn't lying. She wasn't joking. She was telling him that his father was dead. He shook his head. No, she was just wrong. His father would be in his office. He turned to run out and down the hall, but he could only make it a few steps before falling to his knees. The world was spinning. He tried desperately to breathe, but it was like his body didn't know what to do with the air. He got shakily back to his feet and tried to run again, but his vision clouded with heat and the next thing he knew he was in the strangest fever dream.

He was falling, falling through hot air as creatures like enormous bats with scaly wings flew all around him, snapping at his limbs that seemed too sluggish to move. He fell for what seemed like an eternity, and then the scene around him of red air and red walls in the distance began to fade into blackness. Once it was completely black, he opened his eyes. He had no idea what he was looking at. It was white. There was crown molding. It must be the top of a wall. Moving his head seemed like the most difficult thing he had ever done, but he turned it to his right and saw Fiona's face, looking down at him with concern.

As the rest of his senses returned, he realized that his head was cradled in her lap. She was sitting on the floor in the hallway outside his apartment. How odd that she would be sitting on the floor. He'd never seen Fiona sit on a floor before. Her flowy pants were splayed all over.

"Ezren! Ezren! Are you alright?" she asked once he turned his head.

"What?" he asked dazedly in reply.

"I don't know, you seemed as though you were panicking, and then you just collapsed."

He looked around some more, then started slowly moving his fingers and toes. Satisfied that he could do so, he started to get shakily to his feet. Fiona's grip on his head tightened for a moment, then released as though she had decided not to stop him.

"Ezren, you need to listen to me. Please come inside so we can talk."

"No," he said, shaking his head to clear the fog. "I'm going to go find my da right now."

Fiona's eyes tightened in sadness, and she put her hand on his cheek kindly. "Your father is dead, Ezren," she said. "And we have much we need to discuss."

"That's ridiculous," he replied. "He's just working, he's always in his office at this time of day." He started off at a slow, lumbering run, but the longer he went the more of his strength that he got back. He still had a nauseous feeling in his stomach, but it didn't get any worse as he ran faster and faster. He'd go get his father and bring him back to show Fiona that she didn't need to cry anymore – his father was fine. His father was always fine.

He ran the whole way to the other side of the complex where his father's offices were and ran in past Werbal's desk, who stood as soon as he saw him.

"Ezren!" Werbal yelled after him, but he did not stop. He could not stop. He threw open the door to his father's office without knocking. Sure enough, sitting behind the desk was...wait...what was Lieutenant Daut doing in here?

Daut leaped up with a hand on his sword hilt as the door flew open, but he loosened his grip when he saw that it was Ezren. Ezren, however, was enraged.

"What are you *doing* here, Daut? How dare you take my father's office?! When he gets back he'll be furious. Get off me, Werbal! What are you doing?!"

He looked back at Werbal, who was tugging on his arm.

"Captain Daut has a lot of work in front of him today, Ezren," Werbal replied in that odd, just-above-a-whisper way he had of talking. "I know this is all coming as a shock, but he has done nothing wrong."

"Where is my father?" Ezren demanded. "And why is *Lieutenant* Daut sitting at his desk?"

Werbal looked around, surprised and anxious. "Ezren...I...did the ambassador not find you? I know I'm not the one you would choose to hear this from...but Lieutenant Daut has been promoted to Captain because...your father...he died three nights ago."

Ezren shook his arm free and shocked himself by shoving Werbal away from him. He was *never* to treat a member of the Guards that way. His father would understand, though, as soon as he found him.

"You're wrong! I'm going to go find him and when I bring him back you'll- you'll- you'll..." Unable to finish the thought, he took off at a run out of the office. If his father wasn't in the office and he wasn't in their apartments, he might be out in the city somewhere, but it was more likely that he was in one of the audience chambers, like the blue room or the Jucundus chamber.

He ran through hallways where anything above a stately pace was frowned upon -- those frowns going double for a teenage boy -- ignoring the perturbed looks from the servants, Guards, and others who walked the halls. Without even thinking to knock, he threw open the door to the Jucundus chamber, but found it empty.

He continued his run to the blue room, his heart pounding in fear that he refused to accept. Once at the blue room, he once again threw open the door, but this time found a small group of men.

Captain Bagon, the wizard Mellion, and King Radomir, all staring at him standing in the doorway. He didn't know any of these men well, but of the three only Captain Bagon had ever spent any time with the Kimoraes outside of his work responsibilities. Ezren looked to Captain Bagon.

"Sorry for the intrusion, Captain, I – I'm looking for my father. He's not in his office and he's not in our rooms. Do you know where he is?"

The three men looked at each other, seeming to not know what to say. The king pensively put a hand over his mouth and Captain Bagon stroked his face as though he expected to find a mustache there. Mellion looked as though he would rather be anywhere but here.

"Ezren...did Ambassador Bura not find you?" The captain replied in a tender voice. "I'm so sorry to be the one to tell you this, but...here, come have a seat, son. Let's talk for a moment."

Ezren felt his knees weaken. "Please, Captain...just tell me."

Bagon sighed, his eyebrows drawing together as he stared into Ezren's eyes. "Your father is dead, Ezren. Mellion is here trying to help us learn why."

Ezren shook his head. "No. No, Captain, I'm sorry but you're wrong. My father *can't* be dead. You're wrong, and-and Fiona is wrong, and Werbal is wrong."

"You've already spoken with Ambassador Bura?" Bagon asked. "And Werbal as well?"

King Radomir stepped towards Ezren, first lifting a staying hand towards Bagon, then placing it on Ezren's shoulder.

"Maybe they are, my boy. Maybe they are. Why don't you walk with me for a little while?"

Ezren had seen the king on many occasions, had spoken with him on a few of those, but had made a point recently of staying out of his sight. Mostly this was because he was afraid how King Radomir might react if he heard that there were feelings between Asteri and him.

Asteri! After the king was done talking with him, Ezren could go find her. She would tell him the truth.

The king didn't say anything as they walked purposefully down the hallway and a short flight of stairs. They were going into a part of the castle that Ezren had never been before, and he had no idea what was down here.

They descended another short flight of stairs to one end of a long hallway, where lamps lined both walls all the way down. The glass of the lamps was painted blue, so the entire hall was illuminated with a bluish light. It was so quiet. He had never known it to be this quiet in the castle; even in his room he could always hear someone shuffling down the hall outside, or something happening on the ground far below his window.

Here it was...silent. Their steps echoed as they walked along the halls. Instead of paintings, pottery, or other types of art, the hall was lined with busts on small podiums. Underneath each bust was a plaque that seemed to list off the accomplishments of the man or woman whose bust sat above it.

"Where are we?" Ezren asked.

"This is the Memoriale Mimeio," King Radomir replied. "This is one of the places where we commemorate the great deeds and accomplishments of those who came before."

Ezren wanted to ask why they were here instead of looking for his father, but being impolite to the king could only end poorly. About halfway down the hall, they came to a door on the left. The king motioned for Ezren to stop, then pulled open the door and gestured for Ezren to enter. Ezren did.

Inside the room was a stone table, just long enough for a tall man to lay flat on it. On the table was…his father. He was wearing a long white robe and appeared to be sleeping. Ezren wanted to dash forward and shake his father awake, but something inside him knew what he'd been denying…his father wasn't sleeping.

He stepped forward slowly, his eyes never leaving his father's peaceful face.

"I thought it best to pull the arrow out quickly for you. Your father *is* dead, son, and the entire castle is in mourning. I asked Mellion to stave off the decay until you were able to see him. Now that you're back we will perform his funereal rites and entomb him here in the Memoriale Mimeio. He earned his place here even before everything he'd done as Captain of the Castle Guard. Your father was a great man."

Ezren reached tentatively out to touch his father's hand. It didn't feel like his father. Maybe it wasn't. But…this was *clearly* his father. He supposed he should feel something, now that the fear and anxiety had disappeared, but he was…empty. Shouldn't he feel sad?

There was a stool next to the stone table, and Ezren sat on it, not letting go of his father's hand.

"How did he die? Fiona said he was murdered."

He heard the king shift behind him. "Yes. He was stabbed. As far as we can tell it was a short, triangle shaped blade much like the kuno used by Meand assassins."

"Is that who did it?"

"We do not think so, but we don't know much. Mellion arrived too late to do much more than read the emotional residue and see the inside of the wound channels. Ezren, one of your father's main responsibilities was to root out treachery or other wrongdoing within the Guards themselves. He was exceptional at it, and made many enemies, some of whom were never caught. Most likely, whoever did the deed used a kuno deliberately to cover their tracks."

Ezren didn't answer. He felt...numb was the best word he could think of.

The silence stretched. After a time, he felt the king's hand on his shoulder, giving him a squeeze, then heard his footsteps as he left the room, closing the door behind him. The king likely had far more important things to do than sit with an orphaned waif.

What would his life be like now? Would he even be allowed to continue living in the castle? Wouldn't their apartments eventually be needed for Lieu- Captain Daut? Did Captain Daut have a family? Would Ezren be allowed to continue attending the Royal Academy? Maybe Raban and Sergeant Kennard would take him in. Maybe Fiona would. He didn't want to live with Fiona; her mother hated men. He didn't want to live with the Kennards, either; he'd have to go back to the barracks academy, or else just go start an apprenticeship somewhere. He had no skills or training in any trades, unless you counted the sword, or letters.

He could go back to their land in Berengaria, but he did not know how to build a cabin, or how to farm, really. He had done it for two summers years ago, but under the direction of his father, who in turn was learning from an herbalist in town whose name Ezren did not know.

The last time they'd spoken had been just a normal morning before Ezren left on his scouting trip. He should never have gone. If he'd been here...he could have done something...no, that was silly. What could *he* have possibly done? He was a child...a child who'd done nothing of value for anyone, including his father, for years.

But why wasn't he crying? Why wasn't he angry? He sat there, slouched on the stool, holding his father's lifeless hand, wondering numbly why he was wondering numbly. He did not feel the need to stay, but he could not bring himself to move.

He sat.

He did not know how long he sat; they were down beneath the level of the ground by at least a story so there was no window to help him, and the oil lamps lighting the room all had wider-than-normal containers of oil, so he wasn't able to tell by how much they'd burned either.

Had it been midday when the king brought him down? That seemed right. They had ridden in to town midmorning, so that was probably close. His best guess was that he'd been here for at least a few hours.

He still didn't care to stay, but saw no reason to leave. Occasionally he would feel a tear slide down his cheek, but it almost seemed as though it were someone else's cheek. That was an odd thing to think; he wouldn't be able to feel a tear slide down someone else's cheek.

He sat.

He had held his father's hand long enough that he no longer felt it. Strange how that worked; how your body adapted to something after it was exposed to it for a long time. Maybe people who lived by the ocean stopped noticing the sounds of the waves. Maybe people in Comperr stopped noticing how wonderful their art house was.

At some point he felt his head start to droop. He jerked his head up. His head drooped again, but he jerked it back up. He should probably go.

He sat.

His eyes closed slowly and he imagined that he heard the door opening, as he imagined the floor rushing up to meet him. It was a startling dream, but he did not startle. In his dream, someone caught him before the floor got to him and cursed in a woman's voice. The woman in his dream sounded like Fiona. That wasn't a surprise.

The woman called out and he felt himself being carried, the sounds of people huffing up the stairs all around him. This was a silly dream – if people had really been carrying him like this, he would have woken up.

The dream ended when he felt himself dropped unceremoniously onto something soft, probably a bed. His awareness of any more dreams snuffed out.

Ezren woke as sun began to shine through his window onto his face. He brought a hand up to shield his eyes and opened them, sitting up. His window did not face east. It faced South. They were far enough

North that the sun did rise in the southern part of the sky, even more so in Winter, but he could not recall ever having slept in late enough for the sun to already be shining onto his bed.

He looked around, confirming that he was indeed in his own room, and wondering how he had gotten here. He remembered the details of his last dream...perhaps it hadn't been a dream after all. He stared at the ceiling for a long time, seeing his father, lying on that stone table dressed in white. He wished the vision would go away.

He got up, stretching his neck, then washed his face in the wash-basin next to his mirror. He scrubbed his teeth, ran a comb through his hair, and got dressed, letting himself get lost in the routine to avoid letting his thoughts wander.

He stepped out of his room, wondering if the kitchens had brought up breakfast as usual, but stopped when he saw Fiona. She was fast asleep, slouched back in one of the front room chairs, still fully dressed. He watched her for a moment, trying to sort out his feelings. He was grateful that she was there...wasn't he? She must have spent the night outside his room. He blinked back a sudden dampness in his eyes.

His emptiness from the previous night lingered, but deep down he felt a simmering anger.

Trying not to wake Fiona, he walked over to their kitchen. The mornings were still chill in Spring here, but not so bad that it was worth lighting their stove, and he had no need to cook because the kitchens had indeed brought up food. How they had entered, brought food into the kitchen, and left, all without waking Fiona, was beyond him.

He went to the table and pulled the cloth off of the tray, revealing two helpings of bacon, bread, cheese, and eggs, along with a pitcher of milk. They must not have been told it was just him now. Or they could have just brought some up for Fiona. Or maybe they just thought he'd be really hungry. In the center of the tray was a folded piece of paper. He picked it up and unfolded it. It was a note.

Ezren – we are all so sorry to hear about your father's passing. He was a great man. Please tell us if there's anything we can do for you during this difficult time.

- All of us here in the kitchens

He felt his eyes water, but his jaw clenched. His father hadn't *passed*; someone had killed him. Someone had *murdered* his father, and nobody knew who.

He felt the anger rising inside him. After the numbness, he welcomed the anger – fanned the flame to the best of his ability. Someone had taken his father away from him. Someone had purposefully killed him, and with him went *everything* Ezren knew about his own life. The note crumpled in his hand. His arm shook with the tension of squeezing it as hard as he could.

"Ezren?" Fiona's voice said from behind just before he felt her hand on his shoulder.

He jerked away from her hand and stepped away. He hadn't meant to; it had been reflexive, but his anger continued to grow so much he felt his face getting hot. Feeling angry was better than feeling helpless, which is how he'd felt yesterday. His father had always helped him understand what the right choice was. With him gone, how would Ezren know what to do?

"Who?" Ezren asked, forcing the word from his mouth.

Fiona sighed and her shoulders sunk lower. "We don't know, Ezren, and we probably will not ever know."

"Someone killed my father, got away, and everyone is just willing to accept that?"

She held out her hands. "I know it's hard to understand, Ezren, but no one saw it happen, and all Mellion could do when he got here was read the emotional residues. We know that at the time of his death, your father was feeling deep sadness and love, but no hatred or anger."

Magic allowed Mellion to read what emotions a person had been feeling? How did that work?

"What about the killer?"

She shook her head. "Mellion detected no emotional residues from the killer, which is why we are so unsure of who may have done it. Your father's emotions suggest that he knew his killer, perhaps even cared for them, but having no emotion from the killer suggests that it was an assassin-for-hire with no personal connection."

"Mellion can detect emotion but nothing else? He can't...read the... the...physical residues or something?"

"You'd have to talk to him about that, Ezren," she replied, her hands coming back down to her sides. "I don't really know what's possible and what's not with magic. Often it seems that things that should be simple aren't possible at all and others that stretch credulity are easy even for young wizards."

"How are we going to bring the murderer to justice if we can't catch him? Do you even have any suspicions?"

"Ezren, that's not something you need to worry about right now. You must be scared...worried about what's going to happen to you. Let's sit down, eat some breakfast, and talk about it."

She gestured to the table, but Ezren didn't move.

"Who do you suspect might have done it?" He asked.

She sighed and smiled a sad smile. "I should know better than to try and distract you. We have a few parties we're looking into. There was a Guard whose brother talked him into trying to steal some of the tax dollars a few months back, and that Guard escaped the labor farm about a tenday before your father was killed."

Ezren waited for her to continue, but she did not.

"You said a few," he said, hoping that would prompt a response.

She seemed reluctant to speak for some reason. "We believe that it's also possible that it was Comperr. Either trying to weaken us or send a message to stop what we're doing on the Northern Highway. Your father's name is well-known in Comperr for his exploits during the Border War."

She put out her hands placatingly again. "Please, Ezren, I know your first instinct is going to be running full speed until you find the person responsible for your father's death, but there's a lot more going on here and I'm going to need you to trust me and focus on taking care of yourself."

A lot more going on? So. That's what was behind all of her reluctance, all this dancing around the subject – they had more *important* things to worry about. King Radomir, Captain Bagon, even Fiona were willing to send justice to the Inferno because they wanted to focus on *larger problems*.

Not Ezren. His father had given up *everything* to bring him out of Ambarta alive, had lived a life of near-starvation and destitution for years and eventually subjugated himself in joining the guards – all to give Ezren a good life and a good education. His father had not and would not have ever let other concerns become more important than Ezren, and Ezren could not and would not leave justice for his father's murder for the wolves.

He found himself shaking his head. "No. No, we need to find out who did this for certain. I will not allow my father's death to go unavenged."

He strode purposefully towards the door. Fiona reached for his arm. "Ezren, wait, stay and have breakfast. We can keep talking about it."

Shaking her off, he continued his stride towards the door and threw it open.

"Ezren, wait!"

But Ezren did not wait. He strode as quickly as he could without running, straight out, across the courtyard, and down a side street within the castle complex to the library where the wizards kept their offices.

He entered the library through the front door and turned to climb the staircase to the second floor.

Neither of the wizards had actual offices, just desks in their own areas that no one else went without permission or summons. Because they were rarely bothered, they also did not employ secretaries, so there was no one to stop Ezren from marching up the flight of stairs and straight to Mellion's desk where the wizard sat studying an old parchment, a pair of spectacles perched on the end of his nose.

Ezren had never interacted with Mellion before, and knew nothing about him, but his logic was simple – there had to be some kind of magic that would allow them to know what had happened that night, and Mellion was the most likely to know what that was.

Mellion looked up as Ezren approached, sitting back and taking off his spectacles, a look of consternation on his face.

"Ah, Ezren." He looked around, avoiding Ezren's eyes, but that may have just been his manner. "What brings you here?"

"I want to know what kind of magic could be used to find out what happened to my father."

Mellion's eyes flicked up to Ezren's for a moment, then back to his desk as he began shuffling papers, seeming to be merely picking up piles in one spot and putting them in another.

"Surely Ambassador Bura has spoken to you by now...? She was supposed to..." he trailed off, looking anxiously at Ezren again before going back to needlessly arranging his stacks. He moved a stack back to where it had been originally.

Ezren felt his face tighten in anger. "She was supposed to *what?*" his words were ice, but he was all fire inside. So they had been talking amongst themselves about how to *handle* him? His father gone, and their first act was to try and *manipulate* him?

"Ah...she was supposed to explain everything to you. Did she tell you about the emotional residues?"

Ezren nodded, his jaw clenched, eyes focused.

"Then you already have your answer. There's nothing more I can do."

"You're a wizard, aren't you? Or is that just something you pretend to be?"

That got his attention. He looked Ezren dead in his eyes now, sat back and folded his arms.

"You've just been through a tragedy, boy, so I will let that pass, but you'd do well to remember that being in mourning does not grant you a license to do and say whatever you wish. I've been studying magic since around the time your father was born, and I know of no spell that

I can use to learn what happened that night beyond what I have already done. Now, please, I'm very busy here."

As though to demonstrate how busy he was, he leaned forward and began shuffling stacks of paper again, once again putting stacks back where they had started.

This man was not going to help him, that much was clear, so Ezren turned on his heel and strode out. He walked purposefully, thinking wildly for a purpose to walk for. If magic wasn't an option – rather, if Mellion was unwilling or unable to use magic to find out what happened – then Ezren would just have to hit the streets.

He stopped in the middle of the tunnel that led back into the rest of the castle complex. He could ask all around to the people in the area where his father was killed. With how flippant everyone seemed to be being about it, maybe no one had done that yet. But he didn't know where his father had been killed.

He couldn't just march into the King's chambers or Captain Bagon's office and demand answers, and he would absolutely *not* ask Fiona for anything, so he strode off purposefully once again, towards his father's old office, where Lieutenant Kindo should still be working, along with 'Captain' Daut.

The complex was far from deserted, and he strode past the Guards, workers, and other people who worked or lived at the castle. More than one hailed him, but Ezren ignored them, not interested in hearing how sorry they were, like it was somehow their fault, or that their being sorry would somehow make him feel better. He almost wished one of them would react to his rudeness so he'd have an excuse to get in a fight.

As he walked, he clenched and unclenched his fists – a habit he'd picked up over the years when he was angry or scared.

The door to the Offices of the Captain of the Castle Guard was open, and Ezren marched in and right past Werbal. Werbal was nice enough, but the only man his father had worked with that Ezren felt close enough to trust even a little was Lieutenant Kindo. He might have trusted Daut if the man had not just usurped his father's position.

Kindo's door was open, as it usually was -- the men in these offices most often communicated by shouting over at one another – and Ezren walked in as Kindo looked up.

"Ezren," he said in surprise. "I didn't expect to see you."

"Why?" Ezren asked combatively. "Because Fiona was supposed to *handle* me?"

Kindo looked taken aback. "No, I thought you'd be trying to comfort the Ambassador. She and your father were...close."

Ezren shifted his feet uncomfortably. He hadn't even considered how Fiona might be taking all this. But...if she was really that broken up over it then she wouldn't have been making plans with the others on how to deal with him.

"I want you to tell me everything you know about what happened," Ezren said, looking Kindo dead in the eye.

Kindo sighed, leaned back in his chair and smiled sadly, a small... knowing smile.

"Why?"

It was Ezren's turn to look taken aback. "What?"

"Why do you want to know?"

"Isn't that obvious?"

"Well, yes, but not in the way you're thinking," Kindo said.

Ezren narrowed his eyes, trying to understand Kindo's point. It was very difficult to think about anything other than his anger.

"You want to find the person who did this...and kill them," Kindo clarified.

What was Kindo blabbering about? Ezren wanted *justice*. Sure, he imagined that justice coming as he rammed his sword through the chest of the despicable coward who killed his father, but he would be just as satisfied if someone else found him and took him to the dungeons...wouldn't he?

"I just want to make sure that whoever killed my father is brought to justice!" He replied defensively.

Kindo leaned forward and put his elbows on the table, rubbing his face with his hands.

"Right. As long as that justice comes at the end of your sword, correct?" He replied.

The near-echo of his own thoughts repeated back to him was distinctly uncomfortable. For a brief moment he considered his own motivations and whether Kindo might have a point, but after a moment he realized...

"Well, if anyone else actually seemed to care then maybe it wouldn't have to."

Kindo looked at Ezren, hands still on his face, with an eyebrow raised.

"Ezren, you're a smart kid. What in all Quilara has given you the ridiculous notion that no one else cares about what happened to Captain Kimorae?"

"Well, look at you!" Ezren responded, his voice raising. "You're just sitting there working like nothing happened! Fiona is trying to manipulate me into doing what she thinks is best, Mellion is at the library refusing to lift a finger to find the killer, and Daut has already moved into my father's office with no respect at all!"

Kindo sighed, staring at Ezren for a moment. To Ezren, Kindo's eyes had a faraway look as though he were remembering something. Kindo rested his hands on the table. When he spoke, he spoke quietly, thoughtfully.

"I suppose you're also angry at everyone in the city for going about *their* lives. Perhaps you're even angry at the sun for rising this morning just as it always has. When it comes night you'll curse the stars for shining, the wind for blowing, and the mountains for standing, unchanged from yesterday."

Kindo fiddled with a ring on the little finger of his left hand, looking down at it instead of at Ezren.

"I can't tell you how you're supposed to feel right now, Ezren. Anger and vengeance are the frequent companions of loss, and I don't know if you could avoid them even if you wanted to." His eyes looked back at Ezren, staring hard. "But I can tell you that the worst thing you can do right now is funnel that anger towards the people who are mourning with you. Don't push away everyone who can help you recover from this loss."

Something inside Ezren wanted to break, wanted to give way to these words, but he knew that if he let it then he would break down in tears right here in Kindo's office. *No!* Tears would not bring justice to his father. He *had* to find who had done this and avenge his father's death. Nothing else mattered.

This gave him purpose. This gave him strength. He didn't have to worry what was to become of him because he had a job of work to do. He would do whatever it took to find his father's killer and mete out justice. He refocused on Kindo. This conversation had gone far afield from where he had wanted it to go.

"Can you tell me where it happened?" Ezren asked.

"What?" Kindo asked, surprised.

"Can you tell me, or maybe show me on a map, where in the city my father was killed?"

Kindo opened his mouth to say something, then closed it and turned to the wall behind him which was full of small cubbies holding rolled up pieces of paper. He pulled one out and laid it out on the desk on top of all the papers that were already there. It was a detailed map of Novis Terram. Kindo pointed at a spot down a ways from the barracks complex, where a small alley went between an inn and a large shop with apartments above.

Ezren stood without a word to go, but Kindo stopped him, rolling up the map as he spoke.

"What are going to do next?"

"I'm going to go ask everyone in the area what they saw that night," he said, biting off what he'd been about to say about all the people who should have already done that.

Kindo shook his head. "Nobody saw anything. At least not anything useful. A few people remembered seeing the Captain, but only two people saw him go into the alley, and all they saw was a cloaked figure follow him in. No one saw the figure's face, and no one saw him come out."

So they *had* asked. That was something, Ezren supposed. Any goodwill that might have earned them had been lost by the fact that no one had told him anything until right now. The wind came out of his sails a bit, but he couldn't think of anything else to do and he refused to do nothing, so he turned and left without another word and began the walk out to the alley Kindo had indicated.

If he wanted to get answers out of these strangers, though, he had to be polite. He sighed as he walked. He could hold in his anger. For his father, and to find his father's killer, he could hold in his anger.

~

Fiona watched Ezren storm out of the apartment with one hand on her forehead, wondering how she was supposed to help a boy that refused to be helped. She had gotten to him just in time the night before – catching him right as he collapsed off the damn stool he'd been sitting on. She still couldn't *believe* that Radomir hadn't told her he'd taken Ezren down there. She'd been searching for him the entire day!

Well, what was done was done. She supposed it was normal for someone in Ezren's position to be angry, though she had little experience in the area. Getting away from her father had been a relief, and her mother was still alive, though getting on in years.

Her heart was broken for Ezren, though. His bond with Timot had been so unbelievably strong. They had been through the Inferno together and came out all the stronger because they had had each other. Ezren had to be scared, worried, and *devastated*.

She felt tears well up in her eyes and she shook herself, adjusting her divided skirts and her blouse; they'd gotten twisted from sleeping in the chair.

Paying attention to that seemed almost like breaking a dam – she suddenly noticed the pain her neck and lower back, probably also from sleeping in the chair, how foggy her mind was -- likely from sleeping in the chair -- and how unrested she felt, most likely from…sleeping in the chair.

She knew Ezren well enough to know that haring after him right now would be the wrong course of action. He was a smart, thoughtful young man and he would come back. She had several important meetings today and had to draft her recommendations for dealing with Comperr from a diplomatic standpoint to Bagon and Radomir by the end of the day.

Her stomach rumbled and she forced herself to turn to the food that the kitchens had brought up. She had no real desire to eat, despite the hunger, but knew that she had to have her strength today, of all days. The last few days between Timot's death and Ezren's return had been a privilege; she had had her own opportunity to mourn her loss, had already spent her hours down in the Memoriale Mimeio weeping next to his body.

Now it was time to help Ezren work through his grief, and she was ready. Well, as ready as she would probably ever be.

She ate quickly, jotting down some thoughts for her first meeting, and Ezren still had not returned when she had finished. She should just wait, shouldn't she? It had only been a quarter of an hour. Ezren would certainly need more time. She had a leather satchel with paper and graphis. She could use Timot's washbasin and mirror to freshen up.

Instead, she got up from the table and left the room at a brisk walk.

Her feet took her to Lieutenant Kindo's office. She considered approaching Captain Daut, but Ezren had a more friendly relationship with Kindo, so he was more likely to have seen him.

The Offices of the Castle Guard looked the same as they always had, and yet it felt so different. She knew it was just her imagination, but something about it just seemed...empty without Timot. She strode through the open door into Kindo's office, who, oddly, threw up his hands in exasperation as she entered.

"I'm going to start closing my door. I don't care how much oil I go through keeping enough lamps to see properly."

"Stop blabbering, Kindo," she said lovingly. "Have you seen Ezren?"

"He just left," he said, indicating the door with a nod of his head.

For some reason, panic gripped her. "Where did he go?"

Something must have shown on her face, because Kindo's became one of concern. "It's alright, Ambassador, he just went to ask questions around where the Captain was killed."

He just *went to go ask questions about his father's murder?!* Why had Kindo let him go? Hadn't Kindo told him that they had already asked questions of everyone in the area and that no one could say anything for certain?

She paced back and forth along the length of Kindo's desk. She had her hand on her forehead again. This had been a nervous tick for her entire life, though she did not know why; she just expected her head to hurt when something stressful was happening.

Was it best to just let Ezren ask his questions? He wasn't likely to get close to what they suspected was the truth, and perhaps it would be good for him to go through the steps on his own, even though others had already gone through them.

She tried to imagine what it would be like to lose her mother at a young age. Her immediate reaction was summed up in a single word: fear. She would be terrified that she would be forced to go back to her father or that she would lose everything she and her mother had built up.

Ezren had to know that sending him to his surviving parent was not even an option, didn't he? Exactly *what* to do with him was the subject of one of her meetings today, but everyone agreed that he should be allowed to continue attending the Royal Academy and be given a place to stay.

The sound of Kindo clearing his throat brought her attention back to him.

"Is there something else you needed, Ambassador? Or did you just want to continue using my office to pace?"

"Did Ezren say anything about what he was after?" She asked.

Kindo shrugged. "Nothing beyond the obvious. He wants revenge. He wants to kill the person who killed his father."

Right...revenge. Obvious. But wait, Ezren wasn't vengeful! She had heard other boys from the Academy make fun of him when he had first come to the castle, but he had never wished harm on any of them. He *did* have a strong righteous streak in him, though, and had often taken it upon himself to right some wrong that he had seen.

There was certainly a difference between being bullied and losing one's father, but people didn't just change who they were overnight, did they? She wracked her brain, trying to think of other times she had seen someone go through something similar to what Ezren was going through now, but no, while there had, of course, been death and misfortune in the village where she and her mother lived, nothing approaching the circumstances of this had happened to give her any guidance.

Kindo cleared his throat again.

She looked at him, unwilling to admit that she had once again forgotten she was in his office. This time he didn't say anything, he just raised his eyebrows and looked at her.

"Yes, lieutenant, thank you. I will leave you to your work now."

He nodded briskly. "My thanks, Ambassador. I wish you luck with Ezren and with your meetings today."

She left the office, looking at the rough clock on the wall in the foyer above Werbal's desk. She had just enough time to rush up to the Chordus chamber for her first meeting with Bagon and Radomir.

It was going to be a long day.

She hurried down the hall, then outside along the wall walk, through the door in the turret, and up the circular stairs that would take her to the level the Chordus chamber was on.

She entered through the double doors of the Chordus chamber and was surprised to find that she was the first one here, other than a maidservant dusting off an artifact on a plinth.

The clock in the Offices of the Castle Guard must be ahead. She took the time to gather her thoughts. This meeting was for her to ask whatever questions she needed answers to before drafting her recommendations for dealing with Comperr, but her mind was far away from that.

Bagon and Radomir entered together, chatting amiably as the doors swung shut behind them.

Their faces turned serious as they saw her, however.

"Did something go wrong with Ezren?" Bagon asked.

Now how had he known *that?*

"Yes...and no," she said. "He's angry. I'm not sure he even knows exactly who or what he's angry at, and I'm not sure he cares to figure it out. According to Lieutenant Kindo, he is currently out on the streets asking the same questions our investigators asked after it happened."

"Did Kindo tell him anything?" Radomir asked.

"I don't believe so. He knows that we've got to keep our suspicions under lock and key for the time being," she replied.

They all three turned to look at the maid, who was already on her way out the door, having finished her dusting. After she left, the conversation resumed.

"Do we have any more details to say whether it really was Ezmith?" Radomir queried, looking from Fiona to Bagon.

Bagon shook his head, his eyes downcast. "No, sire. There seems to be no more evidence to be had. Mellion did some spell to see if there were traces of steel in the wounds, but he found nothing."

"Doesn't that make it more likely that it was Ezmith using some kind of magic to kill him?"

Shaking his head again, Bagon replied, "Mellion wasn't sure his spell would detect the tiny amounts that would have been left by even a reasonably sharp blade. He wanted to try anyway, but I'm afraid we can draw no conclusions from the results of the spell."

"A shame," the king replied. "Instruct Mellion to keep trying to think of any other ways to confirm whether it was Ezmith. If it was him, then it was an act of war, and we need to respond accordingly." He turned to Fiona. "Now, what questions do you have, Ambassador?"

The man could certainly change directions quickly. She thought back to all the thoughts she had jotted down – the ones she'd left in Timot's apartment.

"We've received only two pigeons from the battalions that were sent to secure the highway, correct?" She asked.

"That's correct," Bagon replied.

"And both reported the same thing, that they have seen neither hoof nor hair of Comperr soldiers?"

"Yes," Bagon confirmed.

"But they *have* both reported skirmishes with raiding bands of brigands, which I would wager my horse are simply Comperr soldiers in disguise."

"And how are you so confident of that?" Radomir asked.

"The same way we knew it was soldiers in disguise before we sent troops – Raanan would never let anything threaten the tariffs he gets by letting merchants pass through his land unless he had a specific goal to accomplish. Also, I've spoken to every merchant caravan that has come from Admone or Meand and they have not heard of any of their caravans being raided. Raanan is clearly trying to wage a war while appearing not to do so."

"That seems a fair assessment," King Radomir responded with a nod of approval. "What other questions do you have?"

The rest of the meeting passed quickly, with all of her questions being answered by the two men with the characteristic brevity of a soldier and a ruler. During the meeting, she almost managed to forget about Timot and her concerns about what to do with Ezren, but the moment she stepped out of the Chordus chamber and began walking, the issue came flooding back, and she still had no idea how to help Ezren in this moment.

~

The sun was beginning to set, and Ezren was *tired*. He'd been on his feet all day, which wasn't unusual, but he'd also been talking to person after person the entire time, and that wasn't something he was as accustomed to. Most people had little to say, if they even bothered responding at all. He was just a teenage boy after all, and the few times they had seen a teenage boy hailing people in the street, it had been to hawk wares.

Through the course of the day he had been able to track down a few individuals, one man and two women, who remembered seeing his father, but they could offer no more information than Kindo had provided: they'd seen him enter the alley, which he did of his own volition, and was followed by a shadowy character in a black, hooded cloak. None of them had seen the cloaked man exit, or could even confirm whether it was indeed a man.

All this work, all this asking, all these questions, and the only thing he could confirm was that his father's killer was a being that walked on two legs and was of an unremarkable height. He couldn't even confirm that it was a human!

The fire that had stayed with him most of the day was dying out, and what was left was a bone-deep sadness. He trudged up the slight incline throughout the barracks complex and into the castle complex. He should get some food and sleep as long as he still had a home to rest in.

The hangings and paintings on the walls of the hall moved past him in a haze as he walked. He turned to go up the stairs that would take him to his apartments, but a voice called his name. He stepped back down to the floor and looked down to see Princess Asteri running to him, followed by her two massive, hulking guards.

Another time, the sight of those two enormous men in full armor clearly disgruntled at having to jog to keep up with the diminutive princess might have brought a smile or a chuckle to Ezren's lips, but this time he barely noticed them.

The moment Asteri reached him she threw her arms around him and squeezed him tight. He was surprised at how comforting it was to be in her embrace.

"I'm so sorry, Ezren! How are you doing?"

Oh. So she was sorry. Like everyone else.

"I'm, uh, just, really tired. I was just going to eat and get some sleep," he replied, wanting to get away from this conversation.

"I'm sure you are. Everyone is so sad at your father's passing. We all loved him," Asteri said, pulling away but keeping her hands on his shoulders.

Passing? There was that word again. He found himself grabbing her hands and taking them off of his shoulders. "No, Asteri. My father didn't *pass*. My father was *murdered*. He was stabbed. Five times. With a knife."

"I-I know that," Asteri said, her eyebrows drawn up in confusion. "It's just- I don't know, I – I just want to try and help you feel better."

He wanted to believe her. He wanted desperately to believe that she cared for him in some kind of altruistic way where her help would not be contingent on some kind of benefit for her.

"Then help me find my father's killer," he said, staring directly into her eyes.

"What? What do you mean?" She asked.

"I've been out all day asking questions around where he was killed, but no one seems to know much of anything. I need to find some way to figure out who it was that killed him. Will you help me?"

"Oh, Ezren..." she reached out with her hands again and began rubbing the tops of his arms. "You need to *mourn*. You need to *grieve*. Why don't we go up to your apartment and we can talk about whatever you want?"

Ah, so she didn't *really* want to help him feel better. His anger spiked again.

"I don't need to mourn, I need justice. You just asked how you can help me feel better. Well, finding who killed my father will make me feel better."

Something in his voice must have betrayed his anger, because she had brought her chin in and seemed suddenly on the defensive.

"What good would that do? It's not like it will bring your father back to life."

His anger exploded. How *dare* she?

"Of course it won't!" he yelled, not even noticing her two guards coming a step closer as Asteri took a step back. "Nothing will! My father is gone! Forever! But I will damn myself to the Inferno before I let his *murder* go unanswered! I don't care how 'sorry' you are! I don't care how 'sad' you are! If you're not going to help me then leave me alone!"

He turned and stormed up the stairs, not even bothering to look back to see how she had reacted. His blood boiled, and after reaching the top of the stairs he considered turning around and yelling a few more things that had come to mind, but his yelling had already drawn more attention than he wanted. He didn't want attention, he didn't want to talk to anyone, he just wanted to be in his apartment by himself and get some rest.

He opened the door to their rooms and found Fiona, sitting at the table with a stack of papers in front of her, her hand on her forehead. She leaped up from her chair after seeing him enter.

"Ezren, I'm so glad you're back."

With great force of effort, he sublimated his rage. His voice was quiet, almost pleading. "Please, Fiona, please just leave."

A look of pain came across her face.

"I asked the kitchen to send up your favorite, bacon with shrimp from Bahadir," she forced a smile. "I still don't understand how you can enjoy the combination, but to each their own, I suppose."

Did she really expect him to laugh? Right now? At that? After ignoring his humble plea? He didn't want to plea, he wanted to demand. He wanted to shout and rage at her, he wanted to get her out of his rooms using as much force as was required.

"I asked you to leave. I…I need to be alone right now," he said, rage boiling so hard inside he worried it would come out his eyeballs.

Fiona sighed, putting her hand back to her forehead. "Ezren, we need to talk about what's going to happen to you now. You're still young enough that you shouldn't be on your own, and we all want you to be able to finish at the Royal Academy. The king considered taking you in, but…" she attempted another smile, "…he wasn't sure he wanted you sleeping in such close proximity with his daughter."

He stared at her. Despite wanting her gone with every fiber of his being, he also very much wanted to know what she was about to say next. It was not a shock that the king had declined to take him in, it was more shocking that he had considered it at all. Ezren supposed he should be touched by that. He was not.

"You have a choice, Ezren. We've reached out to Sergeant Kennard and he'd be happy to take you in. You would then come up to the castle each day for school. I am also happy to take responsibility for you. You'd move into the dormitories with the other children who live too far to come each day and I would become your guardian, at least until you come of age."

She looked at him, waiting for a response, but a response was not something he was prepared to give at this moment. He wanted to scream at her but could think of nothing to shout. He wanted to hit something, destroy something, but the things around him were among the last connections he still had with his father. He couldn't *do* anything!

He *hated* feeling impotent. He needed to be able to do something. He settled for getting Fiona out.

"Get out, Fiona," he said, pointing to the door. Part of him knew she didn't deserve this treatment, but he hadn't deserved to lose his father, either. At least, he didn't think he had.

"Ezren-," she began.

"GET OUT!" he yelled even louder than he had at Asteri, his rage pushing tears out of his eyes, pouring all of itself into those two words. He pointed to the door as he shouted, his arm muscles so tense he couldn't bend his elbow.

Fiona's eyes welled up with tears, and Ezren felt tears running down his own cheeks. She gathered her cardigan, put her papers in her satchel, and walked past Ezren and out the door, closing it quietly behind her.

Alone. He wanted to go collapse on his bed. He was hungry, but he still didn't want to eat. Eating seemed like a tacit endorsement of this pathetic attempt to placate him. He lost the internal battle, however, because the truth of the matter was that he had little chance of ever finding his father's killer if he didn't keep his strength up, and for that he needed food.

Eating also gave him an opportunity to consider what his next moves would be. Asteri wouldn't help him, Fiona wouldn't help him. Kindo and Mellion either couldn't or wouldn't. Raban, though...Raban would definitely help him. He would go find Raban in the morning. He looked up at the hand-drawn calendar on the wall. Raban should be in school tomorrow, but he could catch him on the way and get him to sluff it off.

By the time he finished his meal he was too tired to wash up, so he dragged himself to his bed, kicked off his boots, and threw himself onto it.

He tossed and turned most of the night, waking each time he found himself dreaming and taking a while to fall back to sleep. He must have slept some, however, because sunrise came much sooner than it would have if he'd been awake all night.

Getting up, he certainly did not feel as though he had slept. His fatigue did not make a great deal of sense to him – walking and talking should hardly have this effect on him. Could it be that feeling angry made you more tired? Perhaps the same strength required for walking and moving your body was required for your emotions. An interesting idea that he would have to think on more later.

For now, he had a clear goal. He had to get out quickly to make sure he was in the barracks complex early enough to catch Raban on his way to school.

He put on his boots, staying in the same clothes he had worn the day before, and didn't bother with washing his face or brushing his teeth. He was out the door only minutes after waking up. Of all the inhabitants of the castle, only the servants were out this early, and most of them avoided looking at him. Apparently word of his outbursts had spread. Ezren wished he could find regret for that, but he was more relieved that no one was attempting to make themselves feel better by feigning attempts to console him.

His feet took him out to the barracks complex where he stopped, pacing back and forth on the road, dodging people walking and the occasional wagon or cart, waiting for Raban. But Raban never came. Ezren started to walk slowly towards Raban's apartment, still expecting to see him coming up the street, and probably running since he'd be late at this point. He walked all the way to the barracks where the Kennard's had their apartment and still no Raban.

Just as he was considering going in, Sergeant Kennard and Raban came out carrying saddlebags and backpacks that looked full. They saw him immediately and put down their bags, The Sergeant coming over and pulling him into a tight hug.

The hug felt nice, but he didn't need or deserve comfort right then. Raban didn't hug him, but put his hand on his shoulder and asked the one question that everyone *should* have been asking:

"Have they found the man yet?"

Ezren shook his head. Finally, someone who knew that it was pointless to ask how he was doing and wanted to focus on what mattered.

"I need to talk to you, though. I need your help."

Raban looked at The Sergeant, who nodded and stepped away to pick up his things, giving them a little bit of privacy.

"What do you need, Ezren? How can I help?" Raban asked.

Good man. "No one seems to even be trying to find the man who killed my father, so I'm going it alone, but I'm out of ideas and I need your help to come up with something we can do to figure it out," Ezren replied.

Raban's face was troubled. He looked back to his father. "Hold on a moment," he said to Ezren, then walked away. Ezren gave them the same courtesy The Sergeant had given them and turned to try and pay attention to something else while they talked. They were far enough away that there were other sounds he could focus on, but he still heard snatches in angry voices.

"...last time..."

"...we have to leave today..."

"...care so little...?"

He glanced over as the conversation died down and Raban came trudging over. His posture told Ezren everything he needed to know about how things had ended.

"I'm sorry, Ezren. We're leaving for Inara today. My grandmother, she's ill, and she's getting pretty old, and we think she might die so we're going to see her one last time."

"Oh," Ezren replied. He wanted to feel sympathy for Raban, but having never met his own grandparents on either side, he had no idea to what extent one might feel sad over losing one. It certainly wouldn't be as bad as losing a parent, right?

"I'm really sorry. We'll be back in about a tenday, maybe less knowing how fast The Sergeant gets tired of being around my aunts and uncles. He's the speckled calf in the family; the rest of them are all shepherds."

Ezren sighed. Raban was exactly who he needed, but he had his own problems to deal with.

"It's alright, Raban. Thanks for trying, I know what you would have been sacrificing to stay here and help."

"Well hopefully you find the miscreant before I get back but if not I'll be able to help as much as you need," Raban replied.

"Thanks. Have a safe trip. Wait, if your da is riding Thumb, what horse are you riding?" Ezren asked, trying to keep Raban as long as he could.

"Oh one of the remounts in the barracks stable. The Sergeant called in a favor, and it's good for the horses to get out as much as they can anyway."

Ezren nodded, trying to think of another question. It was silly, but he didn't want Raban to leave. He couldn't think of any legitimate ones, so they did a one-armed hug they'd seen the soldiers do and Raban went to pick up his things. He waved sadly as they walked down the road. Ezren stayed where he was, watching them leave.

He felt distinctly alone as he watched them disappear in the crowds. Fiona didn't understand, Asteri didn't understand, and no one else cared enough to even try to do so. His best friend couldn't help him.

His father was dead. There was no one. He was so desperate that he briefly wondered if his brothers Eztas and Ezrote might be willing to help him.

He'd seen neither of them since leaving Ambarta six years ago, but they had helped him escape instead of killing him, and he'd always had a good relationship with them. Well, with Eztas. Ezrote didn't really have a good relationship with anyone. It didn't take long to dismiss the idea, however; he had no idea where to find them now that Ambarta had conquered most of the Western Region, and small chance he could manage to enlist either of their help without being discovered by his mother or his oldest brother Ezmith. The last time he'd seen *them* they had been the ones ordering his death.

The feeling of powerlessness was creeping back. He stamped on it with the only tool he seemed to have right then: anger. If Raban couldn't help him, he would just go back to the beginning. Something that Sergeant Kennard often said came to his mind: "the squeaky wheel gets the grease".

Well, he would just have to be the squeaky wheel, then! He turned on his heel and stormed back up to the castle complex, under the archway and down the little cobblestone road that led to the front door of the library.

Once in the library, he started up the steps to where Mellion had his desk, thinking over what he was going to say. Despite his efforts over the years to find reading material on the matter, he had little idea what was and wasn't possible with magic.

He got to the top of the stairs, thinking that if he could be a bit milder this time around, perhaps Mellion would stay in a better mood and be more amenable to helping him. That hope got much smaller, however, as he tuned in to what he was hearing and seeing.

Mellion was standing behind his desk, his closed fists resting on it, and yelling at a young woman who appeared to be a worker in the library.

"...my notes on the goblin wars?! They were nearly finished!"

"Yes, sir. I'm sorry, sir," she replied in a timid voice.

"GO FIND THEM!" Mellion bellowed, sender the young woman skittering away.

Mellion watched as she ran past Ezren, rolling his eyes as Ezren walked closer.

"*Now* what do you want, boy?" Mellion asked rudely.

Well, so much for keeping him in a good mood. May as well not bother anymore.

"I want to know everything you've done to figure out who killed my father and figure out what else we can do."

Mellion slammed his fist on the desk, then started rubbing his knuckles, wincing. "I've done everything I *can* do! I can't just invent some new magic that can reveal what happened in the past! You are all asking far too much of me!"

"There has to be *something!*" Ezren yelled back. "I had no idea the castle would retain such an incompetent wizard!"

Mellion leaned forward on his fists much like he had with the young woman. This time, however, he spoke quietly, his words sounding much like a sword sliding from a scabbard.

"I tell you, boy, there is no known magic that can tell us more about that night than we already know."

Something inside Ezren clicked. He knew what to do next. He leaned forward, resting his fists on the desk in imitation of Mellion.

"Then I will go find some *un*known magic that will."

Mellion surprised him by laughing out loud. The laugh was sarcastic and patronizing.

"Go on, then, go find this unknown magic! Ezren Kimorae the Discoverer. You have no idea how absurd your claim is."

Rather than reply, Ezren turned and stormed out. He was angry, yes, but even more than that he was *focused.* He needed to go to their apartments and pack everything he needed, but he had to do it quickly. If someone figured out what he was up to, they would most certainly stop him.

Once in his rooms, he grabbed his saddlebags and stuffed in a few changes of clothes. None of the thin stuff he normally wore around the castle, though. Only thick stuff that would stand up to the elements. A few changes of trousers, some good shirts, his cloak. Spring was officially over now, but nights were still cool and it would likely be even colder where he was going.

The clothes took up more room in his bags than he wanted, so he took out all but one extra change of everything; if he fell in a creek or something he would need something to change into. Clothes packed, he went to the kitchen and grabbed all the food they had that would keep on the road. There wasn't much; Ezren could not remember a time when they had had to leave unexpectedly with no time to gather provisions.

There were a few pieces of waybread, one pouch of dried meat, and a waterskin that Ezren could fill up on his way out. He'd have to buy more on his way out of the city.

After the kitchen, he went to his father's room. He paused involuntarily as he entered. The bed was made and everything was in its proper place, as though his father had only just left to go to work. He went to the wardrobe and pulled open the drawer closest to the floor.

Clothes flew as he tossed them indiscriminately, looking for the row of small chests his father kept. In the chests was a small fortune. His pay as Captain of the Castle Guard had been substantial, and with all of their living expenses, including Ezren's schooling, paid for by the King, they had never had much to do with the money his father had made. Now Ezren had a use for it...well, some of it.

If he could find a way to take all of it, he could live like a Lord during his entire trip, but while it may all fit in the saddlebags, the added weight would be significant. Altogether, the neatly stacked coins kept in neatly arranged rows might weigh as much as Ezren did, and he didn't want to overburden Asteri.

He took two of the small chests after checking their contents to make sure they weren't full of bronze pellets. Each had a mix of gold, silver, and bronze, so Ezren wouldn't have to flash gold everywhere he went. Between the two, he could still probably stay at inns the entire way, though he wouldn't do so. You never knew how long a little bit of coin would have to last you.

He stuffed the chests into the saddlebags, then rearranged the contents so that the two sides were relatively balanced. He threw the saddlebags over his shoulder and headed for the door. He stopped on the way, looking around.

This would be the last time he saw these rooms. He'd be gone long enough that the king would have no choice but to clear the rooms and give them to the new captain. What would become of his things? He had few possessions, not even his own sword.

A sword! He needed a sword!

He considered for a moment sneaking down to the Memoriale Mimeio and retrieving his father's sword and shield, but he wanted them to stay with his father, and he didn't want to risk being caught.

He dropped the saddlebags and dashed back into his father's room, pocketing what he figured would be enough gold to buy his own sword and shield on his way out of the city. He considered just kifing one of the training swords, but he had overheard Stark and Juildar bemoaning at how poor of condition they were in and how badly they needed replacing. Better if he bought a new one.

He didn't like having coins in his pockets; they weighed him down noticeably and his pockets swung disconcertingly whenever he tried to rush. Not to mention how much they clinked; it would be impossible for him to walk past someone without them knowing that he had something worth stealing.

It couldn't be helped, though, so he shouldered the saddlebags again and left his rooms for the last time, poking his head out and looking down the hall both ways before coming out and shutting the door behind him. He took the back way, down the narrow servant staircase and small hallways normally reserved for workers.

He was out of the castle proper and on his way to the stables before he knew it. The horse handlers wouldn't bother him; they were used to him handling Asteri on his own. He entered the stable where his horse was boarded, and saw not one, but two Asteris, the one patting the other on the nose.

Princess Asteri looked up at him as he entered and smiled sadly. Conspicuously, her normal guards were nowhere to be seen. She noticed him craning to look around for them and smiled.

"They are probably just now realizing I'm no longer in the latrine."

He stepped forward cautiously. He had no intention of abandoning his plan, but what could he do, tie the princess up? He'd be lucky to escape hanging, no matter that he knew the king and queen personally.

"How did you know to be here?" He asked, as much because he was genuinely curious as because he was buying time to think.

"I overheard you with Mellion. Those library walls are so thin, I think everyone in the building heard you."

"Did you tell anyone?" Ezren asked with trepidation.

"Of course not!" she said, shaking her head. She looked down. "I think I owe you an apology for yesterday. I don't...I don't understand what you're feeling, and I don't understand why you need to leave. But I understand that you *do* need to."

"So you're not going to try and stop me?"

"No I'm not, are you even listening?" She asked, trying to appear grumpy. "I actually thought about going with you, but I can't imagine it would be helpful to have ten thousand Mountain Home Guards hot on your trail. Do you really think you can find some kind of new magic?"

Ezren shrugged. "That's my only choice now. I have to find out who killed my da."

"Well, then," she said, stepping forward so she was right in front of him. "I'm going to miss you, Ezren. And I expect you to come back. I forbid you from being gone forever."

Ezren hiked the saddlebags higher on his shoulder, not meeting her eyes. He hadn't really thought that far ahead...he supposed he would have to come back once he found the magic. He met her eyes and nodded somberly.

Asteri leaned in, standing up on her toes, and kissed him softly on the cheek. He couldn't deny the thrill that shot through him. Whether she'd meant to or not, she had just made it a lot harder for him to get on his horse and ride out of the city.

Her cheeks were red and she was smiling as she lifted something up something wrapped in cloth about a foot long and handed it to him. He unwrapped it, still feeling the cool wetness of her lips on his cheek.

"It's a Skyfire," she said at the same time he recognized it. "I don't know if it will come in handy, but I seem to remember them being part of one of your da's most famous exploits."

Ezren smiled sadly, remembering the story. How much had changed since then.

After that there wasn't much to say, at least not that Ezren was prepared to say, so he pulled the equine Asteri from her stall and saddled her, his practiced hands going through all the necessary steps to get it just right, just as Ben had taught him. He leapt into the saddle in front of his full saddlebags, reminding himself that he needed to stop at an armorer and get a sword and shield.

His bow, about shoulder height on him, was unstrung and tied onto the side along with a quiver of arrows. Princess Asteri watched in silence as he prepared. Once he was on his horse ready to go, she smiled a sad smile.

"Ezren, I-..." she hesitated, seeming unsure of what to say. "I wish I could change what happened to your father. Just...make him proud, alright? And come back. Come home."

Ezren felt a lump in his throat. He swallowed, trying to force it down, but his eyes began to water and he felt powerless to stop his tears. He wanted to speak, to tell Asteri that he would miss her, that he really did care for her.

"Thank you," was all he was able to croak out, and his voice broke in the middle. Ashamed, he turned his horse to leave the stable out the end that would take him to the rest of the city. He nudged his horse, who took a few steps, but he pulled up on the reins just inside the doors. He turned his head to the side, just able to see the princess out of the corner of his eye, trying to think of something he could say to reassure her.

"I will come back," was all he could think of.

He kicked his horse in the ribs to a trot, trying to get moving before he ended up changing his mind. He rode out of the stables and onto the street that took him through the barracks complex and into the city proper.

The city looked different. Oh, everything was the same, the same faces, the same storefronts, the same workshops. The ting-ting of a blacksmith's hammer, the steady clacking of a weaver using...whatever weavers used. But something was different this time. Maybe it was just him that was different.

There was a shop just outside the barracks complex, likely not by accident, that boasted the finest weapons made purely from Mountain Home steel. He turned Asteri that direction.

There was a beam out front to tie horses to, but there wasn't much room in the street for it. Ezren had to tie Asteri to the beam and push her to stand parallel with the flow of traffic. The more out of the way she was the less likely someone would try to steal something out of his saddlebags.

He walked into the armorer trying to keep his pockets from clinking too much. The armorer looked up expectantly, then rolled his eyes before settling back on his elbows on the countertop.

Ezren wasn't offended; like every young man living in the barracks complex, he'd been in this shop multiple times with no money to spend, and the armorer was very used to young men taking up his time with questions then not buying anything. Unlike most youths that came in here to fantasize, however, Ezren actually had coin to spend this time.

"What can I get you, young sir?" The armorer asked. He was a balding, overweight man with an unpleasant face. He had the best weapons in the city, though, and knew it.

"A sword and shield, sir," Ezren replied. "I'd love to see your best, please."

The man smiled condescendingly. "My best, eh? Well alright, over there." He pointed to the far wall, and Ezren followed his finger, walking past the single-edged blades used for dual wield and the enormous swords as tall as him used for two-handed sword.

The swords and shields were hung on the wall, apparently being sold in pairs; the hilts of the swords designed in a way that matched with the front of the shield. One pair had a green, swirly design. Another was blue with straight lines drawing intertwining boxes.

The idea that one might actually design their sword to be fancy had never occurred to Ezren; the swords he used at the Academy were all plain-hilted, as was the sword and shield his father had been issued. He had no need for his equipment to be decorated, but then he saw a pair at the end of the wall that had a simple eight-pointed star design on the shield, and yellow wrap-arounds entwining the hilt.

A star. That made sense. That would be the one, then. He pulled the sword off the wall and hefted it in his sword arm. It really was well-balanced, it almost felt light compared to the training swords he was used to, and it was a suitable length for him, a blade length of just under 30 inches with a comfortable handle. Hefting the shield next, he checked that it gave him good coverage and was angled back slightly from the center, which would make it better for deflecting hits to either side.

The star design was formed in the steel, which at first Ezren was leery of, but the design was shallow and all the edges were well rounded, making it highly unlikely that a sword tip would get lodged and knock him off balance. Still, he felt the entire surface with his hand to make sure that there were no places where that could happen.

He carried the sword and shield over to the armorer and put them on the counter.

The armorer raised his eyebrows and looked up at him, eyes impatient. "That set there is three gold coins," he said, clearly disbelieving that Ezren could afford it.

Without a word, Ezren reached into his pocket and fished out three gold coins, laying them on the counter.

It was remarkable how quickly the armorer's attitude changed. He went from mild annoyance to shock, then to warm and welcoming almost in the time it took Ezren to blink. He immediately retrieved a plain leather scabbard and put the sword in.

"Why, good sir, have you need of more sword oil or a sharpening stone?"

Oil? Oh, right. He'd heard Master Juildar talk about keeping the swords oiled, but why?

"I do need oil, and a sharpening stone as well," he replied, trying to sound confident. "I need...everything that one needs to properly care for a sword."

The armorer nodded with a knowing smile and bustled away from the counter. He returned with a small leather satchel that he opened to show Ezren the contents.

"You've got your large vial of oil, two oiling rags, a pick for getting dirt and grime out of the hilt and handguard, and a whetstone just the right size for a one-handed sword."

"That looks like exactly what I need. How much for the satchel?" Ezren asked.

"Two silver coins," the armorer replied.

"Done," Ezren said, digging two silver coins out of his pocket. Most of what was left in that pocket was bronze now, but he had some gold and silver still in his other pocket, not to mention what was in his saddlebags.

"I trust the young sir already has a polearm? A sword and shield are a wonderful choice, but are usually taken up only after the warrior's polearm is broken or lost."

Ezren shook his head. This, at least, he had thought about. "I am an archer. My first weapon is my bow, the sword and shield are just for if something gets close."

The armorer nodded respectfully. "As you say, young sir."

Ezren started to gather up his purchases, but stopped. He needed someone to explain to him the purpose in oiling the sword, and how to go about doing it. Did the whole sword need it? Wouldn't oil on the hilt make it too slick to handle?

"Armorer," he asked, using the man's title. "How long would you expect this vial of oil to last? I plan to be on the road a long time."

The man's eyebrows raised. "That would depend on much. You only need to oil the blade every two to three tendays unless you see fighting. Sharpen and oil after each use. The purpose of the oil is just to prevent the blade from rusting, so you don't need much. And don't get the oil on the leather grip, but you can use it on the metal portions of the hilt and handguard."

That was wonderfully informative.

"Thank you," he said, nodding to the man and gathering up his things again.

He stepped out of the armory and looked around, watching the faces of the people walking past in each direction. The throng was not cheek-by-jowl as it often was down in the marketplace, but there were plenty of people. This close to the castle, he expected to see someone he recognized, but despite watching for nearly a minute, he saw no one.

He didn't really want to see anyone he knew, didn't want to argue with them about whether he should leave, didn't want them to try and stop him. But at the same time...he kept hoping someone...maybe Asteri...would come walking down the road, flanked by her guards.

He tossed his new purchases on Asteri's saddle for a moment, buckled on his sword belt, stuffed the maintenance kit into his saddle-bags, and looked for a way to tie the shield on the outside. He could wear the shield on his back, he supposed, but why bother if he could find a way to tie it to his bags?

Finished, he jumped up into the saddle and took one last look around before pulling Asteri into the flow of traffic and riding out of the barracks complex. The buildings changed from multi-story apartments and offices to a line of workshops, then to the pop-up stores and markets that lined the main thoroughfare through the city.

He took his time, for some reason not worried about someone from the castle catching up and stopping him. He drank it all in, seeing alleys where Raban and he had scaled walls, rooftops they'd run on and jumped from, and the rolling shades that many shops had in the front to cover their goods during the day.

As he rode under the West gate, he did not look back, and once clear of the throng, he kicked Asteri up to a gallop, the dust puffing up behind her hooves.

He leaned forward, the wind running through his hair. No fences, no running in circles, no more training in lieu of doing. He was on his way. Whatever it took, he would find out who had killed his father, and if it took finding new magic, then that's what he would do.

CHAPTER 8: THE QUEST

They were somewhat of a pathetic rabble, as far as Ezmith could see. An *enormous* pathetic rabble. Nearly 18,000 of them according to the ledger that Captain Beaumont carried. The rabble had camped on a plain three miles East of Mhairi, far enough that Perivon shouldn't discover them unless he already knew they were there. Training them was going to be a nightmare.

A vast array of tents large enough to rival most cities was spread out before him. There was a conveniently placed plateau here where Ezmith could stand and look out over the camp. Looking out over the incredible mass that had rallied to their banner, Radomir's words echoed in his mind...power alone does not loyalty breed.

How many of these men had come for him, and how many for the greatly-cherished Lady Virtesa? His mind understood that it didn't matter; these soldiers were barely more intelligent and sophisticated than animals and their respect and admiration amounted to little in the grand scheme of things.

Still, though...it nagged at him. How many of these men, if he were on the run, would give him shelter? If he had nothing to threaten them with, would they, as Radomir had said, deny him even the loft of a barn to sleep in?

He rolled his eyes at his own distractibility. These speculations didn't matter! He *did* have much to threaten them with, and they loved his mother besides, so they *had* answered his call, and they *would* fight for him. That begged a more important question, though:

How was he going to train all these men? The short answer was that he had to lower his standards of what he considered training. Official instruction in swordplay and one-on-one combat was out of the question beyond the bare basics, but they could be taught how to use the polearms they would be issued and taught basic battlefield strategy so they would be less likely to question their orders.

That was the main thing that Ezmith was worried about. How many of these soldiers would have the discipline and the courage to face almost-certain death for the good of the army rather than flee? If they were ordered to a fight that looked like they might lose, would they simply refuse to go? How quickly could they be trained to follow orders faithfully regardless of how things looked?

He turned and walked away from the edge of the plateau, throwing a Fold in front of him. He strode, without missing a step, into the designated place in the Mhairi Mayor's place. He stepped through into the foyer, already looking for the man who had the information he wanted…what was his name again?

"Riut!" He called, remembering. "What is the status of the siege?"

The lieutenant, recently promoted from sergeant came rushing up.

"Still no siege weapons, my Lord. They seem content to surround the city and wait us out."

Foolish strategy; Ezmith could simply create a Fold to bring supplies in, though that would require much of his time and attention, and even then it would be next to impossible to predict exactly when a merchant caravan would be arriving. He'd have to send soldiers out to establish checkpoints to detain merchants and then create a Fold at a set time every day. That would at least get supplies in, and they could likely use the same process to get the merchants back out.

They had plenty of time before Mellion returned if they wanted to push back, though Ezmith wasn't sure that was wise yet.

"I want the current count of soldiers in the city. *Trained* soldiers, ones who were soldiering before we sent out the proclamation."

He continued to walk briskly, making Lieutenant Riut scramble to keep up, shuffling papers to find the one he needed.

"Yes, sir, I have it right here, sir. We have near enough 2,000 of our original force here. Less the four hundred in Redwood, that would make just about our entire remaining army."

Ezmith ground his teeth. 2,000 trained soldiers. Not so many years ago it would have been considered a mighty force, but Perivon had half again as much outside the walls, and likely another thousand or so stationed in Bahadir.

Cleononia had maintained that army for decades if not centuries; they used it for peacekeeping throughout their land and held it in reserve to reinforce Mountain Home in the event of wars against the much larger nations East of the Berg.

He was tempted to just hand each of the men in the rabble a polearm and yell 'charge!', since 18,000, even untrained, could wipe 3,000 from off the face of the earth, but just a little bit of training could spare them thousands of casualties in the process. His mother would not approve of throwing men away.

They walked through a door to a side room. It had been a sitting room before they had commandeered the building and turned this room into Ezmith's office. He sat down while Riut stood in front of his desk.

"Do as we discussed, Riut. Each of our 2,000 trained soldiers will be given promotions. Captain Beaumont will receive the title of Captain-General, his two lieutenants will be raised to Captains and each given charge of half the army under Beaumont. Sergeants will be raised to lieutenants and each given a tenth of the armies under the captains, and we will have to create a number of smaller positions. Have the officers determine which of the soldiers are the best fit for bannermen, hundredmen, and squad leaders. I expect most of the trained soldiers will be needed to fill all the leadership positions in the new army."

Riut nodded excessively as he was taking notes. He seemed intelligent enough, but he was so eager to please that it was often *dis*pleasing.

"And what of training, my Lord?" Riut asked, continuing to write even as he asked and waited for the answer.

"Captain-General Beaumont will be in charge of training, but I expect him to focus on polearms and general battlefield tactics. Squad leaders and hundredmen can run drills and exercises to teach the men to fight together. How many of the new recruits brought swords and shields?"

Riut quirked his mouth to the side. "Not many, I'm afraid. According to the number I have here, only 4,792 have reported having both a sword and shield. Another four thousand brought only swords, though in varying states of disrepair, and another thousand brought only shields."

Riut may be disappointed, but that was better than Ezmith had been expecting. Once he'd seen the first group arrive carrying mostly pitchforks and hoes his expectations had not been overly high.

"Put the men who have both sword and shield into their own companies as much as possible. Those without shields will eventually be issued longswords," Ezmith ordered, watching as Riut continued nodding and taking his notes. Was the man transcribing their entire conversation? Perhaps he was.

Riut did pause for a moment, though, and looked up cautiously at Ezmith. "My Lord, I've been told that sword-and-shield is easier to learn than two-handed sword."

Ezmith nodded impatiently. "Yes, but shields require more steel, and I'm sure you've noticed how prices on Mountain Home steel have gone up?"

Riut nodded, eyes wide in agreement. Likely he'd had gone into more than one fit over the cost of steel, not to mention other goods.

"Besides," Ezmith continued, "Even if we engaged every armorer in our lands and could supply them the necessary steel it would take months to get all the shields we need. Most armorers have longswords pre-made and on display. We may be able to get all the swords we need in under a tenday."

"Very wise, my lord," Riut replied, nodding again and going back to writing his notes.

"What of bows?" Ezmith asked.

"Bows, my lord?"

"Yes, Riut, bows," Ezmith said irritably. "How many of the men brought bows and arrows?"

"Oh!" he yelped, trying to leaf through his notes and having to tuck them close to his chest to avoid dropping them. "I've got the number here somewhere, sir."

He continued to look for a bit, his face getting redder the longer it took.

"Forget the number," Ezmith said curtly. "Just give me an estimate from what you remember."

Riut looked at him gratefully. "I believe it was most of them, my lord. Nearly 8 in every 10 brought a bow and claimed to know how to use it, and most of those brought arrows as well."

"Very good," Ezmith said thoughtfully.

"Will that be all for now, sir?"

"Yes," Ezmith replied, anxious to have the room to himself. "Close the door on your way out."

Riut left, clutching his notes to his chest, and closed the door behind him, bowing in an almost groveling way.

Then it was quiet. Ezmith sighed gratefully at the silence that surrounded him. Silence was so wonderful it almost made him believe that it had to have been given to them by a creator of some kind.

He looked around, moved his shoulders a bit, then looked down at his hands.

Shouldn't he feel...different?

Since killing his father a few days ago, he'd felt none of the thrill that killing someone normally gave him. Certainly no sadness, regret, or pain either, but no adrenaline, excitement, or energy. Since coming back he'd waffled between feeling...freer, he supposed was the word and...regret.

He'd puzzled over those feelings of regret as a scholar would study an ancient text, and had come to the conclusion that the regret stemmed from his father's skills and talents going to waste instead of helping in their conquest. After all, with his battle experience, the former Kimorae patriarch could have been a great asset against Perivon, and Ezmith had not even tried to bring him back over to their side.

Yes, the regret was easy enough to understand. In truth, it was the absence of the adrenaline that concerned him more.

Perhaps he'd fantasized too much about what it would feel like? Had he worked it up too much in his own mind? His father had not played an active role in his life for some time now, and even before his escape he hadn't been a particularly large part of Ezmith's existence. Perhaps he just didn't have any strong feelings towards his father.

There was another disturbing possibility: had he now killed so many that the thrill was simply wearing off? If that were the case...well, for now he just needed to find out if it was. He could worry about solutions once he'd properly identified the problem. First, he would find someone in the city to test the theory on that night. If it was true, he'd have to find something else to excite him.

He leaned forward and looked at the papers on his desk. Somewhere here there should be an estimate of how long it would take to properly train the new recruits. Beaumont and he had already discussed everything Ezmith had just told Riut, and Beaumont was supposed to have provided an explanation of how the training would go and how long it would take to be completed well enough to push Perivon back. Ah, there it was.

A *single* tenday?! That seemed absurdly optimistic. Ezmith read through the rest of the document, trying to understand how the training could be done so quickly.

Ah, the tenday was only after all the men had been sorted into companies – garrisons, hundreds, and squads -- and assigned a role –

archers and infantry – which Beaumont estimated would take 3 to 4 days.

Even so, ten days still felt optimistic. Beaumont had listed only a single day for the soldiers to be taught basic battlefield maneuvers – forward push, flanking, and pincers, with a portion of each day following dedicated to practicing them. Weapons training was under-emphasized, as they'd discussed, since there simply wasn't enough time to focus on it. The men would be trained on the use of a halberd, pike, and spear only. Since Cleononia did not field much cavalry, the polearm that the vast majority of the men would be using was a spear.

He considered for a moment whether the men equipped with shields should be distributed throughout the companies so that they could be a defensive front line for the entire army...but no, unless they were full body shields, they wouldn't be large enough to be effective, and then they wouldn't have any full companies of specialized swordsmen to send into city streets and buildings for close-quarters fighting.

A horn blew from outside and Ezmith jerked his head up. Another attack. Perivon had been doing these small sorties for days now, at least a couple each day, though Ezmith could not reason why. He supposed it might be to wear down his men and condition them to treat the warning horn with less urgency. That was a tree that would take a long time to bear fruit, however. Much longer than the tenday that Ezmith needed to wait before he could begin pushing Perivon back into the sea.

He got up from his desk quickly and went out to get a sense of the attack. A messenger in a leather jerkin with steel discs sewn on the outside came running up to him.

"My lord! Attack on the north wall!" he exclaimed, only a little out of breath.

"Another sortie?" Ezmith asked as he walked briskly down the steps of the manor and onto the cobblestone road that would take them to the north wall.

"No sir," the messenger replied, staying one step behind him. "At least, well, if it is then the wizards are getting involved. Only Guillame being there right when it happened stopped them from blowing a hole in the wall. When I left he said he was putting up some kind of shield, but I didn't see anything."

Of course he hadn't seen anything, it wouldn't be visible to anyone who wasn't a wizard. Obviously. Honestly, the idiocy and ignorance of some people.

"Go fetch Flimbast and bring him to the wall. Tell him to come with all speed."

The messenger nodded, bowed quickly, and took off at a run.

Ezmith continued on his way, doing the math in his head. Even if his enemies had broken their word, Mellion could not have returned by now, so they faced Leir, Paavali, and the three guild wizards. Five versus three, but one of the three was Ezmith. He smiled. Not only could they hold, but he might be able to test his theory earlier than this evening.

Long before he reached the wall, he heard the thuds and booms of magic trading hands. Excited, he broke into a run and took the stairs two at a time. Guillame was at the top of the wall, doing a packhorse's work in keeping all the wizards at bay. The strain was showing on his more aged face, however, and sweat was running down his cheeks.

It was clear to see why – it was a bombardment of the elements. They had likely chosen the North wall because the shore of Lake Mhairi was nearby, and the air was more humid here. Fireballs were all well and good, but Waterballs were more powerful in many ways because they had actual weight and mass.

A Waterball as tall as a man came hurtling towards them and Guillame threw both hands up, fortifying the shield about ten feet from the wall. When the Waterball impacted, the Shield trembled and Guillame slid back on his feet as though he'd personally felt the force of the impact, which of course he had.

"I'll take the Shield!" Ezmith yelled, reaching out with his magic for the threads going from Guillame to the Shield. "Take a moment to rest and when Flimbast gets here you two take defense and I'll strike back."

Guillame nodded, releasing the threads to Ezmith and wiping the sweat on his face onto his sleeves.

The bombardment continued unabated, and Ezmith put his focus on adjusting and modifying the Shield to withstand whatever was coming next. Lightning bolts, Fireballs, and Waterballs were soon accompanied by Greatwinds so strong that only a reflexive cast of Iron Boots kept himself and Guillame on the ground.

Magical shields were not simply a solid barrier against any incursion; they had to be crafted to defend against a specific type of attack. Many novice wizards made the mistake of forming the shield so tightly and densely that it resembled steel, but such a shield was too difficult to maintain for longer than a few seconds, and the magical energy was too much like steel – when it could not bend, it broke.

So a Shield had to be woven densely enough to keep out the attack, but loosely enough for the shield to have room to flex and bend as needed to properly absorb the attack. Easy enough with something like a Fireball, but against water attacks you needed more room for the shield to flex, while Lightning required the tightest weave you could manage since it could so easily pierce through any gaps.

Luckily, Ezmith could see the attacks coming before they arrived, and as long as he stayed vigilant, he could adjust different portions of the Shield to properly protect against each different elemental attack. There was no keeping the Greatwinds out, though, so the Iron Boots stayed cast.

Ezmith didn't know how long it took for Flimbast to get there, but he was glad that he had relieved Guillame immediately; this was taxing even for him, so Guillame must have been near to death. Indeed, as Ezmith quickly glanced over at him, the man looked much older than normal and as though he could sleep for a tenday.

"Flimbast!" Ezmith barked as soon as the plump, long-haired wizard from Orjan got to the top of the wall. "Run a Detection to make sure that all five of our enemy wizards are here. We don't want anyone sneaking up on us.

It was doubtful that this bombardment could be done by fewer than all five, but Ezmith had no interest in taking chances. After a moment, Flimbast yelled back over the sound of the wind.

"Yes, sir, they're all there!"

"Good!" Ezmith yelled back, tightening up the Shield as twin Fireballs impacted it on either side. "I want you and Guillame to take the Shield while I go on the attack. Once I'm returning fire the bombardment should diminish and the two of you should be able to hold it."

He let Flimbast take one of the threads and Guillame take the other and he relinquished it, trying to decide on the best way to strike back.

These elemental attacks were effective, but also simple. Perhaps they just wanted to keep their strength up, or perhaps they didn't know any other means of attack. He had found it was common for wizards unaccustomed to using magic in warfare to not realize all the ways that magic could be used. Ezmith loosed a few lightning bolts, which were stopped by an overhead Shield that might have been in place the entire time; this far away it was difficult to tell, especially with all the magical energy clouding his vision.

The bolts were mostly a distraction though, as he created a Scry box and dropped it where he could be confident it was far enough to be behind the attacking wizards. Only a fellow wizard could see the Scry, and only if they were looking for it; it didn't use enough energy for them to sense it. The Scry opened up to show the orderly camp of the Cleononian army, tents in nearly perfect rows. By Clayara, even the firepits were in straight lines.

He threw another Bolt, just to keep the wizards' attention forward, then began moving the Scry up the camp towards the staging area where he expected to find the attacking wizards. He had to be careful with this; he'd likely only get one chance to pull it off.

There they were. They stood just in front of a pavilion about twice as wide as it was long, in a concerted row. Ezmith looked away from the Scry and out across the field, squinting. This would work best if he could see where they were. Even had he walked that ground before – which he had not – the changes to the area from the tents, pavilions, and people would have made it difficult to Fold exactly where he wanted to go.

Ah...he was fairly sure he could see them among the trees, a couple hundred yards away.

He closed the Scry and gathered himself. He had to be careful with this Fold; if he ended up Folding into a tree or something it would feel like the world's largest gong had just been hit with the world's largest hammer inside his head, and he'd be unable to do magic for days. The Scry had shown him that one of the guild wizards was on the end of the row. A shame, he would have liked to get Vewen himself, or Leir, but this underling would have to do.

Hopefully none of the wizards had made a Dome around them, which could be made to stop one or more energies being used for magic. Most likely not, since none of the enemy wizards had ever been close enough to one of his Fold's to sense what energies it used. Assuming this worked, it would be worth giving up that advantage.

As quickly as he could, he made a Fold about waist-high above the ground, and not large enough for a person to walk through. It worked! Suddenly, he was looking directly at the profile of the guild wizard. A young man, with shoulder-length light brown hair, lifting one arm high to call down a Lightning Bolt. The wizard must have sensed the Fold open because his head jerked to the side and his eyes widened at the sight of Ezmith on the other side of his Fold.

With a flick of his wrist, Ezmith sent a razor-sharp thread of air across the wizard's neck, decapitating him instantly. The other wizards went into a panic as the body and head fell separate from one another. Ezmith closed the Fold just as they noticed him, sealing it up before any counterattacks could come through.

That went about as well as it could have. Now it should be simple enough for them to make a Dome where one of the types would not form. Of course, that would mean that they could no longer attack Ezmith with whatever energy type they chose, but they would likely consider that a fair bargain.

The attacks stopped, and Ezmith stood on the wall with his two wizard companions waiting in silence to see if they would begin again. He hadn't expected them to stop the attack after losing one of their comrades. Perhaps they were sad about the loss and had lost focus on their objective as a result. He sighed. Despite all the years he'd spent observing people and learning how others behaved, obvious mistakes like that still confused him.

Oh well, the attack stopping completely would be even better than he had hoped for.

He had delivered a decisive blow against Perivon, and the remaining wizards would not be as severe of a threat until Mellion returned, which should not be for quite some time yet. He considered again sending the rabble now, but he schooled himself to patience. Mellion would be much longer than a tenday returning, so he had the time he needed to let Beaumont bring his new recruits up to an acceptable standard and *then* wipe Perivon's army off the face of the earth.

Despite being in a besieged city, Ezmith once again felt as though he had the clear upper hand in this war.

~

The light from Ezren's fire was just enough for his eyes to make out the words on the page of the book he had taken from the library: "The History of Glacies Castle".

This was his first night out from Novis Terram, and he was halfway to Berengaria. He may not be able to travel as quickly as Ben Rider, but Ben had taught him enough to enable him to move faster than most travelers. The road was fairly well-maintained, but it traversed difficult terrain as it went around, and occasionally straight over, large hills. As the crow flew, Berengaria was only perhaps 70 miles from Novis Terram, but because of the endless rows of hills that the road had to curve around, the distance by foot was as much as twice that.

Glacies Castle was an incredibly fascinating place, and Ezren couldn't take his eyes from the page:

"...was revealed by the melting glacier, the first explorer – a woman by the name of Indrada Meesh – was able to enter the castle. Her journal explains that the castle was still partly submerged in the glacier, and her attempts to break an exposed window were fruitless. Instead, she was able to find a door on an upper level whose lock had rusted, allowing her to break it open."

Ezren couldn't help but imagine what it must have been like to be Indrada Meesh. It seemed like a dream come true, discovering an ancient castle that no one in living memory had ever seen and getting inside to see what secrets it held. He was excited about going, even though he would technically be a fugitive from the law there; his family had conquered Disote years ago. He still hadn't worked out how he was going to keep himself hidden, but he had at least another tenday on the road to figure that out. He kept reading.

"Inside, she found a collection of books, a library, larger than any other in the known world. Most of the books were written in Old Ankonite, but many were also written in our own modern tongue, and still more were in tongues that no scholar has been able to identify."

That right there is what pulled Ezren to Glacies Castle. He needed to discover some kind of new magic, and if new magic were to be discovered, or old magic *re*discovered, it seemed like Glacies Castle was where that would happen.

But also...Glacies Castle was where the book containing the prophecy about his brothers and him had been discovered. It was still there. While he was at the castle, he wanted to read the prophecy for himself in its entirety. He was going to Glacies Castle already, and since the prophecy just happened to be there, he would take the time to read it and see if it gave him any insight on what was coming next for him.

Judging by the stars, it was getting late. He stood up and put his back to the fire, looking around as his eyes adjusted to the blackness. He realized, with a start, that this was the first time in his life that he had camped completely on his own without shelter of any kind. He'd camped with his father plenty on their way from Lugos to Berengaria where they had first settled, and most of the two years they had spent in Berengaria could rightly be called camping as well, but then they had a semi-permanent shelter that they'd built that had provided a degree of protection.

And his father had made sure he was safe.

He pushed down the emotion that started to rise up into his throat and busied himself surveying everything around his campsite, walking a ring around the edge of the firelight to look outwards for any sign of predators. He wanted to keep the fire going all night to keep away animals, but he couldn't guarantee that he would wake up often enough to throw another piece of wood on the fire.

He tried not to let his imagination run away with him. According to Ben, wolves steered clear of people for the most part, and wouldn't attack a human unless provoked, even if the human was sleeping and defenseless. Skicks only attacked when they needed to lay their eggs, and humans weren't their first choice, anyway. Bears could be a threat, but Ezren had tied the saddlebags with the food up high in a tree to hopefully discourage that.

Asteri was hobbled by the base of the large pine that Ezren had camped next to, and he ended up laying his bedroll right next to where she was, finding comfort in her presence.

Sleep was a long time coming. He flushed with anger each time he thought on his father's murder and how ambivalent the adults in his life had been about it. When he wasn't angry he was scared and kept jumping at every sound in the woods, and when he wasn't scared he was excited about finally being out on his own and sojourning to Glacies Castle.

He only slept a little, but he was up at the first hint of dawn, breaking camp. He saddled Asteri and got on the road before the sun was up.

Throughout the morning he felt fresh and energetic, but after stopping for his midday meal the lack of sleep the night before began to catch up with him. He had originally planned to travel until nightfall every day, since making camp was quick and easy with just him and Asteri to worry about, but he gave in before the sun finished setting and found a nice spot a few hundred yards off the road to make camp.

He had time, so he decided to see about finding some fresh food. He wasn't staying in one place long enough for snares, and he couldn't pack a large kill in addition to all his other supplies, so he decided that small game would be best.

He hiked a little ways away from his campsite and climbed a maple tree with his bow and arrow, planning on shooting the first animal he saw that was small enough to last only a few meals.

A large rabbit would be perfect, though a beaver, coyote, or even a squirrel could work. Squirrels were impossible to shoot, though. Most people he had talked to had found it odd, even unpleasant, to think about eating a coyote or fox, but Ben explained that was because most people didn't know how to prepare the meat properly. Indeed, on one of their forays they had nabbed a coyote and Ben and cooked it for them and it had tasted fine. You had to cook it slow, though, and Ezren was already hungry, hence his hope for a rabbit.

He remained perched in the tree for the better part of an hour, keeping silent and moving as little as he could manage. Being up high made it harder for most critters to smell or see him, so as long as he didn't give himself away with noise, he should be able to shoot down at them without them reacting too much.

It was remarkably pleasant sitting up in the tree in the woods, not seeing or hearing another person the entire time. Even on the road he was rarely alone for long; a merchant caravan would be coming the other way, sometimes a family with a single wagon or cart, or he'd catch up and pass one going the same direction as he. Being in the woods, though, felt like coming back home.

That was probably because of the years they had lived in Berengaria. Strange that he would look back on that time with the most fondness of any in his life. In reality it had been the time of greatest deprivation; he and his father had been on the cusp of starvation for nearly a year, and the work his father had found that turned things around had required his father to spend many nights away, leaving Ezren alone in the woods for days at a time. He had been only 11 at the time.

A rustle in a bush interrupted his thoughts. He looked more closely and saw a rabbit foraging under the leaves. He raised his bow, with an arrow already knocked, took aim, and loosed.

The rabbit was delicious.

He passed through Berengaria the next day, marveling both at how little had changed and how different it all looked from up on a horse. He contemplated taking the Oanez road North up to where their plot of land was, but that would delay him unnecessarily. He wanted to make Salimelish by the following night so he could stay in the same inn that he and his father had stayed at when they first came to Mountain Home.

He wondered if the inn still didn't allow Ambartans in. It seemed like the events of the last six years would make enforcement of that policy much more difficult; since the Ambartan empire now included people of a wide variety of ethnicities. Not to mention the threat of reprisal that it seemed Ambarta was more than capable of delivering on.

He certainly didn't notice any overt animosity toward him as he rode through bustling Berengaria.

He rode out the other side of the city, and the sound of the good-sized town faded behind him, leaving only the clop of Asteri's hooves on the road. Was it wrong to see some personal benefit in Ambarta's conquests? The closer to the border he rode, the fewer people looked at him scornfully, and it was unlikely that anyone in a town as close to the border as Salimelish would dare to treat him differently than any other person.

Fiona had a saying – every rainstorm has a rainbow. What she meant was that when bad things happened, there was always some good to be found if you looked hard enough. He imagined it was a city saying; he had said it once to Raban, whose family were all shepherds and farmers, and Raban hadn't understood – *"Isn't rain a good thing?"* he'd asked.

Regardless, perhaps this was his rainbow. It didn't outweigh the rain nor did it change the effects of the storm, but it was an advantage he could use and appreciate with gratitude.

The road here had fewer hills to wind around, but the road also wasn't as wide, and it was more common for livestock crossing to cause extensive delays. An enormous herd of hundreds of cattle delayed Ezren for more than an hour. That would have frustrated him to no end, except that this road did not seem to be nearly as long as he remembered it.

Granted, the last time he'd traveled this road had been on foot at the age of 10, so it would stand to reason that his perception of it might be skewed. Without the delays, he would likely have arrived at Salimelish in the middle of the next day instead of the end. Arriving early would not have been a bad thing, but arriving when you had expected to in the first place was fine too.

He spent the night a few hundred yards off the road again, this time in a small stand of trees, since the forest grew gradually less dense as you left Berengaria. There wasn't good hunting that night, so he dug into his saddlebags for some waybread and dried meat and made a fair enough dinner out of that. He decided that wasn't a bad way to handle things when he was traveling – try to eat off the land when possible, but always have rations handy in case doing so was either unsuccessful or impractical.

The following day proved similar, in that he found himself once again waiting while another herd, this time of sheep, crossed the road. It was getting close to the official beginning of summer -- did that have some significance in why it seemed so many ranchers were moving their herds?

Riding into Salimelish, he realized he really had no idea whether much had changed. His general impression of the town was the same – small, somewhat run-down, though you could tell what was important to the people here based on what was well-maintained and what wasn't. The posts of the palisade wall still had not been painted or replaced, and there still was no gate. The town was built all along the two roads that intersected here, but now that Ezren had spent some time studying maps and understanding them, he knew that the roads going North and West were rarely trafficked.

The road leading North led straight into the mountains and eventually ended up in Oanez, and the road leading West went through the Heran Hills to Robinton, which was a far longer and more difficult road than simply going South from here to the Northern Highway and going around. His own path would be the Northern Highway.

On the Highway, it would likely take the better part of a tenday to get the rest of the way to Glacies Castle. He didn't know how much time going through the Heran Hills would add, but it would likely be days. Then there were the stories...of course, Ezren didn't take much stock in them, but there were children's books about a great monster who lived in the Heran Hills, a creature with the coat of a grizzly bear but the gait of a man.

The only other time the monster was mentioned was in stories meant for entertainment, not education, so Ezren wasn't worried that they might be true. Of course not.

One thing he knew was different, though, was the grouping of Guard tents along the North road on the outskirts of the town. It didn't seem to be a large garrison, perhaps a hundred soldiers, most of whom seemed to be working on the palisade on the South entrance. Ezren stopped in the main intersection, watching as a group of Guards lifted half of a thick wooden gate to hang onto where the wall stopped short of the road.

The inn wasn't hard to find, though he did not remember the name of it. It was the only inn right on the corner of that same intersection in the town. When they had come through nearly seven years ago he had not noticed the name of the inn, though he would never forget the name of the innkeeper – Adal Nirari, a man who had shown them kindness when he had not been required to do so.

Ezren wasn't in particular need of kindness at the moment, but he did need a place to stay and the least he could do was patronize this man's inn at the same time.

Seeing the inn as he approached, he looked for a name somewhere on the outside, but there wasn't one. The inn didn't seem to have a proper stable either, but there were horse stalls built against the back wall, each with a heavy lock on the gate with a roof providing shelter for the horses there. For the time being, Ezren tied Asteri to the hitching post and went up the couple of stairs to the entrance to the inn. He noted that there was no longer a sign banning Ambartans from entering.

Once inside, he saw the round tables in the dining area, with a long bar across the way that ran the whole length of the room, and the booths that lined the other three walls. Behind the counter was the man he remembered – Adal Nirari, but there was also a young woman, pretty, older than Ezren by at least a few years.

Nirari was wiping down the inside of mugs then handing them to the young woman, who put them upside down on a wooden carrying tray. Ezren could see several full trays stacked one on top of the other behind them. He walked up to Nirari.

"Good evening, sir," he said politely. "I'd like a room for the night, please."

Nirari turned and spat chewing tobacco into a mug that seemed to be set aside for the purpose. That explained why the small man's teeth were rather stained.

"One silver coin for a room, two bronze coins for a horse stall."

The man clearly had not recognized him. Ezren smiled to himself and dug in his pockets for the coins.

Nirari swept the coins off the counter and pulled two keys out from under the counter.

"Little one's for your room, big one is for the padlock on your horse stall. You'll be in stall number four. Keys only work on your locks, so don't be getting any ideas."

Ezren smiled and nodded, taking his leave without saying anything. On the one hand, the man was exactly as Ezren remembered, but on the other hand, it would have been nice to be recognized. Then again, what was Ezren to this man? If Ezren died a horrible death tomorrow, Nirari probably wouldn't shed a tear if he ever even found out about it. Ezren was used to being...what did Fiona call it? A small boat on a big ocean, but at least everyone he'd been around had known who he was and cared for him to one degree or another.

It was jarring to go from a world where virtually every authority figure in his life was there for his benefit back to a world to where no one gave two bronze coins what happened to him.

He led Asteri back to her stall and got her settled, retrieving some hay from the pile off to the side under its own small section of roof and giving her a thorough inspection. His thoughts wandered aimlessly as he did the work.

What *had* Rider meant when he joked about rubbing Princess Asteri down afterwards? He wondered if he would ever be able to rub his horse down without remembering that. Rider had certainly seemed to think it the best joke he'd ever made, but his sense of humor was always strange.

Going back to the inn, he ordered dinner at the counter and refused ale, surprised that it had been offered him. His father only rarely drank, and then only when he was expected to on social occasions. Ale had never been much of a temptation to Ezren – why would someone *want* to make themselves less intelligent for hours at a time? A lot of soldiers drank, and Ezren had seen plenty of examples of the incredibly stupid things they'd done while inebriated. He had no interest in becoming like one of them.

He continued to ponder, as was his habit, as he ate his dinner. It was a cut of chicken along with some potatoes that had been sliced and cooked in some kind of oil. There was also a helping of carrots, and when he was about halfway done the young woman brought over a small plate of strawberries. Did all inns have this great of food? It was wonderful! All the food from the castle kitchens had been only moderately seasoned, and the barracks kitchens had served the same basic porridge and cuts of meat the entire time they'd lived there.

It might be worth staying more nights in inns just for the food!

Just as he was digging into the strawberries, which he had saved for last, Nirari came over, squinting at Ezren.

"Have you been here before, boy? Something about you seems familiar, and I try to remember my customers faces."

Ezren quickly swallowed the strawberry. "Yes, sir, my father and I stopped here on our way out of Ambarta almost seven years ago."

Nirari nodded slowly, still squinting but seeming to remember him. "That's right. I think it was your father I was remembering. You have his look about you. You two were on the run from some trouble. That get all straightened out?"

Now how was he supposed to answer *that*? "In a manner of speaking, sir. We went to Berengaria for awhile, then my father joined the Guards," he said, trying to be cryptic without appearing to be trying to be cryptic.

"Well, where is he now? You're still a little on the young side to be traveling alone."

Ezren looked down at the table. "He, uh, died. He was killed five nights ago."

Nirari was silent for a moment. He put one hand on his hip and looked down as well.

"Well, I'm sorry to hear that, boy," he said. Nirari fished in his apron pocket and tossed Ezren's two bronze coins back onto the table.

"I can't go giving rooms away every time something bad happens to someone, but I can manage giving a horse stall to a lad who just lost his father."

Ezren looked up at him in surprise. "No, it's alright, please, I didn't mean to…I wasn't trying to-"

Nirari held his hands up and smiled. "I know, I know, boy. That's half the reason I chose to do it. Now relax and enjoy the rest of your strawberries."

Ezren *did* enjoy the rest of his strawberries, and he slept well on the comfortable mattress in a room with its own fireplace and window. Sure, the night was cool enough that he wanted the window shut and warm enough that he did not need the fire, but having his own room with them made him feel distinctly...adult.

He went down to the common room for breakfast the following morning feeling in better spirits than he had since he'd found out about his father. He took a seat at the bar rather than taking a booth, which led to more conversation with Nirari, this time about where Ezren was going and why. Ezren felt, for some reason, that he could confide in Nirari without fear. After all, he supposed, who was Nirari going to tell?

"No one knows who killed my father. Whoever had done it had made it look like the work of Meand assassins," Ezren began.

Nirari's eyebrows shot up. Ezren supposed that *was* fairly surprising.

"What kind of trouble you boys been getting into since you passed through?"

Ezren barked a laugh. "You have no idea, sir. Anyway, no one could figure out who had done it and, frankly, no one seemed to care all that much. I spoke with the wizard who was supposed to be helping investigate it, and he said that no magic exists that could tell us what happened that night. So, I decided if no one else was going to do something, I would. I would go find new magic that could tell us who killed my father."

Nirari's eyes were squinted a bit, and he rested on his elbows as he listened. "New magic," he said when Ezren was done. Ezren nodded.

"I'm going to Glacies Castle. I don't know where to find any new magic, but it seems like the best place to start."

"Well, good on you, boy. Can't tell you whether you'll ever find that magic, but I think you made the right choice nonetheless. There's a...a need to get away when something like that happens. And it's not just your feelings it's..."

Nirari stood up straight, looking embarrassed.

"Well, boy, if you're going to Glacies Castle I wouldn't take the Northern Highway. Ambarta's got a checkpoint set up on the border and they check everyone going in or out. I don't know if you're still wanted in Ambarta but that would likely be the wrong way to find out."

Ezren slumped. He hadn't even thought of that. How was he even supposed to get into Ambarta if he was still wanted? Would the soldiers recognize him? At most, they could have seen a sketch of him as a 10-year-old, but they would certainly ask for his name, and may want some kind of papers or something.

Looking at Ezren's apparent distress, Nirari shrugged. "Just take the west road through the Heran Hills. They used to have a check there as well but since the war with Cleononia heated up they pulled their troops away. The soldiers there spent most of their days throwing dice and playing foxes, anyway."

"Right. Yes. The west road through...the Heran Hills," Ezren said, nodding.

He didn't believe the stories, of course. If such a monster existed then the locals would certainly know of it, and Nirari wouldn't have just advised him to take that route – certainly not all alone. Right?

He paid for his breakfast, gathered his things from his room, saddled Asteri, and found a store selling provisions where he stocked back up on waybread, dried meat, and some cheese. He was out of town before the sun was all the way above the mountains.

He took the west road which, as Nirari had suggested, would take him to the capital city of Robinton by way of the Heran Hills.

~

To the Lady Virtesa, the last tenday had gone by quickly. She left her apartments in the Mhairi Mayor's Palace at a stately pace, her head held high, surrounded by a small cadre of guards. She approached the Eastern gate and gracefully ascended the stairs that would take her to the wall walk. She was performing, as surely as a bard, musician, or newsman.

So much of ruling was appearing to rule, and so she maintained the same small, confident smile that she always had when in public. It had become so much of a habit that she had caught herself doing it in private on more than one occasion.

As she reached the top of the wall, only her discipline kept her eyebrows from rocketing to the top of her forehead. A roar greeted her, the roar of 20,000 soldiers who had flocked to her banner and assembled to the East of the city. She allowed the smile on her face to grow wider as she walked to where Ezmith was standing. She waved to the soldiers, though she knew many of them were too far away to see her hand waving.

Knowing that they now had an army twenty thousand strong was one thing, but seeing it assembled and standing before her was something else entirely. Organized into companies of 500, the mass was six companies wide and about the same deep, though the army stretched too far for her to see clearly.

Ezmith had observed the army the past several days and reported that the soldiers knew their jobs well enough that he was comfortable beginning to push.

The truth of it was that they didn't need professional soldiers. Or, at least, they didn't need all 20,000 to be fully trained. All the officers were, and Perivon was unlikely to even attempt to stand and fight against such an enormous mass, which meant that the army would march unopposed to the walls of Dazbog and then sit there for who-knew-how-long before Perivon surrendered. There was a decent chance that this army wouldn't have to fight at all. Besides, they could always continue training exercises during the siege, each day making their army more dangerous to their enemies.

Lady Virtesa was already running numbers in her head, trying to calculate whether it was feasible for them to maintain this size of an army indefinitely. Without Cleononia's ports it was certainly out of the question, but *with*...perhaps.

At the very least, it was worth considering the possibility of keeping the army together and moving on Mountain Home immediately after Cleononia's surrender.

Ezmith, using magic to amplify his voice somehow, began a rousing speech to inspire their men and give them confidence as they marched to the other side of Mhairi and all the way to Dazbog. Lady Virtesa did not listen closely to the words he was saying, but instead focused on the faces of the soldiers that she could see.

Ezmith was an inexplicably competent orator. His command of language wasn't the surprise, but his ability to say what the soldiers needed to hear and inspire them. His words never seemed to fall flat. How many hours must he have spent studying the great speeches of history and analyzing them?

As Ezmith continued, Lady Virtesa reflected on their plan of march. It was simple enough – the wizards and the archer battalion with the longest range would lead the way, with infantry immediately behind, followed by more archers, more infantry, and so on. They did have the light cavalry from Disote, two battalions worth, but there wasn't much for them to do in a march such as this.

They had discussed having the light cavalry harry Perivon as they retreated, but even sending a wizard with each battalion would not prove sufficient defense from Perivon's wizards. So one battalion of cavalry was being sent back to Disote to resume patrolling the roads there, while another battalion would march with the army to provide a flanking force should Perivon ever decide to turn and fight. In the meantime, they had more than enough scouts to keep an eye on things in every direction.

"...stand no longer for Cleononian tyranny!" Ezmith yelled. "We will liberate this people and bring them into our fold! The years of Cleononia intimidating and forcing our nations to its will are over! It stops today! For today...we march!"

Deafening cheers rose up, the fainter yells from soldiers further away adding noticeable depth to the louder cries closer up. The very earth seemed to be rising up in support of their conquest. Ezmith created a Fold there on the wall walk and stepped through, appearing at the head of the army next to his horse. Eztas was already down there, astride his horse and looking either bored or sullen. Probably sullen.

They were on the East side of the city and would need to go around the walls to the South to begin their march. Perivon had moved his army's camp from the North by the lake to the West on the highway. Lady Virtesa and Ezmith suspected it was because his scouts had discovered the training grounds of their new army and he wanted to be in a better position to retreat. Smart man.

A single horn blew from the front of the army, calling out in a strong, yet mournful tone, and the call was repeated throughout the army. Then the army began to march. The captains and wizards along with Eztas and Ezmith walked the horses at the front, then the first six battalions began to march, then the second six, the third six, and so on.

The first few steps were in perfect unison and made an impressive rhythm that filled Lady Virtesa with both exhilaration and trepidation. Such a force was a wonderful thing to control, the rhythm seemed to say, but what did it mean for the world? This part of the world had never known armies of this size. It had never known war of this scale.

Lady Virtesa's jaw tightened. She was the master of the four winds spoken of in the prophecy, and it spoke of change. She *would* continue fulfilling her destiny.

As the army continued to march and the battalions struggled a bit in curving around the wall, getting in each others' way, the sound of the marching feet got more muddled. She stayed on the wall walk until the last battalion had marched around to the side, going back and forth between gratitude for Clayara's blessing in raising this army, fear for the precedent she might be setting, and humility as she felt the burden of the people's loyalty.

Some of those men would likely die. They would die for a good cause, yes, and their deaths were not too high a price to pay for bringing the western region under her banner, but each one that died was another husband, father, or son who would be missed by their loved ones.

～

Perivon heard the galloping steps of a horse outside his tent and sighed, knowing what the news would be. He had been once again staring at a map of Mhairi, showing the walls and trying to solve the impossible puzzle of breaching the walls and taking the city. The guild wizards were getting antsy, and no wonder; they had thought to capture Ezmith that first day he returned from securing Redwood. This extended siege was not to their liking.

The problem was simply that the wizards created a stalemate. His wizards prevented Ezmith from moving out, and Ezmith's wizards prevented him from moving in. Vewen and Hindari were still mourning over the unexpected loss of their younger companion, Enaro, but they were more resolved than ever to bring Ezmith to justice.

But *how?* Especially with the news he knew he was about to receive, this was going to be one long, drawn-out conflict that he was no longer confident he would eventually win, despite the aid from the other wizards.

The tent flap flung open and Scout Hanley, out of breath, rushed in.

"They've begun marching, my Lord."

"How many?"

"We couldn't get close enough to tell for sure, but there could be as many as 10,000."

10,000? How is that possible? That was nearly three times what he had here – he'd left two companies in Dazbog and had another stationed in Bahadir.

He began running through scenarios in his mind – their army couldn't possibly be well-trained, so if the numbers were even his army would come out the better, but with such a large difference in numbers...his force would be wiped out, and they probably wouldn't even take as many Ambartans with them as they lost. A numbers advantage had a way of increasing in size during battle much like a storm over water.

Maybe if he found the right terrain...and could delay the battle until closer to sunset so the sun would be in his opponents eyes...no, it just wasn't possible. Too much to lose and far too little to gain. If he retreated back to Dazbog he could likely hold with the increased magical power he had gotten since the previous siege.

As long as trade was still flowing through Bahadir, he could hold Dazbog indefinitely, since he could be supplied by sea and most, if not all, the trade coming in could be diverted and still taken advantage of with only a little delay. Besides, Disote's ice trade had to be hurting with every merchant being forced to take their product by land all the way down to Redwood's port ever since the armistice ended.

Of course…there was the possibility that Ezmith would divert part of his huge army to taking Bahadir as well. With a Fold he could be there in an instant and have the city completely taken before Perivon even received word that something was happening down there.

Ezmith seemed too single-minded, like a horse with its blinders on, for such a move, and there wasn't much Perivon could do if he wasn't, so he just had to hope that Ezmith wouldn't think of that option. With luck, perhaps he would assume that Perivon had prepared for such an attack and decide it wasn't worth the risk.

"Sound the retreat. How much time do we have?"

"Perhaps an hour before they're on top of us."

"Order the men to break camp and be ready to march in 30 minutes. Anything not tied to a horse, wagon, or cart by then is getting left behind," Perivon ordered Hanley.

Hanley ran out of the tent as Perivon began rolling up the map. Back to Dazbog they would go, returning like the curved sticks used for hunting in Lierrey, the nation down on the other side of the mountains from the Wood Coast.

Perivon's two attendants entered the tent and began packing things up. Perivon started to pack up as well but was so bombarded by questions and issues as the army prepared to leave that he soon found himself outside his tent as the attendants gathered the rest up by themselves.

His men were well-trained, and the army was formed up and ready to march at exactly 30 minutes. Perivon ordered the retreat to begin, and a horn blew one short note followed by one long one. Perivon rode to the top of the hill that the highway curved to avoid, carrying a huge spyglass. A strong one, perhaps the strongest that any of the spyglass-makers made. It was two feet in length and had its own legs.

Holding the thing steady enough to see anything at distance was impossible even when you weren't astride a horse, so he quickly dismounted and set the three legs up on the top of the hill, then swiveled to look at where he could just see the approaching army in the distance, some two miles away.

The army leapt into view, and he had to turn the dial that brought the image back down in size a little to get a good view. His breath caught. He was not looking at an army 10,000 strong...he quickly did a rough count of one row of soldiers, then how many rows there were... By Clayara, there had to be double what Hanley had said!

How in the Inferno had the Virtesas been able to recruit such an army?

They must have sent riders to every corner of every land they controlled! With that many soldiers...Ezmith would still likely try to focus his efforts and take Dazbog first, but as soon as the siege stalled out for a few days, certainly no longer than a tenday, he would almost certainly move to take Bahadir.

Perivon hurried to take down the spyglass and get back on his horse. At least it would take a little longer for Ezmith to arrive at Dazbog; an army of 20,000 moved slower than an army of 10,000. Even so, he felt greater urgency to get behind his city's walls. Could they hold a siege against that many? He may have to emulate the Ambartan strategy and conscript all the able-bodied men in the cities. Dazbog and Bahadir were larger and more populous than any city in the West besides Novis Terram, and he could probably raise an army in each city that approached the size of Ambarta's.

How effective they would be...that would have to remain to be seen. How long he could pay and feed an army that size...that would also remain to be seen. He could likely secure loans from the nations they traded with across the Eres ocean. Cleononia had good relations with them and such assistance had offered in the past.

None of this pleased him. One of the ideas that had led Cleononia to prosperity was avoiding debt whenever possible. Cleononia had been debt-free since Perivon's grandfather's reign. While such a thing wasn't rare in this region, that was largely because none of the nations had anyone from whom they *could* borrow money. Most countries in other parts of the world seemed to think carrying debt to be part of the natural course of life.

He trotted his horse to the front of his army, being sure to wave and project confidence into his men. He didn't have much confidence about how things would move forward, but it was important that he pretend to at this moment. He needed his men to believe that they weren't retreating because they were outmatched; they were retreating to find the right spot to rain death upon their enemies.

Once at the front of the army, he slowed to a walk, and stared down the road, across relatively flat land with stands of trees following along small streams. His home. His lands. Ambarta would not keep them.

~

This road was spooky: there was no point in denying it any longer. The way the road narrowly cut along the natural ravine between hills so densely packed with trees and foliage made it seem like each day had only a few hours of sunshine. A fog hung over the road that made it difficult to see anything further out than about twenty yards. Ezren didn't recognize many of the trees and shrubs, though the woods he had lived in for two years were only a hundred and fifty miles away from here.

There was an odd chill in the air along with a humidity that was like entering a different world from Salimelish and the rest of Mountain Home.

It was late Planting, so it should have been much warmer, but Ezren tucked his cloak around him as he rode, holding the reins with one hand.

Alright, so the road was scary. That was that. It was just a scary road. So what? He'd been in scarier situations than this, situations where his life was *actually* in danger.

A rustling in the brush over to his right made him jerk on the reins so hard that Asteri snorted and whinnied, pulling to the left. Ezren kept her moving forward as he stared as hard and threateningly as he could at the bush that had rustled, the hand that had been holding his cloak closed now on his sword hilt.

He looked and listened as hard as he could, and it seemed that he could actually hear his horse's footsteps echoing. But that didn't make any sense. Sounds wouldn't carry nearly as far in that brush, and there weren't any rock faces or anything to create an echo. He listened harder.

No, what he was hearing was a second set of hooves, and they were getting louder. He peered ahead, squinting, with his hand still on his sword hilt in case the creature in the bush leapt out to eat him. It would be a relief to see another person.

Soon he began hearing the creak and thumps of a wagon, and soon after that the horse and wagon began to materialize out of the fog. Ezren let his breath out. It was just a merchant.

The horse-pulled wagon continued, and Ezren pulled Asteri to the right to make room for them to pass each other. The road was barely wide enough, and Ezren wondered what happened when two wagons met here.

He smiled at the merchant, but the man glowered back. He was a short, squat man with a face that had more rolls of fat on his cheeks and neck than made sense compared with the rest of his body. He was very tanned, as most traveling merchants were, and he glared at Ezren as they rode past each other, never letting his eyes leave Ezren's.

Ezren's smile faded as the merchant passed, wondering what on earth he had done to earn this man's suspicion. Perhaps suspicion was a safer norm on this road than friendliness. Ezren looked back several times after the merchant had disappeared into the fog, making sure that nothing and no one was coming up behind him.

It had been dark since early afternoon, but the darkness began to become more...complete, as though there had been small amounts of light reflecting into the ravine and now even those were fading. He didn't want to spend a night here alone in the woods, but he would rather spend the night by a warm, bright fire than continue to ride alone in pitch blackness.

He approached a small hollow in the side of the ravine, which looked to have been used as a campsite many times before. There was a firepit ringed with stones in the center and three or four flat spots that had been cut into the slope for sleeping. There was even a small pile of firewood stacked against the Northern wall of the enclosure.

With how steep the slope was all around, Ezren didn't want to go traipsing around looking for more deadfall, but he *did* want to have a nice big fire all night long, and that small pile of firewood was not nearly enough.

There was room for Asteri in the hollow as well, so Ezren dismounted, led her into it, then unsaddled and hobbled her. The darkness was getting more and more complete as Ezren stretched his legs and back. After several full days in the saddle riding, he was realizing that he wasn't as accustomed to horseback as he had thought. He wished he'd thought to pack a cushion or something.

He had, however, thought to pack an axe, which had proved to be a wise addition to his supplies. He took off his sword belt, putting the magnificent sword down on the ground next to the saddlebags, then removed the shield from his back and placed it alongside.

He pulled the short-handled axe from the pack and looked around, trying to see if there was any deadfall that would be easy to reach. He walked a little ways back down the road the way he had come and, sure enough, there was a fallen tree that he could chop limbs off of and get himself plenty of fuel for his fire.

He got lost in the work for a bit, letting his mind wander as he chopped and chopped, then took armfuls of wood back to the enclosure. The darkness continued to creep in, but each time he stopped to notice and think to himself that the sun must be fully down by now, it seemed he was wrong as the darkness continued to grow. Perhaps he had stopped earlier than he thought.

Well, no matter. Assuming the maps he'd seen of these hills were accurate, this ravine was not long enough that he would need to spend more than one night in it, even if he had stopped early.

He brought the last load of firewood back to his campsite and got the fire going. He had a healthy fire and was just beginning to dig in his pack for some food when he heard hoofbeats coming from up the road. He froze, listening. It wasn't just one horse. It was at least two, perhaps three or even four horses. He adjusted how his sword rested on the ground so that it was near his hand, ready to be drawn at a moment's notice.

The hoofbeats came closer. Because of the wall of the hollow, Ezren couldn't see very far up the road, but it didn't take long for the horses to begin to materialize in the fog. It was a group of riders. Four men, riding down this road at night. They had probably been making for this hollow, which meant that they knew the area fairly well, and they probably would want to share the site with Ezren.

Some company wouldn't be amiss, in Ezren's mind, though he would have preferred men he had met before. Then he remembered the merchant he'd passed earlier, and wondered whether men like these four were why suspicion was the standard response when meeting a stranger on this road. Or maybe the merchant was just a curmudgeon.

The four men, whom Ezren could hear having a quiet conversation, led their horses towards the enclosure and Ezren's fire. Only as they approached did the fire provide enough light for him to see details.

They were rough men, unshaven with long hair, wearing simple clothing. Their faces were scarred in multiple places and one man was wearing an eye patch. Truthfully, they looked an awful lot like soldiers. What made Ezren uneasy, though, was that their leader had a big, almost wicked smile, while the other three glowered at him.

He considered giving up the campsite preemptively. If he didn't sleep here, though, where would he go? If there was another hollow or place to sleep further up the road, then these men would probably have stopped there.

He tried not to look like he distrusted the men and stood to greet them.

"Hello," he said as they looked at him, four frowns with four sets of eyebrows drawn down.

The lead rider dismounted without replying and looked around, his eyes stopped at the much-larger wood pile and at Ezren's saddlebags full of supplies. His smile stayed big. Not a friendly smile, though, the kind of smile that made chills go up Ezren's spine.

"Hello, boy," he said, looking up at Ezren. "Thank you for resupplying our campsite for us. If you leave now we'll let you keep the horse."

What was the man talking about? "Pardon, good sir," Ezren began, "but this is my campsite for the night. I arrived hours ago."

"Ah, but you see, you broke the rules, boy," the man said, smiling and wagging a finger. "This is *our* campsite. We made the firepit, we leveled out the spots for sleeping, and we cut the firewood. We appreciate you adding to our stack, but we'll need to take your supplies as payment for the time you've spent using our spot."

Ezren bent down and pulled his sword from his sheath. He doubted he could take all four men at once, but if it came to fighting hopefully they would try him one or two at a time. He stood, about to speak, but stopped with his mouth open as he heard the sound of three bowstrings creaking, almost in unison.

He looked past the leader to the other riders, letting his eyes adjust for a moment, and seeing that each of them had an arrow nocked, drawn, and pointed directly at him.

"There're two ways out of this, boy. You leave right now, without a fuss, and you can still keep your horse, or we put three arrows in you and we dump your body in the woods. You choose."

Ezren was stuck – he had no idea what to do. He was terrified of being shot; that was apparently a very slow and painful way to die, but he could not leave all his supplies behind. Did the man mean his sword and shield as well? His flint and steel? His axe? His bedroll? His food? How was he supposed to survive for the rest of the trip without even his bow and twine to hunt and trap food? How many days was it to the next town? Would it matter how close if he didn't have any coin either?

He had to take some kind of risk, so he took the safest one he could think of. He raised his hands defensively, stuck the tip of the sword in the ground and rested it back against the wall of the hollow, then bent down slowly. In a sudden, swift movement, he grabbed his shield and threw it in front of himself, squatting down so that it provided coverage for his entire body.

The sudden movement caused one of the riders to shoot, the arrow bouncing off the shield in two pieces.

"Hold, fool," the leader said casually to the rider who had fired. Looking back at Ezren, crouching there with only his eyes showing above the shield, he chuckled. "Please continue. I'm very curious as to what the next step in your plan is. Are you going to try and throw rocks at us while squatting behind that shield? Perhaps you're one of those young sword prodigies and you'll take on all four of us at once if we come close."

Ezren didn't respond. He couldn't think of anything to say because he had no plan beyond what he had already done, and he suspected that the leader knew that.

The leader shrugged. "Well, I'm tempted to let you squat there for as long as you can. I'm sure we can take our ease for longer than your legs can hold you up there, but I'm tired *now*, and I want some dinner *now*. So," he said, turning to his men, "Terrel, come around to this side, Anton, go to the other side, and Rees stay with me. He can't cover himself from every angle. Kill him and let's get on with the night."

Ezren watched, terrified, trying desperately to think of what he could do. The men dismounted and began to move to either side as Ezren looked from one to the other. Suddenly, he heard a loud rustling in a bush at the top of the back wall of the hollow. Everyone looked up, then a bowstring twanged and Anton, the one who had been coming around the outside to shoot him, stumbled backwards and fell, an arrow sticking out of his chest. A second arrow passed right where he had been standing, then, just a moment later, a knife came spinning out of the darkness and thudded into a tree root right next to the leader's shoulder, missing him by a hair.

Ezren leaned back against the dirt wall of the hollow, staying as small as possible with his shield angled towards where the arrows had come from.

"Run!" The leader yelled. "It's a trap!"

Anton got himself to his feet, arrow still sticking out of him, and ran to his horse, only a bit slower than the other three. Ezren watched Anton in amazement. With an arrow in his chest he should be barely able to move and dead within the hour. He watched as the riders rode away as quickly as they could, then looked everywhere around him – up where the bush had rustled, then out towards where the arrows and knife had come from.

A full minute after the riders had left, Ezren heard the clip-clop of a single horse's hoofbeats coming closer. Ezren stayed squatting behind his shield, though his legs felt as though they were on fire, and looked under Asteri's belly to see the legs of the horse as they walked towards the center of the hollow. He looked up as the rider passed beyond Asteri and saw the newcomer's face.

It was Ben Rider! Wearing one of his signature smiles, casual and just a little smug. Ezren felt his eyes widen in shock. What was Ben doing here?

"Evening, Ezren," Ben said. "So, uh, what are you doing out here all by yourself?"

Ezren stood, shaking out his legs. "How did you find me?"

Ben laughed, but stayed on his horse Fengari. "Oh, well see that was the easy part. The hard part has been figuring out what in the Inferno you think you're doing running off by yourself like that. So why don't you save me the trouble and just tell me what's going on?"

Ezren lowered his shield arm and nodded. As Ben dismounted and began to unsaddle Fengari, Ezren explained.

"So, you know my father was killed, right?" He asked.

Ben gave him a sarcastic look. "No, Ezren, you see for the last tenday I've been hiding in a tree in Meand with my eyes shut and my ears plugged with wax. Of *course* I know about your father. So why are you out here futzing around? You know you missed his funerary rites?"

The man's demeanor was infuriating sometimes. It was very Ben-like for him to make light of all this, but this was *his father* they were talking about, and what Ezren was doing was very important. He put the shield down and leaned back against the wall as Ben continued to work on his saddle.

"I'll thank you not to make jokes right now, Ben. I'm on my way to find some new magic that can tell us what happened that night. Mellion said there was no magic that existed that could do it."

Ben put the saddle down, looked at him incredulously, then sat down on top of his pack, gesturing as he spoke.

"You're telling me that you left everything, your entire life, without telling any of the people who care about you, and came on a dangerous journey all alone to try and find something that the one expert you have talked to says doesn't exist? Where are you going to even find this new magic?"

Ezren started to sit, then thought better of it, wanting to stay in control of the conversation. "I'm going to start at Glacies Castle. Seems like if there's any place that would have a record of some magic no one knows about it would be there. And I've been doing just fine on my own so far, thank you."

Ben scoffed. "Yes, you'd be finely dead by now if I hadn't shown up when I did."

"Well, yes..." Ezren started, frustrated that Ben seemed to be intentionally missing the point. "But other than that I've done fine. Now, even *if* I meet anyone else who means me harm, I'll be more prepared."

"What do you mean 'if', Ezren? Those men I scared off for you, that's how most men are. It takes society and usually a woman or three to stamp that out of most men. You were raised by an incredible man surrounded by exceptional people. Men like that Walsh you and your father caught a couple years ago, men like these jackknives," he jerked his thumb behind where the men had fled, "they're the rule. You and me, we're the exception."

That seemed clearly wrong to Ezren. No matter how many people he'd met there had always been more good ones than bad.

Ben held his hands out wide. "Why do you think I chose a job where I don't have to talk to anybody? More people than you think will take from you just because they can, and the ones who fancy themselves good people will still stand by and let you get robbed by someone else just so they don't get robbed themselves."

This conversation seemed to have gotten off-track. "Fine, Ben, I'll be more careful as I go, but I'm still going." He paused, trying to think of what else he could say. "I have to find out who killed my father."

"Eh, Inferno, Ezren, they already think they know who it was!"

Ezren stood up straighter, giving him a clearer view of Ben over the fire. "What are you talking about, Ben?"

"They think it was your damn brother! Ezmith!"

"What?! That's ridiculous! Why would they think that?!" Ezren cried, sitting down abruptly as his knees gave way.

Ben sighed and rubbed his face with his hands. "Look, they didn't want to tell you because they thought you'd do something stupid like, I don't know, *run off by yourself*!"

After a pause, Ben continued. "Your brother was there earlier that day. He came to threaten King Radomir that if he didn't take his wizards off the battlefield with Cleononia that Ezmith would kill him. Your father was in the meeting at the time. Ezmith left right after and had been gone for hours when your father was killed, but with those Folds of his he could have come back to the city with no one knowing."

Ezren tried to think this idea through, sorting his thoughts as they whirled. His heart was beating as fast as though he had just run a mile. Ezmith had visited? He knew where they were? Could Ezmith have killed his father? He was surely capable of it...but how would Ezmith have known where his father was going to be?

"Do they know it was Ezmith, or just think it was?" He asked quietly.

Ben took a deep breath. "They just think it was," he replied just as quietly. "They have no proof, and there isn't really a way to get any, either. No one saw anything but a hooded figure enter the alley after your father."

Ezren stared into the fire. It was starting to get low again. Did his brother kill his father? He could believe that, sure. But there were reasons to doubt as well. His brother had a reputation for being a harsh commander and had ordered the deaths of captured soldiers, but rumors always exaggerated. He had a hard time envisioning Ezmith killing someone in cold blood. His father had told him that Ezmith had killed their old messenger, the one whose murder had been falsely blamed on Ezren and his father. But Ezren hadn't seen him do the deed, and the Ezmith he remembered was impatient, apathetic towards him, sometimes antagonistic, but never truly malicious, and certainly not *murderous*.

No, this was not enough to condemn Ezmith, nor enough to relieve Ezren of his responsibility to find out who killed his father. He needed to be sure. He needed to continue on.

He looked up at Ben, who was shaking his head already. "You're going to keep going, aren't you?"

Ezren nodded.

"Why, Ezren? Why do you need to know? Do you crave revenge so badly?"

The why was simple – he may not ever be able to see or speak with his father again, and it was not right that the man responsible would walk free. That was it, wasn't it? He continued to stare into the fire as though it would have answers for him.

"Because…" he began. "Because I don't know what else to do. If I don't do this, then what? Just go back to the Academy? Classes are about to stop for the Midsummer break. If I had stayed, then everything I saw would be reminders that my da was gone."

Ben looked at him, waiting for him to continue.

"I guess...I guess I just didn't know what I was *supposed* to do. I've never *not* had my father with me. I thought I would have a lifetime to repay him for everything he sacrificed for me, but now, the only thing I can still do for him is find his killer."

He took a breath, then finished, "At least doing this I know what I'm supposed to do."

Ben rested his head back against the dirt wall of the hollow. "Yes, I can see how that makes sense."

They were both silent for a time, with only the crackling of the fire breaking the stillness.

"Thank you," Ezren said, breaking the silence.

Ben eyes flicked up at him without his head lifting up. "For what?"

"Saving me from those men. I can't believe they would just kill me and take all my stuff. Are people really like that?"

"Honestly? Yes. People are really like that. Not all people, and maybe not even as many as I think there are, but in my experience, when most people are offered an apple they run off with a bushel."

Ezren didn't reply as he considered Ben's words. As he thought, his stomach grumbled. Oh! He'd never eaten! He turned and dug in his pack to get some of the waybread and dried meat he had packed up.

He asked Ben if he wanted any, but Ben had already supped and was ready to sleep. The scout wasn't worried about those men returning because they would assume Ben was part of a larger party. Even so, he suggested that Ezren stay up a while longer to take a watch. If the riders did come back they probably wouldn't wait longer than the first watch.

Ezren was tired, but he had plenty to keep his mind occupied while he kept watch, so he didn't mind staying up a little while longer.

Ben settled into his blankets and Ezren threw another log on the fire. There wasn't much wind, and the hollow kept a lot of the heat from the fire in, so the otherwise chilly night was quite pleasant.

He was surprised that Ben had come all this way to find him. How long was the scout going to stay with him? It hadn't sounded like he was going to try to drag Ezren home against his will, but he hadn't said anything about accompanying him either.

His answer came in the morning, as they prepared their breakfast over a fire. Ben had brought a sack of oats and, surprisingly, a small bag of sugar. Combined with water heated over the fire, it made a delicious breakfast. Ezren had eaten this before in the castle and in the barracks, but he had no idea it was so easy to make.

They discussed Ezren's plans, and Ben explained that he had tracked Ezren of his own accord, to learn for himself what Ezren was planning and ensure that he was well. The king had other duties for all his scouts, as a second war with Comperr was seeming more and more likely, so he could not accompany Ezren on his quest.

They would part ways upon breaking camp; Ben back on his way to Novis Terram to report that Ezren was alive and well for the moment, and Ezren on his way to Robinton, and then to Glacies Castle.

As they each saddled their horses, Ezren found himself reluctant to leave Ben's company. He had to, of course; he couldn't accompany Ben back to Novis Terram any more than Ben could go with him to Robinton. He looked over at Ben as the scout tightened the saddle on Fengari carefully.

"Ben," Ezren said. "Please don't tell anyone where I'm going."

"Wasn't planning on it," Ben said without looking at him. "Though the ambassador might put me under the knife to get it out of me. They'd just try to stop you."

"And why aren't you stopping me?"

He paused, resting one hand on the saddle. "You need to learn for yourself how stupid this idea is. I can tell you over and over how hot the fire is but, in the end, you'll have to stick your hand in it to truly understand. If I tied you up and dragged you back, you'd just escape the first chance you got and be right back out here. If we managed to keep you in one spot long enough to give up, you'd spend the rest of your life resentful and bitter. At us, and at yourself too, most likely."

He resumed his work, shaking his head.

"Nah, much better for you to go on this quest of yours. Who knows, maybe you really will find some kind of new magic, and then you'll have your answers. And if you don't, you'll still learn a lot about surviving on your own, and that's a good thing to know a lot about."

Rider mounted up, clicked his tongue to Fengari and nudged him with his heels. After going only a few feet, he pulled up and turned himself in the saddle to look at Ezren.

"Be careful in Robinton, Ezren. They're very...passionate...about their rules."

Ezren watched him turn and continue on, then pulled himself onto Asteri and turned her the other direction.

The strange ravine began to smooth and level out when the sun was highest in the sky, and Ezren took his midday meal a little ways off in the trees. The road seemed even more lonely after Ezren bade farewell to Ben. His thoughts were jumbled; he thought about his friendship with Ben Rider, how Ben had followed him all the way here just to make sure he was alright, and what he'd said about Ezmith.

He tried to focus his thoughts on more important things like how to avoid confrontations like what had happened the night before and firming up his plans for the rest of his trip, but it took effort. He didn't *have* to travel on the road at all. He knew how to survive on his own in the wild just fine, and he was much less afraid of a bear or skick than he was of a group of bandits.

He made the decision to make his way to Robinton city using the road, then travel through the wild between Robinton and Glacies Castle. Stopping in Robinton would allow him to resupply and pick up some oats and sugar to supplement what food he already had.

He also committed to take time each day to practice the sword forms, and each night to take the time to scout out a defensible camp-site and take precautions should ill-intentioned people come upon him. He couldn't let himself slack on his skills just because he was traveling. He wished he'd thought to bring more books; it would be nice to have something to read about when he was too tired to stay on his feet.

He rode through the afternoon, following the walk, trot, gallop, trot, walk pattern that Rider had taught him, and the city of Robinton soon came into view. He considered staying in the city for the night, but decided to camp just outside instead. He still wasn't sure whether the soldiers would be on the lookout for him, but he felt safer just going through long enough to buy supplies and heading straight back out.

Stopping early made it easier for him to start his new commitments; he took a solid half an hour to find the right campsite, a hollow with a massive fallen log across the top that created a nook he could stay in, so that any danger would have to come from the front. There were no signs that the spot had ever been used as a campsite before. He strung his bow and placed it conveniently next to his arrows within arms reach.

He probably shouldn't keep his bow strung every night, but it was old anyway and he'd been considering either buying a replacement or even taking the time to make a new one of his own.

He kept the fire small and put it out as soon as his food was cooked. The nights this far north were still chilly, and would be until the height of Midsummer, but he had plenty of blankets to keep him warm without a fire. Once the sun went down, the fire would probably be a beacon to his location. His goal now was to come and go without it ever being clear that someone was there. If Ben Rider could track him all this way, maybe someone else could too.

Despite, or perhaps because of, the precautions, Ezren slept well that night, and woke just as the sky was beginning to lighten. It was the sounds of the birds that woke him. They were exceptionally loud today, at least in comparison to the previous night in the ravine, which had been eerily silent. Today the birds seemed to be shouting gleefully at one another in an unending barrage of sound.

After a quick breakfast, he led Asteri back to the road and mounted up. He could have ridden to the road, but there was no need to increase the risk of an injury to his horse. His plan to stay off the roads after Robinton was going to be risky enough.

The city of Robinton, capital of the nation of Robinton, had gleaming, pristine white walls perhaps half the height of the walls of Novis Terram. According to one of his school books, the builders had hired wizards to seek out only white granite all throughout the Western region. The outside of the city wall was almost perfectly smooth.

It looked like it would hold up well enough against an invading army, but it certainly wouldn't stay so pretty. The builders had clearly never expected to actually use the wall to keep enemies out, and so far, some 300 years later, they hadn't.

The gates to the city were thrown open wide, and the closer Ezren got to the gate the busier the road became. He rode in only a few paces behind a man walking next to an ox pulling a cart and only a few paces ahead of the beginning of a long caravan of wagons that all had the same merchant's crest painted on them.

There were shops set up outside the gate, but none seemed to be selling any of the things Ezren needed.

Just inside the gate, the first thing Ezren noticed was how quiet it was. There were plenty of people around, though less than he was used to in Novis Terram, but nobody was shouting. Shopkeepers stood pleasantly, or in the case of one small, spindly man, unpleasantly, looking around at passersby. When people approached, they spoke quietly, and there was a little paper stuck on or near everything for sale that listed the price.

A large bulletin board came up on his right, and he pulled up on Asteri's reins to read it.

"Let it be known that within the walls of Robinton City, in addition to the other laws of Robinton Country, there will be no tolerance for:
1. Loud noises or shouting
2. Haggling
3. Horses or pack animals not equipped with a stercore bag

Well that explained the lack of shouting, but what was a stercore bag? Stercore meant feces, so were they talking about some sort of sack to catch the horse's feces? He looked around, and saw that, indeed, every horse besides his own had a small bag that cinched to their saddle and hung right on and under their horse's rear end.

A sign like that would have been a lot more useful *before* he entered the city. He looked around, hoping to see a vendor that had these stercore bags for sale, but none of them appeared to sell them. Then he realized – *that's* what the shops outside the gate had been selling!

Looking for a way to turn Asteri around, he noticed two guards frowning at him, wearing uniforms that looked like they could blend into the outer wall like chameleons. Well, one of them was frowning at Ezren, the other was frowning at Asteri's hindquarters. They started for him.

Should he run? He hadn't known about the rule until now! He'd buy a bag as soon as he could! He looked around furtively. There was no way he could turn Asteri around and get back down the cobblestones and through the gate before those guards caught him. He dismounted, hoping to be able to speak with them face-to-face.

"Boy," a gruff voice said just as he landed. He turned and smiled at the guard.

"Yes, Captain?" Ezren replied in his most innocent voice.

"Are you aware that you are in violation of city code three by not equipping a proper stercore bag on your horse or pack animal while within the walls of Robinton City?" Asked the one with a bushy mustache over his frown.

"I- uh, I just became aware, sir. This is my first visit to Robinton City and I just stopped to read the sign. I was just looking around to find a place to purchase one. Perhaps you could point me in the right direction?"

The guards snorted in unison. "We weren't born yesterday, son," the mustached guard replied.

"Besides, ignorance of the law is not an excuse for violation of the law," the other guard, shorter and clean-shaven, said, sounding as though he were quoting someone.

"Punishment for the first offence is three days in the city jail. You'll be returned your horse and belongings after you're released," The mustached guard said casually, as though three days in jail were of no consequence.

"Three days? That's absurd!" Ezren yelped without thinking.

To his shock, the guards' hands went to their sword hilts. He took a deep breath, remembering Ben's warning and wondering what could possibly make these guards behave this way.

"Please, good sirs, I simply want to buy a stercore bag and continue with my business. I'll get it on my horse as quickly as I can find one," he said, trying to keep his voice calm. "I mean, it's not like she's dropped her stercore yet so no harm done, yes?"

No sooner had the words left his mouth than he heard Asteri whinny, sounding suspiciously like a snicker, and the tell-tale soft splatter of horse manure falling to the ground. He closed his eyes. Curse this horse.

"I suppose there's no chance of me just...cleaning that up?" He asked, opening his eyes.

The guards were both red-faced and livid. They shook their heads without speaking.

Ezren knew he needed to think clearly. He needed to be able to weigh his options, but all he could think of were the riders who had tried to attack him two nights ago, and what Ben had said about most people being that way. Who was to say these guards weren't the same? Putting a uniform on didn't change a person, did it? Would they even give Asteri back? What about his supplies? Would they even let him out of jail?

Panic rose in his mind. He couldn't afford to lose everything; he'd have to pick up from nothing and he'd never figure out who killed his father. There was nothing in this city that he needed. Plenty that he wanted, sure, but nothing he couldn't finish his journey without, thanks to his stop in Salimelish. His eyes leapt to the gates, perhaps fifty feet away, and all the people in between.

The guards must have been able to tell what was going through his mind, because they each grabbed one of his arms and turned him around roughly.

Looking back, he could not believe what he did. It was as though he didn't have control of himself anymore, and it felt more like he was watching it happen than actually doing it.

He let them turn him around and push him up against Asteri, but he widened his feet, and as they tried to put his wrists in irons he kicked backwards with his right foot, hitting the shorter guard in the shin, which caused him to loosen his grip on Ezren's right wrist. Ezren yanked his wrist free and swung his hand back at the other guard's neck, which was exposed under his helmet.

Ezren ducked the punch that came from the guard he'd kicked, then dived and tackled him to the ground. At this point, people around began to notice, and he heard the gasps of several people. Ezren knew he had no more than a second or two before the mustached guard was on him, so he rolled to the far side of the shorter guard and hopped to his feet, much more spryly than his fully-armored combatant.

Now he needed another idea. He unsheathed his sword to keep the guards at bay for a moment while he looked around for options. He may not have been to Robinton before, but he had plenty of experience running around the market at Novis Terram, and all these permanent shops had rollout roofs with…yes! A thick rope tied off at about shoulder-height on the wall just to his left.

The shorter guard had gotten to his feet and both guards had drawn their swords.

"Think about what you're doing, boy," the mustached guard growled. "You're digging yourself a lot deeper than just a code three violation."

"You will not imprison me over a minor, unintentional, offense," Ezren replied.

"Oh, it's not minor anymore. Now you've attacked Guards. If you do not come willingly, we will be within our rights to cut you down where you stand," The shorter guard replied warningly.

Cut him down?! Should he surrender and take his chances? Even if he could beat these two guards at once, he had no desire to kill anyone. Certainly not over something so trivial, at least. Maybe he should just put down his sword.

No! My life is my own!

"Well, come on then!" Ezren yelled, surprising himself with his ferocity.

The guards stepped forward, staying together. Just a bit further now...Perfect. Ezren lunged, let his arm swing wide at the predictable parry from the mustached guard, then did two light slashes at the shorter guard, both on the guard's right side, then stepped back to dodge the predictable thrust from Mustache, and back again to dodge the slash that came from Shorty.

Ezren turned from the guards, tossed his sword from his right hand to his left, grabbed the rope tied off on the wall, and cut the rope with the sword all in one smooth motion. He gripped the rope as hard as he could, flexing every muscle in his upper body to keep himself straight as he launched upward with the rope, kicking off the wall to give himself momentum in the direction he needed.

Once his feet were about level with Asteri's head, he let go of the rope, falling forward and down towards Asteri's saddle. He landed almost perfectly, though a bit too far to the front. The pain coming from his crotch nearly made him swoon and give up right then and there, but he managed to get a hand out to grab on to the reins and gave Asteri a nudge.

People right next to his horse jumped out of the way immediately. For the others... "EVERYBODY MOVE!!!" he roared in his loudest, meanest voice. People looked to him, saw the horse moving their direction, and scattered.

He rode Asteri at a full gallop to the gate. Behind him he heard Mustache shouting: "Stop him! Stop that boy!"

He had no idea how far they would pursue him, so he veered off the road immediately after leaving the gate and only slowed Asteri to a trot after they were under the cover of the trees. Once safely in the shelter of the foliage, he turned to look behind to where the city gate stood, about a half mile away.

There was no sign of pursuit, so Ezren paused to catch his breath and process what had just happened.

What on Quilara had he just done? He was now officially a criminal, though at least he hadn't told the guards his name. They should have no way of identifying him beyond a rough sketch.

He went North, around the city walls, and turned to head West towards the Thousand river. There were a few smaller communities farther up the north road from Robinton, but as far as he knew, crossings were fewer and farther between up there, and he was anxious to cross the river into Disote as soon as possible.

Not only that, but those communities consisted mostly of secondary estates of the wealthiest nobility and merchants. If there was anywhere he'd stand out like a nug beetle in a bowl of oats, it would be there.

The maps he had found had not been detailed enough to include unofficial crossings on the Thousand river, so he had no idea how far up or down river he'd have to ride once he got there. At the moment, he just wanted to avoid conflicts, and going cross-country seemed the best way.

He could always veer back south after passing the city and take the highway to Orjan and then up the rest of the way...but he felt more comfortable out here away from the highway. On the road were more people who could try to take his stuff. More guards and soldiers who he would risk offending. On this route, he could virtually guarantee that he could pass unnoticed, perhaps all the way to Glacies Castle, but at least to Orjan.

He looked forward. The land trended downhill from here, as he was riding away from the base of the mountains and towards the flatter plains of the rest of the Western region.

CHAPTER 9: THE TURNING OF LUCK

Perivon led his force in through the gate at a trot. Hopefully the word he'd sent ahead to have all able-bodied men armed and ready to defend the city had been promulgated. He glanced up and around as he rode past and saw that there did indeed seem to be a large number of men manning the wall and towers on either side of the gate.

Perivon dismounted and handed Dansher's reins to an attendant, already walking as quickly as he could to the top of the wall.

"Lieutenant Nyou!" He barked, unable to keep the anger and urgency out of his voice.

The head of Lieutenant Nyou appeared above the rampart on the rear of the wall.

"I'm here, my Lord," he called back.

"Is the city ready to defend?" Perivon asked as he continued to climb the stairs, two at a time.

"Yes, sir. All posts are manned with as much again in reserves, and that's without the soldiers you bring with you."

Perivon reached the top and stared out, where he could just barely make out the Ambartan army off in the distance. It looked much smaller and less threatening from this far away.

"What of the engineers? Have they had any luck with the Ambartan war machine?" Perivon asked, staring out.

"Not yet, sir. Last they told me, they thought the assembly was missing some kind of counterweight."

"Well," Perivon began, "For now we hope that Ezmith is too impatient to wait for them to build another one of their own. He may think he can take the city quickly with sheer overwhelm. That could buy us at least a few days."

Lieutenant Nyou was staring out at the approaching mass, his mouth open. The sight was a different sort of terrifying; where it seemed there wasn't just a risk of injury, failure, or death, but an inevitability of it. Like trying to stop a taifeng with an umbrella.

This city was filled with defenders, however, and he had a lot more than just an umbrella to stop this storm.

He stood next to Nyou in silence, watching as the army came closer. By Clayara, he was tired. He should go get some sleep, but he continued to watch, standing straight with his shoulders back, as the army approached, fanning out to completely fill the width of the peninsula, well out of bowshot.

His mind whirled with defensive ideas, and he had half a mind to try every single one and hope that something worked. One thing was for sure, he would get no sleep tonight.

The second siege of Dazbog had begun.

~

With the army once again on the march, Mhairi felt almost empty and quiet compared to how it had been when filled with soldiers. The Lady Virtesa and her escort went down to the mayor's palace to the main audience chamber, where the mayor of Mhairi should be taking petitions.

It was almost always best to leave the existing power structure in place after conquering a nation. Keep things as much the same as you could, then make sure that any changes were seen as overall for the better. Mhairi's loyalty was already nearly complete. Even if Ezmith were to fail in taking the rest of Cleononia, Mhairi's own citizens would likely choose the easier and better lives that came from being part of Ambarta.

The walk wasn't a long one, but it gave her a few minutes to reflect. Things had changed a great deal since their first conquest in the Wood Coast years ago. She'd gotten much better at claiming the loyalty of a conquered people.

She had just entered the mayor's palace when a messenger came bearing a silver tray with an envelope on it. The messenger bowed low and held the tray up so she could take the letter from it.

"A letter for you, Lady Virtesa," the messenger said with her face to the floor.

She really needed to have another conversation with the Mayor. She had told him already that insisting on such formality was unnecessary. She wasn't Clayara, after all, and didn't expect servants to avert their eyes and fold themselves in half. And a *silver platter?* For a *letter?* Couldn't they just hand it to her?

She held in her sigh, the messenger was likely just doing as she'd been instructed, and took the letter off the tray, taking it into a side sitting chamber to read. She was glad she did. She reached a chair just in time for her knees to give way.

Timot was dead.

She kept reading. Killed in an alley in Novis Terram.

What of Ezren? She frantically scanned the rest of the letter, searching for his name. Finally, there at the very bottom...his current whereabouts were unknown. He'd disappeared from the castle several days after Timot's death. He had been alive the last anyone had seen him, but he'd been missing for several days when the message was written. She let out a breath she hadn't realized she'd been holding. The boy had probably just run off, perhaps to grieve.

She double-checked the signature line. Yes, this was her informant within the castle itself. He would have the most accurate information.

Timot, her husband of over 20 years, was dead.

Tears welled up in her eyes. Timot had always been a good man, and by all reports had become a great one after leaving Ambarta. She would not have believed the stories of his exploits in Mountain Home's war with Comperr if they hadn't been corroborated by multiple sources.

But was that the source of her sadness? Partially, yes, but some came from how this would affect Ezren. She had not seen him since he was only ten years old, but he'd been a compassionate, sensitive child and likely still was. How would he fare now that he was, in effect, orphaned? She knew enough of the court in Novis Terram to know that he'd be looked after, but there would undoubtedly be a hole in his heart moving forward.

Should she send for him? No, of course not. He would be an unnecessary distraction for the time being, and would be in real danger from Ezmith. Perhaps after taking Cleononia she could reach out.

She didn't regret sentencing them to death all those years ago, though she very much regretted that it had been necessary, and she'd found a certain...peace...in knowing that they were actually alive and, by all accounts, thriving. It had brought her happiness that fate had decided they hadn't needed to die in order for her to fulfill her destiny.

So she let herself weep. Ezmith was far away and occupied, and she was alone in the sitting room while her attendants waited outside. She wept for Timot's fate, for Ezren's predicament, and for her own loss.

As she re-read the letter looking for details of Timot's death, it was clear to her that Ezmith had done the deed.

She recalled his behavior in the days after his 'diplomatic' visit to Novis Terram. He'd been...off. There had been moments where he seemed unburdened and had actually made a joke, which she had rarely known him to do, then other moments where he snapped disproportionately to setbacks or bad news. It had faded over the last few days, and now she had an explanation for his behavior.

He'd been conflicted over what he'd done.

Part of him had felt a great weight lifted off his shoulders at the death of his father, and satisfaction that he had been the one to cause it. The rest of him had likely been filled with various negative emotions –

sadness at his own loss of the father he'd known his entire life, resentment at Timot for not being the father he'd wished he was, and perhaps a bit of guilt for doing something so clearly wrong and unprovoked.

Lady Virtesa wiped her tears and sat up straighter. This revelation was indeed disturbing, and represented a significant escalation in Ezmith's concerning behavior. She'd looked the other way when he'd killed before because he'd been strategic – removing individuals who stood in their way somehow, like the former Lord and Lady of the Wood Coast.

But this...Timot had been no threat to them. They had discussed it at length and reached the conclusion together. His death would serve no valuable purpose until and unless they actually came to conflict with Mountain Home directly, and even then there was little advantage that Timot could have given Radomir that he wouldn't have already provided.

So what had happened? Why had Ezmith done this?

She thought back to a conversation she'd had with Timot long ago, when Ezmith had still been a teenager, that now seemed chillingly prophetic.

"Look," Timot said, hefting what looked to be a dead cat onto the table in their dining room.

"Inferno, Timot! Get that disgusting thing off the table!" Kimaya replied.

"This disgusting thing is Ezmith's handiwork," Timot replied, looking down at her from a standing position.

"What do you mean? Ezmith killed this cat?" Kimaya asked, concerned.

Timot nodded. "I caught him just now. He didn't lie about it, just told me that he wanted to see what happened when a cat died."

She stared at the cat. It had been sliced open down the entire belly, and by the looks of it, a few of the organs were missing. Perhaps they'd just fallen out as Timot had recklessly flailed it around on his way here. Why would Ezmith have done this? He was a very intelligent and inquisitive boy. More than likely he'd just been curious about the insides of a cat. That was all.

"It's just a cat, Timot," she said, meeting his gaze and shrugging.

His eyes widened in surprise and he sat down unceremoniously. "Just a cat,

Kimaya? Just a cat? Before it was just an ant, just a fly, just a butterfly. Then it was 'just' a mouse, 'just' a rat. Now it's 'just' a cat? There's something terribly wrong with that boy, and we can't afford to ignore it any longer."

She waved his protests away. "Stop being so dramatic. He's not hurting anyone, and we'll just tell him not to do it again. He always obeys the rules."

Timot slumped back in his chair, and spoke, almost to himself. "How do you tell someone the sky is blue when they insist that it is green?"

She didn't respond, and started to go back to her meal, then stopped as she once again looked at the dead cat on the table. Her appetite was nowhere to be found. She put down her silverware and Timot rubbed his face with his hands.

"Someday, Kimaya," he said. "Someday, it won't be a cat. Someday it will be a person."

She waved him off again. "That's ridiculous and you know it."

"Ridiculous? Kimaya, there was a boy in the village I grew up in who did much the same. In the end, he killed his mother and father and almost escaped. I still remember the day he was hung. Something has to change, or Ezmith may be the death of us as well."

Kimaya rolled her eyes. "We're his parents, Timot. He knows we love him and he loves us. He's just trying to learn about the world around him. You know how much he likes to learn."

Timot shook his head and stood. "I won't be party to this anymore, Kimaya. I can't keep helping you train him to be a killer just so you can claim more land. I fear the cost has already gotten too high, and will only go higher."

She said nothing, just stared at him until he picked up the dead cat and left the room. What if he was right?

But no, the prophecy was clear enough, and she had faith in her calling.

Looking back, it was clear that Timot had been right...but so had she. Here she was, fulfilling that very prophecy, which Ezmith had been instrumental in bringing to pass.

But now...now perhaps she had to consider how things might move forward if Ezmith had to be...dealt with. After Cleononia was brought under her rule, the only other Western nation would be Mountain Home, and while she was sure she *could* defeat Radomir, what would be the point? She would already control the majority of the exports of this region, all three ports, and the Southern Highway from the coast to Comperr.

If Ezmith could still be safely relied upon when it came to that stage, then she would move forward with invading and make Novis Terram her new capital, but if she began to feel in real danger of Ezmith's wrath...well, it was certainly time to start making contingency plans. She clapped her hands and the door to the sitting room opened, revealing Enoak, looking in earnestly to see what she needed.

"Bring me paper and graphis," she said to him. He nodded and dashed away, closing the door as he went.

Her mind whirled, thinking through what needed to happen. She needed to extend a diplomatic arm to Radomir right now. Ezmith had probably not left sufficient trace that it could be proved that he had done the deed, but Bagon and Radomir were shrewd enough that they certainly suspected. She would send a letter of consolation, which would show her ignorance of the plot, and be careful to phrase the message as from her specifically. Not Ambarta, not the 'court', and certainly not from Ezmith, but from her as an individual.

If they read between the lines, they should see that she was intentionally distancing herself from Ezmith on this. For now, that would have to be enough. Slowly over the course of the next months she'd reach out in various ways. Perhaps she could arrange a large order of Disote ice to be cancelled unexpectedly, then use that excuse to give a gift of that ice to the royal court of Mountain Home.

Then, after the pleasantries that the gift of the ice gave them the opportunity for, she could compliment Oana on her fashion and ask after her seamstress. People always liked you more when they felt they'd helped you with something.

All this would make a conflict feel less likely. After all, why go through all this effort and bother if you were just planning on conquering them? None of this would make the war any easier should it happen, of course. Radomir and Oana weren't foolish enough to let their guard down just because Lady Virtesa seemed to be interested in fostering relationships.

It would, however, make it feasible for her to avoid war altogether if Ezmith became a threat to her and she had to arrange for him to be taken by the guild wizards. And she wouldn't even have to hide her activities from Ezmith because she could explain her reasoning almost in full. He would understand the value of having options besides war with Mountain Home after all the resources they will have expended by taking Cleononia.

By the time Enoak had returned with paper and graphis, she had her plans fully formed in her mind. She would never write those plans down; anything written was at risk of being seen, especially in a situation like this, but she immediately pulled a paper and graphis towards her on the refreshment table and began penning a consolation letter to the court of Novis Terram.

～

Ezren kept expecting his luck to turn bad again, but it stayed inexplicably good. The gentle downhill slope continued all the way until he reached the Thousand River, which allowed him to travel almost as fast as he could have on a road, and he arrived at the river in a spot where he could cross immediately. There, the river must have been at one of its widest points before reaching Cleononia, because it was shallow enough that he could simply ride on through the river.

The water did not even reach past Asteri's knees. The river was about half a mile wide there, and the water was cold, so after reaching the other side he took the time to dismount and rub his extra shirt up and down Asteri's legs to warm them back up. He wasn't sure if such a thing was necessary, but he did it anyway and he made a mental note to ask Ben Rider the next time he saw him.

His good luck continued as the days passed. Around him the terrain changed from the green mountains of his homeland to paler green hills with sporadic clumps of trees, and then to the grays and browns of the open tundra that made up most of Disote. He opted to stay off the road and skip Orjan altogether, but that required a little bit of guesswork to make sure he was going the right direction.

His guess wasn't perfect, but his error veered him towards the road, which he was then able to use as a rough guide, traveling a mile or so off the road the rest of the way to Glacies Castle.

As he went further North, the air got colder, much like the time he'd accompanied his father to Wael, but there were no mountains or forests here; just the open tundra, and the wind made the cool air feel much, much colder. It wasn't long before he donned the thick clothes and gloves he'd brought along with his wool cloak.

He counted his blessings that he was traveling towards the end of Planting instead of a winter month like Twilight or Dawn.

What was more, there was plenty of game that he was able to hunt and skin for their pelts. He didn't have the time or tools to deal with any large game, but setting snares for a single night got him two rabbits and a fox, which he dried out on makeshift stretchers as he continued riding North. Between the snares and what he got hunting, he was able to stitch together a warm hat and attach furs to the outsides of his boots to keep his feet warm.

He knew he likely looked a fool with his ridiculous hat and boots, but he knew very well the importance of keeping his extremities warm.

As they continued their slow plod Northward, the wind was relentless, but Asteri did fine with her blankets and Ezren's hodge-podge of warm clothing kept him comfortable.

He didn't see another soul, besides a handful on the road a mile to his left, until he reached Glacies Castle.

By then, it had been two tendays since he'd left Novis Terram. Not a long time, by most measurements, but it seemed to him that a lifetime had passed. Shortly after breaking camp the next morning, he topped a ridge and saw his destination only a couple miles away.

He'd learned at the academy that Glacies Castle was now essentially a public library. The Lady Virtesa had opened it up to anyone who wanted to read the books within, and only books written in no known language required special permission to peruse.

The castle was just one large building; it wasn't a town with walls or anything, though a small community had cropped up along the road leading up to it. The community had the look of a shanty-town, as though it started out because there were more visitors than the castle could accommodate, then had gradually gotten more permanent as subsequent campers built upon what had been left by the prior ones.

There were a few shops selling basic goods like candles, flint and steel, needles, cloth, and furs. Puffs of breath were everywhere in the chill morning air and Ezren dismounted to see if there was anything that interested him. None of the basic goods appealed to him, though he supposed he could use another length of flint. What *did* catch his attention, however, was a small cart selling meat pies hot off the griddle. The waybread and dried meat and cheese he'd spent the last 20 days eating was fine, but a hot, juicy, spicy meat pie was irresistible.

He bought two and wolfed them both down before even reaching the enormous double-doors that gave entrance to the castle. Maybe it was just because it had been so long since he'd had anything like them, but those meat pies were the most delicious things he'd ever eaten. He committed to buying more on his way out.

Looking up at the castle-turned-library as it loomed above him, the question came to his mind – what now? He couldn't possibly stay long enough to read every book here; he'd be graying and feeble by the time he finished. As he went through the double doors leading through the outer wall, he decided he needed to establish some means of measuring success.

The answer was simple enough: he'd stay until he found the new magic, then if he hadn't found it within five days or so, he'd be willing to settle for hints of where to look next, but he also didn't want to spend the rest of his life traveling back and forth between Glacies Castle and wherever he went chasing down hints.

Maybe he could search until he found three solid leads and then leave to pursue them. That should be more efficient than haring after one at a time. Only if he didn't find the new magic here, though.

Just after he entered the castle through the enormous, iron-bounded doors, he came into a grand entry hall that was much more extravagant than he had expected. It reminded him much of the castle at Novis Terram, though this was even bigger. A majestic chandelier hung suspended from the ceiling like a miniature sun. It was the largest chandelier he'd ever seen, and he watched as two men worked together to ease the chandelier down closer to the ground. It appeared to use oil lamps instead of candles. That would solve the problem of candle wax dripping, but wouldn't it be much more trouble to fill each lamp with oil?

He watched as they tied off the rope and walked over to the chandelier that was now almost touching the ground. One man went around the chandelier, quickly giving each lamp's knob a half turn to raise the wicks a bit higher, which made each one just a little bit brighter. The other man unfolded a step stool and hefted a large vat of oil up to the top of the chandelier, where he unscrewed a cap and began pouring the oil in at the top.

Now *that* was interesting. The chandelier must have been designed to allow just enough oil to reach each of the lamps. How on Quilara did they manage that?! There must have been a hundred separate lamps on that chandelier! He turned away as the men continued their work and took in the rest of what he was seeing.

What he had taken for the entrance hall seemed to be a massive open space that took up the bulk of the castle. The room went back at least a hundred paces, and was five stories high, and each level could be seen ringing the outside of the large space in the middle, containing tall shelves full of books. He was so enthralled as he looked around that he didn't hear a thin, wizened man calling to him until he came up and tapped Ezren on the shoulder.

Ezren jumped, which caused the man to jump.

"Oh- dear, boy, I just need to check you in," he said to Ezren.

"Check me in?" Ezren asked, confused.

"Of course," the man replied. "You will be staying at the castle while you research, will you not?"

Why, yes, yes he would. That would be much better than camping outside in the cold. Ezren straightened and tried to speak confidently.

"Yes, good sir, I will."

The man nodded. "Very good, very good. We have several rooms available at the moment, and you'd be welcome to your pick of them. They are all the same price, just a silver coin per night."

Ezren was beginning to get suspicious of all this luck. *Nothing* was ever this easy. A silver coin per night was a fair price, even if it didn't include food.

The man turned slowly and beckoned Ezren to follow. "Just come this way and we'll get you signed in."

Ezren followed, still leading Asteri, though as he looked around he realized there were no other horses anywhere that he could see. His heart started beating faster. Was this going to turn into another Robinton? He *really* needed to pay more attention to whether he could bring his horse places.

The man reached a podium with a thick ledger and turned to the current page.

"And what is the subject of your research?" The man asked.

That was easy enough to answer truthfully. "Magic."

The man nodded and jotted down the answer. "And your name, young sir?"

Ezren opened his mouth, then closed it again. He couldn't use his real name, could he? What if Ezmith or his mother came here? Why did the castle keep a ledger at all? How often was it reviewed? Did they compare it with a list of known criminals?

The man glanced up at him, likely wondering why he hadn't responded yet.

Ezren panicked. "Raban," he said quickly. "My name is Raban Kennard."

The old man quirked an eyebrow, then shrugged as though he knew Ezren had given a fake name and did not care. He jotted the name down, then looked back up.

"Would you like to see the room options, Young Kennard?"

Ezren shook his head. "Anything with a window will be just fine." A window would be a handy thing to have if any of his family arrived.

"Very good," the man said, looking at his ledger again. He pulled a key out from inside the podium and handed it to Ezren. Your room is on the third floor, number five. A good room with a West-facing window. If you have any needs during your stay do not hesitate to ask."

Taking the key, Ezren nodded and thanked the man. As he turned away, the man cleared his throat. Ezren looked back at him. He was holding out his hand.

Of course! He needed to actually pay for the room! He apologized and fished a silver coin out of his saddlebags.

"Where can I stable my horse?" Ezren asked the old man.

"There is a fully-staffed stable out behind the castle. Just tell them your name and room number and they'll take good care of your horse."

Ezren nodded and led Asteri that direction. There was little chance he would leave the tending of her to the horse handlers, but it was good to know that she would at least be warm and comfortable while he was staying here. The old man clearing his throat turned Ezren's head around to look at him.

The man gestured to the front door. "Please, young sir, if you would not mind taking your horse around the outside. You are welcome to use the rear entrance to come and go, we just try to keep the inside as clean as possible."

"Oh, of course," Ezren replied embarrassed that he'd even needed to be told. He took Asteri around the outside and to the stable.

The horse handlers were also aged, but in high spirits, and a woman took Asteri's reins from Ezren with a welcoming smile directed at the horse.

"And what is this beautiful horse's name?" She asked Ezren, rubbing up and down his horse's neck.

"Asteri," Ezren replied. "It means 'star'."

The woman nodded knowingly. "It's a lovely name. We'll keep her here for as long as you need, young master, but we don't exercise the horses beyond leading them around the corral at a walk. If you're going to be here for longer than a day or so, we would appreciate if you came down to give her a bit more."

Ezren nodded. Of course, he had already planned on coming down, and he opened his mouth to tell the woman that, but she had already turned away and was talking quietly to Asteri as she led her to her stall.

"Oh, wait," he called, laughing. "I need my saddlebags."

The old woman laughed pleasantly and pulled Asteri to a stop. "Yes, I suppose you do."

Saddlebags in hand, he watched as Asteri was taken next to a rack where her saddle would be placed while she was rubbed down. She'd be fine, right? Of course. These people were kindly. At least they *seemed* kindly...Ben's advice echoed once again in his head. He resolved to come down at least once a day, and always at different times so he'd be able to see how Asteri was being treated when the workers weren't expecting him to show up.

For now, Asteri seemed fine. Ezren walked backwards for a few steps then turned and hefted the saddlebags higher onto his shoulder.

He found his room easily enough, up a few flights of stairs to the third floor and over to the West side of the building. He opened the door with the oversized key and stepped into the room, looking around. It looked much like the other rooms he'd seen at inns, but somehow...cozier. Everywhere he looked, there just seemed to be a little bit more of an extra touch than an innkeeper would bother with.

Instead of a plain writing desk, the edging had been carved. The blanket on the bed had a design of blue and yellow triangles on it. As he looked and walked through the room, he continued to notice small details like that. Overall, the room felt wonderfully like home, or what he'd always imagined a grandmother's home would feel like. There was even a doily under a vase with fresh flowers on the writing desk.

He dropped his saddlebags on the bed and went immediately back out to begin looking around for books, pocketing the key after shutting the door behind him. He looked out at the vast library. It was difficult to imagine this place being submerged in a glacier. How had the books all survived? Wouldn't the water have ruined them as it melted? Or, however many centuries earlier, wouldn't it have ruined them before it froze?

He sighed. He didn't really know where to start, but he supposed he could try looking for the section on magic. There were little signs all over that indicated specific subject matter, but he didn't see 'magic' anywhere on this level. All the signs he saw were subjects like "wolves, coyotes, and the like" and "Eastern coastal plants".

He walked all the way around the ring, not seeing anything closer than "Magical Creatures". Then he noticed five large signs hanging out from the banister of each of the five levels. The one for the floor he was currently on said "Flora and Fauna". He read the two below on levels one and two. Level one was "Historical Records & the Craft of War" and level two was "Mathematics and Sciences". He looked up to the floor above him. Its sign said, "Fiction". Leaning out and craning his neck, he made out the sign for the fifth floor: "Magic".

Oh. There wasn't a *section* about magic. There was an entire *floor* dedicated to it. On the one hand, he thought as he climbed the stairs, that made it more likely that the answers he was looking for were indeed here somewhere, but on the other hand, it seemed less likely that he would happen to pick the exact book that had the answer.

He came out on the fifth level and stopped at the top of the stairs, looking around. Each of the other floors seemed to have lots of people milling about, but up here there were very few. Likely that was because magic had little relevance for anyone not a wizard, and even if every wizard in the Western Region were here at the same time the huge space would still feel empty.

He walked around, looking at the smaller signs in hopes that he could narrow down what he was looking for a little bit. Unfortunately, the signs didn't make a great deal of sense to him. One said, "Nature magic". Others just said, "Life", "Chaos", "Water", "Fire", and "Order". On the opposite end was one labeled "Combat magic".

He was beginning to feel a little bit overwhelmed. He did another loop around the ring, and a sign caught his eye that he hadn't seen before. It had "Prophecies" written on it. He had been told that the book that contained the prophecy supposedly about his brothers and him was at Glacies Castle. He made a mental note to check on it at some point.

After standing around for a bit, he decided that he would simply have to pick up a book and start reading. Hoping against hope, he went around the level once more looking for a sign that said something along the lines of "Basic" or "Introductory" or perhaps "Explaining What the Inferno All This Means".

Shockingly, there wasn't one.

He turned into the Nature Magic section, scanning the titles of the books on the shelves. He stopped at a book entitled, "A Beginner's Guide to Nature Magic".

Why not?

He pulled the book of the shelf and went to one of the small round tables with chairs around it that had been placed nearby and opened up the book.

Reading it proved harder than he had hoped, and if this was the beginner's guide, maybe there was a level *beneath* beginner? The book spoke of things that made no sense to him. What was a conduit? Reading further...a conduit was an object that had been enchanted and attuned specifically to nature magic, which the book claimed was a useful tool for beginners and practiced hands alike.

But that didn't make any sense. He distinctly remembered an occasion where he had asked Ezmith if he could do a spell so his swords wouldn't break anymore, and Ezmith had laughed at him, saying that it was impossible to enchant an object permanently. You could put a spell on it, but you had to maintain it constantly or it would dissipate. So why was this book talking about enchanting things?

He didn't doubt Ezmith; Ezren had lived in the castle at Novis Terram long enough that he would have known if Mellion or Paavali had been enchanting objects.

Not long after picking up the Beginner's Guide to Nature Magic, Ezren snapped it shut and replaced it on the shelf. Whatever that book was about, it wasn't what he was looking for. Why weren't any of the sections labeled "new magic" or "mysteries of magic" or something like that? He supposed it wouldn't make sense for someone to write a book about something they did *not* know.

He continued to go up and down the rows of books, grabbing volumes that sounded like they might contain something that would propel him to the next step. He tried, "Why Fire?", "The Dangers of Experimentation", and "Are Potions Magic?"

None of the contents made more than a little sense to him. What did it mean to "worship" fire, and why would someone do so? He was quite sure he'd never heard Ezmith say anything about that kind of thing.

"The Dangers of Experimentation" seemed like it might touch on what he wanted, but it turned out to be a passionate, occasionally belligerent, essay decrying those who tried to, as the author called it, "do foolhardy, irresponsible experiments beyond the known capabilities and framework of the *silindarion*".

It would have been wonderful to know what the *silindarion* was, but the book took the definition for granted.

His hope with "Are Potions Magic?" was that maybe there was something in there about a potion that could reveal who had killed his father.

If there was, he didn't find it.

Flipping through those books took all morning, and his stomach rumbled dangerously around midday. He closed "Are Potions Magic?" and put the books back on the shelves where he had found them, or at least close. It was hard to remember *exactly* where they had gone.

Four meat pies later, Ezren was back on the fifth floor, feeling revitalized and ready to keep moving on his mission. He would not be defeated by four books! He knew this was going to be difficult when he started out on it. He moved throughout the floor and grabbed a book from each section, each time selecting a book that seemed like it would give him at least a little information that he would understand. He was beginning to worry that he simply didn't know enough about magic in general to find any kind of new magic.

He sat down at a table to read, and made an effort to give each book a fair shake before discarding it. He had been reading the second book for just a few minutes when he started to nod off. He shook himself, trying to stay awake, but the full belly from the meat pies combined with the extra warmth from being on the highest level of the building dragged him mercilessly down to sleep. He was powerless to stop it.

An hour or so later, Ezren awoke with his arms folded on the table and his face buried between his arms. He straightened slowly. His shoulders didn't seem to want to work properly. Something in his position must have restricted the blood flow to them. He shook them out, trying to wake them up. After getting up and walking around a bit, he sat back down and felt ready to keep reading.

He went through each and every book he'd selected. Some of them had a listing of the different chapters in the front of the book, so it was quicker to scan through and make a reasonable guess on whether it contained anything of interest to him.

As the squares of light coming in from the windows moved across the floor, Ezren continued to read, sometimes sitting, sometimes standing, or even walking to remain awake. He even slapped himself a few times. It was easier to focus and switch books while he was sitting, but it was easier to stay awake while he was walking. He needed a way to keep himself awake while sitting as well.

He remembered Ben's trick again, about holding his breath to keep himself entertained. That might work well to help keep him awake. He took to holding in his breath while he read a page as fast as he could, then reading the next page while gasping for breath.

It was silly, but it helped him focus, and that was the important thing. That was why he persisted even after a man so old he was bent and walked with a cane gave him a scandalized look when he suddenly let his breath out after finishing a page.

The first day passed, and Ezren had found little. He tried to look on the bright side. He'd come up against many of the same, unfamiliar words multiple times, and he thought he was starting to understand some of them better from the contexts in which they were used. That was a start! If he needed to learn more about current magic before he could discover new magic, then that's what he would do.

Books were not allowed to leave the reading areas, not even to a guest's room, so Ezren found himself with remarkably little to do in the evening. He could have kept reading on the fifth floor, but he wasn't sure he'd be able to force himself to keep reading. Instead he went out to the shanty town to buy some more meat pies.

A space had been cleared for dancing, a group of musicians were playing a lively tune, and it seemed that the entire population of the community was out there, except the shop owners, of course.

The man selling the meat pies, who knew Ezren by the name Raban already, suggested that he go out and dance with some of the young women out there. He politely declined but continued conversing with the man; it wouldn't be right for him to...revel. He needed to stay focused.

He took his meat pies back to his room and ate there. After finishing, he went down to visit Asteri and took her for a trot around the corral as the sun was setting. The temperature dropped quickly at night here, so he hurried Asteri into the stable and handed her off to a different horse handler, a gray-haired man who nevertheless seemed younger than the woman he had first given her to.

Back in his room, Ezren did some exercises that he'd learned at the academy, and even practiced a few sword moves that he could manage without endangering the furniture, then turned in early, only a little after the sun had gone down.

The struggle to stay awake continued into the next day, and the next after that. Ezren developed a system to make it easier. First, he procured a large glass of water, which he could fill in the castle kitchens, and would take a sip every time he started to feel drowsy. This had the added benefit of making him need to use the lavatory more frequently as well, which gave him an excuse to be on his feet.

He also came up with three different things he could do when he needed a break: go visit Asteri, practice sword-and-shield in one of the courtyards, or simply go walking for a while. One of them he would do immediately after lunch, since that seemed to be when he was most tired, and the others he would do later in the afternoon and one in the evening after finishing his researching for the day.

His study felt painstakingly slow, and he had no idea how to speed it up. The hard truth was that he wasn't a wizard. Things that a wizard would understand intuitively would take him hours just to get a basic sense of from an academic standpoint, and even then he was unlikely to be able to predict the implications of it.

Book after book went through his hands, and he occasionally glanced towards the "Prophecies" section, which he had avoided so far. Of all the sections, it seemed like "Prophecies" would be the least likely to have instructions on how to discover new magic. He recalled the few prophecies he'd read, and they were distinctly unhelpful and vague.

It seemed to take both a lifetime and the blink of an eye to reach the end of his fifth day at Glacies Castle, and he was very concerned about his lack of progress. He still had a small fortune in his saddlebags, so being able to afford staying here wasn't a problem, but he was having a harder time fighting down the discouragement at how little he had discovered.

Even more pressing, he was starting to not enjoy the meat pies as much. Luckily the kitchens were fully staffed, also with elderly people, and the food there was quite good. Much how he imagined a grand-mother's food would taste, as a matter of fact.

It turned out that the kitchen food *was* included in the cost of his room, which, when combined with the stable services for Asteri, made Glacies Castle the most affordable place to stay that Ezren had ever heard of.

After his head hit his pillow on the night of the fifth day, he stared up at the ceiling. When he had made his plan to settle for a few leads after looking for five days, he had assumed that he would have some leads to settle for. So far he had absolutely nothing, and he had no idea what to do about it. His eyes began to feel heavy, and he resolved to figure out what to do the following day.

The next morning Ezren traipsed back up the stairs to get up to the

"Magic" floor. He stood at the top of the stairs for a moment with a sigh, then stepped forward.

A walk through the bookshelves in different sections yielded precious little that sounded promising, but he grabbed what seemed the most likely and took them to his now customary table, cup of water in hand. He had just barely started reading, however, when he read yet another passage that might as well have been in a different language, and he dropped the book in frustration.

This was a silly thing to get angry about, wasn't it? It wasn't the book's fault that it was written for a more knowledgeable person. This stagnation was no one's fault but his own.

Still, he supposed, five days of fruitless research would probably try the patience of most people. His eyes wandered over to the "Prophecies" section again. Oh, why not?

He went over and began looking through the books. He wasn't finding any information on new magic anyway, so why not see if he could learn a bit more about the prophecy that he and his brothers were supposedly the fulfillment of?

What was the name of the book again...? *Proleesi*, which meant 'origins' if Ezren remembered correctly. He scanned the shelves. The books seemed to be in roughly alphabetical order, but by the author's last name instead of the title, which made his quest much more difficult; he had no inkling of what the name of the author was.

Eventually he found it, on the furthest possible shelf from where he had started. Unlike the books all around, there was no thin layer of dust resting on the top of the book. He pulled it gently from the shelf. It was leatherbound, as most of the books were, and not as thick as many of the others. He carried it back to his table and set it down carefully.

After sitting, he stared at the book for a moment before opening it. His entire life had followed its course based on the words in this book. Everything about his existence right now would have been different if these words had never been written. His mother wouldn't have set out on her conquest, she wouldn't have hated him so much...Perhaps he wouldn't even have been born; it was uncommon for most people in this region to have more than two children, especially Lords and Ladies.

The book didn't have a listing of the contents, but there was a folded sheet of paper that had been inserted behind the front cover that had very helpful notes on where specific prophecies were to be found.

After a closer look, the handwriting sparked recognition in Ezren. This looked like Ezmith's handwriting! That made sense; Ezmith had probably spent a great deal of time here after their conquest wanting to better understand his own powers and destiny.

Ezmith's notes took Ezren only a little ways into the book, and he found the exact passages he was looking for right where the notes said they would be.

He recognized the first passage in the section immediately – he could have recited it by heart:

And it shall be, that in the day when the sons of the Forgotten land ride
forth as the four winds, they shall be as a cyclone in a field of corn.
Rulers kneel, and the land will sing with one voice, and the Blood of the
Forgotten shall lead them.

That was the passage his mother had quoted unceasingly as he was growing up in the castle at Lugos. She had interpreted "the forgotten land" to be Ambarta, since it had, in essence, been forgotten and cast aside by all of the nations surrounding it. "Sons" and "Four winds" she had interpreted as needing to have four sons, which seemed to have come true.

Rulers kneeling and the land singing with one voice seemed to be coming true as Ambarta continued it's conquest, but the last part was interesting to Ezren. "The Blood of the Forgotten shall lead them". On it's face, it seemed to be saying that the sons of the Forgotten land would rule all the nations, but wasn't that just redundant with what had been previously said?

Also, why were 'Blood' and 'Forgotten' capitalized? Forgotten was capitalized earlier in the passage as well, so perhaps it really was referring to the same thing. Something about it seemed off, but Ezren could not put his finger on it. He continued reading:

The Blood of the Forgotten will rise from weakest to strongest, and make vassals of those who once scorned it...

More rambling that sounded exactly like Ambarta's rise to power. He continued reading through the prophecy, disappointment beginning to settle in. He didn't know what he expected, exactly, but he was hoping for a little bit of insight or guidance about where to go next, not just in his quest for his father's killer, but after that was completed.

He had no doubt that he would find the killer eventually, but then what? If it took too long, he might not be able to go back to the Royal Academy at all, and he couldn't live off his father's savings forever.

He shook himself and kept reading. He needed to stay focused on the task at hand. He could worry about tomorrow...tomorrow.

As he read through the rest of the section, he started to understand why his mother had always just quoted the first paragraph. It seemed to be saying the same thing in different ways. He almost gave up, but continued reading.

It was the very last paragraph in the section, and it had a large question mark written next to it, presumably by Ezmith, that made Ezren's eyes go wide and caused him to lean forward in interest. It was a short paragraph, only a single sentence:

Though sword shatter and light shrink from view, the master of the four winds shall release a new magic, in form of the long forgotten, much changed by frenzied isolation.

He felt his heart beating faster. *This was it!* He'd found the new magic! Now came the hard part of comprehending it. "The master of the four winds..." sounded like Ezmith. If the four brothers were indeed the four winds of the prophecy, then Ezmith would certainly be the master. The rest he didn't understand at all. Sword shatter? Light shrink from view?

And this time, 'forgotten' *wasn't* capitalized. Did that mean something? Was he reading way too much into this?

Well, as to that, he didn't have much choice. If he was going to decipher this then he'd have to read as deeply into every letter as he possibly could. This was the lead he'd been looking for! Now he just had to figure out exactly what it meant.

The old man he'd seen several times over the last few days shuffled past, and an idea struck Ezren. He called out to old man.

"Pardon, good sir, are you familiar with this prophecy?" He asked as he scooped up the book and dashed over to show him.

The man turned slowly and looked at the book without looking at Ezren. He read for a moment.

"Ah, yes," he said in a frail voice. "The Evil Lord has come here many times to study that prophecy. Looking, I suppose, to justify bringing death to so many."

Ezren was taken aback. This old man better not say that in front of Ezmith or his mother; they would not react well to such a thing.

"This last passage here," he said, pointing. "Do you know what it means?"

The old man chuckled without looking. "No one knows what any prophecy means for sure. If prophecies were easy to interpret, then we might find ourselves slaves to destiny."

Ezren felt his eyebrows furrow. "Well...aren't we already? If prophecies have written what's going to happen, aren't we already slaves to destiny?"

The old man smiled and shook his head. "Knowing what choices a person is going to make is not the same as taking that choice away from them, especially if the person who knows is powerless to affect those choices. Prophecies do not tell us what to do, they simple tell us what someone has seen us choose to do."

*So...*Ezren thought, looking down at the last passage. *Maybe the* *"master of the four winds" doesn't have to be Ezmith. Maybe I can release the new magic.*

"Thank you, sir, would you mind telling me any thoughts you've had about this last passage?" Ezren asked again, holding up the book for the old man to see it.

The old man peered at it and his mouth moved silently as he read through it.

"Ah, yes, this is the most important passage in the entire prophecy. At least based on my reading of it."

"How so?" Ezren asked excitedly.

The old man finally looked slowly up at Ezren, with his face showing surprise.

"Well, because it tells us the whole reason the four winds come. Why else would this prophecy exist? Nations' borders change all the time: it is hardly worthy of premonition. Conquerors come and go, and any prophecies about them do not center around their conquest, but, um, something else. Something else that the conqueror does or causes to be done. In *this* case, I believe that the new magic referred to is, in fact, the old magic that existed before the War of the Intelligences."

"The War of the Intelligences?" Ezren queried. He'd heard of the war, but only so much as an explanation that the first settlers of this region had been fleeing it. It had happened on the other side of the Berg.

The old man nodded, now seeming more eager to talk. He likely did not have many people to talk to if he spent all his time up on this floor. Were it not for this old man, Ezren could have run around naked and no one would have known.

"Much of what was known about the war has been lost, and even more has been lost about life before it, but based on what I've found, I believe the war centered around restricting the use of magic. Locking it away so that none save a select few could access it."

"A select few?" Ezren asked.

The old man gestured to the table and chairs and they both sat before continuing.

"Down on the histories level, you can find a number of volumes about life starting about 1,500 years ago and going further back. You can also find a number of books covering the history of both sides of the Berg since about a thousand years ago and coming forward." He leaned in towards Ezren, his posture straightening some to allow it. "But there's a 500 year gap, boy. A 500 year gap where precious little can be found that gives real insight to what happened during that time."

"But why?" Ezren asked.

The old man shrugged. "That's the trouble. The only thing we know for certain is that there was a great war, the war to end all wars, and it was called by the people then 'The War of the Intelligences'. We can, however, compare how historians wrote about life long before the War with how historians have written about life since. Doing that, we can reach a few more safe conclusions. Number one, we can deduce that magic, or the use of it, was far more ubiquitous prior to the War than it was after. Number two, we can deduce that the victors of the War, whoever they were, made a concerted effort to destroy any records of it. The gap in knowledge is too complete, too thorough to have been merely the result of wanton fighting and destruction, no matter how widespread."

The old man did not speak quickly, but Ezren found himself hanging on his every word, drinking in this information as though he were a man dying of thirst.

"Is there anything else we know?"

The old man smiled. "'Know' is a powerful word, boy. At your age, you think you know when you merely believe. With that said, I *believe* a number of things about that era, that I think are well-supported by the fragments we have left. I'll not share them all with you right now, but suffice it to say that the passage you asked about, I believe it references a restoration of sorts, bringing back the magic that was sealed away."

Ezren looked down at the passage. "Then what does it mean, 'in form' of the long forgotten? Why would it be changed by 'frenzied isolation'?"

The old man's face grew serious, and he spoke much more solemnly than he had up this point. "Magic has never operated simply as a water pump, where you leave the pump as long as you like and all you have to do is pour a little water down it first then pump to your heart's content. Wizards describe using magic much like...a negotiation. The wizard says this, thinks that, or does something, and the magic 'agrees' to do something in response. I've always thought...if *I* were imprisoned alone, unable to communicate with any besides those who imprisoned me, for a thousand years...I would emerge much changed myself, and not in all ways for the better."

The old man got up slowly, using his cane for support, and gradually walked away, leaving Ezren to ponder. It wasn't until he'd gone out of sight that Ezren came out of his thoughtful reverie and wondered if he had been rude by not bidding farewell to the man. But then, he had left without a word as well, so perhaps he had just sensed that Ezren had no further questions. Besides, if Ezren *did* have more questions, it's not like the old man would be hard to find.

Ezren slumped back in his chair. He'd been at this for *days*, and one short conversation with the old man had given him infinitely more valuable information than he had found up to this point. Why hadn't he just talked to the old man earlier? The first day he arrived, for example?

Oh, well, there was no point in dwelling on missed opportunities, though next time he was in a situation like this he made a note to just ask someone who might know before spending days and days faffing around.

Now, though, he was ready to start taking the next steps. He had to figure out how to release this new magic, that might be the same as the old magic, that might be different now, and he might not be able to release the new magic because Ezmith was supposed to do it. Maybe it required magic to do it. Well, if that were the case, perhaps the other Mountain Home wizard...Paavali, was his name...perhaps he'd be able to help.

Ezren grabbed his sheaf of papers that he'd been taking notes on and started scribbling with his graphis, outlining what he knew. Well...*believed*, but whatever.

'Though sword shatter and light shrink from view.' That sounded like hints to how to find the magic. Light shrink from view…maybe blackness? Something black? Somewhere dark? Sword shatter…swords all broke eventually unless they were never used, but *shatter*? That wasn't something that happened often. When *would* a sword shatter instead of simply break into two or possibly three pieces? Maybe if it was already weakened from years of use, then it was swung against something flat, as long as the blade was, so the blade impacted all along it's length instead of just one point.

Ezren found himself nibbling on the end of his graphis as he thought, and had to rinse the taste out of his mouth with his water.

With what he understood now, it seemed possible that the new magic would be found by finding a dark object, or maybe something in a box, and shattering a sword against it. Hardly the only interpretation, but it was the best Ezren had, and he could think on other possibilities while he pursued the one.

He decided to copy down the entire section of the prophecy, word-for-word. He forced himself to write slowly and to do it very carefully, making sure to copy every punctuation, every capital letter, with exactness.

It took a little while, but after finishing, he read it through, comparing his version with the book's version, and they were truly identical. He considered keeping the book handy, or perhaps trying to find another copy of it, but decided against it. With how much interest Ezmith apparently had taken in this book, who knew how much time Ezren had before Ezmith would come looking for it again.

He could always read more of it later. If the prophecy about his brothers and him was near the beginning, how much more information did it contain about the future?

Putting that thought process aside for the moment, Ezren asked himself where he might start looking for this artifact. If it was Ezmith who was supposed to find it, maybe it would be somewhere Ezmith was likely to frequent. Considering that, here at Glacies Castle might be the right place to start. He immediately got up and went to the stairs, leaving his notes spread out on the table.

He wasn't worried about them going missing; he'd accidentally left them overnight once and found them undisturbed in the morning.

He went down the stairs all the way to the ground floor of the entrance hall and approached the same old man that had checked him in. The old man looked up and smiled. They had exchanged several niceties over the last half-tenday, but Ezren had not yet learned his name.

"Young Raban, how can I help you today?" the man asked.

"I was wondering if there were any artifacts or objects of historical significance here? Perhaps a room of items that were in the castle when it was discovered?" Ezren replied questioningly.

The man thought for a moment, narrowing his eyes. "We do have a small room with a few items, may I ask what you are seeking?"

"Anything related to magic," Ezren replied.

"Hmm...I believe all the items here are rather pedestrian. You're welcome to peruse them but if you're looking for objects rumored to have magical properties then you may be best served by traveling to Robinton. Many of the land's...wealthiest people have taken to collecting items thought to have magical properties. I believe it has become quite the trend."

"Robinton?" Ezren asked, disappointed.

The man nodded. "Yes, over the last few years the upper estates in Robinton especially are said to have amassed quite a number of supposedly-magical artifacts."

Ezren sighed. Right back the way he had just come, and right into a land where he might be a known criminal. It had taken him days to get here from the North Road in Robinton that led to the upper estates. Maybe he could save some time by cutting straight across instead of following the road south to Orjan first. Summer was getting stronger each day, so maybe cutting across this far north wouldn't be a problem.

He thanked the man and went to check the room he'd mentioned, just in case there was something of interest, but as the old gentleman had said, all the items were simple and set up on pedestals for display. None of them looked like they would shatter a sword *or* have anything to do with light shrinking from view.

He walked around the castle, thinking carefully about his plans. He was surprised to find that he was a bit trepidatious about going back out traveling by himself. Glacies Castle was safe, warm, and comfortable.

He sighed. He would never find his father's killer if he stayed here, though. He would leave with the sun first thing in the morning.

The creaking of the wheels on the battering ram grated on Ezmith's nerves even more than Eztas' heavy breathing. The enormous man wasn't enchanted yet; Ezmith wasn't sure how long it would take for the ram to break through, and he wanted to maximize the amount of damage his brother could do by waiting until the last possible moment to start the enchantments. The sweat ran down his face as he walked, slightly hunched over, under the wooden ceiling of the ram that provided shelter for the men pushing it forward. Ezmith did not push, of course, he was here for a far more important reason.

It was the 12th day of the siege, and so far it had been much more of a standoff than Ezmith had expected. First, despite his worries about being ambushed or Folding into something solid, he'd tried to bypass the wall by Folding his army to the courtyard outside Perivon's palace. When he'd tried, however…it hadn't worked. His Folds were working fine elsewhere (he'd tested exhaustively), but for some reason he could not Fold into the city. The wizards must be maintaining a Dome that stopped one of the elements he used for Folds.

But if that were the case, why couldn't he sense it? Had they come up with some new way to prevent his Folds?

Since Folding wasn't an option, they'd built another slinger to bring down the wall again but Perivon's wizards were prepared for that too. The boulder had impacted on a magical barrier instead of the wall, leaving the wall itself unharmed. Stopping something so heavy moving so quickly had likely taken three of the four wizards, so he'd ordered his engineers to continue firing the slinger at the walls.

Eventually the wizards would get tired, or so he thought.

The wizards managed to keep up their strength for long enough, however, right up until a massive, solid iron bolt had suddenly rocketed out from behind the wall, arced slightly as it flew, and slammed right into one of the support bases for the slinger, splintering it beyond repair.

An entire tenday of building, slinging, and waiting...wasted.

Now they were going back to basics. A good, old-fashioned battering ram, but with him along to maintain a shield against magical attacks. He was hoping that the wizards didn't attack at all; they might assume that the regular soldiers could handle a ram on their own, and that magic would not be required. If the ram could break the gate open without Ezmith or Eztas revealing themselves, then they'd have an immediate advantage.

Arrows thudded against the wood above their heads. It was made with thick wood, and they had soaked it all in water just before moving out to reduce the effectiveness of flaming arrows. It wasn't perfect, but it should help enough that Ezmith could use just a trickle of magic to keep the flames from spreading.

The plan was simple: break the gate open, then Eztas and Ezmith would hold it against the defenders for the time it took for the army to run in from where they waited just out of bowshot. It would have been faster for them to have been here already, but Ezmith had no interest in pitting his untrained archers and soldiers against the well-trained Cleononian defenders until their numbers could make a difference.

If the ram didn't work...well then it was probably going to be ladders. With how many soldiers he had, it wouldn't matter if he lost a thousand or two while getting the ladders set and scaled. He could have enough ladders made to cover the entire wall, using their numbers to overwhelm the defenders quickly.

The ram finally reached the gate. The men moved from their

handles along the walls to the handles inserted along the thick log that had been sharpened to a point, then plated in steel.

The soldier in front counted off, and the men pulled the log back, then pushed it forward with all their might, slamming it into the closed, iron gate in the wall. Arrows continued to thud, but Ezmith didn't detect any magical attacks coming. Eztas breathed loudly. Eztas always breathed loudly.

Ezmith continued looking up at their ceiling for any flames visible between the cracks. A flaming arrow would sound much the same as a regular one from down here. Strangely, none of the arrows he could see had flames coming off them. He would have thought that the flaming arrows would have started being prepped the moment the defenders had seen the ram approaching.

He felt the rushing wave of magic approaching with only moments to react. He threw his arms up, unsure of what was coming his way, and put all his strength into making a Shield that should be tight enough to keep most elements out but loose enough to bend instead of break under other elements. It was an impressive Shield, and he wouldn't be able to hold it indefinitely.

Theoretically, he shouldn't have to.

The soldiers operating the ram continued their work unabated, having no idea how close they had all just come to complete annihilation. The magical attacks kept coming, and since he was functionally blind anyway, Ezmith closed his eyes, focusing on what magic he felt and how it was interacting with his Shield.

It seemed to be a variety of attacks, which would have made sense even if only one wizard had been attacking, but the attacks were coming from two very different directions. Only two. They had not predicted that Ezmith would be here personally.

With his eyes still closed, Ezmith put his hands up on the ceiling of the ram to keep a sense of where it was. The worst thing he could do would be to try and counterattack but originate the spell on the inside of the ram. He was about to begin counterattacking but stopped after considering the advantage he had. His Shield, while impressive, could be done by another wizard, who would likely be completely expended afterward. If Ezmith also turned to attack at the same time, he would reveal himself.

If he waited, however...Perivon might assume that he was Guillame, and would be next to useless once the gate was breached. They would not be expecting the wrath and destruction Ezmith could wreak once they were through. They would under-commit both their wizards and their troops to holding the gate while Ezmith's army came running for the opening.

He smiled, his eyes still closed, holding the Shield against the barrage of attacks that kept coming.

The steady thud of the ram continued for about a half an hour as Ezmith continued to hold the shield against the barrage of magic. Flaming arrows had still not come, but that might be because the oil that had been poured from the top of the gate had been diverted by Ezmith's shield instead of soaking the ram.

Even as he thought it, he heard arrow thuds in the ground to both sides of the ram and heard the whoosh of oil catching fire. It seemed that they had decided it would be worth it to try and scorch them out from under the ram. They were fools, though he supposed they had to try *something*.

With one final slam, the gate swung open. The soldiers operating the log seemed confused, so Ezmith peered around their heads to see what was inside. Was that...a catapult?

His eyes widened as the catapult released, launching a group of head-sized rocks from only a dozen feet away. He had no time to do anything besides create a Bubble Shield around himself and Eztas, and the rocks rocketed straight into the ram, smashing it to bits and crushing the men inside. Ezmith and Eztas were thrown backwards. Ezmith scrambled to his feet and created a Fold for them to dive through as he felt the magical barrage coming.

Sparse, but soft, grass cushioned his fall as he emerged a few hundred paces away from the city walls next to his brother. He got to his feet and stared angrily at the walls of Dazbog.

"Why...won't...you...just...ACCEPT THE INEVITABLE?!" He bellowed at the city. The large gates slowly closed back up in response.

He clenched his fists so hard his fingernails began cutting into his palms. He felt immense pressure rising up through his body like magma through a volcano. As the pressure reached his head, he found that he had no choice but to let out a prolonged yell, a scream, really, of pure rage. He yelled as loud as he could until he no longer had breath to continue.

Only after he ran out of breath did he pay attention to his surroundings. He had fallen to his knees, and he was surrounded by his soldiers, all of whom were staring at him in shock. Beaumont was there as well, where he'd been waiting to call the charge. Ezmith raised his hand in anger. *Kill them! Kill them all!* He held his hand up, but did nothing, fighting an internal struggle that none watching likely understood. Somewhere beneath the rage he knew he still needed these men.

His pragmatism won out, and he lowered his hand as he struggled to his feet. These simpletons had no idea how close they had just come to death.

"Call the retreat," he ordered in a whisper. "Pull everyone back for now." He strode, head down to avoid seeing how the soldiers stared at him, back towards his command tent. After the hundred or so yards to the tent, he flung open the flap angrily and stared down his captains. His eyes settled on Captain Aberdeen, the one who had suggested the battering ram.

Ezmith pointed a finger while using Air to lift the man and pin his arms to his side.

"You," he said softly, before his rage boiled back up and he bellowed the rest: "...ARE A *TRAITOR!*"

The man's eyebrows rocketed up and he looked around, the extra pudge on his face making him seem more innocent and earnest than most soldiers. Captain Beaumont entered the tent behind Ezmith.

"Sir, no!" Aberdeen squeaked. "I have never- I am loyal to Ambarta!"

Captain Wallitz, of a height with Ezmith and more battle-seasoned, stepped forward.

"Lord Ezmith, what has happened?" He asked softly.

Ezmith slowly lowered his hand, and as he did so pudgy Captain Aberdeen came back down to the ground.

"They were prepared for the ram," he said, forcing himself to speak softly. "They *knew*." His volume rose suddenly as he finished. "And the ram was this one's idea!" he finished, pointing at Aberdeen.

Wallitz shook his head. "That is indeed bad news. I can see why you are enraged, Lord Ezmith. However, I am willing to personally vouch for Captain Aberdeen. If there is a traitor in your command structure, it is not him."

Ezmith looked hard at Wallitz and lowered the hand pointing at Aberdeen. Wallitz was his best Captain. He had not *really* intended to harm Aberdeen anyway, unless he was proven to be a traitor. At least not in front of his other officers.

"Very well, Captain, I will refrain, for now, from executing Captain Aberdeen. Now how would my command structure recommend we proceed next? Ladders, I presume?"

All around the room, men nodded, clearly eager to please. Ezmith sighed internally. Idiots. How was he supposed to make the best decisions when the other minds in the room simply said 'yes' to whatever he suggested?

One head, however, was not nodding. It was the head of Captain Wallitz. Ezmith looked at him angrily.

"You disagree with the rest of the Captains, Wallitz?"

Wallitz took a deep breath and nodded. "I do, sir. From what I've seen, Perivon is entrenched here, and has conscripted most of the city's able-bodied men to defend the city from attack. This means that he will likely have enough to have several rotations of guards, keeping the defenders constantly fresh *and* allowing the temporary troops to continue with their day-to-day work, which means he could keep up his defensive numbers during an extended siege. Ladders would require wizards to combat the enemy, which would in turn require our wizards to be far more exposed than theirs, making it more likely that ours will fall to a well-timed arrow." He shook his head, looking down at the large map on the center table. "Ladders would work, yes, but the cost would be high, perhaps higher than we have the stomach for."

Ezmith felt his frustration boiling up again. He spoke through gritted teeth. "Then what would you suggest, Captain?"

Wallitz paused for a moment, seemingly unaffected by Ezmith's temper. He thought for a long moment before speaking. "Perivon can't move out. He has the same advantages, but also the same problems we had at Mhairi. We could cut our force in half and still easily hold the siege here."

Captain Endith stepped forward. "But we'll never outlast them while they have their port open. They can get food and supplies into the city as easily as we can get them to our army."

Wallitz nodded. "Exactly...as long as their port is functioning and they have willing trade partners. I believe we have two options, my lord. Both of them require moving a significant force to lay siege to Bahadir. The first option is to simply maintain a siege on both cities at the same time. If Perivon is not able to move trade out of either of his ports, then eventually he will run out of resources to trade for the things he needs. If he's found a trading partner to borrow coin from, eventually even that will run out. His people will slowly starve, and at some point he'll surrender for the sake of his people. It could take a year or longer."

A year was far too long. "What is the second option, Wallitz?" Ezmith asked.

"Once the army is there, you send General Beaumont along with an enchanted Eztas to begin an immediate attack on the city. Perivon has likely warned Bahadir of the possibility of attack, but I do not believe he would risk sending any of his wizards there just on the chance of it. General Beaumont and Eztas can break into the city quickly, without encountering any magical resistance, and our force can overwhelm the defenders there. Once the city is taken, we can commandeer the Bahadir navy and work to raid ships carrying supplies to Dazbog. We avoid direct confrontation with the Dazbog fleet and do our best to disrupt the trade well enough that Perivon surrenders."

Ezmith thought about it. Despite the rationale, and the well-thought out plan, it still felt like a retreat. It felt like admitting failure here at Dazbog and simply changing the battlefield to somewhere else. But... the plan *did* make sense. Perivon likely wouldn't be able to do anything about what happened at Bahadir because word would take at least a day to reach him by water, and it would take at least another day, likely two, to marshal forces and send them back over water down to the other port, if he was even willing to pull from his forces here at all.

Not only that, but maybe he'd be able to Fold to inside Bahadir the way he'd tried with Dazbog.

Without a word, he turned and tried to open a Fold just behind him to the Bahadir docks. The Fold would not form. He cursed inwardly. How was Perivon always managing to be everywhere at once? They would just have to resort to siege weapons again. Another ram, most likely. The plan was still solid, and worth the sacrifice.

Even if they could not find enough sailors to harry the supply ships going to and from Dazbog, they could immediately begin using the docks, which would save most of the merchants in their realms a tenday per trip and significantly improve trade throughout the lands they controlled. He suspected his mother had been presented with numerous complaints of merchants having to trek all the way down to Redwood since the armistice had ended.

"I agree to this plan," Ezmith said, forcibly relaxing his hands at his side. "But I'm placing *you* in charge of the attack on Bahadir, Captain Wallitz."

Wallitz looked surprised, but bowed his head in agreement. The other captains looked surprised as well. Ezmith had no interest in sharing his thought process with them.

"How much time do you need to prepare?" he asked Wallitz.

Wallitz bent over the map, and Ezmith spent the next hour with the captains working out the details of the attack. Since they weren't sure what they would find there, and scouting and scrying would only reveal so much, they agreed it was best to take half the army along, a full 10,000. Bahadir had more land around it to cover, and even though besieging it was not the plan, it would be best to give Wallitz the ability to adapt as the battle unfolded.

Bahadir's walls were similar in size, scope, and even design to the walls of Dazbog, so they had a fair idea of what to expect. The real question became how to break into the city quickly, so that word could not reach Perivon in time for reinforcements to be sent. A slinger could break down the wall in a single volley, but it would also take time to assemble and position.

A ram was an option, but without magical protection, it would fall very quickly to oil and flaming arrows. That was simple enough to solve, however. He would just send Guillame along with the army, and he could provide the same defense that Ezmith had. With no magical attacks to defend from, keeping the ram protected would be a simple matter.

They ended up sending a scout anyway, since they had to decide whether the ram should attack the gate or the wall, and therefore how it should be designed, and many other questions that could be better answered after getting additional insight into how things were laid out there.

They decided that the ram would be built prior to Folding there, and all other preparations would be made here so that the attack could begin the moment the army arrived, giving the defenders as little time as possible to prepare.

CHAPTER 10: JOURNEY

It was interesting how the terrain changed as one traveled between Disote and Robinton. Ezren stayed as far north as Glacies Castle, or at least close to it, as he traveled. Something besides distance from the equator must have affected the temperature, because it got gradually warmer as Ezren moved East. Maybe it had something to do with the mountains. As he got closer, the elevation of the land did continually go up, but wouldn't that normally make it colder?

Crossing the Thousand river this time around did not go as smoothly as before. It was smaller this far up, but still wide and deep enough that it would take a lot of searching to find a crossing like the one he had found on the way to Glacies Castle.

He approached the river a few days after leaving the castle but could see long before he arrived that he was not in a place where he could cross. He opted to head upriver, since it was possible the river would narrow more as he got closer to its headwaters.

He had been traveling for about half a day upriver when he found a place that should work. It was a waterfall, but at the top the water was wide and fairly shallow, only reaching about as high as Asteri's knees. He examined the area for a long moment, looking for places where it might get deeper unexpectedly or cause problems. He didn't want to walk Asteri too close to the edge.

He nudged his horse into the river and they began their crossing. As they walked, Ezren noticed a series of larger rocks that jutted out above the water level at almost regular intervals along the entire width of the river. A few in a row like that might not have been worth noticing, but across the entire river? It seemed like someone had placed them there. Whoever they were, they probably weren't traveling by horse; those rocks would have been worse than useless if you were trying to get a horse across the water.

The placement was odd for another reason as well; when the water was already shallow enough to cross, who would go through all the trouble of adding large rocks for a crossing?

He looked around as much as he dared while making sure that Asteri didn't slip on her way through the water, but didn't see anyone around. On the other side, he rubbed Asteri's legs down for warmth again and then continued along their way. Only a few dozen yards from the shoreline on this side, the surroundings turned to dense forest.

Ezren didn't mind that, in fact he preferred it. It was easier to feel like you were passing by unnoticed when anyone further than a hundred yards away would have no idea you were there. Even for those closer, being heard would be a higher risk than being seen.

Perhaps it was just thinking about who had placed those stones, but he kept feeling this itch on the back of his neck like he was being watched. He found himself whipping around on occasion, looking along the ground, up in the trees, and everywhere else to see who was there.

He was just being nervous. A forest like this would likely have predators, including bears, so it was good to be on his toes. There probably wasn't another person here, though. There wasn't a settlement of any kind for days in any direction.

As though intending to prove him wrong, the forest opened up to reveal a clearing that was clearly a campsite. Ezren pulled Asteri to a stop at the edge of the clearing to look around. There was no cabin or other structure, but there was a good-sized and well-used firepit in the center of the clearing with a tripod erected and even an iron grill hanging from it, positioned so that a small fire would be able to cook whatever was placed on top.

At the moment nothing was on it, and there was no fire in the pit. Ezren looked up at the sky. It was getting close enough to sunset that if someone was nearby they should be thinking about making a fire, both for warmth and for preparing dinner.

Of course, he had thought the same thing about the last campsite he had chanced upon.

He considered staying; there was an overhang of dense pine branches that had been made using a combination of live branches from a pine tree and cuttings from others. It would be a perfect place to sleep. If he stopped now he could take a little time to try and hunt up a rabbit or a fox or something to cook fresh over the fire...

No, he would *not* make the same mistake twice. He nudged Asteri forward. They would continue on their way and stop a couple miles from here. As he reached the middle of the clearing, he heard the unmistakable sound of a branch snapping. He grabbed his bow, only just remembering that he hadn't strung it this morning.

Cursing, he hopped off Asteri and strung the bow as quickly as he could, nocking an arrow and looking around.

The source of the noise was not apparent, but Ezren knew what he had heard. If it wasn't the person whose campsite this was, then it was a large animal, possibly a bear. What if it wasn't just one person? He remembered the feeling of being slowly surrounded, with arrows pointed at him...He moved up against Asteri and pulled her to the side of the clearing. Maybe if they saw him leaving they'd let him go. If not...

Another branch snapped, off to Ezren's left. Here they came! Terrified, he immediately drew his arrow to his cheek and loosed into the trees where he had heard the noise. The arrow disappeared into the brush, and he didn't hear the sound or effect of its impact. He pulled another arrow from the quiver tied to Asteri's saddle and nocked it while backing up, continuing to stare hard at the place where he'd shot.

Listening for all he was worth, he thought he heard a *scoffing* sound, but it was hard to tell for sure. As he backed away, a person dressed in furs with a hood up stepped out, holding a bow aimed at Ezren. The person said something, but Ezren could not hear what over the yelp that escaped his own lips as he raised his own bow and fired at the person.

The figure in fur leaned quickly to the side to dodge Ezren's arrow and shot right back. Ezren shied away in fear as he worried that he was about to die. He felt a solid 'thunk' against the side of his head and all went black.

Everything was dark. He couldn't see anything. What was that sound he could hear? A creek burbling by? No. Someone walking on dry leaves? No. A fire crackling? Yes. That was the sound of a fire crackling. Why was everything dark? Wait, were his eyes closed? Oh, yes. That must be why it was dark.

He became aware of pain in his shoulder. Was he hurt? No, it was just the position he was in. He struggled to change positions, but found that he could not move one hand without moving the other. He was tied up!

His eyes snapped open as panic filled him, and he began to flail at his bonds. His hands were tied together behind his back, and his feet were tied together at the ankles.

"Eh, calm down," a woman's voice said from the other side of the fire. "Yeh look like a fish flopping around on the shore."

He took a deep breath and tried to see around the fire. Had he been rescued? Then why was he still tied up? A woman sat there, older than Ezren, perhaps in her late 20s or early 30s. Her light brown hair was pulled up at the back of her head. Her face was pleasantly featured, but dirt marks on it served to accentuate the harsh angles.

"That's better," the woman said. "Now, yeh mind telling me what yeh're doing in my forest?"

Oh, so he had *not* been rescued. This woman must be the figure wearing fur that had shot him. Wait, if he'd been shot...He looked down trying to see his body, wondering where the wound was before he remembered that he'd been shot in the head.

"O, yeh're not hehrt," she said, waving an arrow to the side where he could see it. "Not permanently anyway."

The arrow was tipped with a small iron block instead of an arrowhead. "It was clear as day that yeh thought I was going ta kill yeh. Yeh might not be all that that dangerous on a nehrmal day but even the tamest cat'll bite when it thinks it's in danger."

That arrow must have been what Ezren had felt hit his head right before he'd lost consciousness. He shook himself, trying to sort out his thoughts. Who was this woman? He'd never heard that accent before and could not place it. Her next question interrupted his frantic thoughts.

"Now, I'll ask yeh again...what're yeh doing in my forest?" She asked.

Hold on...a tame cat? Not all that dangerous on a normal day? He was plenty dangerous! He narrowed his eyes as he glared at the woman and clenched his mouth shut.

She chuckled. "So, it'll be like that, eh?" She shrugged. "Stay tied up, then. I'll take yeh and yeh're horse out tomorrow and let yeh go, s'long as you don't come back."

Ezren grunted. His shoulder was quite uncomfortable. "If I answer your questions, you'll untie me?"

"Well, truth is that'll depend on what yehr answers are," she said, raising an eyebrow. "But my guess is, yep, I'll probably be able to let yeh go."

Fair enough, Ezren supposed. He doubted he'd get a firmer agreement than that.

"I'm on my way to some of the estates in Robinton."

She gave him a confused look. "'Some of' the estates? Not a specific one?"

Ezren tried to shrug, but it didn't work very well with one shoulder in the ground and his hands tied behind his back.

"I'm looking for...magical artifacts, and someone told me that people in Robinton collect them."

"What're yeh looking fehr magical artifacts fehr?"

Sighing, Ezren considered how to respond to that question. It's not like the truth would get him in more trouble than he was already in. Besides, she might be able to tell if he lied. Telling the truth had worked fairly well so far on his journey.

"I'm trying to find out who killed my father. A wizard told me that the only way to learn the truth would be to discover some kind of new magic."

"A wizard told yeh that?" She asked, seeming incredulous.

Ezren nodded defiantly.

"And yeh're sure he meant yeh should go out and hunt some down? He didn't mean for yeh to just let it be?"

Ezren looked away, blinking at the dull ache in his head that accompanied the sudden movement. "I don't have time to explain everything to you."

She threw back her head and laughed. "Oh, yeh've got somewhere to be, do yeh? Looks to me like yeh're not going anywhere til I say yeh can, so I think yeh've got all the time yeh need."

This was embarrassing. How do you explain something to someone who seemed intent on misunderstanding? She'd heard him say his father had been killed, right?

Without looking at her, but unable to keep the heat from his voice, he replied, "There is a prophecy, and it talks about a new magic being released, alright? I know what I'm doing. You don't have to understand, but you can at least stop hindering me."

She held up her hands bracingly. "Alright, alright, I didn't mean offense, boy. Now, I'll untie yeh, but I'll need yehr word that yeh won't try to harm me or mine, yes?"

"I give my word," Ezren said, nodding. "I'll make no attempt to harm you or anything of yours."

She crossed her ankles and stood without using her hands. "Eh, that'll do. I figured yeh were harmless."

He refrained from arguing her last point. It just didn't seem productive.

She untied his wrists first, and the relief that came immediately as he moved his arms about caused him to sigh. Once his ankles were free he brought himself shakily to his feet and swung his arms, trying to get his blood to flow properly again. His shoulder still ached a little, but it would most likely go away soon.

"Thank you," he said to the woman, nodding to her, then began walking toward where she had tied Asteri on the other side of the clearing.

"Well, hold up there, boy," she called out, stopping him.

He turned, confused. "You said you would let me go."

"Well, yes, yeh can go, I just thought maybe yeh'd want some dinner first."

Dinner? As though the word were a cue, his nose suddenly caught the scent of meat cooking over a fire, and he noticed properly the first time the skinned rabbits roasting on the grille above the campfire. He stared hungrily at the rabbits for a moment.

"I got us a brace of coney's to share if yehr interested. Only one good way to eat a brace of coney's, and it ain't boiling 'em."

He heard Ben's warning in his head about how 'most people' were, and there were plenty of reasons why he shouldn't trust a woman he'd just met, but something about her…earthy demeanor was beginning to put him at ease. It was just dinner, after all. He wasn't going to stay the night here and make himself vulnerable to being robbed. Besides, if she wanted to rob or harm him, she had already had ample opportunity to do so. Even Ben had admitted that he might be wrong about people.

He agreed to stay and sat down by the fire. Silence reigned for a bit as he tried to think of what to say. The woman seemed relaxed and had lain on her side, propped up on her elbow, as the rabbits sizzled.

"So, what's yehr name, boy?" she asked finally, looking over at him.

He opened his mouth to say his name was Raban again, but he was out of Glacies Castle now, and it seemed unlikely this woman would have heard of him, and even less likely that she would have any contact with his family, so why not just use his real name?

"Ezren. Ezren Kimorae," he replied. "What's yours?"

"Aminah," she replied. "Just Aminah is fine."

He nodded. "So I told you why *I'm* out here, but why are *you* out here?" He asked. "Are you a scout?" He was thinking of Ben, the only person he knew of that might be found out in the woods like this woman.

She laughed good-naturedly. "Heavens, no. No, this is my home. I live here."

He looked around, bewildered. "But there's no cabin, no house or anything."

She pointed. "That hill right there, next to the clearing? I've hollowed it out and made a space that's good enough fehr me."

"Why do you live out here?" He asked, still confused.

"Well as to that...I don't know yeh well enough to tell yeh that. Besides, it's not one of those good stories, the kind that keeps yeh on yehr toes wondering what's going to happen next."

She got up into a squat and poked at the rabbits.

"Alright, Ezren, I think these coneys are 'bout ready," she declared.

She pulled them off the fire while Ezren retrieved his tin plate from his saddlebags. Aminah dished them both up and they dug into the rabbits, eating around the bones.

While they ate, Aminah asked him more questions.

"So these estates," she said around a mouthful of rabbit. "Yeh think they'll have the magic thing yeh're looking fer?"

Ezren shrugged. "I don't know," he said honestly. "But I hope so. If they don't, then I'll have to go back to Glacies Castle to do more research."

"Oh, yeh've been to Glacies Castle, have yeh?" she asked, smiling excitedly. "Wonderful place. So much knowledge."

"Wait, *you've* been to Glacies Castle?" He asked, surprised.

"Of cehrse!" she said, holding her arms out. "That's half the reason I live out here."

Ezren looked at her for a moment, trying to figure out what to make of her. Why was it so surprising that she frequently went to study at Glacies Castle? Well...she just...*sounded* like she hadn't done very much reading, that's all. And it was perfectly reasonable to assume that someone living in the woods away from everyone else would not be particularly interested in books.

Looking for a way to cover his awkward silence, Ezren continued explaining his plan. "The prophecy I read said that a new magic would be discovered or...well...it might be an *old* magic being *re*discovered, but either way, it would be discovered when 'sword shatters and light shrink from view'. So my guess is I need to find something black, that would break a sword, that's also connected to magic in some way," he said, looking to her to see her reaction.

There wasn't much of one.

"Sounds as good an interpretation as any to me," she replied, shrugging. "How are yeh planning on getting into one of those estates to look at all their stuff? Those places are like miniature fortresses."

"Oh, I'll be able to sneak in," Ezren said confidently. "I grew up on the streets of Novis Terram, I had to sneak into places all the time."

She raised an eyebrow at him again, speaking slowly. "Those places are like miniature fortresses," she repeated. "How many fortresses yeh snuck into in Novis Terram?"

He tossed his head angrily. "None, obviously, but I know how to snea-"

"It's a bad idea," she interrupted, shaking her head. "Here's what yeh do – yeh bribe one of their servants to get yeh a uniform, then waltz in like yeh belong and no one will look at yeh twice cuz they think yeh're s'posed to be there."

"Is that right?" Ezren asked, defensive. "And how many fortresses have you snuck into, then?"

Aminah shrugged casually. "Three or fehr. 'Cehrse it's a bit easier fehr me. No one ever suspects a woman as much."

She took another bite of her rabbit, which reminded Ezren to do so as well. Aminah's suggestion sounded like an awful lot of trouble that would take more time than he wanted. He'd have to scout out the estate he wanted to look at, make friends with a servant somehow, then bribe them to get him a uniform, and only then would he be able to get in to see if that one single estate just happened to have what he was looking for.

No, his way might be riskier, but it was much faster. He'd be in and out in a single night and could move on to the next estate immediately if he had to.

He shook his head. "Thanks for the advice, but I don't want to take that much time. I may have to search through every estate in Robinton."

Aminah shrugged, yet again, casually. "It takes the time it takes. Doing it the wrong way first'll just make it take even longer."

Ezren had nothing to say to that, so he merely continued to eat. They ate in silence for a while, then Aminah gestured behind her and to the left.

"There's an estate real close that way. The Lord there has the most magical stuff of anyone nearby. Maybe half a day's walk fehr a horse. Yeh seem like a nice boy, Ezren, and I'd hate to see yeh get caught sneakin' around. If they catch yeh they might lock yeh up, send yeh off with a beatin', or maybe even kill yeh."

Ezren forced a smile. "I guess I'd better not get caught then, right?"

She looked at him, gave a small chuckle and shook her head. "I like yeh, boy. I think yeh're an idiot ten times over," she looked hard at him for emphasis. "But I can't help but like yeh."

Ezren felt his smile get a little less forced. Aminah might be a bit rough, but he couldn't help but like her too. In some ways, she reminded him of Fiona. They were completely different people, and yet they both had a way of seeing past the words he said and understanding what he was thinking.

They sat in silence as the fire crackled. Both had finished their rabbits, and it seemed as though the silence *should* be awkward, but it wasn't. The sun disappeared behind the horizon and stars began to peek out. It was a perfectly clear night, and the only things obscuring their view of the cosmos were the trees and the light from the fire.

After night had settled and the fire began to die down, Aminah stood and brushed herself off. Now that she was standing, he could see that she was about of a height with him, and perhaps a little broader in the shoulders than it had appeared while she'd been lounging.

"Well, yeh're welcome to stay the night out here under the overhang. Not enough room in my home fehr the both of us and I don't trust yeh that far yet anyway, but yeh can sleep out here if yeh want."

She walked off towards the little hill she called home, straight to a large bush. Ezren furrowed his eyebrows as he watched. Surely she hadn't actually planted a bush in front of her door…

It made sense as soon as she bent over and picked up the bush. The trailing leaves and branches had kept hidden the shallow but wide pot that the bush was kept inside. Moving the bush revealed a small door, short enough that she would have to bend over to get through. He watched her go in and straighten up once she was inside. She closed the door without another word.

Ezren turned his eyes back to the fire. He should leave, shouldn't he? Find somewhere else to sleep the night. Ben's warning echoed again in his head. But…hadn't it been his assumption she meant him harm that had led to him getting shot and tied up in the first place?

Had Ben given him bad advice?

His bedroll was with his saddlebags, so he trudged over there to retrieve it before going to the overhang. Inspecting the overhang, he saw that it was well built, and sloped and layered properly that even if it rained the shelter would keep most of the water off. He nodded in approval, laid out his bedroll, and climbed into his blankets against the chilly night. He considered putting out the fire, but there may still be warm coals in the morning that would make it much easier to rekindle.

Aminah had said that there was an estate within a half a day's walk from here. He'd head that way in the morning. With that decided, he closed his eyes and sought sleep. He found it easily, as calm as he had been at Glacies Castle.

The following morning, he tarried long enough to breakfast with Aminah, then bid her farewell. She waved once as he mounted up, a look of mild concern on her face, then turned to get back to…whatever she did all day. Ezren led Asteri out of the clearing, using a faint trail that Aminah had pointed out as a deer path that she often used when heading this way.

The forest continued on for about five miles, so Aminah had said. While part of him wanted to rush, with how uneven the terrain was, Ezren chose not to risk anything faster than a walk. He didn't emerge from the forest until mid-morning, when the landscape opened up before him. There were still trees, sometimes stands of them, but he was looking at a long, narrow valley that ran from north to south for miles and miles in each direction.

Running right through the middle of the valley was a road, presumably the North Road of Robinton. There might be patrols on that road, with orders to be on the lookout for a young boy who had violated Robinton City codes one and three.

From this vantage, he could get a clear picture of how the Robinton Estates were laid out, and a better understanding of just how many there were… Some were separated from others by less than a mile, and they went all the way up and down the hollow, which itself extended out of view in both directions. There had to be at least a hundred, all told.

The estate closest to him was situated exactly how Aminah had described that it would be – in the middle of a few acres that looked like it had been painstakingly flattened out in a square around the building. The entire square was fenced in. From here, it looked much like the fences Ezren had seen around animal pens on farmland. The building itself had tall outer walls, but plenty of windows that Ezren could see.

He walked Asteri down the gentle slope that led into the valley, not going directly toward the estate, but rather to a stand of trees a little north of it. He would tie Asteri there and then sneak his way to the estate. If he was lucky, he could be in and out with enough time to at least get to the next estate before the end of the day. Who knows, he might even have time to sneak into that one as well.

The stand of trees was farther than he had thought, and it took him until about midday to reach it. Once there, he took a break to eat a little food and give Asteri an opportunity to graze. He also made the decision to hobble her instead of tying her so she could continue to graze while he was gone.

There wasn't much cover between the stand of trees and the estate, so for the most part Ezren tried to walk purposefully, then use the cover when it was available. It was not likely that anyone was watching out here with enough scrutiny that they would notice him approaching the fence, but if they did he wanted them to see someone who had every right to be there. Nothing suspicious here.

As he approached the fence, he realized that it wasn't like the livestock fences at all; those had simple 'A' frame supports with three or four logs going across one side with lots of space between the logs. This fence was also of logs, but with far more going across, making the gaps too small for him to fit more than his wrist through. He could climb it easily enough, he supposed, but he would have no idea who might be looking out a window right at that moment.

It was tall enough that he was mostly hidden from view of the estate, so he walked up and down it a ways to see if there was a tree anywhere on the other side that could block him from view as he came over the fence. He found one such tree and took a deep breath to steady his nerves. This was it. This was worth it. He needed to find this new magic.

Making sure that the tree was between him and the house, he climbed the logs and peered over the top of the fence, scanning the entire area to see if anyone was there. It would be much better to do this at night, but he didn't want to wait that long, especially after seeing how many estates he might have to search through.

He swung his legs over the fence, then noticed how close he was to the tree and decided to jump from the fence into the cover of the dense branches. From there he could take all the time he wanted to look around.

There really wasn't much to see once he was in the tree. The grounds were immaculately maintained with bushes, trees, and flowers planted all around. It looked like a too-perfect version of what one might find in the wild. Perhaps that was the point.

To the north side of the estate a gardener worked, but from this vantage point there wasn't another soul in sight. This might be easier than he had thought. He stayed in the tree for several minutes, keeping watch and practicing holding his breath again. He'd used Ben's breath-holding trick a number of times, and it was remarkably effective at keeping his mind occupied, especially when he realized that he was getting better at it and could do it longer than he had before.

Over the course of his observation, nothing changed at all. The one gardener he could see was slowly working his or her way up towards him, watering flowers and skipping over bushes and trees. No other gardeners, guards, or other workers came into sight, and he noticed no one walking past any of the windows that had open curtains.

Well, that one gardener was only going to keep getting closer, and Ezren had no interest in waiting long enough for them to come and go, so the sooner he made his move the better. He plotted out a path in his mind, then dropped carefully from the tree and ran, hunched over, to the cover of a nearby bush. He then watched the gardener for a moment to make sure that they hadn't reacted to his movement, then dashed to the cover of the next bush.

He continued this pattern all the way to the back wall of the estate. There were first floor windows within easy reach, so Ezren began testing each window to see if he could find one that wasn't locked from the inside. The first three he tested wouldn't budge, but the fourth one swung open silently. He crouched down below the window and raised his head slowly to peer over the edge to see if anyone was in there. He saw the back of one man walking away wearing some kind of uniform and carrying a short spear.

Why would anyone carry a spear that short? It was barely taller than the man was. Maybe it was intended to be a one-handed weapon.

He took a deep breath and swung himself inside, grateful that he had decided to leave his sword and shield with Asteri. He wished no ill on any of the people here, and his weapons would only get in the way as he sleuthed.

After hopping in through the window, he belatedly remembered to check the status of the gardener. He turned, still squatting, and looked to see if the gardener had noticed him. He looked all around, and even stuck his head out and craned his neck searching, but the gardener was nowhere to be found. That might be a bad sign, or it might not mean anything.

Either way, there wasn't much he could do about it that he wasn't already planning to do: find where the magical artifacts were kept as quickly as possible and search for one that fit the description in the prophecy...preferably without anyone seeing him.

He pulled the window shut and looked around, remembering to stand straight and behave as though he was supposed to be there.

In the castle at Novis Terram, the pieces of art and sculpture had been scattered in different rooms throughout the castle, but the King and Queen didn't really *collect* anything that Ezren knew about. If they did, they didn't keep the collection somewhere public. It would have to be in their apartments in the castle...That seemed as good a lead as any, so Ezren opted to search for the Lord's private chambers. He walked forward, down the hall he'd watched the soldier go down, looking for a staircase going up.

If *he* were a lord, he'd have his rooms on a higher floor, probably the highest floor in the building. And he wouldn't have anything else on that floor besides his living quarters, which would display his most prized collections.

The hallway opened up on his right to reveal a staircase that curved slowly to the right. He stepped purposefully up the stairs, hoping that no one would see him. A servant, probably a maid based on the stack of linens she carried, came down and started upon seeing him. He did the only thing he could think of – he smiled and waved.

"Hello," he said cheerily as he continued walking up the stairs.

The maid stared after him, confusion on her face, then gave herself a shake and continued down the stairs. She seemed to have bought the deception.

The stairs opened up onto the second floor but also continued up to the third floor, which should be the uppermost based on what Ezren had seen from outside. He climbed the rest of the stairs and found a pair of brass-bound doors, closed, but thankfully with no one guarding them. It made a certain amount of sense – why guard the lord's rooms when the lord was not in?

He tested the doors and cursed softly. Locked. He felt around in his pockets. He'd never been particularly good at picking locks – Raban had been much better on the few occasions they'd had to do it for one of their pranks.

As he dug in his pockets for anything that might be useful, he heard a sound from the other side of the door and panicked, ducking behind the suit of armor on a stand to his right. The door opened, and another maid left the room, using her foot to push the door closed behind her. Without thinking, he shot his hand out from behind the armor and caught the door before it closed.

This was his chance! She was already going down the stairs so he ducked out, slid through, and shut the door behind him before she had looked back. Once in, he looked around and smiled. Arrayed throughout this front room were numerous objects on pedestals and stands that all seemed unusual in one way or another.

In one spot was a giant chest that looked like it was made out of solid cement and was large enough for him to climb into. Next to it was a sword that curved back and forth along its length like a snake, which seemed both unnecessary and impractical, and a pot that seemed normal except it was very shiny – certainly the shiniest pot Ezren had ever seen.

He walked carefully through the artifacts, looking at each one and seeing if any might fit the words of the prophecy in any conceivable way. Most of these things were quite obviously junk – an old horseshoe that just happened to have a crack in the shape of a lightning bolt, an old, tattered cloak that may have once been fine based on the embroidery up and down the front edging – but some of them were genuinely bewildering like a solid, white box with a sheet of glass on the front, and something that looked like one of those blacksmith puzzles except it was three times as large and far more intricate.

Nothing he saw seemed close at all to "light shrink from view" or "sword shatter". The closest would have been that strange chest if he climbed in and closed the lid.

He was just beginning to contemplate his departure when the door suddenly flew open. Three burly guards stood there, their short spears pointed at Ezren. For the briefest moment he considered trying to talk his way out of this one, but one look at their faces told him they knew full well that he was not supposed to be there.

He dashed to the nearest window and started fiddling with the latch. He'd take his chances climbing down the outside.

The men yelled and came after him. He had just gotten the window open and was starting to climb out of it when a hand grabbed his foot. He kicked out and heard a cry of pain, but before he could get the foot all the way out another pair of hands grabbed him firmly by the shin, and try as he might, he couldn't get his foot free. The third guard grabbed his other leg and together they pulled him in, struggling like a caught fox.

"Stupid waif!" Yelled a guard. He had a hand to his face, not quite covering a large foot-shaped red mark.

The hurt guard leaned over and punched down at Ezren's face, hitting him so hard that Ezren's vision darkened for a moment. Then the guard grabbed Ezren's chin and forced his eyes to his own.

"This is how we treat thieves around here, boy."

His other hand balled into a fist and socked Ezren in his side. Ezren jerked back and cried out.

"I wa-wasn't trying to steal anything," he said, coughing.

"Oh, shut up, boy. The gardener saw you sneaking in through the window. She came and got us and where do we find you? Hiding in the master's quarters!" the guard replied.

Was there anything he could say to convince them? Another fist impacted Ezren's side, and he tried to curl up in pain.

"Ple-please," he gasped, "I'm sorry."

"Sorry?!" yelled the guard Ezren had kicked. "Oh, you're not sorry yet, but you will be."

Blows began to rain down on him. He fought back as best he could, but darkness quickly took him.

A cough escaped Ezren's throat, startling him awake.. Under him was a cold, unforgiving floor. He didn't remember losing conscious-ness, though maybe that was normal. He tried to move, and his entire body protested. He groaned in pain. The guards had worked him over quite thoroughly, that much he remembered. It seemed his entire body was bruised. His legs would barely move and his arms weren't much better.

He laid where he was for a few minutes, but now that he was awake the floor was simply not comfortable enough. He pulled himself to a sitting position, a moan escaping his lips, and leaned against the wall, displacing some straw to do so. Where was he? He looked around.

He was in a jail cell, lit only by an oil lamp hanging on the wall outside his cell. Straw was piled on the floor in lieu of a bed. High on the back wall of his cell was a window that gave a little light as well. He used the wall to push himself to his feet and limped over to the window. The sun was going down. He must have been unconscious for hours.

Looking down, he tenderly lifted his shirt. His stomach and chest were a mass of bruises, already showing an angry red and purple. He shifted his weight from one leg to another. Well, he tried to, but his right leg buckled with a sharp pain and he fell to the ground.

That worried him; that pain had felt like more than just a bruise. He wondered if something had happened to the bone. His back was once again to the wall, and he was sitting on the straw now, so he leaned his head back and rested, trying to take stock of his options.

There was no way out of this cell anytime soon. He could probably fit through the window if he could find some way to get the bars out of it, but not in his present condition. He would need days, perhaps even a tenday, to get to where he could leap and climb and pull himself up. He tried to open and close his fists, and winced in pain at just opening them less than halfway. What had they done to his fingers? Hopefully they weren't broken...

He sighed. He hadn't even taken anything.

He should have listened to Aminah.

He sat there, one hand on his ribs -- they felt better with a little pressure on them -- and listened to a drip repeating in the distance. His stomach rumbled, so loud he jumped. He hadn't even realized that he was hungry, as though the pain throughout the rest of his body had drowned out his stomach. A quick look around the floor told him that there was no food to be had here in the cell, and based on his treatment so far, there may very well not be any forthcoming.

There had to be a way out of here. He didn't know how long Asteri would go undiscovered in the stand of trees he'd left her in, though she should be able to find enough grazing to last her for at least a few days. The trouble was, every way he could think of to get out would only be feasible if he were in good condition, which he absolutely was not.

The sound of a heavy door slamming brought his head up, looking to the door of his cell. A young woman appeared who looked rather familiar...ah yes, it was the maid that he'd passed on the stairs, the one that had looked confused when he smiled at her.

She carried a plate with a generous helping of meat and mashed potatoes on it. She froze outside the cell, looking in on him with wide eyes. Was she scared of *him*? He could barely move. He brought his hand from his side and gave her a wave, wincing at the pain of shifting.

"Hello. Don't suppose that's for me, is it?" he asked.

"The shambaya said that you should only be given half at each meal," she started, her eyes looking over him quickly. "But I...I think maybe you've been punished enough already."

She swallowed nervously, knelt down, and pushed the plate through the gap at the bottom of the bars.

Ezren looked at the plate of food hungrily. It seemed so far away. It might take him the rest of the night just to retrieve his food. He looked back up at her.

"Thank you," he said sincerely. This girl did not have to show him kindness and had little reason to believe anything but the worst in him. "Do they treat all thieves this way?"

Still kneeling, she shrugged. "I do not know. You are the first they have caught since I began working here."

"Well," he said wryly, "perhaps now I know why no one attempts it."

He tried to shift so he could sit up higher and ended up back where he'd started.

"What were you trying to steal?" she asked.

He shrugged. "I wasn't trying to steal anything. I'm looking for a magic artifact, a specific one. If I'd found it here I might have borrowed it, but I would have brought it back."

"What does it look like?" She asked.

"Uh, well...I...don't actually know," he replied, realizing how foolish that probably sounded.

She gave a small laugh. "Well then how would you know if you found it?"

"That..." he said, a small smile coming to his face. "...is a very good question."

The sound of the same, heavy door opening came and she looked down the hallway.

"I need to go," she said, getting to her feet quickly and brushing off the bottom of her skirt.

"Thank you," he said again. "Truly."

She looked at him, nodded, then walked away. Ezren looked back down at the plate of food. It was simultaneously the object of his greatest desire *and* his greatest adversary. Of all the things he'd accomplished in his life, getting to that plate and successfully eating the contents seemed like it would be the greatest.

Hands and knees were probably best. His ribs would hurt like the Inferno, but he should be able to make it to the plate without collapsing. He leaned forward and caught himself with his hands, but his left wrist buckled and he came down onto his shoulder. Instead of trying again, he brought his foot up and pushed against the wall he'd been leaning against, which moved him a foot or so closer to the plate. His right hand he used to slide himself across the floor the rest of the way until he got to it.

How bad had the beating *been*? He'd gotten in his fair share of fights and had been beaten before, but he'd never experienced anything like this. It was like every inch of him had been pummeled to a pulp. He managed to eat the food on the plate, making a point to eat all of it so that no one would be able to tell the maid had given him more food than she was supposed to. When he was finished, he dragged himself back to where the straw was thickest on the floor and laid down, trying to find a position comfortable enough to sleep.

The night did not bring much rest. His body was exhausted and wanted nothing more than to recover, but the pain all over his body kept him awake. The straw poking through his clothes didn't help.

He eventually found sleep, but it was fitful, and he found himself painstakingly rolling over several times during the night. For that reason, he was already awake when light was beginning to show on the eastern horizon, perhaps two hours before the sun would actually rise. He heard a loud click, and then the sound of the same heavy door opening. He rolled himself over to see out the cell wall and was surprised to see the same maid come, this time with a stout ring of keys.

"Come on," she whispered, waving him over before looking for the right key.

He propped himself up on his elbow.

"What are you doing?" He whispered back.

She looked at him like he was an idiot. "I'm getting you out."

"Why?"

She looked around furtively. "I heard the guards talking. They said that…well…the law in Robinton is that a caught thief can be beaten, but he can't be killed unless he attacks someone in the house. They're saying that since you kicked one of them that…they can kill you."

"What?!" Ezren exclaimed. The maid held out her hands to shush him as she looked around to make sure no one was coming.

"What kind of men does your lord hire as guards?!" He whispered incredulously.

She shrugged helplessly. "I don't know if they'd actually do it! Maybe it was all talk, but I think they're anxious to have something big to tell Lord Mehum when he returns. A violent, dangerous thief is a bigger story than a young, innocent one."

Ezren had no interest in taking any chances. He used the wall to help him stand up shakily. Despite his fretful sleep, the night seemed to have done him at least a little bit of good; he could stand and shuffle forward as long as he was leaning against the wall.

She tried a handful of keys before finding the right one, and the door swung open with a loud creak. They both froze and listened, hoping that no one had heard the noise. She waved him out. He shuffled forward as best he could, but he tripped on his way out. He flung his hands out to catch himself, but the maid caught him first, grunting with the impact and grumbling under her breath.

"I know it hurts to move," she said, straining, "but do you think you can just, I don't know, live with the pain for a little bit? I can't carry you the whole way, and I certainly can't toss you over the wall."

He looked at her disbelieving; she clearly had no idea how much pain he was actually in. Gritting his teeth, he straightened out and pushed off her shoulder until he was standing on his own. It felt like lightning was going up his right leg. His left leg hurt as well, but nothing like his right. He clenched his jaw to keep from yelling in agony. The pain caused him to take deep breaths, which in turn caused his chest and stomach to seize up in pain as well.

He took shallower breaths, which helped a little. As they began to step forward, beads of sweat popped out on his forehead. How was he supposed to get over the wall in this condition?

"This early," he whispered. "Could we make it out the front gate instead of going over the wall?"

The maid shook her head. "It's guarded all day long. But it's alright, we received a delivery of summer flowers yesterday, and the gardener had them put the crate right next to the wall. Should be easy enough to get over once you're on top of the crate. Easier than climbing straight up, for sure."

He grunted noncommittally, very much *not* sure about how this was going to go. They reached the end of the short row of cells. There were only four in total, which still seemed excessive for a single estate that apparently saw so little crime that the guards would consider committing murder in order to prove their value.

Outside the door to the cell block, there were no guards. Either the maid had lured the guards away or they just knew how immobile Ezren was and saw no point in guarding him.

The maid continued to lead him through the dimly lit hallways, each one with only a single oil lamp lit to provide just enough light to see. As they neared the end of the hallway, the ground began to rise up toward a door. The maid opened the door first and peeked out.

"It's all clear. Come on," she said, waving to Ezren.

He made it to the top of the ramp, gasping for breath and soaked in sweat, and stepped out onto the grounds lit softly by the dawn sky.

"Come on. The crate is this way," the maid said, pulling gently on his arm.

He followed painfully, as quickly as he could. The maid was bouncing on the balls of her feet and kept getting ahead of him and then having to wait.

She baffled him. She was clearly afraid of the guards, and from the sound of it she had good reason to be. Helping him escape would at minimum get her put out from the estate, and she might even find herself in a similar, or worse, situation than he himself currently was. He stopped, partially because he needed a break, and partially because he wanted answers.

"Hold on," he said, shuffling a few steps to a tree trunk to lean on and take the weight of his right leg. She stopped and looked around furtively.

"Why are you helping me?" He asked.

She looked at him, confused. "I already told you."

"Yes, but, this is so much risk for you to take. Couldn't they do all the same things to you if you get caught helping me escape? Why take the risk? How did you know I wasn't as bad as they say? A violent thief?"

She thought about what to say for a moment, then spoke without looking at him. "You smiled at me." She laughed when she saw his face. "Oh, that makes me sound like a filly. No, I did not go weak at the knees at a smile from you. When I saw you on the stairs, I didn't recognize you, but you gave me a big smile and said hello. If you were violent or dangerous, wouldn't you have...I don't know... knocked me out and stuffed me in a closet or something?" She shrugged, her face red. "Maybe it was silly, but I just didn't think that someone who could give such a genuine smile could be that bad of a person."

Ezren looked at her. She may not be a...filly, whatever she meant by that, but she certainly had a helping of naivety in her. He truly hoped she never met someone like Mir Walsh, who could have given the most innocent grin while shoving a knife in your ribs.

"Well," he said, straightening. "Thank you." He forced a smile. "It's good to hear that my smile can still make a woman swoon."

She scoffed, but smiled as well. "Oh shut up, you-" she paused, a look of confusion on her face. "I don't know your name."

The false name began to form on his lips, but he stopped himself. The least he could do was give her his real name. "Ezren," he said.

"Well, it's nice to meet you, Ezren," she replied. "My name is Sarrah."

He inclined his head in the closest thing to a bow he could manage. "Nice to meet you, Sarrah."

"Now, can we get on with this, please?" She asked, gesturing forward.

He nodded and began moving forward, trying his best to ignore the pain.

What seemed like an eternity later they arrived at a crate up against the base of the wall. It was not a difficult wall to climb anyway, and with the crate, he could probably make it. She helped him clamber up onto the crate, which was about waist high, then she climbed up next to him to help hoist him over the top.

He didn't realize their mistake until he was straddled on the topmost log and his weight started shifting towards the other side: his hands could not grip the uppermost log on the fence long enough to ease himself down. His weight pulled too hard and he fell the full height of the fence, a new sharp pain forming on his left side. He laid there, trying to breathe through the pain and get himself under control.

"Are you alright?" Came Sarrah's voice from the other side of the wall.

"Yes," he gasped. "I'm fine, just...you go back in now, before you get caught."

"Alright," she said. After a moment she said, "Good luck, Ezren. I hope we meet again someday."

"Me too, Sarrah," he forced out, as naturally as he could. "Thank you."

He listened to the light scraping of her getting off the crate, then a few moments later he tried to roll onto his right side. As he did, his alarm rose as he felt the stub of branch that he had fallen on pull *out* of his body. He had assumed it was just a rock, but now he felt himself bleeding out of what seemed a sizable hole in his left side. He moved his hand to his back, feeling the wound. Blood was coming out at a worrying rate. He could barely move.

If he didn't figure out a solution soon, he was going to die.

That realization hit him like a falling boulder. How could he do anything when he couldn't even move?

But...he *could* move. It hurt so badly he thought he'd either throw up or pass out, but he had walked from the cell block to the wall successfully. He could get to Asteri, leave his supplies behind and ride bareback to Aminah. Maybe she'd be able to help him. That was his only chance.

He gritted his teeth and forced himself to his feet, moving his left hand to push on his wound to hopefully slow down the bleeding. The feeling of lightning moving through his right leg persisted and his vision blurred, his mind threatening to lose consciousness, but he persevered, forcing himself to look forward and walk as quickly as he could.

He didn't know how long it took, but he eventually reached Asteri, unhobbled her, and threw himself across her back, unable to get astride. He gasped into Asteri's ear.

"Aminah. Take me to Aminah. Back where we came."

Asteri understood the urgency. She took off at a gallop, nearly throwing Ezren off, but not protesting when he tightened his grip on her mane.

Ezren put everything he had into staying on his horse. Every step sent a jolt through his leg, and he felt the blood seeping between the fingers of his left hand.

Asteri ran through the forest as sure-footed as a stag, and took him with incredible speed to Aminah's clearing, where Ezren slid off the saddle onto his feet and looked for her.

She was nowhere to be seen.

He hung his head, resigned to his fate. This had been his only chance. He had neither time nor somewhere else to go. His vision darkened, and he distantly realized that he was falling. He collapsed onto the ground. All went black.

For the third time in recent memory, Ezren came slowly back to consciousness, coming out of a strange, ethereal dream that seemed just raw colors, shapes, and feelings. His first thought was that he was too hot. It felt as though he were asleep inside of a stove. He forced his eyes open and looked around.

He wasn't in an oven. That was a relief. With his luck lately, he would have no trouble believing that a clan of ogres had found him and were cooking him up for dinner. The view of the night sky was familiar. It seemed we was in Aminah's clearing, or at least, somewhere close by. It was night.

"Yeh finally awake?" A voice said, coming from a few feet away.

That was her voice. He closed his eyes, saying a quick prayer of gratitude. He turned his head, unwilling to try any other part of his body yet. He was back by the fire in almost the exact spot he had been when she'd tied him up.

Without another word, she got up and brought a waterskin to his lips, pouring before he had a chance to protest.

As soon as the water hit his lips, his body seemed to realize how much he needed water, as he drank and drank. She didn't stop pouring, so he kept drinking. He almost emptied the waterskin before needing time to breathe, but she was still pouring and he couldn't move his arms to stop her. He shifted his head back and tried to shake his head, which just got water all over him.

"Agh- what- stop!" He cried. "Stop!"

She finally lifted the waterskin and sighed.

"What are you doing?!" he gasped.

"Yeh need water. Honestly, yeh needed water a day and a half ago, but yeh can't give water to an unconscious person. I've only been able to give you sips when yeh woke up enough to swallow."

She peered at him, her eyes narrowed. "Looks like yehr fever has finally broken. I was worried it would overtake yeh."

"Why is it so hot?" he asked.

She laughed out loud. "Well probly 'cause I have every blanket I own on yeh right now." She started taking blankets off, and Ezren realized how much combined weight the blankets had been putting on his body. He could move his arms now, though not much.

"Thank you," he said weakly. "I didn't know where else to go."

"Yes, well," she said, not looking at him as she took the blankets to the other side of the fire. "It's a good thing we met on yehr way there, or yeh wouldn't have had anywhere to go at all."

He waited for a moment, but she simply settled back on the ground with her back to a log, looking at him sternly with her arms folded. Yes, she reminded him very much of Fiona.

"Aren't you going to ask me what happened?" Ezren asked.

She snorted. "I know what happened, boy. I know *exactly* what happened. Yeh went to the estate, tried to sneak in, got caught and beaten within an inch of yehr life. I assume the open wound on yehr side came as yeh were trying to escape? Doesn't look like a sword or spear wound."

He struggled to prop himself on his right elbow. He wasn't in nearly as much pain now as he had been before, and found it much easier than expected to get up to that position.

"You told me that would happen," he said.

"Yes, I did," she replied, nodding.

"I didn't listen. I'm sorry."

She snorted again, but more softly this time. "Well, yeh seem to have been punished enough. Yeh should consider the price cheap fehr the lesson learned."

What did she mean by that? Surely she couldn't mean that his current state was the cheap price? Felt pretty expensive to him.

"What I *don't* understand," Aminah said, "is how yeh managed to get all the way back here, hehrt as yeh were."

She shook her head. "Yeh must have the willpower of a mountain. Or the discipline of an Enderian."

Ezren tried to shrug but, being propped up on one elbow, he found it too difficult and gave it up. So much for Aminah's theory on willpower or discipline.

"So yeh still going to try and find this magic artifact of yehrs?" She asked.

"Of course," Ezren replied, working to get up from his elbow to a sitting position, pain surging from the wound on his back.

"Yeh wise enough now to do it my way? Or yeh need another beatin'?"

He shook his head, settling with his back to the rock behind and his legs straightened out before him. His right leg had two thick, straight branches that had each been flattened on one side tied tightly to it, making it so that he could not bend his leg at all even if he had wanted to. He reached gingerly back to the wound on his left side. There was a layer of leaves on top of it. Based on the numbness, it seemed that she had made some sort of poultice to help with it.

"Where did you learn to do all this?" He asked.

She looked into the fire. "I've been around a bit longer than yeh, Ezren. Livin' out here by yehrself, yeh pick up things like that real quick."

"Can you teach me?" he asked.

Laughing, she said, "Yeh even have time to be taught?" She shrugged. "It ain't magic; the bone in yehr right thigh I think is cracked, 'cause it was swelling too much to just be bruising. Not very bad though, or we'd be able to tell because it would be all…" she made a disconcerting jerking motion with her hands. "With swelling…yeh mostly just gotta wait until it goes down by itself, but those branches will stop yeh from bending or putting weight on it and making it heal wrong."

Ezren swallowed, remembering all the walking, climbing, and lurching-in-lieu-of-running he'd done since his leg had been injured.

"What about this?" he asked, touching the poultice on his back.

"Oh that's nothing," she said, waving it away. "That's just Cleanlily to fight the infection and Yarrow to numb the pain. I use it all the time."

"I also sewed yeh up as best I could. Still, yeh'll have a real ugly scar."

It was his turn to snort. "If all I have to worry about is a scar, then I'm not worried at all."

She looked at him. "Yeh say yeh're going back to keep looking for this artifact."

He nodded.

"Well, maybe yeh could be a bit mehre strategic in yehr choice of targets."

"What do you mean?" he asked, confused.

"When I was down in town the other day, while yeh was getting' yehr ass beat, like as not, I took time to listen to what everyone was sayin'. Galdrach is comin' to visit. His tower is a ways away but he's good friends with one of the lords around here. Don't know the lord's name, but I know which estate is his."

Galdrach. The wizard who had given his brothers powers. His father had described Galdrach as a very old wizard even back before Ezmith had been born, and Ezren had just assumed he was dead, though he hadn't given it much thought. Galdrach was the only wizard Ezren had ever heard of who experimented with magic. If any artifacts could release new magic, it made a lot of sense for them to be either with Galdrach or his good friend.

"Can you show me where his estate is?"

"Yes," she said tentatively. "On one condition." She held up her finger. "Yeh take my advice and do it right. Scout out the estate, learn the workings of it, find a servant who can get yeh in, and do things that way instead of sneaking around and ending up back here again."

"I promise," Ezren said, nodding. "When can you show me?"

"It'll have to wait until yeh're healed up a bit more," she replied. "I want yeh off that leg fehr at least a tenday."

"A *tenday?!*" Ezren exclaimed. "But I need to go faster than that!"

She held out her hands. "I can't very well change how yehr body heals, now can I? Besides, I *told* yeh that if yeh try to do something the wrong way first it'll take longer than just doing it the right way would have."

Ezren leaned his head back on the boulder behind him, looking up at the sky. An entire tenday, stuck waiting in this clearing. By the sound of it, he wouldn't even be able to train or practice.

"What's yehr hurry, anyway?" She asked. "Yehr pa isn't gettin' any deader."

He pulled his head up to look at her incredulously. He should feel offended by that, shouldn't he? He'd been enraged when Asteri had said something similar back in the castle.

Aminah had a point, though, no matter how crassly she had put it. The only reason for urgency he could think of was what Mellion had said about how the passage of time can make it harder to use magic to investigate, but it had already been long enough that any magic he found would have to be able to help regardless of time passing anyway.

"What am I supposed to do for the next ten days? What are *you* going to do for the next ten days?" Ezren asked.

"Well, I'm not goin' to wait on yeh hand and foot, if that's what yeh're asking. First I'll make yeh a crutch so yeh can get around without using that leg too much. Yeh can lay yehr own snares and keep yehrself comfehrtable just fine. I'll be around, checkin' on yeh to make sure yeh're not dyin'."

She got up, dusted off her leggings, and started walking to her little hill-home.

"Good night, then," she said as she went.

"Good night," Ezren replied. He sighed as she closed her door behind her.

He was going to get a lot of practice holding his breath over the next tenday.

CHAPTER 11: BAHADIR

When Beaumont had reported that this next ram had been "over-engineered", Ezmith hadn't really understood what he'd meant. Now, seeing it with his own two eyes, Ezmith understood. A part of him simmered in anger; his engineers had delayed the attack for two extra days to do *this?*

The front of the battering ram was no longer shaped to a point and covered in a layer of steel, it was shaped as the head of an actual ram, as in a male goat, and seemed to have been fully cast in solid steel. The ram itself was larger in every dimension, fitting six men on either side instead of four, and had steel plating on the outside and on the roof.

He ground his teeth, thinking about how much all that steel must have cost, and how many swords and polearms he could have made with it, especially when the ram didn't *need* those extra defenses; the thing was going to be accompanied by a wizard, for Clayara's sake!

The engineers assured him that the ram-head design would be more effective at not only breaking through a specific point, but also weakening the wall throughout a larger area. They had determined to attack a portion of wall about a quarter of a mile away from the gate. There was a section of Bahadir's wall that was not as heavily defended, and based on what they'd seen when scrying, the wall itself narrowed at that point, though it wasn't clear why.

Regardless, it made for the perfect spot for a surprise attack with a battering ram.

Ezmith could hear the engineers making bets amongst themselves about how many hits it would take to knock down the wall. Idiots.

He glanced down, and saw that someone, either an engineer or a soldier, had tied a cloth with two large stones in it to the bottom of the rearmost portion of the ram. He rolled his eyes and turned to face Eztas, the army fanning out behind him and out of sight.

Eztas, as usual, looked angry. More than ever the huge man seemed to resent his own existence.

"You know your mandate?" Ezmith asked curtly. He had exchanged few words with his turncoat brother since finding out that he and Ezrote had helped their father and brother escape.

Eztas nodded and shifted his enormous shoulders, adjusting his grip on his massive war hammer and shield.

Giving Eztas a mandate before putting him under the enchantments was a lesson learned from hard experience. Eztas could be as destructive to their own forces as the enemy's when he was under the berserker enchantment, but as long as he only had one mandate to keep in his mind, it seemed to keep him focused on the objective instead of killing everything around him.

The timing for making the Fold was crucial. Ezmith checked with Captain Wallitz to make sure that everyone was ready, then stepped forward, in front and to the side of the battering ram.

The sun was shining, luckily, but the smell of the rain from the last several days was still in the air, making it feel more like a fresh spring day than one in the early days of summer. It rained more here near the coast than Ezmith was used to. He raised his arms dramatically, remembering what his mother had often said about theatrics, and created the Fold, as wide as it could go.

They were less than 100 paces from the wall. The battering ram immediately creaked forward and began picking up speed. The thing could never go truly fast, but the men could get it up to almost a jog after a bit.

Guillame walked immediately behind the ram, a look of distaste on his face. Likely it was the smell of the soldiers operating the ram. Guillame had a sensitive nose.

The moment the ram was through the Fold, Ezmith began casting his enchantments onto his brother. Eztas began to quiver, then to shake, and his skin turned bright red. The ram was only halfway to the wall when Eztas leaped through the Fold and ran after, overtaking the ram and reaching the wall before it.

The rest of the army poured through after him. With a little luck, the army wouldn't be exposed to arrow fire long enough to take a significant amount of casualties. The heavy, repeated 'thunk' of the ram mingled with another, more frenzied beating sound. Eztas must be hitting the wall with his hammer in his impatience.

Silently, held the Fold open as thousands of soldiers continued to march through. He maintained a look of stoicism, nodding to soldiers who caught his eye. After the last row of soldiers marched through, Ezmith waved the Fold closed.

It was out of his hands now, and Eztas had his mandate. He stopped for a moment to consider the feeling that a weight had just been lifted off his shoulders. He was responsible for holding the siege on Dazbog, which should be simple, and Wallitz and Eztas were responsible for taking Bahadir, which should also be simple. If they failed, it would be on their shoulders instead of his, and there was something…relaxing about that.

～

Why is the ram so slow?!?! Eztas thought frenetically as he leapt around it. Banging on the wall with his hammer had cracked one of the bricks, but had not come close to bringing it down, so now he leapt. Leapt as high as he could to try and grab the top edge of the wall. He needed to get in! He needed to kill!

Though he could leap much higher than a normal man thanks to his natural strength, he could not quite reach the top of the wall. He jumped over and over as the ram continued to pound the wall. Archers had come in defense and were raining arrows down on him and the ram, but he was protected by a Stone Skin enchantment, and the ram had thick metal and wood to protect it.

At the top of one leap, he saw several defenders running along the top of the wall with buckets of oil and arrows. He needed to kill them! He leapt again, as hard as he could, his every landing leaving another pair of deep footprints in the soft ground. So close!

Must get higher! He landed next to the ram.

Must get higher! He landed next to the ram.

Must get higher! He landed next to the ram.

Then he looked at the ram. Ram was higher. Ram was strong.

He jumped on top of the ram, now about six feet closer to the top of the wall. He squatted down, then leapt upwards with all his strength. The fingers of his left hand closed on the parapet! He was there! Immediately a sword came down on his fingers, but he had Stone Skin. The sword broke in two pieces. Eztas pulled himself up with a roar, feeling the arrows bounce off him.

Nothing could hurt him. He landed on the wall walk with both feet and pulled his second hammer off his back. The defenders on the wall looked at him, eyes wide in terror. With a primal yell, he ran forward just as another tremor ran through the wall. The ground beneath his feet began to give way. He leapt forward, swinging his hammer as he flew, sending the bodies of defenders in both directions.

The wall crumbled behind him, the ram having *finally* finished its work, and battle cries from the men in the rest of his army came closer as the thunderous sound of 10,000 running men got louder.

Eztas looked back up to the long wall walk in front of him that led all the way to the other side of the city. Time to kill more.

He took off at a run, barely slowing as he knocked defenders off the wall to either side. He had to find *more*, had to find a big group of soldiers. He could only keep one thought clear in his mind: kill as many enemy soldiers as possible before the enchantments wore off.

As he approached the towers flanking the gate, he saw in the courtyard below a mass of soldiers. Without thought, he leaped from the battlement and crashed with both hammers down in the very middle of the mass. He hardly noticed the blood, the noise, or the feeling of men's bodies crunching under his merciless swings. No, it was the *smell* he noticed. Blood had a smell, though he never noticed it when he was normal. It had a taste too, but he could *smell* it when he was like this, and the smell made him ravenous for more.

The panicked screams and shouts from the soldiers around him didn't even register as he laid about himself, his hammers snapping bone and hurtling men with every swing. Many soldiers dashed in, striking with spears or swords only to find that they could not penetrate his skin. They died even more quickly than the ones who fled.

As he finished with this group, the survivors attempting to flee, a new wave of troops rushed into the courtyard. Enemy reinforcements! He turned and immediately began to strike, killing perhaps ten or twelve before noticing the color of the uniforms. These were not *enemy* soldiers. He stopped and turned, looking to where the enemies had fled.

He ran forward, glancing to his left and seeing a small face looking out through a window. His grip on his hammers tightened. *Not* an enemy soldier. The face ducked down out of sight. He continued his run through the city streets, finding pockets of enemies and killing them.

After some time, he did not know how long, he felt his rage beginning to diminish.

His mind became clearer. Yes...he was coming out of it. He looked around. He was on an elevated walkway that did a ring around another courtyard deeper in the city. Bodies were all around him. The battle rage was always the first to fade. He thought that Ezmith did that on purpose, so that he would have time to leave the battlefield before the Stone Skin and Sustain wore off.

He turned on his heel and began walking purposefully out of the city. There was no fighting going on around him. There was no one around at all, as a matter of fact. Just bodies. Dead bodies of enemy soldiers he'd killed.

Now that he thought about it, it had been a long time since he had seen any soldiers on his side either. Hopefully they'd won and hadn't been routed. The pockets of enemy soldiers he'd been finding the past while had been small and isolated as well. No matter. He was done. He walked through the courtyard just inside the gate to the city. The gate was closed and unmanned. With only a little effort, he lifted the thick bar that held the swinging doors in place and dropped it to the ground, stepping over it to push the gate doors open.

He walked out towards where the army tents were being erected, knowing there would be a tent designated for him. As his rage faded completely, he wished the walk were longer. He just wanted to be alone.

~

Captain Wallitz watched Eztas step through the gate while it still swung slowly open. The battle rage seemed to have finally worn off. The battle had been won an hour ago, and the surrender given, but no one had been able to calm Eztas down or stop him from killing enemies who had already laid down their arms.

Wallitz had been forced to order the enemy soldiers to hide wherever they could and use his own soldiers to try and keep as many enemies out of sight as possible until the enchantments wore off. Now that the rampage was over, perhaps they could start processing the surviving enemy troops.

All things considered, the taking of the city had gone even more smoothly and swiftly than Wallitz had hoped. The defense had been unprepared; clearly the steward of Bahadir did not have the same mind for warfare as Lord Perivon himself did, and the engineers truly had done a wonder with that battering ram. The wall had come completely down in under a half an hour. Never in his years of soldiering had he seen an operation of this magnitude go so perfectly according to plan.

A scout rode his horse out of the now-open gate towards where Wallitz stood outside the command tent. With the city already taken, it might seem foolish to have spent the time to erect the tents, but Wallitz had his reasons.

This scout should have the news he'd been waiting for. Wallitz watched and waited as the scout came closer at a gallop. It was Doming.

Scout Doming pulled his horse to an abrupt halt just short of Wallitz.

"It's confirmed, sir. Perivon had a boat ready to push off if the city was under attack, but we were in quickly enough to stop it from leaving."

Now *that* was downright wonderful. So wonderful, in fact, that Wallitz had to question whether there was a trap hidden where he could not see it.

"It still must have taken our forces two hours between beginning the siege and reaching the docks, how was the ship not already gone? Was there another ship that had already left?"

"As to that..." Doming shrugged. "There are plenty of open spots on the docks where ships could have left from, but the captain of the boat we stopped said that they were to flee to alert Dazbog if Bahadir were under assault, and they had not yet received word from the Steward to do so."

Wallitz nodded to himself. Most likely a redundancy then. It was wisest to assume that a boat did make it out of the harbor and was currently on its way to Dazbog. At least they had stopped the rest of the sailors from getting to the warships and pushing off. That had been his biggest worry; take the city only to be blockaded by the fleet.

He turned his head to Lieutenant Emer, who stood behind him. "Have my horse saddled. I need to go into the city."

In a matter of minutes, Wallitz was riding through the front gate of the city, surrounded by a guard of 50 soldiers. Normally he'd be grateful for a guard like this as he moved into a just-conquered enemy city, but he had no fear of assassins or hidden archers this time. Every man, woman, and child in this city was likely still shaking at the knees at the threat of Eztas. He doubted any but the most defiant would find it in themselves to even glare at him as he rode by.

It was the docks that he wanted to see. He rode through the densely-packed corridors and wound his way following the signs directing him towards the docks.

He did not like Bahadir, he decided.

Like all cities, it had grown over time, but for some reason the streets had never been widened, and were instead still just wide enough to pass a single wagon or two horses riding side-by-side. As though to compensate for this, courtyards were placed frequently throughout the city, and traffic was only allowed to move in one direction on each road.

It made sense, in a way, but it also made it so that if you happened to need to go one block in the wrong direction, you'd have to travel at least four blocks in a circle of right or left turns to get back there. And Clayara have mercy on you if you were simply distracted and accidentally walked past your destination.

The road opened up into yet another courtyard that ran steeply down to the docks, the cobblestones set smoothly into the hill and providing reasonably sure footing for the horses as they moved down. Something like this would never have worked in Orjan; the winter freezes would have made this a death trap.

At least a thousand men in the uniforms of Cleononian sailors knelt at the bottom of the slope, under a guard of Ambartan troops. He hoped his soldiers had been treating these men well. The sailors' cooperation was essential to their plans. They couldn't hope to utilize Bahadir's fleet without their loyalty.

Wallitz stopped a little ways up the hill, where he hoped if he raised his voice that all the captured sailors would be able to hear him. Before speaking, he surveyed the sailors and noticed, to his surprise, that many of them were women. Indeed, it seemed that about one in every five sailors was a woman. Suddenly the speech he'd prepared felt wrong. He sat on his horse for a moment, thinking quickly about what to say.

"Hello," he began. "My name is Captain Wallitz. I represent the Lady Kimaya Virtesa of Ambarta and I hereby declare the city of Bahadir to be the newest part of her realm. Surely you have heard word from residents of The Wood Coast, Robinton, Disote, and even your own Mhairi that life under the rule of Ambarta is better, not worse, than you are used to."

He paused to swallow and take a breath.

"We would like your help in preventing as many unnecessary deaths of your people as possible. Your Lord Perivon has entrenched himself in Dazbog with a group of wizards who break their own code by using their magic against our soldiers in battle. Lord Ezmith has been forced to marshal all the wizards from our own realm to combat them. Taking the city will be a long, bloody affair in which many Cleononians, good, strong men and women, would lose their lives."

The majority of the sailors he could see had deeply suspicious looks on their faces. Not at all the 'thoughtful consideration' he'd been hoping for.

"However, Lord Perivon can only maintain Dazbog's defenses for as long as he is supplied by sea. If you are willing to man your ships and blockade the port of Dazbog, you can save perhaps thousands of Cleononian lives."

It was a potent argument, or at least he thought so, but the faces of the sailors did not look convinced. There was no response, except for one sailor, one of the women, to lean forward slightly and spit on the ground.

There was a brief pause, then, almost in perfect unison, the rest of the sailors leaned forward and also spat on the ground.

Their opinion on his proposal seemed quite clear.

He turned his horse and leaned his head to Lieutenant Emer to speak quietly with him.

"When Lord Ezmith opens a Fold for a report on the status of the battle, inform him that the city is taken with minimal Ambartan casualties, but that we will need the Lady Virtesa to convince the sailors to move against their own people."

Emer nodded and they rode together, out of the city. He could have commandeered one of the palaces in the city, with their odd architecture of towered domes topped with a spiral of rounded spikes, but it was bad luck to sleep the first night in a newly-conquered city. Everyone knew that.

The city dungeons were not large enough to house all the sailors, let alone all the remaining Cleononian defenders, so they pulled most of them out of the city to house them in prison camps. Most of the defenders were not professional soldiers, so after relinquishing their weapons they were permitted to return to their homes. The rest of the soldiers were interspersed with the sailors and separated into smaller camps of a hundred.

Wallitz and the rest of the captains had learned through hard experience that there were a few ways to lower the likelihood of an uprising. First, don't keep enemy soldiers in large groups. Second, do not organize them by their existing battalion structure. Intermingle them as much as possible, which would confuse the authority structure and take soldiers away from the comrades they trusted the most. Third, have a *heavy* guard presence, as heavy as is practical.

In this case, the prisoners shouldn't need to be held for very long. The Lady Virtesa would be here in no longer than a couple days, and then she would see to smoothing over any bad feelings.

～

Lady Virtesa smiled with pride as she listened to the report from the messenger that Ezmith had sent through a Fold. Ezmith really needed to teach the other wizards how to make Folds; he couldn't keep making them himself for every messenger that needed to go out, and it made sending replies take much longer by comparison. She'd solved that to a degree by ordering that a flock of pigeons be given a cote with Ezmith's army, and each messenger sent through a Fold bring a pigeon that could then be sent back if a response was needed.

Pigeons weren't as fast as Folds, of course, but they worked well enough for now, until she could convince her son to teach at least one other wizard how to make a Fold. She refocused on what the messenger was saying.

Bahadir had been taken in a matter of hours. The plan that Ezmith and Captain Wallitz had schemed up had gone perfectly. Ezmith had easily held the siege against Dazbog so far and saw no issues looming that needed to be addressed. Best of all, Captain Wallitz had requested her assistance in converting the Cleononian sailors to their cause so they could blockade Dazbog's port.

She'd been in Mhairi for some time now and for days had been thinking that there was little more need for her here. The mayor and city council had things well in hand, and the people's loyalty to her was assured. It was time to move on, and this provided her with not only the perfect excuse to give Mhairi's leadership, but also with a very interesting and fulfilling challenge.

How on Quilara was she going to convince enemy soldiers to fight against their own countrymen? The basic idea was simple – they needed to feel more appreciated and indebted to her than to Perivon. But that was a process that could take a great deal of time, even with regular citizens. There were plenty within her realm, she knew, especially older folk, who simply held their tongues and tolerated her rule despite everything she'd done to earn their loyalty.

With soldiers...yes, this was a very interesting challenge, indeed.

She sent back a pigeon with instructions for Ezmith to create a Fold to the foyer of the Mayor's palace the following day just as the sun was beginning to set, then immediately began preparations, thinking through every aspect of what she was about to do – what time should she arrive? Should she make an address immediately or wait until the following day? Should she walk instead of ride...?

That's an interesting idea...

What if she wore a simple gown and slippers with her crown and walked into the front gate of the city instead of riding? She could smile, meet people's eyes without looking down at them, and even take a moment to stop and smell flowers that she passed.

Part of her wondered if it would be just...too much...and feel contrived, but, no, maybe she would wear one of her normal gowns so it would not have the feel of a performance. That should work. It was one of the funny things about people; one of the best ways to get them to see you on a pedestal was by behaving as though you did not need them to.

Preparations went by swiftly and by the time the Fold opened the following evening, she was ready, surrounded by the elite honor guard she'd spent the last month assembling. They had special uniforms and were all mounted on armored steeds. They would provide a wonderful contrast to her own display of simplicity and vulnerability.

They surrounded her in a simple box formation and they walked through the Fold together. As they were coming through, Ezmith quirked an eyebrow at her, in response to which she simply smiled and winked. She hoped for a smile from him, but he just shrugged and opened another Fold from there to just outside the city of Bahadir.

She walked through the second Fold, the city opening up before her, seeming larger from the ground than it would from astride a horse. She was perhaps a hundred paces from the gate, a perfect distance. It would give the prisoners in the camps time to notice her arrival and gather to watch, as well as word to spread inside the city that she was approaching. The streets would be lined with curious people.

She let a genuine smile come onto her face. There was a unique feeling to coming to a newly-conquered city. It wasn't quite like coming home...more like discovering a *new* home. The smell of salt coming from the ocean wasn't particularly pleasant, but it wasn't overpowering and it seemed like something she would quickly grow accustomed to.

Sailors and soldiers under guard came to their feet and watched in silence as she and her honor guard walked past. She looked at them, met their eyes where she could, and kept a natural smile on her face.

She did not wave – there was no way to do so without either appearing condescending or childish – but did her best to truly *see* every sailor she looked at and smile so that they would feel her concern for them.

Before she knew it, she was passing under the large gate to the city and walking the narrow streets. Her guard was forced to constrict uncomfortably around her, so close that her shoulders brushed their horses on more than one occasion. Her smile became a bit more fixed; this was hampering the image she had hoped to convey, but she could still make this work.

Now it was time to wave. With a close-mouthed smile that just barely crinkled her eyes, and a simple open and closing of her hand while making eye contact with small children, she could almost feel the endearment coming from the mothers and fathers of those children. She could almost hear their thoughts:

'She clearly likes children, and will see to it that they're protected.'

'She seems much more kindly than I expected.'

'Now here *is a ruler that understands us.'*

Little things. All the things she was doing were little, but they added up to an overall impression that people would come away with, hopefully without even realizing it.

She walked through the city all the way to the Mayor's palace, which was much larger than its counterpart in Mhairi. She admired the architecture as she passed buildings crafted with care. Where there were pillars, they were carved so that it appeared each was made by combining a number of smaller tubes that gently twisted around as they moved upwards.

That seemed to be the hallmark of Bahadir architecture: gentle twists, hinting at a spiral. The domes atop structures were common throughout Cleononia, but the gently-spiraling formations placed on top set this city apart. She climbed the steps of the palace, taking care to lift the front of her dress.

Entering the palace, she was greeted by an entourage of well-dressed men and women headed by a thick woman several inches taller than herself, her hair tied back in a tight bun. This must be Mayor

Balfe. Lady Virtesa smiled warmly at the Mayor and extended her hand.

Rather than taking it and bowing, the woman glared at her and folded her arms.

"Not much I can do now that you've taken my city, but I can at least keep my dignity."

Her first real test in this city already, and likely with the entire Merchant Council as an audience. Luckily, she had a wealth of experience dealing with being disrespected.

She smiled sadly. "Treating others as befits their station does nothing to diminish our own dignity. But as you wish. For now, I have a great deal to discuss with the Merchant Council. You are welcome to remain if you'd like, or retire to your rooms."

As simply as that, she'd put the mayor on the defensive, where further obstinance would be perceived as petulant at best, and in order to maintain her own relevance the mayor was forced to acknowledge that the Lady Virtesa was the ultimate authority in the room. Leaving the conversation would only end in losing her position as Mayor, and she likely knew it.

The Mayor inclined her head slightly and gestured to an audience chamber off to the side of the entry hall. They moved that way, Lady Virtesa motioning her guards to take positions at the door. She highly doubted she was in any danger from these men and women.

The Council's questions were predictable, and easy to address. No, trade would not cease, even temporarily. Yes, tariffs on goods coming in and leaving Ambarta's provinces would go up, but patrols on all major roads would be increased to make them safer and allow merchants to save money on their own guards. Yes, taxes on trade within the lands Ambarta controlled would increase as well, but a commission of engineers would be formed to maintain, widen, and improve all thoroughfares in addition to making them safer.

Yes, Lady Virtesa's soldiers would man the defenses until the loyalty of the soldiers here was unquestioned. No, she would not be bringing sailors up from Redwood to commandeer the fleet here. She updated them on the status of the siege at Dazbog and informed them that she would be redirecting much of the trade throughout her realm to come through this city now that it was available, but warned them that if the sailors continued to refuse to serve for too long, overseas trade might diminish in fear of pirates and other dangers.

The conversation took the rest of the evening. Dinner was brought to them and they ate while they continued to talk. She clarified her intent to address the city the following morning, then to address the soldiers and sailors afterward. All the little details had to be arranged; scribes to record her address and make copies, determining the best place for such a public address, making sure each member of the merchant council had a place behind her.

That last detail took a great deal of time to sort out.

"With all respect, Lady Virtesa," said one of the merchants, a thin, middle-aged man with an immaculately-trimmed goatee. "It has only been days since your soldiers took the city. I am not sure those of us here are prepared to stand unified with you. Personal loyalties to Lord Perivon and the history of Cleononia aside, it would not be prudent for us to publicly display support for you when it's entirely possible that Perivon will retake the city."

"Tell me, Merchant...?" she asked.

"Tellivor," the man responded.

"Merchant Tellivor, do you happen to know, of all the cities we've taken, how many have ever been retaken by the sitting rulers of the province?"

"I do not," he replied, shaking his head.

"I do," Mayor Balfe replied, defiance painted on her face. "One. When Lord Perivon retook Dazbog. Hence our concern."

Lady Virtesa nodded. There was no point in trying to deny or spin the disaster that the first taking of Dazbog had been.

"You are correct, Mayor. And do you know what has changed since then?"

She gave a moment for her to respond, though in truth the question was rhetorical.

She continued, "Since that time, our army has grown in size by a factor of 10. We are currently besieging Dazbog with five times the number of soldiers that we used to take it the first time, and we used a second, equally large force to take Bahadir. Perivon could summon every ounce of strength he can muster using borrowed coin and still not be able to overwhelm our forces. He is stuck in Dazbog, with no escape, and with no possible outcome besides eventual surrender."

She let them consider that for a moment; it was important they realize that they were aboard a sinking ship and needed to take the hand she was offering. The threat was obvious, so now all she needed was a promise.

"You all have an opportunity here. I have no interest in ruling Bahadir directly, or Cleononia for that matter. The former rulers of every province we've conquered remain the current rulers, the only exception being the Wood Coast, which is ruled by the daughter of the late Lord and Lady. They are vassal-states, yes, and they all recognize my authority, but life goes on much as it did before, only better because of the extra services and benefits that uniting with Ambarta provides."

She sighed sadly. "Lord Perivon, I fear, may be the first ruler that I cannot offer continued leadership over his province. His shrewdness and intelligence would make him a great asset, but this war has already been far bloodier than any of our other campaigns, and much of that is due to his stubbornness. He may escape the gallows, but I do not think it likely we will come to an agreement that keeps him in power."

She watched them as they sat pensively. Some of their eyebrows were furrowed, others stared into their glasses of wine, considering. The choice was obvious here, though it may not seem so to them quite yet. She sipped her own wine as she considered what was going through their minds.

Was their loyalty to Perivon or Cleononia? Was it really in Cleononia's best interest to continue resisting Ambarta? More importantly, she had implied that a new ruler would need to be chosen over Cleononia, presumably taking over Perivon's estates and all the wealth that would come with them. Merchants were not greedier than any other person, truthfully, but they had a prudence about them that allowed them to take advantage when advantage came.

One by one, small smiles appeared on each face and they looked to her and nodded, each no doubt already scheming how they would convince her that they were the right choice to take Perivon's place. All except Mayor Balfe. She would no doubt continue to be a formidable opponent. No matter, it was easy enough to excuse the Mayor for tomorrow's address, so long as the full Merchant Council stood behind her, and it seemed they did.

The conversation ended and they all retired to their rooms. As Lady Virtesa brushed her hair in her apartment, she considered the success. It *was* a success, but it was also the easiest. The Merchant Council had been easy to sway in her favor. The people of the city, and even more so the soldiers and sailors, would be far harder to convince. The worst mistake she could make was to try and snatch their loyalty too quickly without earning it. Tomorrow's speeches would have to be very delicate indeed.

It felt great to be riding again after a tenday out of the saddle, even with the frequent twinges of pain coming from his right leg. Ezren trailed a short distance behind Aminah, who was on foot, into the village. For reasons she had not adequately explained, Aminah had required them to enter the village separately so no one would place the two of them together. She hadn't said it outright, but it seemed clear to Ezren that she wanted to make sure that if he was caught again that no one would think to ask about her and the assistance she had given him.

Once they were in the village, she claimed, no one would notice any two people walking or talking together, so they'd be fine.

Ezren looked around as he rode into the village. Based on her description of it, he had expected it to be run-down, like the slums in Novis Terram, but it was...quaint. White-washed cottages with brown trim lined the main road and stretched out on side roads to either direction. They were small, certainly, but well-kept, and the people he could see seemed a notch happier on average than the people in Novis Terram.

This defied his expectation, as his experience with the rich and powerful had been...mixed, and this village was where the servants of those rich and powerful people lived. For now, though, he had something more important to focus on than sociology. On one of her many scouting trips to this village, Aminah had confirmed the name of the Lord whose estate Galdrach was visiting. It was one of the least-liked lords in the region – Lord Lucke, a man that Ezren had never heard of, which he'd originally found odd, since he had thought that there were only a handful of lords and ladies throughout the Western nations.

That was both true and false, Aminah had explained to him. In the traditional sense, where the Lord and Lady were the rulers of a nation like Disote or Ambarta, then yes, that was true. But Robinton granted the title of Lord to anyone who owned a parcel of land larger than two square acres. They were only known as Lords here in Robinton: everywhere else they'd be known by whatever profession had brought them enough wealth to purchase an estate here.

In most cases it was successful merchant traders, but the occasional craftsman or entrepreneurial farmer would amass great enough wealth to purchase or build a Robinton estate and claim the title for themselves. Apparently there was an entire culture and society between the nobility of Robinton and the nobility of Comperr, who operated under a similar system.

He followed Aminah at a distance as the road curved gently to his right, angling eastward. There were workshops and stores, still with the same white-and-brown-trim design, with more houses being a little further set back from the road. Nearly every family who lived here had at least one member that worked for one of the estates.

After Ezren had told Aminah about the young woman who had helped him escape the last estate, she had taken on a thoughtful expression, said "I s'pose yeh are a bit of a looker", and identified a maid in Lord Lucke's staff that she felt would be most susceptible to Ezren's "charms". He didn't like the idea of deceiving a young woman about his intent, however, and wasn't planning on doing so.

As Aminah passed through a farmer's market, she turned around and took a few steps backward just long enough to catch Ezren's eye and jerk a thumb toward a stand selling tomatoes and bell peppers. He looked over and immediately identified the girl Aminah must be indicating. His breath caught. He had never seen such a beautiful young woman. Princess Asteri would likely grow into a beauty to rival this girl, but Ezren felt like he was seeing a fully-bloomed rose for the first time.

He better not share that metaphor with Aminah; the last ten days had shown her to be...sensitive...to the typical ways people talked about women.

He sat up straight in the saddle and adjusted his sword and shield so that they were both prominent and moved his horse through the wide walkway that led to the stand where the young woman was working. Aminah had told him to stay on the horse, but that he could dismount soon after beginning the conversation. First impressions were important, and young girls were often taken by the idea of a young, handsome, adventurer on horseback.

This sort of thing really wasn't his strong suit – he had always been awkward around Asteri and didn't really talk to very many girls at his school. Over the last year or so Raban had started to talk more about the fun he'd had flirting with this girl or that, but Ezren had been too focused on his studies and practice to do much of it.

Aminah's advice had been simple: smile, make jokes, and don't let her think that she is your target.

He brought Asteri to the stand and put on a smile. He would just try to behave as he had seen Raban do.

"Hello there," he said congenially.

The young woman looked up at him and hesitated, her mouth open for a moment before she tucked some hair behind her ear, shifted and broke eye contact.

"Hello, my Lord, how can I be of service to you?" She replied subserviently.

"Lord?" Ezren spluttered without thinking. "Oh, Inferno, no I'm not a lord"

She looked up at him in surprise. He shrugged.

"It's true, and I can honestly say that is the first time I've been mistaken for one. You have my thanks; flattery on that scale is hard to come by."

He smiled, and on instinct, winked.

It seemed to have the desired effect – her cheeks flushed a little and she dipped the top of her head innocently.

"I'm sorry for mistaking you, mister…?"

"Raban," Ezren replied. "Raban Kennard." Since he was doing his best to act like Raban he might as well use his name as an alias again.

"Mister Kennard," she said with a pause. "How can I help you?"

"Mostly, miss…?" Ezren started.

"Ann Marie," she replied.

"Well, Miss Ann Marie," he said. "Mostly I'm interested in two of your largest tomatoes."

"Oh!" she jumped, as though just now remembering that she was, in fact, operating a fruit stand. "Of course!"

She hurried to retrieve the two largest tomatoes that Ezren could see. He dismounted so that he could proffer his satchel for her to place them in after wrapping them in some thin cloth. She was of average height for a young woman her age, so he stood a few inches taller. He did his best to stand up straight with his shoulders back and keep a pleasant smile on his face.

"Thank you very much," he said as she placed the tomatoes in his bag, stepping perhaps a little closer than she needed to.

He paid her for the tomatoes and turned to grab Asteri's reins. This was it for the first interaction. According to Aminah, the worst thing he could do right now was try to make too much progress too quickly. He felt her eyes on him as he mounted up and gathered the reins. He had a sudden thought and decided to act on it. Before nudging Asteri forward, he looked back down at Ann Marie.

"Pardon me, Ann Marie, but could you direct me to one of the inns here in the village? I've just arrived today and I may be staying for a little while."

She nodded. "Yes, if you just keep on this road until it comes back out on the highway, the best inn in town is on the corner there."

He gave her a cheery grin. "Thank you!"

He nudged Asteri forward and rode away without looking back.

Before he'd gone more than 20 feet, Aminah appeared at his side as though she had materialized there.

"Yeh're shehre yeh've never done this befehre? That was damn near perfect. Could've done without that last bit, though."

"What was wrong with that? I wanted her to know I was going to be in town."

Aminah sighed patiently. "So now she won't be surprised when she sees you again. We'll have teh skip the next step. Yeh have to give her a chance to show she's wehrth yehr notice. She's a maid, so she'll know how teh clean stuff. Tehmorrow we'll have yeh spill something on yehr shirt while yeh're buying mehre tehmatoes. If yeh've got her as well as I think yeh do then she'll jump at the chance to help."

"What good will that do?" Ezren asked.

"Her scrubbin' at yehr shirt will give yeh time for some natural conversation," she said, sounding as though she were explaining that the sun rose every day. "She'll want to know why yeh're here, and yeh can explain that yeh're looking for somethin' powerful, and yeh think it might be here. Then *yeh* can ask *her* how she learned to clean so well, and she'll tell yeh that she's a maid at Lucke's estate."

The following day went exactly as Aminah had predicted it would. Ann Marie was not back at the fruit stand until the middle of the afternoon, but shortly after she got there Ezren purchased a meat pie from a different stand and ate it nonchalantly while walking past her stand. He let his hand slip, and some of the meat and juices dropped out, hitting his shirt.

"Oh, dear…" he said, looking around.

Ann Marie was there in an instant with a dry rag, dabbing at it for a moment, then clicking her tongue.

"Hmm, this doesn't seem to want to come out, why don't you come back here Raban?" she asked, taking his hand and leading him back behind her fruit stand, where there was some space for all the vendors to work. She sat him down on a stool and took a lemon from a neighboring stand, squeezing the juices from it onto the stain and then scrubbing away with the cloth.

The conversation followed nearly line for line as Aminah had said it would. She asked why he was there and he told her, flexing his stomach instinctually when she lifted his shirt high enough to reveal it. Then he asked how she had gotten so good at this kind of thing, and she told him. Despite the awkward feeling of having half his midriff exposed, he tried to maintain a façade of confidence and crack a few jokes.

She finished cleaning the shirt to her satisfaction and released him. He thanked her again for the help and went on his way.

Aminah was insistent that he be out of the village for the next day. He needn't do anything more than wander around the countryside, but they needed to maintain the impression that he was off looking for whatever it was that he sought. He had pointed out that he could simply stay in his room at the inn, but Aminah was adamant that there was still a risk Ann Marie would choose to walk past the inn he was staying at and see Asteri in the stable.

Truthfully, Ezren had had enough lolling about to last a lifetime after the tenday in Aminah's clearing, so he was happy to go out for a Summer's day in Robinton. Summer was still hot even this far north, but not nearly as hot as it could be in Ambarta.

It had rained a couple times over the last ten days, but there was no sign of it as he rode off the highway in a direction chosen at random. He contemplated doing some hunting. He wasn't prepared to do anything with an animal he killed, but there was certain to be a butcher or a tannery in the village that would take it.

He opted to spend the day using his bow. No snares. His main goal was to practice moving silently in the woods and shooting faraway targets. Living with Aminah had shown him that he was still a novice in these areas.

He rode to the edge of the treeline and hobbled Asteri just inside it.

Though he didn't nab any game throughout the day, it still felt like a day well spent. He was able to stretch out his leg more and even jogged a bit through the forest, though that still hurt enough that he stopped shortly after he started.

Over the next several days, Aminah continued to guide him through the 'art of the woo' as she called it, and before he knew it, Ann Marie was presenting him with the uniform of a newly-hired guard at the Lucke estate. New guards were identified by a red stripe on the arms of their uniform, since apparently the shambaya, who was responsible for all hiring, rarely introduced new hires to the rest of the staff before their first report for duty.

He would have preferred something a little less attention-grabbing, but Ann Marie insisted that this would be the best way to get the access he needed. She apparently had little loyalty to Lord Lucke, though she would not give much detail beyond that she was once responsible for cleaning his living quarters. Aminah told him in no uncertain terms that he was *not* to ask further questions.

He had been feeling guilty at the prospect of manipulating Ann Marie, but he should have had more faith in Aminah's 'art'; he had been nothing but honest with Ann Marie. The only thing he had not been forthright about was that he had selected her from the beginning. Everything else – what he was looking for, his suspicions about it being in Lucke's estate, and his request for her help – had been completely genuine. She seemed to know exactly what she was doing, and he found little to justify any guilty feelings.

Then came the day he was to enter the estate. He recited in his mind what Ann Marie had told him to do. Just go straight up to the front gate and tell the guards that this was his first day and that he had been instructed to report to the shambaya's office.

The guards on duty nodded knowingly and opened the gate for him.

He walked through the complex, allowing himself to look around trying to see everything at once. Doing so only reinforced what he wanted everyone to think of him. Once inside, he asked directions to Lord Lucke's quarters, where Ann Marie had confirmed that he displayed his array of artifacts much like the first estate Ezren had gone in.

He approached the guards that were standing watch at the door to the display room.

"Hello," he said awkwardly. "I was told to relieve one of you."

"'Bout time," said the older one, looking Ezren up and down. "Erl keeps takin' em younger and younger, doesn't he?"

Ezren shrugged and took the spear the older guard proffered him. Neither of the guards wore helmets, which seemed like an oversight, but he supposed it was highly unlikely that any of these guards would ever actually see combat.

He took his position outside the door and waited, not making conversation. Eventually, the other guard said it was time to do a walk of the room inside. It had windows, after all, so they needed to make sure that no one had snuck in. Before they entered, the guard stared hard at him.

"Lord Lucke is in there with Master Galdrach right now, so you do your side nice and quick-like, and stay absolutely silent, you understand?"

Ezren nodded, his mouth going dry at the news that Galdrach and Lucke would be in the room as he walked through.

The guard nodded back and pushed open the door. Ezren turned to his right and began walking the perimeter, mirroring the other guard. Lucke and Galdrach were deep in conversation, standing on either side of a large orb that appeared to be made out of rose quartz.

"...been swindled, my friend," Galdrach finished in a slow, gravelly voice. "There is nothing special about this ball of quartz besides the polish."

"Ah, well, as long as you don't tell that to anyone then it can still be of great value to me," Lucke replied.

"Of course, of course," Galdrach replied.

Ezren snuck a look at the old wizard who had caused his life to go the way that it had. He didn't know whether to curse or bless him, truthfully. Galdrach wore robes of a deep black and was hunched over and wrinkled. He looked like the oldest man Ezren had ever seen. Lucke, conversely, looked only about a hundred years old and had taken good care of himself.

In all his preparation for coming here, he had not taken time to learn much of anything about Lucke but seeing the bulk of muscles beneath his shirt, Ezren felt like that might have been a mistake; the vast majority of these artifacts were weapons of one kind or another, and the way that Lucke held himself suggested that he may well know how to use them.

"My apologies that this orb isn't the one you've been looking for" Lucke said to Galdrach. "You still hoping that the Kimorae boy will find this new magic of yours?"

Ezren missed a step, stumbling briefly as his heartbeat skyrocketed. Were they talking about *him?!*

Galdrach shook his head. "No, not *new* magic, Lucke. *Old* magic. From before the War of the Intelligences."

"Right, right, right," Lucke replied.

"And remember, it's not 'Kimorae' anymore, Lucke. It's 'Virtesa'. Slips like that will have you hanging at the end of the gallows."

Both the men laughed as though that were a hilarious joke.

"But to answer your question," Galdrach began as the laughter subsided. "Maybe. Ezmith may very well be the one foretold, but I've studied the prophecies of the Maradra enough to have my doubts."

"And what in the prophecies leads you to doubt that Ezmith is the master of the four winds?" Lucke asked.

"Bah," Galdrach said, waving a hand. "I've got all those notes back in my tower: I cannot pull them from memory. Now, is there anything else you'd like me to Delve to see if it contains any magical properties?"

Ezren passed by the other guard at the back of the room and continued to move around the perimeter. Galdrach and Lucke continued to talk, but Ezren's mind whirled to fast to listen. All of Galdrach's notes, from all the years he'd spent studying this exact topic, were sitting, *unguarded* at Galdrach's tower. Well, he might have guards, but Galdrach himself was not there, so if Ezren could get there quickly, he might be able to find a way to get the notes before Galdrach returned.

Unfortunately, he still had to keep up appearances for the rest of his shift. He stood outside the room with the artifacts for hours before he and his guard companion were both relieved. He then walked purposefully out of the complex and straight back into the village.

Aminah slipped next to him from the other side of the road and he gave her a summary of what had happened.

"So that's it, then?" She asked, stopping on the road with her hands on her hips. "Yeh're not even goin' to stay long enough to get back in and look at Lucke's artifacts on yehr own?"

Ezren turned and shrugged. "There's got to be a hundred estates in this valley, and what I'm looking for could be in any of them...or *none* of them. If I have a lead with more promise than spending the next year or two sneaking into estates and hoping I'll see what I'm looking for -- let alone know it when I see it -- I'm taking the chance."

She frowned, clearly disgruntled. Ezren did not understand her dissatisfaction; she hadn't seemed to really want to help him during all this, so he thought she'd be happy to see his back. Come to think of it, why *had* she been helping him?

She stood there for a moment, then motioned forward and they continued to walk further into the village.

"Do yeh even know where Galdrach's tower is, Ezren?"

Ezren thought for a moment. No, he did not.

He glanced at her and noticed her eyeing him.

"Yeh don't, do yeh?

He shook his head. She scoffed.

"Well ain't yeh a lucky one, then?" she asked with a half-smile. He looked at her, confused.

"I happen to be one of the few who *does* know where it is."

"That's perfect! How do you know where it is?"

She looked away for the briefest moment. "I used to be one of his guards."

"So are you coming with me, then?" Ezren asked, surprised. But she shook her head.

"Nah, I like it here better. Yeh're a nice boy, Ezren, and yeh remind me much of my younger brothers, but I don't like yeh well enough to go back near the city and into the Heran Hills."

It was his turn to stop in the middle of the road. A woman behind him 'tsked' loudly and went around, pulling a small wagon that just fit two small children inside.

Aminah looked back at him and noticed his face. "Ah yeh've been to the Heran Hills, I see. Well then it shouldn't surprise yeh that someone like Galdrach would make his home there."

Ezren took a deep breath. There was no need to be so afraid; his last jaunt through the Hills hadn't been all that bad. Of course, if Ben hadn't miraculously shown up then he would have been dead, but now he knew that such a thing was a possibility and he would be more careful as he traveled through. *And* he'd made it all the way through and there hadn't been any strange monster, so...nothing to worry about. Nothing to worry about.

He'd been stuck in these hills for two days now, making painfully slow progress through the incredibly dense brush and brambles. The map that Aminah had drawn for him was certainly not perfect, but he felt like he was going in the right direction.

He was leading his horse; there was no point in riding when he was moving at a snail's pace anyway. He'd spent each day so far using his sword as a machete to cut their way through.

The work was murder on his sword and, for that matter, on his sword *arm*. He switched arms regularly to give each arm a break and he spent a good chunk of the evening sharpening his sword after making camp. The leather grip was holding up fine, though little twigs and chunks of dust kept sticking into it.

According to Aminah's map, all he needed to do at this point was continue traveling in a northeastern direction and he'd eventually see the tower rising high out of a small, bowl-shaped valley. The tower would be quite tall, about twice as tall as the tallest tree in the area, but because it was situated in the little valley it was impossible to see from a distance.

She had also warned him that the brush would be this thick, but he hadn't quite believed her. After all, how did Galdrach, his servants, and his guards get to the tower? There had to be some easier way to get there, but Aminah did not know it. She claimed she'd spent several years as one of Galdrach's guards and she had never been able to find the path unless she was with the wizard at the time.

The slow pace was infuriating, as he had no idea how much time he had before Galdrach would be returning, or how long it would take to find what he was looking for once he reached the tower. The ground leveled out as he continued to chop his way slowly through the bramble, Asteri whickering in protest as the branches tugged at her body.

His clothes were torn in several spots, his hands, cheeks, arms, and legs were covered in scratches, but as the ground suddenly started to dip down, he looked out and saw the unmistakable shape of black spires atop a solid black tower. He dropped his sword to the ground and gave a somewhat sarcastic chuckle. He was happy to have found the tower, of course, and the scratches and tears were worth it, but he was getting tired of all...this.

He'd been forced into unconsciousness three times in the last month. He'd been beaten, tied up, threatened, attacked, and arrested. That was all *before* the last several days of non-stop hacking that made him wish his arms would just fall off. Dust and twigs had fallen down his face and back, he had a tenday's worth of sweat caked all over him, *and* the pain from his injured leg still lingered.

But he was here. His answers were in that black tower. They had to be.

Moving downhill towards the base of the tower was faster. The bramble was not nearly as thick, as though it was kept under tighter control than the surrounding forest.

Within a half an hour, he was at the bottom of the bowl, which had been leveled out to create a rough circle of cleared land about fifty feet around the tower. Now that he was closer, the tower did not seem as thin as it had when he first saw it. It narrowed as it got higher, of course, but here he could see that there was plenty of space for multiple rooms on each story as it went up.

Looking around furtively, he saw that the entire area seemed deserted. Galdrach *had* servants, right? Aminah had said she used to be one of his guards, so...Ezren supposed it was possible that he had taken everyone with him, but an old wizard seemed like the type of person who would have a lot of people to do things for him. Back in Lucke's estate, Galdrach had looked so old and frail that he might need help dressing himself in the mornings.

Despite not seeing anyone, Ezren pulled Asteri back up the hill a little ways and tied her in a spot with a fair amount of grass. He didn't want to hobble her and risk her grazing too far down the hill, and he would be back soon. It was midafternoon, and he definitely wanted to be back out of the tower before the sun went down.

Back down in the cleared land, Ezren walked around the tower, trying to appear nonchalant. He even picked up a stray watering can he found and made a show of pretending to water some of the plants he passed. It seemed silly given his sword and shield, but recent experience made him feel more comfortable posing as a servant than simply sneaking around.

There was only one door to the tower, facing almost due west. There were windows as well, but they didn't start until the second story, and with so few trees growing nearby it seemed unlikely that he would be able to enter via one of those. As he passed the door he stepped over to it and gave the handle a tug just to see. It was locked. Of course. He did another lap around the tower, this time paying special attention to the windows and trees planted nearby. There might be a ladder or something else he could use to get to a window that high, but a tree would be by far the most convenient.

He had just about given up when he rounded the north side of the tower again and saw, to his delight, that one of the trees indeed grew close enough to the tower that he could probably use its branches to get him in through the window that looked out to it. He dropped the watering can and placed his shield at the base of the tree. His sword he brought along on his hip. It could get caught in the tree, but there was enough that he did not know about what awaited him inside that he wasn't willing to explore it without a means of defending himself. He needed to get better with knives like Raban's da. Knives would be *much* easier to bring along in a situation like this.

The tree proved an easy climb and before he knew it he was inching along a thick branch that angled directly towards the window. The window was a little below the branch he was standing on, so he had to drop down and hang on it with his left hand in order to reach the window with his right. His left arm strained with his weight and he puffed air in and out as he reached his right hand to the window and tried to lift it up.

Blessedly, the window slid right up – it wasn't locked. Thank Clayara!

He tightened his grip on the branch with both hands and swung his feet over to the windowsill. They hooked on, and he pulled himself in through the window. He squatted just below the window for a full minute as his eyes adjusted and he listened for any sounds. There had to be *someone* in here, right? Even if it was just a single maid. Did the old wizard cook his own meals?

As the inside of the tower became clearer to his eyes, he saw what appeared to be a kitchen and dining area. This was the second floor, so that probably meant the first floor was a reception area or sitting room. The upper floors were probably reserved for his bedchambers and, hopefully, a study or library of some kind.

He realized he had no idea how many floors there were on this tower. The positioning of windows outside would probably have told him but he had not thought to count them. He thought it was five, though. Five stories. That seemed about right.

As he looked around him, trying to take in everything, he noticed oddities; there was only one chair at the dining table and the stove did not have a door to shut once the fire was lit, nor was there any indication that it had ever had a fire built within it. There was a large, wooden chest bound with iron sitting on the floor next to the counter, almost as tall as the counter itself was.

Looking around more fully, Ezren saw that there was a layer of dust on the floor, except for narrow pathways, leading to the chest, to the stove, and to the table from various directions. Maybe Galdrach really didn't have a maid.

Regardless, this meant that Ezren needed to be careful about where he walked. He looked down. He was squatting in the layer of dust, having already disturbed it. It was abundantly clear that someone had come in through this window.

He cursed quietly, wondering what to do. The trouble was, there wasn't really anything he *could* do. 'The milk was spilled', as Fiona used to tell him. The only real choice he had was to hurry. There was no way to prevent Galdrach from knowing that someone had snuck in, but he could be in, out, and long gone by the time the wizard returned. Everything should be fine.

Unless Galdrach could use magic to figure out who had been in his tower. That was a chilling thought. *Well, nothing for it now.*

Alright, then, he thought as he stood and strode purposefully up the stairs. *No point in sneaking around. Just get in, out, and gone. In, out, gone.*

The third floor opened up into what Ezren had been looking for: a study. It didn't resemble a traditional study, though. It had plenty of books, sure enough, all on shelves that lined the entire perimeter of the room, but the rest of the space was taken up by a wide variety of beakers, strange-looking machinery, and workbenches with a variety of tools, only some of which Ezren recognized the purpose of.

He walked around, looking for something to save him the time of scanning through all the books Galdrach had on his shelves. On one workbench, next to a capped jar that appeared to be holding human eyes, was an open book that Galdrach appeared to have been reading just before going off to Lucke's estate.

There was a notebook on top of it, and a quick perusal showed Ezren that apparently Galdrach recorded everything he did in almost painstaking detail, even mundane things like what he had prepared and eaten for meals.

He flipped through the notebook, looking for some semblance of organization beyond simple chronology. At first he assumed there wasn't one, but then he noticed little numbers written next to some paragraphs.

One such paragraph, which read, *"Attempted combining the purple mushrooms from the East quadrant with chicken meat. Results were inconclusive,"* had a little number scribbled next to it that matched a page three further than the one he was currently on. He flipped to that page, and found another paragraph: *"Mushroom and chicken experiment deemed a success. Delicious, and with no unintended consequences after consumption."*

He continued to turn pages, stopping at random to read down a page to see what the notes were. Galdrach had said he had all his notes about this new magic, or old magic, here, so hopefully it was in this book.

Indeed, on page 37, he found a paragraph that read, *"Acquired journal. If authentic, may be the only surviving record of the Lost 500 Years."*

There was a number scribbled next to it. '42'. He quickly flipped to that page.

"Journal seems to be authentic. Verifiable details match. Elliadel was known among moon elves as a 'human-lover' prior to the Lost 500, so stands to reason that he would write this record."

Another number. '55'. He flipped to that page.

"Moon elves were nearly unanimous in their plan? Elliadel cast out for refusing to cooperate. Claims there was something significant about the fourth focal point, in the Nadrasah Mountains, what is now known as Mountain Home. See journal for more details."

Ezren cast his eyes about the room, hoping to see the journal immediately so he could stop this rabbit-chase. Not seeing it, he looked back down and saw, again, a number scribbled next to the paragraph. '103'.

He jumped forward to page 103, now almost halfway through the notebook.

"*I have finished Elliadel's journal. Unfortunately, he knew little of what transpired after his banishment, and we have no way of knowing what he meant by landmarks or other references, many of which appear to have undergone significant change since his time. One thing remains unlikely to change, however. The conduit was intended to be an orb, of a pure stone such as topaz or quartz, about 18 inches in diameter. Hidden away where none could find or access it, not even the moon elves themselves. Possibly in deep cave.*"

There was yet another number written next to that paragraph. Ezren scrambled through the pages as quickly as he could. This was exactly what he was looking for! The scrawled number was of the last page in the notebook with writing on it.

"*Lucke has contacted me to request my evaluation of his latest acquisition of a supposedly magical item. However, this time the object is a large orb of rose quartz that he claims was found deep in a cave. I find it highly unlikely that either I or he are the master of the four winds, but my curiosity drives me to inspect. Truthfully, I weary of this search. A careful second reading of Elliadel's journal indicates to me that the orb may reside deep within a lake. Possibly both a cave and a lake.*"

Ezren stood up straight, barely able to breathe. A fourth 'focal point', whatever that was, in Mountain Home? A deep lake? It seemed obvious on its face that the reference was to the Novis Spring. And now he knew what he was looking for! A big rock orb like the one Lucke had.

What he really wanted right now, though, was a chance to read this Elliadel's journal for himself. There were probably so many details in it that could help him. He looked at the bookshelves. Rather than methodically scanning over all the books in the room, he instead looked for spots with the least amount of dust gathered.

He bounced quickly from spot to spot, until he found a book with a strange binding unlike anything he had ever seen. It was stiff, like wood, but thin, thin enough that if it was actual wood then it would just snap. He opened it to its first page, and it read *"The Journal of Elliadel, In Hope That the Future May Be Brighter Than the Present."*

"Don't move, boy," came an old, gravelly voice from behind Ezren. He froze. He thought he had done so voluntarily, but when he attempted to turn his head, he found that he could not.

"Before I kill you, I must know: are you alone?"

Ezren opened his mouth to claim that he was one of many; anything to buy himself some time but found that he could not speak the lie. Instead, he gagged on his own voice until he stopped trying to say it.

He felt an inexorable pressure on his body and mind, forcing him to turn around slowly to face Galdrach. His feet shifted as his body turned, despite his best efforts to stop them.

"Speak!" Came the gravelly command. His mouth opened as his head finally turned enough to see the old wizard.

No! He would not give in to this wizard's coercion! He could not close his mouth, but he managed to stop the words from coming out. Galdrach's eyes narrowed as they considered Ezren.

"You're the Kimorae boy, aren't you? The failure," he said pensively. "You're the spitting image of your father."

Galdrach stepped forward a little ways, as though to get a closer look at a unique specimen.

"So why didn't the enchantment work on you? Was there not enough blood remaining? Perhaps I won't kill you immediately after all. You could be very useful for my research. I can just kill you after I've learned what I can." He sneered. "You're an abomination anyway."

Galdrach turned, waving his arm at Ezren. "Come. Now."

The command was clear and he felt his foot beginning to lift. No! He would not meet his end this way! If he was going to die, he would die sword-in-hand, fighting for his life. He would not stay in some cell until Galdrach got what he wanted out of him.

The pressure intensified, but he shouted "No!" in his mind, and pushed back against it. Galdrach quickly turned to stare at him, a startled look on his face.

Encouraged, Ezren yelled, "No!" out loud, and the pressure went away completely. Galdrach's startlement turned to shock, then was quickly replaced by rage. Galdrach threw out his hand and launched a ball of green fire twice the size of a fist right at Ezren's chest. Ezren dived out of the way, crashing into a small table and knocking various beakers to the ground in a cascading shatter.

"How did you do that, boy?! How did you break my Coerce?!" Galdrach roared.

Ezren rolled to his feet and unsheathed his sword, journal still in his left hand. Another ball of fire shot past his shoulder as he dived and rolled again, hoping that the many tables and workbenches in the room would provide him suitable cover.

He came up close to Galdrach, and it was the wizard's turn to jump out of the way as Ezren swung his sword in an overhead chop. The wizard's nimble jump belied his frail appearance, but Ezren had no interest in fighting against a wizard – he just wanted to escape. Now Galdrach was no longer in front of the door.

Ezren leapt for the opening, hoping he could make it to the stairwell and out the bottom door. From there, he'd have to hope that Galdrach would not be able to pursue him through the woods as fast as Ezren could escape.

In mid-leap, however, he felt an impact and a terrible burning pain on his left hip, close to where he'd landed on the branch outside the first estate in Robinton. His feet wouldn't support him as he landed, and he found himself tumbling down the curving cement staircase all the way to the second floor landing, his sword clattering nearby. Counting his blessings that he hadn't been impaled on his own sword, he struggled to his feet and bent to pick it up.

Hearing Galdrach's angry yells coming down the stairs, he looked around. He could go down to the first floor and hope that the door would unlock from the inside without the need of magic, or he could jump out the window right next to him, the same one he had climbed through. The window came with about a ten-foot drop, but it also got him out of the tower a whole lot faster.

A fireball came shooting down, impacting right next to him and spreading green flames in a foot-wide circle.

It would be the window, then. He had no interest in staying in this tower long enough to get roasted to a crisp. He slammed the pommel of his sword against the window, shattering the lower half, then sheathed his sword. He climbed out the window as best he could, the pain in his hip flaring in protest. He hung by his fingertips for a moment before his strength gave out and he fell, attempting to roll with the impact. The grass was thick and spongy, and the ground was relatively soft, but his roll-turned-tumble left him with a bruised shoulder and a shortness of breath.

His vision blurred from the pain coming from where the fireball had impacted his hip and he cursed under his breath. Wherever people went after they died, his father sure as Inferno better be there appreciating all of Ezren's effort!

He climbed to his feet, scooped up his shield, and stumbled away as quickly as he could, rotating his shoulder as he went. Nothing seemed to be broken, which was a relief, but his hip hurt fiercely. He hobbled to where Asteri waited just inside the trees, untied her, stuffed the journal into her saddlebags, and tried to lead her as quickly as possible up the hill through the brush.

Thank Clayara the brush wasn't as thick on the downslope, but he wished he could find the path he'd made on his way in.

If it came down to a footrace between himself and Galdrach, he liked his chances, but if he couldn't find the path he'd already made, he'd be stuck hacking away a new path while Galdrach could just mosey up behind him.

As Ezren huffed up the hill as fast as he could, a blast of…something…knocked Ezren forward onto the ground. It hadn't felt like anything, except perhaps an incredibly strong gust of wind. At least it wasn't a fireball. Maybe Galdrach didn't want to burn the entire forest down.

More of the same type of blast impacted around him, snapping branches, pushing Asteri forward and almost toppling her, and another slammed him back to the ground. These blasts weren't strong enough to cause any new damage, but they aggravated his existing injuries. Likely the blasts were designed to keep him in one place until Galdrach could summon guards to chase him.

Getting on his elbows and staying low, he turned to look at the tower. Galdrach was leaning partially out of a high window in the tower, making throwing motions as the blasts kept coming. No guards were coming around the tower yet.

He rolled painfully to the side and struggled to his feet. If the beating he'd taken at that first estate hadn't stopped him, then a little burn from a fireball on his hip certainly wouldn't. He continued to struggle through the brush as the gusts of wind started to come slower and cause less damage. Once at the top of the bowl, he unsheathed his sword again and began to hack exhaustedly at the thickening brush. His original path was nowhere to be seen: it would likely take just as long to get out of here as it took to get in.

He hacked for a while, feeling inexplicably drained. He had the strangest sensation in his left foot. It felt like water had gotten into his boot somehow, but he hadn't walked through any swamps or anything. He glanced down and stopped, confused at what he was seeing.

There was red staining his pant leg all the way down from his hip. That was decidedly odd. Oh…he was bleeding. A lot, apparently.

His mind was foggy. Something told him that he had to stop the bleeding somehow. He fumbled at the saddlebags for some linens and stuffed them onto the wound on his hip, tying them tightly in place with a longer piece around his waist. That should stop the bleeding.

Water. Water next. When you lose blood you need to drink water. He'd known that long before Aminah had told him. His father had taught him that. His father had taught him a lot of things.

Tears welled up in his eyes as his fingers struggled to untie the saddlebag containing the waterskin. Whether from the pain, or the loss of blood, the tears began to run down his cheeks.

His father had taught him everything.

He fell to a sitting position, drinking freely from the waterskin, and it seemed to clear his mind. He was obviously injured and needed care that he could not give himself. The wound seemed deep and wide enough that it would be very difficult to completely stop the bleeding without bed rest. He might very well die out here. Again.

He sighed resignedly. Just once he'd like to get something done without coming face to face with his own mortality.

He took a last swallow of water and replaced the waterskin in the saddlebags. He didn't want to die in this dense, ugly, somewhat twisted forest in the Heran Hills. Gathering Asteri's reins in his right hand and gritting his teeth, he swung his sword with his left hand, cutting a path through the bramble.

He hadn't been at it long before he happened upon a miracle – a small trail of cleared ground. He would have to duck down low while riding, but the trail went in the direction of the road, and as long as it went that far, he may be able to get there by evening.

The trees and hours passed uneventfully, with Ezren focused on staying balanced on the horse while leaning so far forward he was resting his head on her neck. The swell of the saddle was pushing uncomfortably up into his stomach, but at least his saddle didn't have a horn like the standard-issue Guard saddles did.

Galdrach would likely pursue him or send someone else to pursue him and retrieve the journal. They'd have to have the same luck Ezren had if they wanted to find this trail, though. If he were Galdrach, he'd just send them out whatever the normal way was and have them take the road.

Maybe taking the journal had been a bad idea, but he very much wanted to know what was in the rest of it.

The direction of the trail stayed true, and in what felt a ridiculously short time compared to how long it took him to get in, Ezren was on the road that went from Salimelish to Robinton City. He pulled himself up to a sitting position and nudged Asteri forward. He felt himself fading again, and had half a mind to kick Asteri to a gallop, but he didn't know how much further it was, nor whether he could manage to stay on at anything faster than a walk. He settled for a canter, gritting his teeth with each bounce.

The sun went down, but the thought of stopping to make camp didn't seem like a reasonable option. If he took the time to spend a night on the road, he might die from his wound. How long he rode into the night he didn't know, but the hills slowly leveled out and the road moved at a gradual downwards slope. The sounds of the wild, so eerily muted while within the Heran Hills, came back in full force. Crickets, owls, and even the occasional howl of wolf or coyote kept the night from being as silent as it was dark. In the distance he began to see the winking lights of the town of Salimelish.

Ezren leaned forward and whispered to Asteri. "The inn, girl, take me to the inn."

The lights came closer in the darkness. Asteri's hoofprints threatened to lull Ezren to sleep. In the darkness, he almost couldn't tell that his hip had been bleeding. The winking light of candles and fires inside the houses disappeared behind the palisade as Ezren rode down the final hill towards the town, re-emerging as he rode through the gap where the gate should have been.

The sounds of the wilderness were replaced, almost instantaneously, with the sounds of the town. Nirari's inn came slowly into view, its shape a black mass against the starry sky. Warm, inviting light came from many of the windows.

Adal Nirari had been inexplicably kind to him on two occasions. He didn't want to risk using up all of his goodwill, but he had nowhere else to go. Asteri's quick footsteps took him to the front of the inn, and he slid off her to the ground, falling to his knees before picking himself back up, both hands applying pressure to the wound on his hip. He staggered up the few stairs to the porch and pushed the door open.

He must have pushed the door harder than he had intended, because it flew open, banging hard against the wall as he stumbled in. A good-sized crowd was inside, including a musician who was up on a small platform Ezren had never noticed before, and every face was turned towards him. Ezren looked through that sea of shocked expressions, trying to pick out the one that belonged to Adal Nirari.

There he was, at the end of the counter setting down a tray of drinks. Nirari's face shared the startled expression with the rest of the crowd. Ezren took a step forward and opened his mouth to explain, but he felt the telltale blackness of unconsciousness coming and closed his mouth to refocus on staying awake.

He would *not* faint *again*! He tightened every muscle in his face and neck, forcing himself to stand straight up, even bringing his shoulders back the way his father had always stood. He cleared his throat.

"I am in need of help," he said.

Nirari's eyebrows raised. "A blind man could see that, boy! Get in here." Nirari gestured Ezren to come forward, turning his head just long enough to shout "Xochi! Bring hot water and rags!"

The short innkeeper ducked under one of Ezren's arms and supported him as they walked out of the common room and into the hallway leading to the rooms.

"Apologies, friends!" he shouted behind him. "Continue on with the performance! More drinks will be on the way!"

Ezren relaxed his jaw. Nirari was going to take care of him. He *wasn't* going to die. He blinked, and suddenly he was being eased down onto a bed. He felt himself smile. This bed was *really* comfortable.

CHAPTER 12: HIGH TIDE

Lady Virtesa rode out of the city gate, surrounded by her full elite guard. They insisted on accompanying her when she went to speak with the imprisoned enemy soldiers and sailors. Truthfully, she didn't mind them guarding her on these excursions, since the enemy sailors were kept under watch precisely because their loyalty could not be assured.

Over the last two tendays the people of Bahadir had warmed up to her considerably, and not in small part because of how much time she spent among them, patronizing inns, hiring seamstresses, and simply speaking with and listening to the people she saw on the street.

The sailors, however…they'd been much more staunch, which was to be expected. After all, for an average citizen of Bahadir, all they were being asked to do was go on with their lives and shift their loyalty to a new monarch. Difficult for the most stubborn, perhaps, but an easy enough choice for most as soon as it became clear she was not a monster.

For a sailor, they were being asked to take up arms against their own countrymen to help complete the domination of their homeland by a foreign power. As Timot had often used to say: it was a tough sell.

But with this, like many other things, all it would take was time. She'd been honest and forthright about what her plans were and why, and the sailors just needed time to see that she was telling the truth. She rode to the large tent that had been designated as the command center for the prison camps and sent for Officer Kidron. Lady Virtesa had spoken with her on several occasions, and felt their conversations had been among the more productive.

Stepping inside the tent, Lady Virtesa helped herself to some of the dark, bitter tea that had grown in popularity over the last few years. It came from some country on the other side of the Eres ocean. She'd been told the name of the country before, but all the countries over there had very similar-sounding names, and it was difficult to keep them straight. Such a gap in knowledge would not continue to do, however, not now that she would rule Cleononia.

Most of the trade that came through the Redwood port was from southern nations on the other side of the mountains, and Aletheia had everything so well in-hand there that Lady Virtesa had never felt the lack of her knowledge of foreign powers up to this point in her conquests.

A woman in a simple prisoner's shirt and trousers stepped into the tent, flanked by Ambartan soldiers. She looked at Lady Virtesa silently. Now was the time to offer more hospitality than she had in their previous conversations.

"Tea?" Lady Virtesa offered pleasantly.

A look of surprise crossed Officer Kidron's face, but she schooled her features quickly. She stayed standing where she was, however, and did not respond to the invitation.

"Please," Lady Virtesa gestured, "Make yourself comfortable. I wanted to continue our last conversation."

Officer Kidron still did not move. "You still haven't brought sailors up from Redwood to commandeer our navy."

Lady Virtesa sat on one of the stiff chairs around the short table. "And I never will. This is Cleononia, Officer Kidron. If the Cleononians won't fight this fight, then it won't be fought."

The officer stepped forward. "But your soldiers, most of them are not professionals. They have lives to get back to: they won't stand for a years-long siege of Dazbog."

Lady Virtesa allowed a small smile. "Accommodations for our troops are already being made. Bahadir is more secure by the day, which allows us to send more and more of our soldiers to join the rotation of the siege, which in turn allows each soldier more time to return home and see to important matters."

"You could just leave."

Kimaya sighed before she could stop herself. "We've talked about that before, Officer Kidron. Regardless of whether you disagree with our coming to Cleononia in the first place, at this point our leaving would do more harm than staying. Mhairi and Orell already want to be part of Ambarta, and sentiment inside your own city of Bahadir is leaning towards us as well."

Putting her cup down and putting her hands in her lap, Lady Virtesa looked straight into Officer Kidron's eyes.

"The simple truth is that we are offering a better life. Safer highways and streets, more support for budding merchants and craftsmen, and the easier exporting of goods. I know that Perivon has not been a bad ruler for Cleononia, but his mistreatment and oppression of anyone not Cleononian is the tree from which the fruit of this invasion has fallen."

There was a prolonged silence as she watched Officer Kidron consider her words.

"You truly mean these things."

It wasn't a question, but Lady Virtesa dipped her head in assent anyway.

"And you truly wish to save Cleononian lives by preventing a prolonged siege?"

That *was* a question. "I know Perivon well enough to know that he will dig in his heels worse than any mule in the Western Region. Swaths of his citizenry will starve to death before he willingly surrenders the city. Those citizens have done nothing wrong and deserve no such fate."

Another long moment of consideration from Officer Kidron, then, "We will not harm any sailors of any ship. We will turn trade ships away from the port, and even damage them if we must, but we will neither board nor sink any ship."

Hiding her surprise at the decisiveness, Lady Virtesa nodded. "I would want nothing more."

Strictly speaking, that wasn't true – she'd have been thrilled if Officer Kidron had been willing to do whatever it took to bring Perivon to his knees, but she had never expected it, and was perfectly happy to settle for what Kidron was offering.

"How many other officers and sailors have you brought along to your line of reasoning?" Lady Virtesa asked.

Kidron shrugged. "Not many. A few. Enough that we can train sufficient deckhands. If you can find Cleononians in the city to sign up, we can get them trained."

"How long would that take?"

"Most people who live here know their way around a boat already," she said with another shrug. "We can get them trained on the differences between a warship and a fishing boat quickly enough, and operating the ballistas is simpler than putting on pants. I'd say...five days, to be safe."

"Five days," Lady Virtesa repeated. Kidron nodded. "Very well. You have five days. Then we sail for Dazbog."

～

Ezren's first thought as he slowly opened his eyes and saw the wooden planks of a ceiling above his head was that he was glad he was still alive.

His second thought was that he really needed to stop losing consciousness. This was getting to be a bad habit.

His third thought was that his left hip still really hurt.

His next thought was wondering how much time had passed since he was laid down on this bed.

The sunlight coming through the window and illuminating the room told him that it was late morning, or perhaps early afternoon... hard to be sure without knowing what direction the room faced. With a little luck, perhaps it was only the day after he'd arrived.

The door opened and a young woman with bright yellow hair came in carrying a tray. Perhaps this was 'Xochi', the one Nirari had called to before.

"Hello," he croaked, then cleared his throat. "Hello," he said again in a clearer voice.

She looked at him with a wry smile. "Glad to see that you're doing better. That was some entrance you made last night. I've never seen my da move so fast."

"So I've only been asleep for the night?"

"Well," she said, looking out the window. "You've also been asleep for about half the day so far, so I'm not sure what you mean."

"I just meant that I hadn't been asleep for more than one day."

"More than one day?" She laughed. "It would take a much more serious wound to keep someone down that long."

He leaned his head back on the pillow, relieved, and chuckled. "I could tell you some stories."

She raised one eyebrow in amusement. "Well, I'm busy at the moment. Not all of us can sleep half the day away."

He raised his head incredulously as she walked out, but she was looking at him with a mischievous smile. Ah, she was teasing him.

She was gone for a full minute before Ezren realized that he hadn't thanked her for the care he'd been given. He tried to get up, but his left hip was still quite stiff. Maybe he'd just stay where he was for a while.

The door opened again and Adal Nirari stepped in, holding a bottle of some dark liquid in one hand.

"Ah, yes, Xochi told me you were awake. Glad to see it." He looked over Ezren a bit as he lay in the bed.

"Are you feeling feverish, boy? I think we got enough spirits down your wound to stop any infection but it could still crop up."

Ezren shook his head. His body ached all over, and there was the deep and abiding pain in his hip, but he certainly didn't feel feverish. He looked up at the ceiling. He was bedridden...again. What had he done wrong *this* time?

Well...maybe he shouldn't have just climbed in through the window as soon as he got to the tower. Maybe he should have looked inside before climbing through, then he'd have noticed the dust patterns before ruining them. Galdrach had apparently returned only minutes after Ezren went in, so a little patience might have stopped him from being caught.

At that point, he could have gone through the same process as he had back at Lucke's estate. He sighed. Why couldn't things be simpler?

Some of his frustration must have shown on his face, because Nirari asked:

"What's wrong? You should be thankin' the stars that you're even alive."

"I just..." Ezren began. "It just seems like I've spent more time recovering than doing anything useful since I was last here."

Nirari snorted. "Well that's likely just because you're being stupid. Do yourself a favor and figure out what you're doing wrong."

Ezren frowned at Nirari, who held up his hands placatingly. "Everyone has their fair share of stupid in 'em, just part of being a person."

Nirari sounded a lot like Aminah. And Ben Rider. And Fiona. And his father. It seemed like there were two types of adults: the type that didn't offer enough guidance, like Mellion, and the type that offered too much, like every other adult in his life so far.

With that observation completed, Ezren could admit that Nirari probably wasn't wrong – Ezren could trace each time he'd woken up recovering from an injury to a mistake that he had made.

The door opened and a middle-aged man with wisps of gray at the temples entered, carrying a small leather bag. He wore a fine white shirt of cotton with embroidery across the chest and shoulders. Nirari leaned over to shake the man's free hand.

"Boy, this is the village medicine man, Endini. He was here in the inn last night and helped us take care of you," Nirari told him.

The bed creaked as Endini sat on the edge and pulled the blanket down to look at Ezren's hip. It was covered in bandages, with just a little bit of red staining the center. Endini carefully peeled the bandages back to take a look. Ezren looked up at Nirari, realizing that he hadn't shown the man much gratitude so far.

"Thank you," he said sincerely. "I know you didn't have to take me in, and you certainly didn't have to take care of me. Thank you."

"Bah," Nirari said, waving his hand, with a smile that belied his dismissiveness.

Endini examined the wound, peering over the top edge of the spectacles he wore on his nose. "It's not as bad as it may have seemed. Don't get me wrong, you were close to death, but just a little bed rest, spirits, and tight bandages were all you needed. The wound wasn't deep except for a small part in the center, which is where all the blood came from. Probably a vein. Everything besides the middle was cauterized by whatever burned you."

"Why wouldn't the center be cauterized as well?" Ezren asked.

Endini shrugged. "It was probably just deep enough to avoid it. There may be a small piece of you lying around somewhere nicely charred." His eyes flicked up to look into Ezren's. "What happened, did someone thwack you with a torch? A...sharp torch?"

Ezren considered his answer. "In a manner of speaking, yes," he responded, finally.

"Well, however it happened, in another day or so you should be on your feet," he said, replacing the bandages with fresh ones from his leather bag and standing up.

"How long before I can ride, do you think?" Ezren asked.

Endini shrugged. "Maybe another day after that. What's your hurry?"

"No-nothing," Ezren stammered after swallowing his initial answer. "No hurry, here."

Endini rolled his eyes. "Whatever you say, son." The medicine man turned and headed out of the room, nodding to Nirari on his way out. Nirari watched him go, then shut the door and looked back at Ezren.

"All right, out with it boy – what are you worried about?"

"I think that...someone might be coming after me. If they find me here then you may be in danger."

He looked around the room, suddenly concerned about Elliadel's journal, then saw all his saddlebags piled in the corner of the room. He resisted the urge to climb out of the bed and make sure the journal was still in the pouch he'd left it in.

"Well, you do like to get yourself into situations, don't you?" Nirari said, chuckling as he pulled a paper out of his apron pocket and unfolded it. "I was about to recommend you stick around here for a while, because our tax brigade just came through and had a couple of these they handed around town."

He handed the paper to Ezren, who scanned it, his eyes getting wider as he read. It had a very good likeness of him drawn on it, and below the photo it read:

"Reward for the safe return of the young man pictured above. Answers to Ezren Kimorae. 100 gold coins offered for his safe return. If you find him, bring him to Novis Castle, attention Ambassador Fiona Bura. Reward is void if Ezren is harmed in any way."

He felt a wave of homesickness and guilt as he thought about what Fiona must have been going through the last...how long had he been gone? There hadn't been much opportunity to keep track of time. It must be two months now. A hundred gold coins?! Fiona was fairly compensated by the King and Queen but he was surprised she had that much to throw around just for bringing him back to the castle.

Something on his face must have betrayed his thoughts, because Nirari seemed to know what was going through his mind.

"Ah, so you know this Ambassador, then," he said with confidence. "I figured you did, what with her insistence upon your 'safe' return. Though how she would expect anyone to take you against your will without harming you is beyond me."

Nirari continued to talk, but Ezren couldn't focus on the innkeeper's words. What was he supposed to do now? He needed to get to the Novis Spring, but the closer he got to Novis Terram the more likely it would be that he'd get recognized and captured. He also couldn't stay here, because Galdrach would most certainly have sent guards after him. Going back to Robinton would take him further away from his goal and potentially closer to danger.

Couldn't go forward, couldn't go backward, couldn't stay here. Certainly seemed like he didn't have a whole lot of options. A hundred gold coins was a lot. Perhaps Nirari had considered taking him in himself. No, nothing the bald innkeeper had done up to this point suggested he would even think of such a thing. He still had to face his problem, though.

"I need to go to Novis Terram," he said. "The object I've been looking for is there. But I *can't* get taken in. If they find me they'll never let me out of their sight again."

"Well, I can't tell you how to get into the city without being spotted, but if you travel into the forest north of here then travel East through the woods, you should be able to at least get *to* the city without running into any guards. Careful, though, there are a lot of bandits who make their homes in those woods for that very reason."

Ezren nodded. He was familiar with that area, having lived in part of it a few years ago and, more recently, been on scouting expeditions with Ben Rider.

Ezren sighed tiredly. At some point, this had to get easier, didn't it? For the first time, he considered whether it was really worth it. He had intentionally been trying not to think about his father all this time and just focus on the next step of his quest. Last night, while tying his bandage and halfway into delirium, the wall had broken briefly and he'd been confronted with how much he missed his da.

Now here, lying in this bed, Ezren felt helpless. His father was gone, *forever*. Not just for a day or tenday or month...gone forever. Nothing he could do would bring him back, and Ezren himself was so...*incompetent* that he couldn't even find his father's killer.

And now he was questioning whether it was even worth continuing to try. He couldn't go back in time and save his father, he couldn't change anything that he had said or done prior to his father's death, and he couldn't bring his father back to life.

Shame turned his cheeks red and made him feel flushed. The *one* thing he could do for his father -- find justice for his murder -- and he was asking himself if it was *worth it?* His father had given *everything* up for him. He'd given up his life at the castle in Ambarta, his other three sons, and his wife. He'd spent years trying to build a life for them in Berengaria, then when it was all ripped away his father had given up the only thing he had left: his freedom. He had joined the Guards, agreeing to go where they sent him and fight who they told him to fight.

He could not remember a single thing his father had done for his own happiness in the entire six years since they'd escaped Ambarta. How could Ezren falter in this one thing that he could do?

He would *not* be a bad son.

He gritted his teeth and tried once again to get out of the bed.

"Ho, hey now," Nirari said. "I didn't mean leave right this moment. You'd have to be mad, boy."

Ezren had every intention of leaving regardless of what Nirari said, but he found that he couldn't get out of the bed without the pain being so severe that his vision started to spot and go dark. He eased himself back on the pillow.

"How long do you think before I can leave?"

"If you do nothing but lay there, the pain may subside enough to be manageable within a day or so."

Ezren nodded, trying not to move any other part of his body. "I will move as little as I can. Hopefully I can be gone before anyone comes looking for me."

"You mentioned that earlier," Nirari said, nodding. "Why would someone come looking for you?"

Ezren considered telling Nirari everything, but what would be the point? What Ezren had done was not only theft, but also breaking into someone's home. Nirari might even side with Galdrach and insist that Ezren return the journal.

"It's probably better if you don't know," Ezren replied. "I wouldn't want to get you involved."

Nirari snorted. "Fair enough, I suppose. At this point I've done nothing but help a wounded patron of my inn. Just answer me this one question – have you done anything that makes you not want to look at yourself in the mirror?"

Ezren stared at him, not understanding what he was saying.

"What do you mean?"

"I mean, is there anything you've done that has made it hard to look yourself in the eyes? Everyone faces the judgment of others, and sometimes we need that, sure, but sometimes those others jump to their conclusions without knowing all the details. You, though, you *do* know all the details. So if you have done something that you, knowing how it all happened, have judged yourself in the wrong, then I expect you to tell me what it was so I can make my own decision on whether I keep helping you."

Ezren thought back, considering all his actions over the last two months in context of this new metric. His escape from Robinton city, his travels to and from Glacies Castle, his attempt to sneak into the first estate, his successful infiltration of the second estate, and what had happened at Galdrach's tower. Of all that, he hadn't really been hurting anyone…except when he'd taken the journal. But, Nirari couldn't possibly mean something like that, could he?

He shook his head. "No, I haven't done anything that makes me not able to look myself in the eye."

"Alright, then," Nirari said with a sharp nod of his head. "Rest up and I'll send someone in to help you use the bedpan in a little while."

As soon as Nirari left, Ezren started breathing deeper in preparation for holding his breath. He had to lie still and had no other entertainment, so it was back to this. He was getting much better at it. He had just gotten close to eight minutes the last time he'd tried.

He didn't know how long he practiced, but eventually he fell back asleep. He awoke as two pairs of hands pulled him up to something between a laying and sitting position, propping him up on extra pillows. It was Nirari and his daughter Xochi, and they had brought a plate of food that Ezren was expected to completely clear.

He didn't feel like eating, but as soon as he'd taken the first bite his appetite seemed to wake up and he had no trouble clearing the plate.

Xochil mixed something into a cup with water and gave it to him, and he quickly fell back asleep.

He awoke to the sound of the door creaking open. Looking outside, he was surprised to find that it was night; he had apparently slept the day away. He must have been more tired than he thought. He looked over to see Xochil come in furtively carrying a single candle for light. He tried to stretch and was quickly reminded of the pain in his side, though it was noticeably less than it had been during his conversation with Nirari earlier.

He started to ask Xochil what she was doing here, but she held her finger to her lips and hurried over. As she got closer, he saw that she was holding a small wad of leaves.

"Here," she said, "chew this."

Without waiting for his assent, she stuffed the wad of leaves into his mouth.

"Erm..." he said, trying to speak around his chewing. "What's going on?"

"There are men downstairs asking about you," she whispered.

Ezren pushed himself up to a full sitting position, pleased that he could actually do so now.

"What men? What did they look like?" He asked.

"Well, they're not soldiers. They look more like bandits than anything else. But they certainly don't seem like they're good friends of yours. Anyway, we have to hurry. My da tried to tell them he'd never seen you before, but one of them said they tracked you here. I think they were starting to get impatient. We've got to get you out of here."

Ezren swallowed the last of the leaves, already noticing that his energy level had risen and the pain in his hip had nearly gone away.

"What did you give me to eat?" He asked, amazed.

Xochil shrugged. "I don't know what it is, Endini left it with us earlier when he came and checked in on you again. He says you're healing wonderfully. As long as you keep the wound bandaged, it should heal on its own now without much trouble. He said those leaves should help with the pain in the meantime."

Ezren nodded emphatically and threw his blankets off, scooting gingerly to the edge of the bed to put on his boots. He looked to the window.

"Are we on the first floor?" He asked.

"Yes," she replied, understanding his intent.

With all the bedrest and now the seemingly-magical leaves, getting out the window would be a simple matter. He buckled on his sword and shield while Xochil opened the window and tossed his saddlebags out onto the ground. As soon as she was done, he lifted one leg through the window, ducked down low, then pulled the other leg out. He heard the doorknob rattle and someone pound on it just as he was through. He dashed to the side, yanking the saddlebags out of sight just as Xochil leapt forward to slam the window closed.

Leaning against the wall, his heart pounding, Ezren listened as the door was kicked open, his hand on his sword hilt. He wanted to run, but what if these men started to hurt Xochil? What had they already done to Nirari? If he wanted to be able to look himself in the mirror Nirari talked about, he could not leave yet.

Both of his questions were answered quickly.

There was a pause after the door was opened, then a gruff, deep voice growled, "He just left. Went out the window. Go straight for the stable *now!*"

Footsteps, then Nirari's voice. "I won't have you continuing to kick down the doors of my guests. This room was vacant tonight. My daughter must have just discovered an open window and slammed it accidentally because you startled her!"

"You're clearly lying," the gruff voice said. "It is nothing, however. We will find the boy and take him. You are lucky that our orders are to harm no one but him."

Footsteps announced the men leaving the room, and Ezren knew that he had to get moving *now*. He raced – as fast as his hip would allow him – to the stable at the back of the inn. It was faster to get there from the outside than inside, so he felt he had a good chance of escaping. To his relief, he found that one of the horse handlers had already saddled Asteri. He threw his saddlebags over her and hopped astride, grunting as his hip reminded him why he should not be leaping about, and kicked her into an immediate gallop out of the stable.

At just the wrong moment, three men in dark clothing that vaguely resembled uniforms came around the front of the stable. Ezren didn't have time to stop, or even really change direction, so while two of the men jumped out of the way just in time, the third was slammed by Asteri's left shoulder and thrown backward. Ezren was fairly sure he heard a crunch of bone.

He kept Asteri riding as fast as he could manage, down the road towards Novis Terram until he got past the palisade wall, then up to the forest in the north.

He knew he was being followed, but he knew that it would be next-to-impossible for them to track him in the dark. Even with all the sleep he'd already had, he didn't feel like he could ride all night, so he settled for going longer than he thought his pursuers would, then found a well-hidden hollow and curled up for the night.

The sky lightening brought him out of his sleep and he climbed onto Asteri's back with a few twinges from his hip. He looked back as he topped the first rise and saw a group of five dark-clothed riders amongst the trees. They were so close! Less than a mile away. The forest here was not dense, and before he realized how visible he must be, one of the riders pointed and he heard a shout. They instantly kicked their horses to a gallop. Ezren spun Asteri about and rode down away from the men.

Not for the first time, Ezren blessed the name of Ben Rider for all the scout had taught him about traveling quickly on horseback. Though Ezren was not able to gain much more of a lead on them, they also did not get any closer throughout the day, despite how often they seemed to be taking their horses at a gallop. He didn't think that his hip was slowing him down much, but it must be or he would have out-distanced them.

Unless magic was involved. Who knew what was possible with magic? Was there magic that could make horses go faster?

Travel through the woods was not as fast as it was along the road, and Ezren didn't reach Berengaria until long after the sun had gone down. He still wanted to avoid the city, so he stopped at their old cabin to camp there. It was two miles up from the city and, from what he recalled, few people went up that road unless they were going to Oanez, so it seemed as safe as anywhere.

He kept going long after it would be too dark to follow his tracks. Once on the road, he rode up North until he reached their old cabin plot.

The road would do an excellent job hiding his tracks, and his pursuers would have to guess whether he turned South to go into the city or North towards Oanez. With luck, they'd split up, and by the time they reached here he'd be gone anyway.

The moon was just rising as he rode into the once-familiar clearing he had called home for just over two years. The moon was waxing gibbous, giving plenty of light to observe the decrepit pile of half-burned logs that had once been their cabin. He continued riding into the clearing, seeing the "temporary" shelter they had constructed upon first arriving. He would have slept in there that night, except they'd converted it into an outhouse as soon as they had started sleeping in the cabin.

He took only another moment to look around, simply too tired for the variety of emotions that threatened to assail him. He hobbled Asteri by a lodgepole pine at the edge of the clearing and laid out his bedroll under a much shorter tree with branches closer to the ground to provide a little more shelter.

He closed his eyes immediately upon laying down, allowing his fatigue to drown out the feelings of loneliness and loss.

He woke before the sun had risen the following morning, and immediately resaddled Asteri. He needed to be gone before any of the riders came up the road. Cutting through the hills above Berengaria should keep him out of sight of the road easily enough.

As he traversed hill and dale all through the morning, leaving Berengaria quickly behind, he wondered hopefully whether he would be able to reach Novis Terram the next day without any problems. He still wasn't sure what to do when he arrived at Novis Terram, or how he was to avoid getting caught by the Guards, but he had some time left to consider that.

What was he so afraid of, anyway? Fiona was clearly worried about him: wasn't it selfish to deliberately avoid her attempts at finding him? Why not just 'turn himself in', as it were? He could keep himself safe from Galdrach's riders, explain everything he'd found up to this point, and then convince Fiona to let him go up to the Novis Spring and find the new magic.

Of course, that was only *if* Fiona believed him. And *if* he wasn't in trouble for stealing a saddle from the stable and the book on Glacies Castle from the library when he'd left. And *if* she ever agreed to let him out of her sight again after he had just run off for months without a word.

No, much better to finish his mission and then go make things right with the ambassador afterward. He still didn't know exactly what he would do when he got into the city, but now he at least had decided one thing he was *not* going to do.

His wound and leg continued to heal as he traveled, such that he didn't feel much pain from it except for when he mounted or dismounted. It would probably twinge if he squatted or sprinted, but normal riding and walking seemed fine. He also did not see the riders throughout the entire day. Perhaps he had lost them.

He camped that night under an enormous rock outcropping jutting out of the ground at an angle, much like the outcroppings that permeated The Berg. Still no sign of the riders.

He woke at first light the next morning and moved on as quickly as he could. He was running low on rations, so he skipped lunch altogether and decided to try and reach Novis Terram before stopping again, no matter what.

He wanted to head straight up to the Novis Spring, but if he still hadn't lost Galdrach's men completely then he'd be much harder to find in a big city. Not to mention he needed to restock on food.

The terrain on the approach to Novis Terram gradually smoothed out, but in a fitful way, where there would be a larger boulder here or a thick patch of trees there, and the huge walls of the city became visible when he was still far away. The first time he topped a rise and saw the entire city visible in the distance, his heart leapt. He was anxious, in both meanings of the word – nervous to return and also in a hurry to do so – but there was nothing to do except nudge Asteri's ribs again to keep her moving.

The Northern Highway stretched out a few miles to his right, and he considered whether he should head straight for it and follow the Highway all the way into the city. He'd have to merge with the road eventually, and travel would be faster on the road than through the rocky terrain. It had been long enough since he'd seen the riders that he worried they'd somehow gotten ahead of him and were waiting for him in the city. On the other hand, if they were capable of traveling that quickly they would have caught him before Berengaria.

Since he'd stuck to the wild up to this point, they would probably expect him to continue doing so. Therefore, heading straight for the road should be the opposite of what they would assume *and* get him to

Novis Terram faster. Decision made, he reached the road just after midday and set Asteri to a trot until he caught up with a Merchant caravan. He fell in at the back, far enough that none of the caravan paid him any mind, but close enough that the Guards at the gate would hopefully take him for a member of the party.

The caravan moved at a snail's pace, but that turned out to be good; they arrived at the gate just after nightfall. The darkness made it easy for Ezren to hide his face under the hood of his cloak and enter without detection. Guards stood at the gate, as always, but they weren't checking faces.

But what to do now? He eyed a patrol of four soldiers armed with spears as they marched briskly past him. Considering trying to get a good night's sleep, he started to pull Asteri over towards an inn, but realized that if an inn all the way in Salimelish had gotten a flier with his face on it, the chances were pretty good that one here in Novis Terram probably had as well.

He could always go to Raban's. Of course! He slapped his own forehead in amazement that he hadn't thought of that sooner! In fact, that might help him with more than one problem. It might create a problem as well, though. Raban's father, Sergeant Kennard, was a stickler for the rules and would most likely haul him up to the castle as soon as he saw him.

Ezren cautiously rode Asteri up the road to the barracks complex, trying to look everywhere without appearing as though he were looking everywhere. Another Guard patrol passed him without incident. His heart pounding, his hood still drawn, he reached the tying post outside the building where Raban and his father lived. He tied Asteri, hoping that no one recognized her, took his pack, left the saddlebags, and went in, still wearing his hood.

Once on Raban's floor, he looked up and down the narrow hallway. No one was around. He snuck quickly to Raban's door, knocked, then ducked back to hide behind part of the wall that stuck out. If the Sergeant answered, Ezren would just hide and see about getting to Raban's window from the outside.

THE POWER OF THE BROKEN | 387

After a moment of tense waiting, the door opened and Raban's head popped out, looking up and down the hallway in confusion.

"Psst!" Ezren whispered, unsure if the Sergeant was inside. He stepped out, pulling his hood back. Raban's eyes went wide, and he beckoned frantically to Ezren.

"What are you-? Get in here! Quick!"

Surprised but trusting his friend, Ezren dashed into the apartment and looked around as Raban shut the door and pulled the bolt lock.

"Where's the Sergeant?" Ezren asked. Raban wouldn't have had him come straight in if his father were here.

Raban put his hands on his hips. "Well, 'hello' to you too, then! Do you have any idea what you've put me through? I got hauled up in front of the King and Queen themselves! They wanted to know where you'd gone, and they really meant business. I still don't think they believe that I didn't know anything. And that Princess Asteri..." he said, shaking his head and walking towards the kitchen. "Ankon have mercy on you, Ezren, if things ever get more serious between you two."

"Asteri?" Ezren asked, confused and trying to follow along. "She saw me off, what did she want out of you?"

"She was convinced that you had told me something that you hadn't told her. She didn't start bothering me until you'd been gone a month, though. Seemed to think you should have been back already. Truth be told, I thought you would be as well. Anyway, not only did I get inter-rogated by just about every important person in the city, but all day today I've had Guards *following me* as if I would lead them to some secret hideout of yours."

Raban froze suddenly, his eyes going wide in realization. "Wait. How did you come in here?"

Ezren shrugged. "I tied Asteri on the front post and walked in through the door."

"Stercore!" Raban cursed, dashing to his room and emerging a moment later with a backpack, already stuffed full, and two large coils of rope in one hand. He tossed one of the coils at Ezren, who caught it, confused.

"What-?" Ezren started to ask as Raban pulled on a loose coat.

"I figured you'd turn up sooner or later, most likely in some kind of trouble and probably in a hurry." He grinned at Ezren as he slung the pack over his shoulder. "Was I wrong?"

Ezren couldn't help but grin back. "No, that's pretty much exactly what's going on. I'm being chased by a few of Galdrach's men because I stole one of his books. But I lost them around Berengaria. What's your rush right now?"

Raban looked at him disbelievingly. "You left your horse at the front of the building and just walked in? I told you that guards have been tailing me, didn't I?"

Everything clicked in Ezren's mind a moment before there was a pounding at the door.

"Open up, Kennard! We know he's in there!" A deep voice called. "The ambassador is on her way right now!"

There was something Ezren was missing here, and he stopped to try and think it through. Fiona had been looking for him for a while, but Raban said he'd only been being tailed that day. What had changed?

He opened his mouth to ask but Raban just jerked his thumb calmly back towards his room. Once they were both there, Raban whispered, "I laid a plank from my window across to the roof of the next building. From there we can get all the way to the wall without touching the ground once. There's a spot on the wall that the Guards only walk by every few minutes. We can get out that way."

Ezren nodded, then looped his sword onto his back underneath his shield and tied his pack securely over both. The rope he tied to the outside of it all. When one was running around on rooftops, one needed both hands and feet unencumbered. His bow was still tied to his saddlebags on Asteri, along with his axe and most of his supplies. Raban likewise tied his pack to his back, then grabbed several knives from his dresser and tucked them on either side of his belt. Ezren hoped Raban had some food in there, because it was looking like he wouldn't get that chance to resupply.

Raban pushed the window open and they climbed out, walking

across the plank one at a time. Raban reached the roof and turned, waiting as Ezren followed suit. Ezren was almost to the end when a focused beam from a lantern on the ground shone up at him.

"He's out here! Stop, Ezren!" yelled a voice that Ezren recognized. It was Lieutenant Kindo. He hesitated, looking down at the light.

"Kindo?" He called down, confused.

"Ezren, we're all just glad that you're alive! We've been fearing the worst! Please don't run, you need to come back to the castle."

Again came the feeling that he was missing something...The Guards at the door, Raban being followed, a Lieutenant in the Castle Guard being sent to fetch him...Ezren looked down, realizing how many Guards there were accompanying Kindo. What was going on?! He swallowed nervously.

"Just tell Fiona I'm all right!" He called down to Kindo. "I'll be back in a few days!"

Ezren couldn't see Kindo very well past the light of the lantern, but his voice called back sadly. "It's not that simple, Ezren. I need to take you in."

Something was definitely wrong.

"Why?" he called down, still hesitating in going to the end of the plank.

Kindo cleared his throat. "We've received a pigeon from the Robinton Guards requesting your immediate arrest. The wizard Galdrach has accused you of breaking into his tower and stealing some of his most valuable possessions. The Guards say you also fit the description of a thief who broke into an estate and attacked one of the guards there, *and* that you assaulted a pair of Guards within Robinton City itself."

Ezren could barely hear Kindo's last words over the pounding of his own heart.

"Ezren Kimorae, I am placing you under arrest."

His thoughts whirled. He looked up at Raban, wanting to see how he was reacting to all of this. Raban just beckoned urgently but silently for Ezren to keep coming.

It was beginning to hit him just how much trouble he was in. What was worse is that he knew he was guilty of everything he'd been accused of. There was certainly a lot of relevant context missing in the accusations, but the cold facts were not on his side.

But...could he still look at himself in Nirari's mirror? Yes, yes he could. Everything he'd done he had done for his father. He had hurt no one who had not attacked him first, and the only thing he had taken was the journal, which he would find a way to return as soon as he was finished with his quest.

He set his jaw and took a step forward.

"Ezren, stop!" Kindo yelled. Ezren ignored him and kept walking. To his shock, the creak of bowstrings being pulled tight came from below.

"Hold your fire!" came Kindo's angry bellow. "No arrows! He is not to be harmed! Catchpoles only!"

As soon as Ezren reached the roof, he pulled the plank away from Raban's window, letting it fall to the ground just as the Guards that had been pounding on the Kennard's door stormed into Raban's room. Feeling impudent, Ezren gave them a cheeky salute as he turned and ran after Raban.

Kindo cursed and called soldiers to help pursue them on the ground. Guards bearing torches came running and spread out into the alleys between the houses. Raban picked up speed and Ezren kept pace; they both had a fair amount of experience with this kind of thing. Ezren felt a twinge of pain come from his hip as he ran, but it was mild and he'd build a home in the Inferno before letting the pain slow him down right then.

Just as Ezren was feeling grateful that no arrows were coming his way, he saw the end of a catchpole lift up to his right and another on his left.

Deep inside he understood that this was the sort of compromise decision that a soldier might make when given two orders that potentially conflicted: capture Ezren, but don't hurt him. Kindo was just doing what he'd been ordered to do, and no one could objectively condemn his actions as wrong, strictly speaking.

Much closer to the surface, though, were anger, affront, and determination. Did Kindo think so little of him? Did he really believe that Ezren had – what – gone on some kind of rampage throughout Robinton? Robbing estates and hurting anyone who got in his way? He'd known Kindo for years! Had Ezren earned so little trust in that time? So little regard? Was Ezren's own will of so little consequence that he could be snapped up like some common criminal?

Well, he thought cynically. *Best of luck to you, Kindo.*

An opportunity for Kindo's luck to prove itself came quickly, as two more catchpoles rose in front of Ezren as he was about to leap a gap between one roof and another. It was a small enough gap that it could be simply stepped over if he were walking, so Ezren brought both feet together and leapt as high as he could, diving over the loops, rolling forward, and sliding a ways down the next rooftop.

Both loops snapped tight as he leapt, the operators no doubt having trouble seeing whether he had jumped into their traps.

He rolled to his feet, ignoring the now-fierce pain in his hip, and worked to catch up to Raban, who was two rooftops ahead of him now.

Looking up, Ezren could see the wall beginning to materialize in the darkness. The catchpoles continued to follow him, but it appeared that Kindo had not sent a runner to notify the Guards-on-the-Wall. The top of the wall had no activity on it, save for a single torch lazily marking the passing of a patrolling guard. Kindo must be assuming that Ezren's goal was to hide somewhere in the city.

Or he just didn't think Ezren had a way out.

He followed Raban to a rooftop that was adjacent to the wall. They squatted on that roof for a moment, listening to the shouts of the guards below trying to figure out where they went. Raban grinned mischievously, then jumped up and pulled himself onto the rampart.

Ezren watched as Raban looked left, then right, making sure that no Guards were patrolling here.

He gestured to Ezren and pulled himself the rest of the way up.

Raban's feet disappeared over the lip. Ezren breathed in deep against the pain in his hip, then leapt and pulled himself up onto the wall.

"That was brilliant, Raban," Ezren whispered, squatting next to his friend. "Now, how are we going to get down the other side?"

Raban motioned to their left, towards the mountains, and they ran at a crouch along the top of the wall, the shouts of the Guards fading into the distance. About a hundred yards up the wall, Raban stopped and peered over the outside edge.

"This is the spot," he whispered, pointing. "There's a cluster of trees that comes almost all the way to the wall. We should be able to go through those on our way out without being spotted.

Ezren peered over the edge, and indeed, the trees stopped only about 20 feet from the wall and continued onward a ways. But there was a more important question on Ezren's mind: how were they going to use the ropes to get down? Wouldn't they have to leave the rope tied at the top? Wouldn't that tell the Guards exactly how they'd escaped and from where?

"How are we going to do this?" Ezren asked, bewildered.

"Simple. We'll tie one end to the rampart and you'll go down, then I'll untie it from the rampart and tie it to my waist, looping it around the rampart once so you can ease me down," Raban responded.

"Is that going to work?! Is the rope even long enough?" Ezren asked.

"Oh, the rope is definitely long enough. The wall is only about 50 feet tall, and just my spool of rope is 200 feet. Yours is too. We should only need one of them for this."

"Then why do we both have one?"

Raban shrugged and grinned. "The ropemaker said if I bought one he'd give me the other free."

"And you're sure it's strong enough to hold us?"

"Oh, I have no idea," Raban laughed softly, adjusting the pack on his back.

"Wait, haven't you done this before?!" Ezren asked in a strangled voice.

"When would I have done this before, Ezren?" Raban asked pointedly.

Ezren nodded with a wry smile. "Fair enough, so you want to go first?"

Raban laughed again. "Inferno, no. You're heavier, *you* go first."

"Why does that matter?"

"Because," Raban began patiently, "the person at the bottom will be the only thing stopping the person at the top from dropping to the ground like a rock and dying. Therefore, the person at the bottom needs to be heavier than the person at the top."

Ezren frowned, but it was hard to dispute Raban's logic. With a sigh, he looked over the edge to see how far away the ground seemed. The wall was only about five stories tall, so he *might* survive if he fell from the top. He would certainly break something though, and possibly a lot of somethings.

Eh, he could live with that.

Raban tied one end of the rope to the rampart and threw the rest down the wall so that it hung down, ready for Ezren to begin his descent.

The ground seemed *very* far away.

Well, nothing for it, Ezren thought to himself. He swung from the inside of the wall to the outside, holding onto the rope as he pivoted, making Raban breathe in sharply. He kept a tight grip on the rope as he stepped down with his feet, finding toe holds as he started down.

After several small steps, he decided to try taking some bigger ones. The Guard patrolling this section of wall could be back any minute. It seemed like a great idea until his left foot slipped out and his shoulder slammed into the wall as he bounced. His hands started to slide on the rope, which was just slightly too thin for him to grip tight enough to hold his entire weight.

Forcing himself not to panic, he dug his toes into a crack and put as much weight as he could on them, shifting his grip on the rope. The sliding had burned his hands, but he kept his breathing under control and thought this through.

He just needed to keep doing what he'd been doing originally. Small steps, find toeholds, try not to put his entire weight on his hands.

After two minutes of slow climbing down that felt like an eternity, Ezren's feet found soft ground and he released the rope. His hands looked rubbed raw from the short slide down. He looked up grumpily as Raban untied the rope from the rampart and tied it around his waist.

Raban would just get to step down all easy-like while Ezren had to once again let the rope slide in his hands. Unless...Ezren looked back to where the trees started. The rope was long enough to reach them, so he pulled his end over and wrapped it once around the tree, pulling it tight. He looked at it, wrapped it around a second time, then a third time, and pulled it tight again.

There. Now the tree would get the friction and Ezren could do the hand-over-hand method.

Raban pulled his end of the rope around the rampart so that it came down through the next gap over.

He could barely see Raban in the moonlight, but he saw Raban's hand wave back and forth as a signal that he was ready to go down. Ezren stepped forward and waved his hand back and forth to signal that he was ready as well.

Raban stayed where he was, though. Ezren watched as Raban stayed there, looking like he was staring down at the ground. What was he doing?

"Raban!" Ezren whispered as loud as he dared. "Come on!"

Raban gave no indication whether he had heard Ezren's whisper. Ezren held the rope tight, waiting for Raban to turn and sit back on the rope.

A glint of light at the edge of Ezren's vision caused him to turn, and he felt the blood drain from his face. The light came from the torch held by the Guard coming back. He didn't dare whisper again, because if Raban could hear him then the Guard most likely would too. He watched helplessly as the guard's light slowly came closer.

Luckily, Raban finally turned and sat back, putting his weight on the rope. Ezren started letting the rope down as quickly as he dared, hand-over-hand, worried that the scraping sound of the rope going around the tree would be loud enough to get the Guard's attention. As soon as Raban was on the ground, Ezren dropped his end and Raban ran towards him, pulling the slack as he came.

Once under the cover of the trees Raban turned and kept pulling as fast as he could. The end of the rope flipped up around the rampart and fell down to the ground just before the circle of light reached where it had been. They both watched from the shelter of the trees as the torch-light walked slowly past, going all the way to where the wall dug into the mountainside, then back where it had come.

They both released their breath in unison.

Untying himself, Raban brushed off his pants and led the way, though Ezren could now guess where they were going. On the other side of a ridge a couple miles away there was a gully where they had frequently laid snares and gone hunting. There was a comfortable campsite there as well.

They stuck to the shadows as much as they could. Clouds flowed past, sometimes blocking the light of the moon and sometimes letting it bathe everything in a soft, white light. They frequently checked behind them, but the small glow of the torch on the wall continued its rhythmic back-and-forth.

Once they passed the first ridge, the ground dipped down enough that they were mostly blocked from view of the walls, and by the time they came up again to go over the next ridge, they were far enough away that no one on the wall would be able to tell them apart from the rest of the shadows.

They reached their campsite and Raban tiredly dropped his pack on the ground, sat on a log, and dug out his flint and steel to get a fire going. Ezren raised a hand to stop him, then reconsidered. They were miles away from Novis Terram and on the other side of a ridge to boot, so there was no way a fire would give them up to anyone who might be looking for them.

Once the fire was crackling comfortably, Raban sat back on the log and folded his arms.

"Alright, Ezren," he said. "Now it's story time. You said you stole a book from Galdrach, but what about all the other stuff Kindo said? Did you really attack a bunch of guards in Robinton?"

"No!" Ezren said instinctively. "Well, not really, at least. *They* attacked *me*. In Robinton city, they wanted to put me in jail because I didn't put a sack on Asteri to catch her stercore, and I just wanted to leave."

"Hold on," Raban said, opening and closing his mouth twice before speaking again. "You didn't put a what on Asteri? To catch her *what?*"

Ezren sighed, setting his pack, shield, and sword down against another log. He bent over gingerly, looking around in the moonlight for some thicker sticks for the fire as he considered what to say.

"I should probably just start from the beginning," he said.

Raban shook his head. "Nah, let's start with - where are we going, and why did you steal a book from a wizard so notorious that even *I* know who he is?"

"Well...I found it, Raban. The new magic, the one that will help me figure out who killed my da. At least...I know where it is."

Ezren paused, brushing some damp leaves off an otherwise good stick. He considered for a moment whether he should tell Raban *everything*. Maybe he could leave out some of the more embarrassing bits.

"That's great," Raban said interestedly, interrupting his thoughts. "Where is it?"

Ezren grinned, his exhaustion taking a back seat. "The Novis Spring!" He replied excitedly, straightening to look at Raban. "I think it's underwater somewhere, and we just have to pull it out and break it open. At least I think so."

"Are you sure?" Raban asked, a hint of disbelief in his voice. "People swim in the Spring all the time. I think if something was down there people would know."

Ezren shook his head. "The Spring is huge, plus the orb we're looking for is probably really far down. You wouldn't be able to see it unless you were in the right spot and you dove down far enough."

"So…" Raban began. "How do you expect to find where this 'right spot' is?"

Ezren held out his hands and shrugged. "I don't know."

"But you are sure that it's there?" Raban asked.

"As sure as I can be," Ezren replied, tossing the sticks he'd found into the firepit.

"And how do you know that it will help you find who killed your da?"

Ezren opened his mouth for a moment, then closed it again, thinking.

Raban's eyes got wide. "You *don't know!*"

Ezren held his hands out. "Now, hold on, I've been following clues across three countries to find this new magic, and this is all actually part of a prophecy, and here, let me show you."

Between the light of the fire and the moonlight, they could see well enough to look at the journal Ezren had taken and talk about what he had discovered in Galdrach's tower. Discussion of the events in the tower led to questions about how he ended up in the tower and how he'd made it back here.

Ezren told Raban the entire story, watching with satisfaction as Raban's jaw slowly dropped more and more throughout the regaling. He did his best not to embellish, though he certainly added more color in places he knew Raban would find most interesting. Raban's face morphed into a wide grin as Ezren told the story of the 'wooing' of Ann Marie.

Raban expressed a strong interest in meeting Aminah and had a nod of respect for Adal Nirari. He shook his head and sighed at how easily Ezren had escaped the guards at Robinton City, bemoaning their incompetence. Glacies Castle was mostly glossed over, as Raban's interest in books was not particularly strong.

They talked for hours into the night, but eventually the conversation came back around to what their next plan of action was. Ezren had not had much time to think about it, since he'd been on the run almost since the moment he had discovered the orb's location. Raban, for his part, was still trying to grasp everything Ezren had shared.

"Explain to me again how you know we need to break it," Raban asked, looking at Ezren quizzically.

Ezren shrugged helplessly. "I guess I don't. It just seems like what we're supposed to do. The prophecy specifically said 'sword shatter' and, I don't know, to release something don't you have to break the thing that's holding it in?"

"I mean…" Raban began with a sort of half-shrug, "Sometimes you can just open it."

"I guess we'll find out when we get the orb," Ezren replied. "If there's a way to open it then great, and if not, I'll hit it as hard as I can with my sword."

"Didn't you say this orb thing was made out of solid rock? It wouldn't even require any magic to break a sword swung against solid rock."

Raban had a point there.

Ezren had no idea how to break open an orb of solid rock. He had no idea whether 'sword shatter' meant what he thought it meant, and the only reason he knew where to look for the orb was because of the research done by someone infinitely more knowledgeable than he. It was discouraging to realize just how little he actually knew about what needed to happen next.

Raban's voice once again pulled him away from his thoughts.

"We also need to consider the possibility that we'll have limited time once we reach the Spring. The men that Galdrach sent to chase you might head that way, or inferno, Ezren, even Guard patrols go up to the Spring on the regular."

Ezren closed his eyes and took a deep breath. Raban was right. There was just no point in continuing to charge headfirst into things. With luck, maybe he could avoid blacking out from his injuries on this venture.

"Alright," he said after a moment. "Why don't we stick around here tomorrow? Hopefully no one realizes we're even out of the city yet, and

I can go through the journal to see if there's anything in there to help us."

Raban nodded his assent, and they continued their discussion.

They agreed that once they arrived at the Spring, time was not on their side. They needed to find the orb quickly and either break or open it before any unwanted parties arrived. They talked so late that light was beginning to appear in the sky before they agreed to lay down and get a few hours of sleep before moving on. A little rest now could make the difference between having to stop early that day or continuing on.

After only a few hours, the brightness and heat of the mid-morning sun forced them both to admit that they wouldn't be getting any more sleep. They got up, stretched, and chewed on some dried meat Raban had in his pack. Ezren sat on one of the logs by the fire and pulled out the journal.

Raban stood up with a sigh, gesturing with his piece of jerky. "I'm going to scout around a bit, maybe backtrack and make sure no one is following us."

He walked out of the camp as Ezren opened up the first page of the journal.

Hello,

These writings may one day be the only hope for every intelligent race on the surface of Quilara. I pray that they will survive the centuries they will no doubt be required to endure...

Hmm. Ominous.

...Read with care, whoever you might be, for the burden of knowledge is heavier than that of the field, the craft, or the mine. Those who read these words with the proper regard for their importance will inside find clues to understand the very nature of their reality and how to usher in its change...

Maybe he could just skip to the next page.

Ezren flipped to the next page just as Raban jogged back into the clearing. Raban jerked his thumb behind him as he leaned forward, other hand on his knee.

"Patrol's coming," he said between breaths. "Looked like five guards.

I didn't get close enough to be sure, but one of them looked like that skinny one that got after us that one time."

"Oh, yeah," Ezren said, remembering. "With the rats, and the, uh…"

"The top hat, yes," Raban said impatiently. "They're still a mile or so out from here but unless we want to risk being discovered we should probably get on our way."

Ezren frowned. When was he supposed to prepare for getting to the Novis Spring? From here it would only take a little over a day to get there, even without a real trail to follow. He snapped the journal shut and stuffed it into his bags.

"Charging headfirst, it is!" He said ruefully as he slung his pack over his shoulders and strapped on his sword and shield.

Raban did likewise and they tromped out of the clearing. Ezren worried for a moment about leaving too clear of trail for the patrol to follow, but Guards stationed at the Castle didn't get a whole lot of practice with that sort of thing. They'd have to go back and pull a scout, like Rider, to come out and find their trail.

They could have anywhere from a few hours' head start to more than a day.

They cut through the brush to a thin deer trail they could use to make their path more difficult to track.

"You know," Raban said thoughtfully from ahead of Ezren. "I wonder if those ruins around the Spring have something to do with it."

Ezren shook his head, though Raban wouldn't be able to see it. "No, I don't think so. Ben explained them to us, remember? They were from some of the original settlers of Mountain Home, before they decided that the bottom of the waterfall was a better place to settle."

"Yes, but that was only *some* of the ruins," Raban insisted. "There were those strange pillars right on the shore that angled in towards the lake."

"Oh, you're right," Ezren said, remembering. He was surprised that those pillars hadn't occurred to him before now.

Ezren needed to take a rest earlier than Raban, which led to Ezren needing to explain that his wound from Galdrach's tower wasn't quite healed yet, which, of course, led to jokes at Ezren's expense.

"I'm sure the princess would be happy to take good care of you."

Then, a few lines later:

"Sounds like she'll have to fight off a lord's maid and an innkeeper's daughter for the privilege, though."

And, lastly:

"Maybe I'll go up to the Spring, scout around for a day or two, then come back while you sit there resting."

At first, Ezren didn't rib Raban back, in large part because…well, because it felt great just to bask in the good-natured insults. He hadn't *bantered* in so long. He'd been alone so long, and his only companions had been people who didn't know him well. Raban's taunts felt so… normal, which brought along hope that such a thing as 'normal' could exist for him again.

He'd have to make things right with Fiona first.

Enough was enough, though, and as Raban continued his ribbing, Ezren started to fire back, the two of them laughing uproariously when one got the other good. The knowledge that there was a patrol out looking for them failed to dampen their spirits.

How long had it been since he had *laughed?*

Thinking back, he realized it had been the last time he had come down these very mountains after a scouting trip around the Spring with Ben and Raban. He had learned about his father's death when they had gotten back into the city.

The thought sobered him a bit, and Raban seemed to detect his change in mood. They walked in silence for a while, not stopping again until the sun began to go down. They stayed off the main trail, relying instead on wildlife paths that found ways through the brush and trees more easily than simply tramping up the hill would have.

Their lack of sleep the night before began to catch up to them fiercely as the sun went down, and they both agreed to stop and make camp before the sun had disappeared completely. They searched around a bit for a secluded spot to camp and found a large pine tree which had branches growing down all the way to the ground in a protective bowl around its base. Sleeping there, someone could pass right along the outside of the tree and not notice them.

Raban still had enough rations for the both of them in his pack. They scarfed down the waybread and dried meat. Once they had lain out on their cloaks, they looked up through the pine branches at the clear sky visible through the small gaps.

They were both asleep before the sky was completely dark.

CHAPTER 13: THE RETURN

The next morning they awoke covered in a layer of dew that had somehow gotten past all the branches above them, and as they shook it off Raban counted on his fingers for a moment, then looked at Ezren and grinned.

"Happy birthday, Ezren!"

"What?" Ezren asked, bewildered. "My birthday? Surely it hasn't been that long."

"You didn't know? How could you not know it's your birthday?" Raban asked, equally bewildered.

"Believe it or not, a pocket calendar was not on my packing list when I left," Ezren said sarcastically.

Raban shrugged and nodded. "Yeah, alright, I guess that makes sense. Well happy birthday!"

"Thanks," Ezren replied, laughing. "I guess that means I'm 17 now."

"You guess?" Raban said with a grin. "Didn't they teach you to count at that fancy Royal Academy?"

It was hard to tell with the thick forest, but it seemed they had camped close to the top. Indeed, after following only a mile or so of switchbacks that took them to the top of the rise, the ground leveled out and the Spring opened up before them.

They stayed a few feet down the slope, hiding in the brush, searching for any sign that there might be other parties here. Bandit groups camped here on occasion, and Raban was right about the regular patrols from Guards. Combine that with the possibility of running into Galdrach's men *and* the patrol that might be tracking them up this way, there was a lot of reason for caution.

Ezren couldn't see a way for Galdrach's men to know he was coming here, though, unless Galdrach had some magical means of tracking him...or he had his own suspicions about the Novis Spring.

They identified the pillars they could see from this vantage point, but it was not immediately obvious how they could be associated with what they were looking for. There was no sign of any other people around, though they did notice a herd of deer drinking from the water's edge on the far side of the Spring. After waiting patiently in the brush for nearly half an hour, they cautiously came out onto the far more visible beach area that led down to the water's edge.

They had emerged fairly close to the falls, and here the Spring narrowed considerably before falling down to Novis Terram. At its widest point, one could hardly make out the opposite shore at all, let alone see individual creatures.

Satisfied that they were alone, Ezren and Raban walked up to the nearest pillar. 'Pillar' perhaps wasn't the correct word, but it was the closest they could come to describing this...thing. It wasn't cylindrical, and it didn't stand straight up. It stood out of the ground at an angle and had almost a hook-like appearance. The base of the pillar was rectangular, with the long sides pointing towards the lake, and once it was taller than either of the two boys, it began to curve towards the water then down towards the ground, almost reminiscent of the head of a grazing horse.

Where the forehead of the horse would have been was a long horn that protruded out, pointing towards the water.

Ezren looked towards the next nearest pillar, squinting to see it more clearly. If one were to draw a line out from where this pillar was pointing and another from where the next pillar was pointing, it seemed they would intersect somewhere in the middle of the Spring.

He pointed this out to Raban, who immediately suggested they go all the way around the Spring, using all the pillars to make sure the intersection point remained in the same place. It would take all day, but Ezren wasn't keen on the idea of choosing a place at random to dive down who-knew-how-deep into the water.

Of course, it was possible that someone could arrive in that time, but in Aminah's words, 'Trying to do it wrong will just make it take even longer.' In this case, diving blindly at different places in the lake could keep them here for days.

So, they circled the enormous lake, Raban drawing out a rough map on a piece of paper he had packed and making lines that matched what they were seeing as closely as possible. Ezren watched with interest. Cartography was one of the few things taught to students at the barracks academy but not the Royal Academy, and was only taught at all because a cartographer volunteered his time.

Raban claimed he didn't know much, but he made them count their steps carefully as they walked from pillar to pillar so he could keep the distance as accurate as possible on the paper.

The trip all the way to the other side of the Spring took the entire day, and they made camp at the base of a steep rise on the west coast of the water just hidden in a small stand of trees. They again chose not to make a fire that night, and each of them took a watch, starting as early as the sunset. Ezren took the first watch, and pulled the journal of Elliadel out to read for only the second time since he had stolen it.

He skipped the first page, which seemed to have no point beyond stoking Elliadel's ego. The next page opened with a passage that Ezren did not truly understand:

"I feel the burden of watching prophesy be fulfilled, though I cry reason with every breath I take. My hope is that this journal, which I now fully expect to be a target for destruction along with every other record of the past several

centuries, may survive and help accelerate the latter half of the prophecies of our days."

Ezren continued to read, though he was honestly not sure what he expected to find. A skilled researcher and wizard like Galdrach would probably have distilled the useful bits in the notes that Ezren had already read, but there was little else to do while keeping watch, and he didn't want to leave any possible due diligence undone.

His impression as he continued to read Elliadel's words is that the moon elf certainly seemed to feel an awful lot of self-pity. It seemed every other sentence was bemoaning that he should be cursed to live in such times, or explaining the hardships of banishment and the 'burden of knowledge'.

This would have been easier to tolerate if the rest of the journal contained a great deal of insight into what he was looking for, but like many of the books he'd read at Glacies Castle, there was much that this Elliadel seemed to take for granted. He mentioned spells by name without explaining what they did, threw out names of geography and cities without context, and even spoke of animals and magical creatures casually as though their presence, and indeed their very existence, were a matter of course.

He supposed he should count it a blessing that the journal was written in his own language at all, unlike many of the books at Glacies Castle, and be grateful for whatever he was able to glean from it.

Exhaustion prompted him to close the book and rise to his feet to avoid sleep long before his watch ended, and he spent the rest of it peering out over the still, dark waters that reflected so clearly the light of the moon and stars.

There were plenty of noises that caught his attention, but they were all perpetrated by nocturnal wildlife of one sort or another, and when he estimated the night to be halfway gone, he shook Raban awake to take over.

The morning came with still no sign of any pursuers, so they took a further look at the map Raban had drawn the day before. The lines intersected at a point just as the lake was starting to narrow, relatively close to their current side of the lake. They hiked back down to approximately where Raban's lines had intersected and looked out across the water.

"I don't know, Ezren," Raban said doubtfully. "This seems too easy. You're telling me that no time in the last thousand years has someone thought to draw out where these pillars are all pointed?"

Ezren didn't respond immediately, thinking. Raban had a point; it's not like this had been all that complicated. The final point they'd determined with the map was fairly close to where Ezren had guessed just by using his eyes.

Even someone who had no idea what they were looking for would likely have stumbled upon the fact that the pillars around the lake pointed to a common spot. He went over the now-memorized prophecy in his mind.

None of what they'd experienced yet seemed like it could be a fulfillment of "light shrink from view" *or* "sword shatter". Maybe they just hadn't gotten that far yet. He looked at the water, out to about where they estimated the focal point to be.

"How deep do you think the water gets at that part of the Spring?" Ezren asked pensively.

Raban shrugged. "My da told me once that some scholar working for the King and Queen tried to dive down to the bottom but drowned."

They considered the spot for a moment. "Looking at how steep the mountains around us are, it could easily be a couple hundred feet deep," Raban finished.

Ezren nodded slowly. "It gets darker the deeper into water you go. Like the light just doesn't go through water very well."

Raban nodded back. "What are you thinking?"

Ezren looked at him. "'Light shrink from view'. I'm wondering if that is a hint that we have to dive down until it's so dark that we can't see the sun anymore."

"How far do you think that is?" Raban asked, eyebrows raised.

It was Ezren's turn to shrug. "I've never dived anywhere near that deep."

"Could someone even hold their breath that long?" Raban asked, skeptical.

Ezren laughed and shook his head disbelievingly. "I think *I* can."

Raban looked at him, confused. Ezren caught his look and explained.

"I've had a lot of time to kill over the last few months. I've been doing that trick Ben taught us about timing ourselves holding our breath. Standing still I can hold my breath for eight minutes now."

"Eight minutes?!" Raban asked incredulously. "No, you're pulling my tail."

"It's true," Ezren said. "When I first tried on that trip with Ben I could only last for about 30 seconds, but I've been able to do it for longer and longer the more I practiced. It was *really* hard to get past six minutes."

"Well eight minutes is plenty of time to get down and back, I would think," Raban said, though he sounded doubtful.

"Probably," Ezren replied. "But that eight minutes is while I'm holding still. I think it would be wise to assume that I can only last for maybe half that long while I'm trying to swim."

"Seems like you could still get pretty deep in four minutes," Raban replied.

Ezren stood up straight, having made a decision. "Let's give it a try."

He took off his pack and pulled out the long bundle of rope Raban had had him carry.

"Alright, so here's the plan," Ezren said, squatting as he uncoiled the rope and tossed one end towards Raban. "I'll tie the rope to my waist and then swim down as far as I can. Hopefully I can get to the orb. You hold the rope and keep just a little bit of tension on it. If I need you to help pull me up, I'll yank on the rope a couple times."

"Are you sure about this?" Raban asked. "What if the rope isn't long enough?"

Ezren hesitated as he tied the rope around his waist. "Let's tie the ends of both ropes together. That should give us plenty."

"What if the rope snags on something?"

"I'll just have to be careful. The rope is just in case I dive too deep and can't get back up on my own, anyway."

Raban put his hand on Ezren's shoulder. "Be careful, Ezren. I know you want to know who killed your da but it isn't worth your life."

Ezren looked out over the water. It was calm, with only slight ripples tickling the shoreline. As he watched, a group of ducks took wing from the water to land on shore and waddle their way up into the trees a little ways.

"Yesterday I turned 17," he said. "That marks exactly seven years since the day I was supposed to die. Seven years that I only had because of my father. He gave up everything to give me those seven years."

Ezren looked at Raban with a sad smile and put his hand on Raban's shoulder in turn. "I don't *want* my life to end, but I have only had life because of him anyway. Sacrificing my own life to give him a measure of justice would only partially repay my debt."

Raban's hand squeezed his shoulder and his eyes bored into Ezren's. "That's very noble, Ezren. It's also very stupid. Your da would never expect this of you. If it's indebtedness you feel, you *know* he would tell you to pay your debt by making him proud, not by throwing your life away."

Ezren felt tears welling up in his eyes. He looked away from Raban. His friend's words rang true, but...could he turn back now? Did he even want to?

He found himself watching the branches of the trees all around swaying in the wind, moving in the direction the wind told the branches to move. In a lot of ways, his father had been the wind and Ezren had been the trees; he'd moved the way his father had told him to. His father had kept him alive, helped him thrive.

Now, with the wind gone...Ezren couldn't see what else to do. If he did not have his quest for vengeance, what did he have?

He wasn't sure he knew how to live in a world without his father.

He didn't know how he was supposed to move forward, or what he was supposed to do with his life from here.

Further...he wasn't sure he *wanted* to. Vengeance was simple, straightforward, and measurable. Learning his new place in the world and figuring out who he wanted to be...maybe he didn't want to do that. He could not bring himself to share these thoughts with Raban, certainly not when his friend already seemed motivated to dissuade him.

He cleared his throat and removed his boots. His shirt and trousers he left on in the hopes that they would keep him warmer while in the cold water for so long. He also kept his sword strapped to his waist. Perhaps it was silly, but he might need a sword that could be shattered. He stepped into the water with his bare feet, feeling the chilly waters between his toes, and took a deep breath along with his next step. He waded until he was about waist deep and perhaps fifty feet from Raban. Just as he was thinking that the water didn't get deep as quickly as they had expected, he nearly fell forward as the ground in front of him dropped off in a sheer cliff.

He looked down, seeing the blue coloring get deeper and deeper in the clear water. There was no way to tell how deep it got there.

He began to breathe deeper in preparation to dive. He breathed in and out several times, each time breathing in deeper and expanding his lungs a bit more. The moment he filled his lungs as much as he possibly could, he jumped forward, headfirst, into the deeper water. The sounds of the outside world were snuffed and replaced with the deafening silence of the underwater world that unfolded beneath him.

～

Raban watched Ezren jump into the water, silently wishing his best friend luck, and secretly having every intention to start dragging his idiot carcass back to shore long before the eight minutes were up. The sound of horse hooves caught his attention, and he looked up as two men rode out of the trees some hundred yards or so down the shoreline. One saw him and pointed, and they both kicked their horses to trot in his direction.

They were dressed in rough woodsman clothing, and they were too far away for Raban to tell if they wore any insignias. Galdrach's men? He was nervous, but only a little.

The two men slowed their horses to a walk as they got closer. Still about 30 feet away, they dismounted and unsheathed their swords.

Raban wrapped the rope loosely around his left wrist, then readied a throwing knife in his right hand. He'd spend the night in the Inferno before he let go of that rope for even a second. What if Ezren tugged on it while Raban couldn't feel?

He brandished the throwing knife as the men continued to close the distance. It was in his best interest that they stay as far away as possible until he knew their intentions. Throwing knives were a lot more useful from range. The men had swords, but no shields, no bows, and it appeared no armor either. Who were these idiots? Who went into battle so unprepared?

But then, maybe they weren't here to battle. Best to find out quickly one way or another.

"Hello, there," Raban called out. "That's close enough for now." He brandished the throwing knife again.

The men paused for a moment and looked at each other. Raban called out again. "Now why don't you tell me why you're coming at me with swords drawn? Did Galdrach send you? I don't have the journal and I don't know where it is."

One of them looked queryingly at the rope going into the lake.

"If you don't have the journal…then how do you know about it?" The one on the left asked.

"Fair question," Raban said. "Why don't you gentlemen just sit back over there until my friend Ezren gets back? Once he gets back and dries off I'm sure we can get everything sorted out to everyone's liking."

The men looked at each other again, then back to Raban.

"The boy who stole the journal is…in the lake right now?" The same man asked, sounding rightfully confused.

"Yes. And as soon as he gets back, I can convince him to just hand you the journal with no problem."

"Just pull him up right now, then," the other said gruffly.

"Sorry, can't do that," Raban said. "He's doing something important, but it'll only be a minute. Well…no longer than eight minutes."

"No," the one on the left said, shaking his head. "We take him now."

The initial shock of the cold water wore off quickly, though the water seemed to get colder the deeper Ezren went. He tried to swim at a measured pace, though his adrenaline tried to push him to swim as fast as he could. The faster he swam, the more difficult it would become to continue holding his breath.

He had only dived to a depth of twenty feet or so when he noticed a bright light rippling down below. Curious, he looked closer…it didn't seem too far away. At first, he thought it was the reflection of the sun above, because it was virtually identical in size, brightness, and shade. He continued swimming, straight down, towards it.

As he got closer, though, the light wasn't behaving like a reflection. He couldn't see anything that would be causing a reflection, first of all, and it matched the appearance of the sun from where he was too perfectly.

Whatever it was, it provided a useful target for him to continue swimming towards. He continued swimming in a nearly straight downward direction, aiming as closely for the light as he could. But something curious began to happen. Though it still didn't make sense for it to be a reflection of the sun, as the sun got smaller and dimmer the further down Ezren swam, so did the light he was swimming *towards*.

Shouldn't the light he was getting closer to be getting brighter? This oddity propelled him forward, and the thought rang in his mind, "*Light shrink from view.*"

He swam….and swam…and swam. It soon became so dark that he

could not properly see his hands when they came in front of him during his stroke. The only thing he could see was the light, which had now shrunk so small that it seemed a small, shimmering jewel. He began to feel the signs his body gave that he needed to breathe...even now he may not have enough time and energy to return to the surface unaided.

But if he could just get down to the light...he was sure it was the orb that he was looking for. He could grab it, then yank on the rope and hope that Raban could pull him up fast enough. The rope had kept a little tension consistently and he hadn't been yanked upwards against his will, so it seemed that Raban was still at the ready.

He continued swimming downwards, fear growing as the light he swam towards continued to shrink in both brightness and size. What if the rope wasn't long enough? Worse - what if the light disappeared? He would be alone in the crushing darkness, unable to see or hear. He would have nothing to swim towards and would fail in his quest. He may even drown.

He continued to swim downwards, panic and a rising loneliness his only companions until his vision started to go dark for reasons unrelated to the depth of the water. The light was so small, as dim and pale as the sun far above him. But was it closer? It almost seemed as though he could reach it.

He stretched out his hand desperately, hoping against hope to reach the light...then his finger touched something hard and smooth.

～

Ezmith watched from astride his horse as the gate slowly opened. He and his honor guard were perhaps two hundred yards away from the wall, mostly out of bowshot but close enough that he'd be able to see what was going on without having to scry. The rest of his army was several hundred yards further back, taking their ease in the camp that had been their home for nearly a month.

He'd been expecting to receive Perivon's message of intent to surrender for days before it finally came. The arrival of the Bahadir fleet to blockade Dazbog's port had been the last shift in the pieces of this particular puzzle, and from then on it was only a matter of time, and indeed a short time.

The message that Perivon had finally sent had been cryptic, saying only that it was time they spoke face to face and come to a proper understanding. Normally Ezmith would be suspicious of such ambiguity, but at this point there was very little Perivon could possibly threaten him with. Dazbog's soldiers and citizens were hungry, their stores exhausted.

As the gate opened, Ezmith looked for Perivon's defeated figure riding out to meet him. Ezmith blinked, then squinted to make sure that he was truly seeing what he thought he was seeing. Instead of seeing Lord Perivon riding out at the head of a small contingent of troops like the one that sat mounted behind Ezmith, it appeared that Lord Perivon was riding out at the head of...his entire army!

Part of him wondered if he should be sounding the alarm, but Perivon was not a rash man...surely he was not about to-

The unmistakable Cleononian battle horns blew the charge and the front ranks of the army spurred to a gallop. The shouts and battle cries of the soldiers were easily audible over the short distance.

"Sound the alarm!" Ezmith yelled, knowing that any help would come too late. "Retreat!" His honor guard and he turned and began to ride away, but his army would need more time to get properly ready before the cavalry charge tore through them. He looked backward as he rode, trying to get a sense of how many Cleononian troops were coming at him.

It was difficult to tell while looking behind you on a galloping horse, but the number could easily have exceeded five thousand – more than sufficient to wipe Ezmith's entire force from the field if they were caught unprepared.

Unfortunately, unprepared is exactly what they were. The *last* thing Ezmith had expected was an all-out assault at this moment. Using every ounce of magical energy he could summon, he did the only thing he could think of that would slow down the entire army: Headwind. Air was relatively easy to manipulate, at least compared to the other elements, but the sheer amount that had to be affected in order to slow down not just one or two riders, but an entire army of them, took everything that Ezmith had.

The alarm was sounding throughout his camp and he saw, looking forward, men dashing back and forth retrieving polearms and strapping on armor. Here and there an arrow arced far above him to land among the pursuing horsemen. Ezmith didn't look back again, trusting the Headwind to do its job. Truthfully, even if it didn't there wasn't much Ezmith could do. He was not a swordsman or soldier, and he needed a moment to recover before he could lend his magic to the battle.

The Headwind seemed to slow the Cleononians down well enough. Looking behind him, Ezmith could see the wind ripping at their uniforms and the manes of their horses. Several riders inadvertently tugged their horses to one side or the other and collided with other riders. He looked forward as he reached the relative safety behind his lines of soldiers. The line was still forming, but he turned his horse to watch the approach. Their enemies were less than a hundred yards off.

The Cleononians mouths roared soundlessly as they closed the distance and plowed into Ezmith's rows of pikemen. Only the front row of riders was equipped with lances: the rest had an assortment of spears, other polearms, and even some longswords to fight with. The hodgepodge of polearms proved effective, however, and the screams of dying Ambartans accompanied those of the impaled horse and stymied riders.

The Headwind would do no more good now, so Ezmith released it. A flood of sound suddenly began reaching his ears, no longer hampered by the heavy wind.

Ezmith watched as a Cleononian went down with a spear through his chest, still swinging his longsword in rage, which sliced into the face of a helmetless Ambartan. The Ambartan line, incomplete as it was, buckled, and Ezmith began backing his horse up as more Ambartan soldiers came running forward to try and reinforce.

At the head of the cavalry, Ezmith saw Lord Perivon, already splattered with blood, throw the broken remnant of his lance at an Ambartan and draw his own longsword. Perivon spat blood out of his mouth and turned to look directly at Ezmith.

The look in Perivon's eyes terrified Ezmith, far more than he would ever be willing to admit. Perivon shouted something, then kicked his horse into a gallop directly at Ezmith. A significant number of his riders fell into step behind and rode with him. At last Ezmith understood: this wasn't a battle, or even a last stand.

This was an assassination.

Ezmith spurred his horse to a gallop down one of the dirt paths through the camp as he thought furiously about what to do. This was absurd! Perivon was well and truly beaten! He could not possibly win this way! Ezmith searched inward, sensing that only a trickle of his magical energy had replenished. Not enough to fight off the thirty or so galloping horsemen that seemed to gain on him with every step.

Here and there a soldier with a polearm noticed the chase and made an attempt to stab at the enemy horsemen. Some were successful, others fell skewered by lances or other weapons.

Ezmith continued to flee, but the simple truth was that he was not as skilled a rider, nor was his horse of as fast as those who pursued them. He knew if he did not change something soon, he would feel the thrust of a lance in his back and it would all end.

~

Galdrach's men charged Raban with their swords, communicating their intent very clearly, as the Sergeant would have said.

He threw a knife at the foremost man, taking him in the chest and knocking him to his back. The other man stopped abruptly, holding his sword cautiously in front of them as Raban readied another knife.

"Easy now," the remaining man said, a grizzled-looking fellow who needed a shave. "Just pull your friend up, and this doesn't have to get bloodier."

Raban quirked an eyebrow. "*You* charged *me* with swords, remember? If you don't want it to get bloodier then go away."

The man just stared at him for a moment, but didn't say anything. That worked for Raban, who just wanted to buy time until Ezren got back. He could fire off one more knife before the man reached him, but if he missed or the man knocked it aside, he'd be left trying to win a swordfight with -- almost literally -- one hand tied behind his back. If he lost...Ezren would be at this man's mercy.

So, he continued talking. The Sergeant had always said that talking was one of his strong suits. "Better yet, why don't you drop your sword here, along with your boots, then go sit on the beach a ways up there," he said casually.

He wasn't truly *feeling* nonchalant at the moment, but it was the one thing he'd seized upon when he started talking and he couldn't seem to let it go.

"Go on, now. Ezren should be back in a little while and you can sort things out with him."

The man narrowed his eyes at Raban thoughtfully. He actually seemed to be taking the proposition seriously. Suddenly, though, the rope looped around Raban's right wrist went slack, and he looked at it, panicked. What had just happened to Ezren?!

The man jumped forward, taking advantage of his distraction. Leaping backwards, Raban threw the knife in his left hand, but the knife went over the man's left shoulder, spinning uselessly off into the distance. He slid his left hand out of the rope and unsheathed a knife out of his belt just in time to turn the thrust of the man's sword. It wasn't perfect, and the sword still got him, barely catching his side, making a superficial cut.

In a flash, Raban whipped out another knife and slammed it home in the man's throat, feeling the hot blood flood over his hand.

Raban stared in shock as the man dropped the sword and fell to the ground in front of him, gurgling with his hands vainly trying to stop the flow at his neck. He stared as the man suddenly stopped kicking and gurgling and his eyes glazed over.

He didn't know how long he stood there, looking between the man's glazed eyes and the blood on his own hands, but he seemed almost frozen in time. He had never watched a man die before, unless you counted sitting with his great grandma in her last moments. That had been very different from this experience.

He expected to feel guilt but didn't. He'd killed this man, sure enough, along with the other one, but it had been their own stupid fault. They'd attacked *him*, and he'd have been happy as a fish in the sea to let them sit patiently and wait for Ezren to come back and sort out whatever was going on between them. He forced himself to look away and scan the tree line all around the lake for signs of more enemies.

～

Ezren gasped for breath as he fell forward onto hard stone. For a moment he did not look around, did not question what had happened, he simply sucked in the air, trying to catch his breath, staring at the ground in front of him. As his strength slowly came back, he brought his head up to look around.

He was in a cave of some kind. But there was something strange about this cave...looking behind him, he could see no indication of how he had entered here. The stone was unbroken from ceiling to floor.

As he looked at the walls, he noticed that they...changed. It was subtle, but their color ever-so-slowly shifted from one shade of grayish blue to another, then back again. He looked around at the color-changing walls, still wondering how he'd gotten here in the first place. There was indeed something very strange about this cave.

He jumped as there was a flash of motion just in front and to his right. It had happened too quickly to be sure, but it had looked like a person.

He held very still for a moment, staring hard directly to his right, where the cave ended only a few feet from where stood. The flash came again, and out of the corner of his eye to his left he saw another flash.

Looking out, he could see flashes all throughout the cave. The flashes *did* look like people, but they started and ended in different places in the cavern. The only commonality between them was that each ended at...a corpse on the ground.

As he watched, he began to register what he was seeing; there was a rhythm to it that he didn't understand, but he was watching rapidly sped-up versions of the moments of their deaths. He stepped forward to get closer to one of the flashes and raised his hand. The flash brought the momentary image through his hand as though either he or it were insubstantial. He turned and walked over to where a skeleton sat, slumped at the bottom of the cavern wall.

As he approached, he saw that the skeleton, somewhat slower than the flashes of people and somewhat faster than the colors of the wall, was also changing. It was gradually fleshing out, going from a bare, mostly decomposed skeleton back to a person who merely looked unconscious. As he watched, alarmed, the body began to decompose once again.

He watched as the body went through an entire cycle, not understanding a thing that he was seeing. He slowly stood and backed away, looking at the other bodies in the room. Some men...some women... one that he thought was a child before realizing that it resembled a goblin but with dark skin...they too were going from freshly-killed to fully decomposed and back again, in concert with the flashes in the room.

He had a lot of questions, but as his heart pounded nearly out of his chest, the most urgent one rose to the top: how had these people died? He unsheathed his sword as he watched one corpse re-flesh, and a long slashing wound on its chest became clear, then began to fade again. Another corpse he watched had no outside markings but seemed skeletally thin even at the fleshed end of the cycle.

Taking his eyes away from the corpses and looking around at everything else, he saw that the cave continued back further, curving so that its end was out of sight. What he *didn't* see was a source of light. There were no openings in the top of the cave that let in any light. There were no torches, nothing, but he could see as clearly as though he were outside during the dawn.

He walked forward tentatively, holding his sword with both hands in front of him. The two-handed sword techniques he'd been taught would work well enough with this sword, but he'd have to be mindful of the shorter reach. He wished he had been able to bring his shield. As he continued to walk forward, he saw several more corpses, some leaning against the wall, and some sprawled on the floor.

As he rounded the bend, he saw at the far end of the cavern a wide pedestal. On top of the pedestal was a glowing orb of a yellowish-pink. It's glow was...feisty – fitful, pulsing in an angry manner – and he watched it uncertainly as he approached. Barring the possibility that this was some other magic orb hidden in both a deep lake *and* a cave, this must indeed be the orb he was looking for.

Ezren stepped up next to the pedestal, staring into the depths of the orb. This was it. The culmination of everything he had suffered since his father's death. His grip tightened on the hilt of his sword. Just break this orb and then...what, actually? Go find Mellion or Paavali?

He was afraid to swing. What if it didn't break? For that matter – what if it *did* break? What if a wizard needed to be here when it was released in order to use it?

Maybe he could take the orb with him?

He sheathed his sword and put both hands under the orb. An immense shock went through both hands that sent him flying onto his back.

He rolled painfully to his feet, groaning. That answered *that* question, he supposed. He looked up at the orb while propped up on his elbows.

He sighed as he got to his feet, trying to think this through a little more. The last thing he wanted to do was botch his only chance at learning who killed his father by being impatient. Did he really *have* to break the orb right now? What if he went and got a wizard and brought them down here?

He had not seen a way out of this cave so far, but he walked past the orb to see if there was any opening in the cave on the other side. The gray-blue, color-shifting walls continued a short way, then ended much like the end Ezren had come in from.

From one end to the other, the cave was sealed. Even had he been able to find a way out, how would he get a wizard to come down here with him? Would he even be able to get back in the same way he had just now?

Apparently breaking the orb was a risk he needed to take.

He unsheathed his sword and let it hang at his side for a moment, glaring at the orb. Stepping back, he let out a roar and swung his sword with all his might at the orb, using the roar to drown out his worries.

The sword struck the orb with all the force Ezren could put behind it. A bright flash of light came from the point of impact and Ezren closed his eyes against the whiteness even as he felt his sword shatter against the orb.

After the brightness faded, Ezren tentatively opened his eyes to look at the orb.

It was whole.

He looked closer, directly at the place where his sword had impacted. There was not even a mark on the orb. *Stercore!*

He held up the hilt of his now-ruined sword and looked at it. The blade ended jaggedly just an inch above the guard. Pieces of his once-fabulous sword littered the ground around the orb. The hilt was as ornate as it had ever been...and completely useless.

"So you're the one," rasped a voice from behind him, making him leap away and hold up his sword hilt instinctively.

There stood a strange-looking creature. It resembled a human, but it was taller, and its skin was deathly pale, glowing a light white color. Its eyes also glowed white. Its ears came up to sharp points and its hair was long and straight. The creature was staring at him with a look of consideration. Ezren didn't know what to say. This must be the creature that had slain the others that were now corpses, unless there was some other denizen lurking about.

How was he supposed to fight it off without a sword?

"Are you going to kill me?" Ezren asked, still holding the hilt up in front of him as if it would be of any use.

"Strange…" the creature said, sounding confused. "No…I don't kill you. Why? You knew to strike the orb, though you used the wrong sword. Hmm…is it time then? Is my imprisonment at an end? I had forgotten such things as beginnings or endings."

This…creature was not making any sense. It looked away from Ezren, muttering to itself. It seemed to feel that Ezren was no threat, and Ezren had to admit that it was right. The creature looked frail, but the glowing skin and eyes could only be the result of magic, and no magic Ezren had ever seen before. As the creature continued muttering, Ezren finally registered one of the things it had said.

"What did you mean I used the wrong sword?" Ezren asked.

The creature looked back at him as though he'd forgotten Ezren was there.

"You need to use *that* sword," the creature replied as though it were obvious, pointing over to the side at…a wall.

Ezren looked from the wall back to the creature. "There's nothing there," he said, confused, and more than a bit worried. How long had this creature been down here? Perhaps it had lost its mind. He shifted his feet, trying to ready himself in case the creature rushed him without warning.

"Place your hand on the markings," the creature said, looking him in the eye for a moment before dropping his gaze to the floor and speaking almost to himself, "But beware, once the door is open, only one with the blood of a moon elf may enter the room on the other side. All others will be struck down in a most painful death."

Only one with the blood of a moon elf? Perhaps that's what this creature was. Ben had mentioned that their skin and eyes changed color when they did magic.

He finally lowered the hilt of his sword and walked over to the wall, making sure not to completely turn his back to the creature. On the wall was a marking of three vertical lines, a triangle drawn using the right-most line as one side and the other two pointing to the middle of the left-most line, and a square turned on an angle so that the middle line pointed up and down directly into two corners of the square.

"Do I need moon elf blood simply to touch the marking?" he asked, turning to look back at the elf.

Instead of answering, the elf walked, turning slowly away from Ezren as he muttered to himself incoherently. Ezren frowned, then turned back to the wall. He couldn't turn back, so...

He cautiously placed his hand on the marking and felt a rumble as the wall split in two right in the center of his hand. He pulled back and watched in amazement as half of the wall slid upwards out of sight and the other half glided down into the floor, so perfectly that Ezren could not see a crack in either floor or ceiling. Through the opening was a narrow side chamber that stretched for perhaps twenty feet. At the other end was another pedestal, lower to the ground, with a sword inserted tip-first into it.

The sword was minimally designed, with a simple, straight hilt and a gently-curved pommel, but it somehow managed to make its simplicity look more elegant and beautiful than any other sword Ezren had ever seen.

He started to enter, but looked down and saw three more corpses, each going through a cycle of death. Unlike the ones in the main chamber, there were no flashes of the moment of death followed by slow decay, however. These corpses writhed in agony, faces frozen in silent screams, for long moments before they grew still and began to decompose. They had died a very slow, very painful death.

"They had not the blood of a moon elf," rasped the voice from behind him.

Ezren looked over his shoulder. The moon elf had followed him here and was looking disdainfully at the corpses.

This was no good; he was stuck now. He didn't have the blood of a moon elf either!

"You do it," the moon elf rasped in disbelief. His eyes were wide, staring rapturously at the sword at the other end of the room. "You suffer nigh unto death, but you reach the sword. You must be of the blood."

Ezren stared at the elf incredulously. He had never had so many questions about a single statement before in his life. Was this creature some sort of prophet? It was speaking as though it had witnessed the event already. That aside, he had the blood of a moon elf?! How was that possible?

But wait...Galdrach's spell. The magic drink that his mother had taken to give his brothers and him powers. Maybe one of the ingredients was moon elf blood.

Did this elf want him to succeed? But then...what if it had said the exact same thing to the corpses now on the ground in front of him?

He stood still, considering his course of action. He stared at the sword, seeming within easy reach. He had made it all this way.

He owed this to his father.

He could be brave one last time.

He stepped forward.

A terrible sensation like the shock that would happen when touching a metal handle started in his feet and began working its way up his legs. It wasn't a brief moment, but a cascade of shocks repeating over and over and growing in intensity. He leaped into the air, but it did nothing to change it, as though now that his feet had touched the floor they were linked.

As the feel of the shockings continued to rise up to his knees, he made his way forward, taking one step forward, and then another.

This was miserable, but all he had to do was get to the sword.

He was three steps in. The pain continued rocketing up and down his legs, but he fixed his eyes on the sword, knowing he had to continue. He took another step, and began to feel an intense heat on the top of his head.

He forced himself to take another step.

The heat began to bathe the tops of his shoulders, and increase painfully on his head. Sweat began to pour out of his forehead, dripping and sliding into his eyes. He blinked rapidly, trying desperately to keep his eyes focused on the sword.

He took another step.

The heat on his head and shoulders intensified until he screamed in agony, feeling that his skin must be peeling away from the heat. His eyes dropped from the sword and he fell to a crouch, placing his hands on the floor.

No sooner had his hands touched the floor than the shocking began in his fingers and shot up towards his elbows, rocketing back and forth in concert with the shocking in his legs.

He ran out of breath to scream, sucked in as much air as he could, and screamed again.

He was in *agony*. He could feel the muscles in his legs seizing up as the burning, terrible heat enveloped his entire head and chest, obscuring his vision.

The sword. He had to get to the sword.

He looked up, rubbing at his eyes with his arms. The sword was still there. He was still alive. That meant he could continue on. He *would* continue on.

He took another step forward.

The pain...didn't get worse.

It did not subside either, and tears leaked from his eyes as he tried his best to hold in further screams, but it *didn't get worse.*

He closed his eyes, feeling his mind trying to fade from consciousness yet again. He fixated on the sword, refusing to give in to the now-familiar blackness, finding grim appreciation for the practical training in enduring pain he'd received over the last few months.

If it wasn't going to get worse...he exploded forward, sprinting for the sword, agony in every step. The pain actually did get worse, but he had momentum now, and a defiant roar escaped his lips as he reached for the sword and felt his hand close down on its hilt.

Instantly, the pain vanished. He gingerly felt the top of his head, his breathing ragged and shirt soaked in sweat. Not even his hair was singed. He pulled one of his pant legs up above the top of his boot to inspect his leg and saw no mark or indication that anything had happened. Still breathing hard, he turned his attention to the sword in the pedestal, gripped it in both hands, and pulled it from its slot.

A strange sound came from the moon elf, and Ezren looked over in concern.

It was weeping. As Ezren walked towards the entrance of the room, it fell to its knees, weeping with its eyes sightlessly staring upwards. Ezren walked past with the sword at the ready, focused on the orb, not willing to take any chances that yet another obstacle lay in his path.

Ezren walked straight to the orb and, without hesitation, pulled the sword behind him and swung once again with all his might. This time, the flash of white was still blinding, but the sword did not break. Instead, the orb shattered, pieces flying outward along with a massive pulse that knocked Ezren off his feet. Rushing wind spun all around him, centered on where the orb had been, and Ezren found himself unable to stand against the raging storm.

The sound of Perivon and his soldiers came closer and closer behind him as Ezmith galloped his horse as hard as he could.

He cut a hard right turn between two tents into a spot of cleared ground that had been set aside for archery practice. Turning his horse to face the riders, he snarled and waved his arms, intending to send a wave of fire that would hopefully scare them away. The fire would likely be too weak even to singe their arm-hairs, but it was the best he could do.

He waved his arms, summoning the magic, and...something happened. All in a rush, magic poured into Ezmith as though a geyser had just been released. The wave of magic overwhelmed him, knocking him from the saddle as he watched a veritable avalanche of fire flow from where he had sat and move towards Perivon and his riders.

Ezmith's entire body felt like it was about to explode. He gripped his head with both hands just to keep it from bursting. The world around him was fuzzy, as though the pressure from inside his body were pushing against the backs of his eyeballs. Blinking, he saw through the blur that the skin of his arms had turned bright red. He attempted to get to his feet but stumbled and fell back to the earth, the pressure in his head continuing to build.

He felt sweat drenching his entire body...

Darkness began to creep in around the edges of his vision, and he let out a long, primal yell, hoping that it would lessen the pressure he was now afraid would kill him.

His last thought before the blackness took him was that he had never before felt such power. He hoped that he would wake, if for no other reason than to feel again the immense strength that he had just experienced.

～

As Raban scanned the treeline, something strange happened. The world...rippled... It was as though, for a brief moment, everything around him was on the other side of a wave of heat. It only lasted a moment, but afterward Raban felt a strange tingling in his fingers and dizziness in his head. He shook it away the best he could and tried to refocus. There was no sign of any other attackers.

Ezren!

Raban dashed back to the rope, still slack, and started pulling on it to see if it would tighten up. He pulled and pulled, but the rope never grew heavier. He pulled it all the way out and saw that the loop Ezren had tied around his waist was empty; it was still intact, as though Ezren had just vanished.

Raban threw down the rope and removed his boots, preparing to jump into the water to find him.

～

With difficulty against the continuing wind, Ezren propped himself up on his elbows to look at where the orb had been. In its place was a cyclone of wind and dust. As he watched, a rock was flung out from around the cyclone and hit him in the arm, drawing blood. He felt hands under his armpits pull him a few feet away, where the wind was significantly milder.

He glanced up briefly to thank the moon elf for moving him out of danger before looking back at the cyclone, but the face he saw wasn't that of the moon elf.

It was his father.

Ezren's eyes widened at the sight of his father's face and he froze, staring in shock. His father's eyes crinkled in his familiar smile. Ezren raised his hand slowly and touched the kindly face. It was real.

Tears came to his eyes as he threw his arms around his father, feeling the strong reciprocal embrace of his father's very real arms as they pulled him up to a sitting position. His face mostly buried in his father's shoulder, only one word escaped from his lips.

"How?"

His fathers arms released him and gently pushed him away far enough that they could look each other in the eye.

"It is a gift," his father said. "I was given permission. But Ezren..." he paused a moment. "I am still dead."

"But," Ezren protested. "You're *real*, you're solid, I can feel you, hear you."

"Yes," his father replied. "All those things are true. But...I have passed through death and am now no longer a being that could exist in the world you inhabit. Please, Ezren," he said as Ezren opened his mouth to ask more questions. "I cannot tell you more. Ignorance, it seems, is a key part of the plan. Suffice it to say that you exist as a creature locked inside time. All you see and know is within the bounds of moments in time. When we die..." he hesitated, seeming unsure of whether he was saying too much. "...we are without those bounds."

"Here, in this place," he continued, gesturing around, "you are outside of time. Because you are a creature of time, what you see is a cycle, the beginning and end of each object to enter this cave. I do not see the cycle, but each person, each rock, in all moments of their presence here, all at once."

"I don't understand," Ezren said slowly.

"No, I would not expect you to," his father said with that same smile. "Now on to more important matters." His face grew serious, stern even, as he regarded Ezren.

"Give up this quest, boy. Vengeance will bring no good and much ill. If you wish to honor me in some way, do so by living the best life you can live. Become all that you can become, and be a greater force for good in the world than I was."

Ezren broke eye contact, blinking away another wave of tears at his father's words. The words being unsurprising did not diminish their impact, but rather enhanced it. His eyes sought his father's hands...the strong hands that had carried him so far in his life. But it wasn't his father's hands that would carry him through the rest of his life...it was the words his father had just spoken.

All this seeking...all the pain and tribulation he'd experienced...and all he had been looking for were the words his father had just said.

He had been given a directive, by the one person he trusted enough to obey. He would do as his father asked, striving to become all that he could become and be as great a force for good in the world as he could.

But there was one thing more he needed to know... "Who?" he asked, looking back up to his father's eyes. "I must know who it was that took you away from me."

His father's eyes saddened. "And if I tell you, Ezren, will you stop yourself from seeking vengeance? *Could* you stop yourself?"

Ezren considered these questions. He was being asked to deny justice. Well...that wasn't exactly true. He was being asked to deny himself vengeance. Could he hold back? Could he restrain himself if he knew the identity of the person who had ripped the foundation of his life away from him?

The answer was simple enough: this was a mandate from his father. Not seeking vengeance was one of his father's last wishes, and though he would rage, perhaps even falter, he knew that he would find it in himself to stay his hand.

He nodded. "Yes, father. I will not deny justice should it come to them, but I will honor your wish of not seeking revenge against them."

His father nodded somberly, his eyes locked unblinking on Ezren's. "It was Ezmith. I attempted to bring the error of his ways to his awareness, and he responded in an unfortunate, if predictable, way."

Ezmith. His own brother. His hands shook with emotion.

"How could he have done this? Is he so evil?" Ezren asked, not really expecting an answer.

"Evil?" his father asked, then said pensively, "Maybe. 'Broken' might be a better word. Whether evil, broken, misguided, or anything else, the time for Ezmith to face the consequences of his actions *will* come, with no need for acceleration from you."

Ezren nodded. Even without his father's express command, he did not think he could have brought himself to seek vengeance against his own brother.

But what now? Could he obey his father's directive if he just went back to life at the castle?

He no longer knew if he could return to live there, perhaps ever. Even if his status as a fugitive was resolved, could he play the dutiful son to a false mother or father? He had one real father, who had given him three instructions: seek no vengeance against Ezmith, become all that he could become, and be a greater force for good in the world than his father was.

That last one, though...Ezren shook his head. "Da, every bit of good I do will only be because you gave me my life. Everything I do will only add to the good you've done, so how could I ever do more than you?"

Tears came to his father's eyes and it was his turn to look down and blink away the wetness. "Very well," he said with a smile. "Do your best."

Ezren looked at the cyclone, which had shown no sign of abating yet.

"I miss you, Atta," he said, using the title he had used as a child.

"I know, Ezren. But you'll see me again. In the blink of an eye."

The wind continued, and Ezren turned, seeing the moon elf, still on his knees but now facing the cyclone from the doorway of the side chamber, raising his arms in grateful exultation.

"What have I done, father? What is the new magic that was in the orb?"

"More than you realize, son. Much, much, more. But take comfort in knowing that it was known, expected, and...everything will work out the way it's supposed to."

Ezren felt his father's fingertips on his eyelids, pulling them gently down to close. The feeling of rushing wind stopped. "Goodbye, son. Goodbye."

A moment later, he felt wetness, all over, and the sensation of rising. Then his back suddenly felt a cold breeze, and his eyes snapped open. He was lying facedown in water! He began to flail, but a hand grabbed the shoulder of his shirt and yanked him over. He turned his head and saw Raban somehow pulling him along. Ezren continued to flail, trying to swim without thinking.

"Just walk, you idiot!" Raban yelled.

Only then did he look around and realize that he was close to shore, where the water was only about waist-high, and that Raban himself was halfway out of the water as he dragged Ezren.

He stood up immediately and looked around. The sun looked to be in the same place in the sky it had been when he left. He didn't know how long he'd been in the cave, but it had been at least an hour, possibly longer.

He followed Raban to shore, who stopped and turned to look at him.

"How did you get there?!" Raban gasped, clearly relieved but incredulous. "I pulled the entire rope up and you were gone! Then as soon as I came running into the water to get you, you were just suddenly right there!"

Ezren hesitated, looking out over the water of the Spring. "I think my father put me there."

"Wait, what?" Raban replied, confused, his voice moderating. "Your father?"

Ezren shrugged helplessly as he looked around. "Uh, yeah."

"I saw my father, Raban. I swear I'm not crazy. I shattered the orb, and he was just there."

Raban nodded, looking out at the lake. "I figured you had shattered the orb," he said quietly. After a moment with a thoughtful expression, his eyes went down to the sword at Ezren's hip, and he squinted, regarding it curiously.

"That's not the same sword you went down with," he asked, pointing.

Ezren looked down and saw that the sword he'd used to break the orb was now in an ornate scabbard he didn't recognize. It had thin gold plating in a crisscross pattern up and down its length, which was of stiffened leather. He thought for a moment before answering.

"No, it's...it's not," he said, looking up. "It's the sword I used to break the orb. Wait, how did you know I'd broken the orb?"

They had reached the shore and were wringing out their clothes as Raban answered distractedly.

"I, uh...I felt a strange...pulse a few moments after the rope lost you, like for a moment I was seeing the world through...I don't know... intense heat. Since then things have felt...different."

Ezren looked at him as they both shook their legs to get the water off. Over Raban's right shoulder, he suddenly noticed the bodies of two men. They were dead, with the blood pooled under them still wet!

"What happened, Raban?!"

Raban glanced at the bodies for the briefest moment then pointedly looked away. "They showed up right after you went into the water. They attacked me. I'm pretty sure they were Galdrach's men."

Ezren nodded, understanding a bit better why Raban had been uncharacteristically laconic during this conversation. He started walking toward the cliff edge, the waterfall some ways to his left. Raban walked alongside him. The crunch of their footsteps seemed to echo ominously. Ezren looked around, realizing that it was strangely silent. No birds singing. No animals rustling in the trees, no wind. Nothing but the still far-off roar of the waterfall, the soft lapping sound of the waves hitting the beach, and the dry, salty, ground under their feet.

Raban's next question pulled his attention back.

"What happened down there, Ezren?"

How was he supposed to answer that question? He wasn't sure he even had the words to describe it. They walked closer to the cliff edge.

"I released the new magic, just like we planned," Ezren said.

The silence stretched as they continued to walk. Raban looked around as much as Ezren did. His next question sounded idle, as though his thoughts were far away.

"Did you find out who killed your father?"

Ezren watched the edge come closer as he wondered about the stillness around them. He nodded.

"Yes."

They stood at the cliff edge, staring out in silence, Raban seeming as wrapped up in his own thoughts as Ezren was. Nearly all of Mountain Home was visible from this vantage. Raban looked from the left side of the valley to the right, shaking his head.

"Ezren," Raban said, eyebrows furrowed. "Something is wrong."

To Be Continued...

ABOUT THE AUTHOR

Cameron C. Porter is happily married and the proud father of three children. He completed his first novel at the age of 12 and became an internationally published poet while still in high school. After serving a 2-year mission for The Church of Jesus Christ of Latter-Day Saints, Cameron started a video production company with a focus on small businesses. He dabbled in wedding and real estate videography but found that his passion was stronger for crafting compelling stories on behalf of solopreneurs and smaller businesses.

As his career progressed, Cameron began offering marketing strategy development, finding that most smaller businesses needed to have a better understanding of their brand positioning, personality, and value-offering before they could capitalize on the value that video could bring to their business.

Throughout this time, Cameron continued to write. In 2014, he spent a summer producing a web series that he still hopes to eventually rewrite and adapt into a full TV series. In 2015, he took six months to produce and direct a feature film he had written himself. Over the years, he continued to make slow but steady progress on a fantasy book he first began while still in high school.

In January of 2021, Cameron found himself in a tough spot – his client base had still not recovered financially from the global pandemic and his attempts at pivoting had not found great success. He turned to freelance writing for a variety of websites, writing articles on a per-word basis.

It only took a few months for Cameron to realize that if he could apply the same amount of discipline and time writing for himself that he was currently spending on clients, he could make the switch to finally pursuing his greatest passion: storytelling.

That was all the convincing Cameron needed, and he immediately began writing the first book in the Kimorae Rift Trilogy, "The Trail of Swords".

Hear about future titles in The Saga of Ezren Kimorae, discover free bonus content, and interact directly with Cameron by following him online!

Amazon Author Page   Official Facebook Page   Website

Made in the USA
Las Vegas, NV
01 August 2022

52539939R00256